## Sweet Savage Surrender

"Don't fight me," Logan said, as he caught her protesting hand by the wrist, and pressed it down onto the bed.

"I hate you, Logan Campbell," she gasped, her voice trembling. "I hate you," but he stilled her protest with his lips.

Poe tried to ignore what she was feeling, but slowly, as his hands slid down her body and his lips caressed her mouth, the hunger and yearning that she'd been trying to deny were there broke loose in her like a storm and sent raging torrents of fire through every nerve in her body.

Poe never dreamed anything could feel like this, so strong, so utterly overwhelming that she could hardly breathe. With every nerve in her body tingling with ecstasy, she let out a soft cry as she melted against him. . . .

# Lady Wildcat

# Lady Wildcat

## June Lund Shiplett

AN ONYX BOOK

**NEW AMERICAN LIBRARY**

# I

# The Telegram

Gaslights reflecting off mirrored prisms in the chandeliers overhead spotted twinkling lights like diamonds all about the huge gambling hall known as Cassie's Place, while beyond the gaming tables, on the stage at the far wall, a voluptuous blond ended the last note of her song and bowed, smiling at the audience, her purple sequined gown glittering ostentatiously beneath the same lights. The throng of men who'd been listening howled and hooted, throwing their hats in the air and whistling their appreciation of her rendition of the latest song to hit San Francisco's infamous Barbary Coast. All but one group of men, that is.

At one of the tables a short distance from the stage, Logan Campbell and the men with him had their minds on other things, and now his gray eyes studied his cards for quite some time before finally looking up to scan the faces of the others. Seemingly satisfied with what he saw, he slowly and deliberately reached out, took three hundred dollars off the pile of money in front of him, and tossed it lightly into the center of the table.

"I'll see your two hundred, and raise you a hundred," he said, his eyes once more moving back to study his hand.

Logan was an attractive man in his late twenties, with dark wavy hair and cynical steely gray eyes. Once more those intense eyes left his cards, only this time they settled on the man at his left, who was staring back at him deep in thought.

Money meant nothing to Logan Campbell really as far as winning was concerned. It was the principle of the thing. He just hated losing. And although he knew most of the men at the table were playing far beyond their means, he wasn't about to let it bother him as he continued to stare at the other man, who was sweating profusely now as he took one last look at his cards, then threw them facedown on the table.

"That cleans me," the man said disgustedly, and leaned back in his chair, jerking a handkerchief from his pocket, wiping his forehead.

Logan turned to the next man. He was much younger than the others, barely out of his teens, with freckles still spattered across his nose, and a mass of sandy hair that refused to lie flat even though it was generously greased with pomade. He'd been drinking heavily all evening, and now his bloodshot eyes narrowed viciously as he looked, first at his cards, then at Logan Campbell, then back again to his hand.

He was holding four kings and a deuce. A gravy hand. Ordinarily he'd bet his life on it, but with deuces wild, he knew the other men could be holding anything. Still, the odds were against Campbell being able to beat him. And all the others except one had thrown in. Yet . . . he bit his lip. Campbell had to have five aces to win, and it wasn't likely. If only . . .

He took a deep breath and reached into his inside coat pocket, fingering his last four hundred dollars. It was all that was left of the whole three thousand, the rest having been lost at cards already. Suddenly he hesitated. Maybe he shouldn't; after all, four hundred was better than going home broke. His eyes narrowed thoughtfully. Still, if he stayed in and Campbell was bluffing, he'd have a chance to get the whole three thousand back, and more. And there was every chance Campbell was bluffing, because he'd bluffed a number of times already tonight. What to do?

He fingered the money desperately, his face flushed, sweat glistening in his curly sideburns; then, before giving himself a chance to change his mind again, he snatched the four hundred from his pocket, slapped it down on the pile of money in the center of the table, and said, "I'll see your three hundred and raise you a hundred," and his jaw set stubbornly.

Logan's expression never changed as his eyes slowly moved from the worried young man to the dealer, who shook his head as he neatly folded his cards and set them facedown in front of him, then reached in his pocket and pulled out a cigar. He bit off the end and made a direct hit with it into a nearby spittoon.

"By me," he said curtly, and reached in his pocket, pulling out a match, lighting it deftly with his thumbnail.

The young man's hands shook slightly as Logan sat quietly, first looking at his cards, then scrutinizing the pile of money between them. Logan was calm and cool, his hands steady as he breathed a sigh, his strong fingers reaching out to slowly pluck another hundred dollars from the stack of money in front of him, and he leaned forward a bit, setting it gently on top of the bills the frustrated young man had just set down.

Not a word was spoken, and now the men who'd gathered around watching grew silent. They'd seen this before, and were staring at the two men who faced each other across the table.

Logan waited motionless, watching, while the face of the young man turned a sickening gray. The young man was swallowing hard, knowing there was nothing left for him to do except show his hand. He took a deep breath. Well, what the hell! He had five kings, didn't he? This was ridiculous. Why was he prolonging it? His shoulders straightened, and he tried to put on an air of confidence as he turned his hand faceup on the table, causing a stir among the crowd just as the blond who'd been singing joined them, sauntering up to stand at Logan's elbow to survey the scene.

There were four kings and a deuce on the table, a pile of money, and a sick-looking young man who was staring intently into Logan's face, and instinctively she knew what was happening. She studied Logan carefully for a moment. Although he was holding his cards against his chest, she could tell by the look on his face that the other man didn't have a chance.

"Well, what are you waiting for, Logan?" she asked rather sarcastically. "Why prolong the execution?"

He glanced up at her, his face hard and unemotional, then looked back at the young man across from him once more before slowly laying his hand faceup next to the pile of money.

The young man didn't move, only stared long and hard at the four aces and a deuce. He felt numb and cold inside as he watched Logan Campbell reach out and begin to slide the pile of money toward him.

It wasn't fair! He should have won! It wasn't

fair! He'd only planned to sit in for a few hands, maybe make a couple extra dollars to take home with him, to prove to his pa he was a good businessman. Now he'd go home broke. Nothing to show for all the horses they'd brought to the city. Nothing to pay the men with until he got back home to face Pa. He'd failed his first time in charge, and he sat motionless, unable to believe what was happening.

"The kid's gonna be sick," the blond said, and Logan glanced over quickly at the young man, then returned his attention to the money, continuing to stack it in front of him, apparently unconcerned.

"Men shouldn't gamble unless they have the stomach for it," he said callously, and reached inside his suit coat, drawing out his billfold.

The dealer stood up, pulling the cigar from between his thick lips, and walked off, giving the young man a rather disdainful look, but still the young man didn't move and only stared at Logan as Logan put the money away, then stood up.

"Don't you have any sympathy at all?" the blond asked. "The poor kid looks like he's ready to die."

Logan straightened his broad shoulders, then shrugged them nonchalantly. "So next time he'll know better."

She shook her head as she gazed up at him. It was typical of Logan. He was a hard man in many ways, yet she'd seen the other side of him too. He'd been in San Francisco at Christmas last year as usual, and had thrown a party for all the street urchins, putting on a feed even better than the one he'd given them the year before. And often she'd see him slip money to the flower ladies who frequented the streets. He seemed generous enough at times, and she guessed maybe that it was just that he couldn't abide stupidity or weakness, and she assumed he thought of the young man as being both weak and foolish.

The young man finally stood up, the dazed expression still on his face, and for a brief moment no one was sure just what he'd do. Then quite abruptly he turned from the table and hurriedly made his way through the crowd, never looking back while both Logan Campbell and the blond stared after him.

"Feel pretty smug, don't you?" the blonde said as she eyed Logan again, her head tilted to one side, studying him.

He frowned, his eyes still on the young man who was going out the door. "It's a hard lesson to learn, I know," he said, his voice a little deeper than usual. "But one I guarantee he'll never forget. As Aunt Delia would say, 'If you can't swim, don't jump in over your head unless you like drowning.' "

The spectators had started filtering away when Logan began counting his money, and now, with it safely tucked away, he took the blond's arm, entwining it with his own as he looked down at her.

"And now, Cass, love," he said, smiling lazily, "since I was so engrossed with the cards that I missed your number, how about a private performance just for me?" and he began ushering her between the tables, toward her private offices to the left of the stage, while she smiled at him seductively, her eyes never leaving his face.

Suddenly he stopped abruptly as they both realized someone in the crowded room was calling him.

"Mistel Campbell, Mistel Campbell!"

It was the Chinese errand boy from the hotel where Logan was staying. He was elbowing his way through the closely knit crowd, waving a telegram above his head.

"Teleglam fol you," he called, and reached them a moment later, holding it out toward Logan, who took the telegram, gave the Chinese a coin, then waved for him to leave.

"I wait fol leply," he answered, and stood stoically, arms folded as he watched Logan open the message and read it silently to himself.

"Logan," it read, "come home immediately. Urgent! Explain later. Help!" and was signed "Aaron."

Logan was frowning as he glanced at the Chinese, then using the edge of the bar near where they were standing for support, he pulled a pencil from inside his suit coat and wrote hastily on the back of the telegram.

"Here," he said when he'd finished, handing it back to the small Oriental man, who next to Logan's six-feet-five-inch frame seemed a dwarf. "Send this," he said, and handed him enough money to cover the return message; then he turned to Cassie.

"Sorry, Cass," he apologized. "I'm afraid your special performance will have to wait for a while."

She was disappointed. "Surely business isn't that pressing."

He bent down closer to her ear. "Only business could drag me away tonight," he whispered soothingly, and put an arm around her, beginning to head her toward the cloakroom near the front entrance.

"You'll be back?" she asked.

"Next time around." He feigned disappointment. "I have to go back to Goldspur."

"You're sure it's not that snob up on the hill?"

He touched her nose with his forefinger. "Your claws are showing, Cassie."

"You went to the opera with her last night."

"And I intended taking her to the theater tomorrow night." He was matter-of-fact as he fastened the neck clasp of his long evening cape, took the silver-handled cane from the black boy who was checking hats and coats, then reached out and tilted her face toward him, his fingers almost hurting as they pressed into her chin. "I've told you before, Cass, don't expect more than I'm ready to give."

She tried to hide her frustration beneath a teasing pout. "Don't worry, I won't. But one of these days you're going to be in for a big surprise, Mr. Logan Campbell," she warned him. "Because I just might not be waiting for you when you return to San Francisco."

"Oh, won't you?" He smiled sardonically, then turned and left, leaving her standing alone with only the raucous noise of her patrons to keep her company.

She watched after him for a long time, the noise from behind her drifting into her thoughts. He was so sure of himself. *The* Mr. Logan Campbell! Well, maybe she meant what she said this time. For five years now she'd always been waiting, looking forward to his visits. Loving him, yet knowing she was only one of a number of women in his life, and now she was suddenly more certain than ever that no woman, including herself, would ever really mean anything to Logan Campbell. He always took everything they offered and left nothing in return, and he never would.

It'd serve him right if she married that mining gent who came by whenever he was in town. He'd proposed often enough, and she just might take him up on it. After all, he did have money, even if he was pushing forty. Besides, she wasn't all that young herself, although she'd never admitted to anyone that she was over thirty. Her thoughts drifted back to Logan. There sure was no future in waiting around for him, that's for sure, and she turned around, heading for her private office, a wicked gleam in her eye as she thought over her decision. Yes, sir, Logan Campbell was in for a big shock when he hit San Francisco "the next time around," as he nonchalantly put it, because if her mining gent showed up like he said he would last time and proposed, she sure as hell didn't intend to stick around here waiting for something that was never going to be.

Logan squared his shoulders as he strolled up the street in the direction of his hotel, his cane swinging as he went. It was a balmy night and he liked walking, especially with the fresh smell of San Francisco Bay filling his nostrils, and he took off his black evening hat so the breeze could cool his head of dark wavy hair. It had been so damn hot in the saloon.

In a way he was glad to get rid of Cassie tonight. She was a diversion for a while, but after one or two nights he grew tired of looking at her painted face. She was starting to show her age, and although her voice was still the best on the Barbary Coast, her figure was getting hippy, and the lines in her face were getting hard to hide, even under all the makeup. Cassie was fun for a night. She owned the best gambling house and saloon on the coast, and the most plush, with its thick carpet and crystal chandeliers, but Cassie was Cassie. A woman to use until he tired of her, and he was beginning to tire more easily each time he came to San Francisco.

His thoughts went back to the telegram, and he frowned. It worried him. Never before had Aaron sent such an ominous message, and with Aunt Delia still away visiting in Scotland . . . He hailed a hack and headed straight for the hotel, deciding he'd better not waste any more time walking.

The Chinese had returned ahead of him and was waiting in the lobby when he walked in.

"You sent the wire?" Logan asked, and the man nodded; then Logan turned to the clerk at the desk, asking if any more messages had come in. Assured they hadn't, he headed up to his room.

Logan always stayed in the best hotel, and he glanced about as he walked up the stairs. It was nice having money. There were things you could do with money. He looked down at the silver-handled walking stick. Even in San Francisco the Campbell holdings at Goldspur were well known. The Comstock Mines weren't all Nevada had. Campbell's Highland Spur at Goldspur, just north of Tonopah, was one of the richest, and Delia Campbell had managed to keep full ownership. She was one of the few people to buck the big banks and win, and he, Logan Campbell, was not only her nephew but also right-hand man and heir.

He kept the men going, Aaron Goldbladt took care of the finances and legal operations, and Aunt Delia was overseer of the whole works, and few people ever put anything over on Delia Campbell. She was a shrewd woman; however, at the moment she was an ocean away, and he couldn't for the life of him comprehend what trouble Aaron could have run into. If he'd gotten them into a financial bind he'd have hell to pay, and Logan prayed it wasn't the mines. They were the safest in the territory, although that wasn't saying much, because any mine was dangerous.

He opened the door to his room and breathed a sigh as he entered, draping his cape over a chair near the door. The room was dark, and he lit one of the lamps in the sitting room, then went into the bedroom. Packing was brief, and three-quarters of an hour later he was in the lobby at the desk again, not having bothered to even change from his evening clothes.

"Do you have something to write on?" he asked the desk clerk as he set his suitcases down.

The clerk handed him pencil and paper. "You checking out, sir?" he asked.

Logan was curt as he handed the man his room key. "I know I'd planned to stay a full week, but something urgent's come up."

He started writing on the slip of paper the clerk had given him, and scowled as he thought of the look that would be on Rachel's face when she got the message. It was bad enough having to break a date with the daughter of one of the richest men in town, but to leave without even saying good-bye made matters worse. He wasn't really too worried, however; he was sure she'd be waiting to fall all over him when she saw him again. Just like all the others, he thought irritably. God damn women anyway! Always trying to get their hooks in a man and drag him down the aisle. Why couldn't they just be happy knowing he liked being with them?

And Rachel was no different from any of the rest of them, either. She'd hinted more than once about white cottages and orange blossoms, and he cringed at the thought. She was all right for a night at the opera or theater and a few kisses in the carriage on the way home, but to sit across from her at breakfast? The thought was nauseating. Rachel's voice was too high-pitched, and if he had to listen to her affecting that animated baby talk of hers at breakfast, lunch, and dinner every day, he'd go insane. She was pampered and spoiled, and would drive a husband to an early grave. That's why a smart man never took a lady like Rachel to bed. That way there was no chance of being subjected to a shotgun wedding.

He finished the note, asked the clerk for an envelope, addressed it, then called the Chinese over.

"I've got an errand for you, Soong Lee," he said, handing him the envelope, along with a generous tip. "See that this is delivered to the lady whose name is on it, and no one else. They may put up an argument, but insist on giving it only to her."

The Chinese grinned. He knew Mr. Campbell real well. If he say give to lady, Soong Lee give to lady. For two years now he run errands for big man when he come to town.

"You no wolly, Mistel Campbell," he chanted, his eyes shining. "Soong Lee give to lady same you bling to eat last night, yes?"

Logan nodded, and grinned. Soong Lee might not have been in the States very long, but he understood English and Americans better than most people thought.

The little Oriental bowed three times quickly as he spoke. "I call cab fol you. You come back, I see you next time"; then he turned quickly and padded out the front door.

Logan watched him through the glass in the door as he stood on the curb beneath the lamplight, the silvery threads of his clothes shimmering slightly as he hailed a hack; then Logan picked up his suitcases and left the hotel, taking the carriage Soong Lee had waiting. It was almost midnight when he was finally able to lean back in his seat on the train and relax some as it pulled out of San Francisco, headed for Tonopah. He'd take the stage from there to Goldspur, but was still wondering, as he settled back to spend a restless night, just what trouble Aaron could have run into, because nothing like this had ever happened before.

He reached Goldspur by stagecoach shortly after sundown the next evening, tired and worried, and was met by a nervously jittery Aaron.

"Am I glad to see you," Aaron said as Logan emerged from the stage, and he grabbed Logan's arm, pulling him aside quickly. "I've been frantic. Afraid she'd arrive before you did."

"She who?" Logan asked.

Aaron rubbed his forehead nervously. "The little girl."

"What little girl?"

"Now, don't explode," Aaron blurted. "I'll explain the whole thing . . . if I can," and he turned around as the driver threw down Logan's suitcases, then climbed back in his seat again and headed the stagecoach out of town. "Stow those someplace and we'll go have a beer," Aaron said, motioning toward the luggage.

Logan had been watching him curiously. "You think a beer will help?"

"It'll help me."

"Maybe it'd be better if we went to the house and I fixed you something stronger."

Aaron sighed. "Oh Lord! Could I use it!"

"Talk as we go," Logan suggested, and they each picked up one of Logan's suitcases and started down the road toward the edge of town.

Aaron started talking in unrelated sentences, all garbled together.

"Hold it!" Logan interrupted him, stopping in the middle of the road. "Start from the beginning, and make sense."

Even in his heeled boots Aaron was shorter than Logan. Of course almost everyone was shorter than Logan, and Aaron was about ten pounds heavier than what he should be, only he wore it well. He was in his early thirties, and even though his kinky brown hair had started to recede, it hadn't affected his prowess with the ladies, so he'd concluded. He rolled his soft brown eyes as he shifted the suitcase from one hand to the other, and they started walking again.

"Well, yesterday when I picked up the mail," he began, a little more calmly this time, as he tried to keep up with Logan's long strides, "there was a letter from an Attorney Wimpole from up Elko way. You ever heard of a Joe Yancey?" he suddenly asked.

Logan shook his head, and Aaron continued.

"Well, seems Mr. Joseph Yancey had a wife named Hester, and a daughter named Poetica."

"Poetica?" Logan asked. "What kind of a name is that?"

"How the hell should I know?" Aaron answered. "Anyway, you're not listening."

"Go ahead," Logan said, and Aaron went on.

"Well, it seems that since Joe Yancey's been dead some nine or ten years and the wife, Hester, just died a short while back, Delia Campbell's been made guardian to Miss Poetica Yancey, who's on her way here right now."

Logan stopped again, and stared at him. "Aunt Delia? Taking care of a little girl?"

"I told you I needed help." Aaron looked rattled. "With Aunt Delia gone, and the kid comin' . . . What do we do with a snot-nosed kid?"

Logan took a deep breath. "You're sure she's coming here?"

"Positive. According to the letter, she'd have left a few days back. Didn't say whether she was alone or with someone. Just that she was comin'. Hell, Logan, I don't know what to do with any kid!"

"Nor do I," he answered, frowning, and they began walking again. This time in silence.

The town was quiet except for the noise from the saloons and the ever-present thumping of the quartz-crushing machines at the mines. The mines were northeast of town, and Delia Campbell had built her home as far from them as possible, yet where she'd still have access to them, and the town had settled on an angle in between the two. All the empty land between Delia Campbell and the mines belonged to Delia Campbell, along with a good section back into the hills and woods. The sound of the thumping grew fainter as they continued to walk.

Besides the mines, Delia Campbell ran a lumber mill and a number of other small enterprises. In fact, practically the whole town lived off Campbell money one way or another, although there were a few lesser mines and businesses. But Goldspur had started with the Highland Spur mines, and built up from there, and Delia Campbell called it her town.

Her house, affectionately called the Highland, sat on a rolling slope overlooking the town, and she often felt like a queen on a throne as she surveyed her little kingdom. Built Victorian style with gingerbread trimming, it was three stories high, and painted pale yellow, with a tower on the north side. Windows graced the room at the top of the tower, and it was Delia's favorite spot.

The moon was just tipping the edges of the trees on the horizon now, and as Aaron and Logan turned into the long drive, it reflected off the tower roof, making it resemble a medieval castle. Logan seldom drove the buggy to town, although it was quite a walk, but Delia never ventured out without it.

"How old is this kid?" Logan finally asked as they started up the front walk.

Aaron shook his head. "Damned if I know. Probably about ten or twelve. The letter never said."

"And we have to take her?"

"We have to."

Logan reached for the front doorknob, and opened it just as the butler arrived in the foyer.

"I'll take the bags, Mr. Logan," he said. "Mr. Aaron said to expect you, sir. There's a tray set up in the library."

Logan thanked him, and watched as the old man, strong for his years, picked up both suitcases and headed for the stairs. He'd been with Delia for as long as Logan could remember, and almost seemed a part of the house. The Highland wouldn't be the Highland without tall, gray-haired, soft-spoken Clive.

Logan sighed a few minutes later as he and Aaron entered the library, and the first thing he did was pour his friend a drink. Aaron had worked for Delia for about nine or ten years now, and he and Logan had become good friends, although there were times Aaron had a hard time understanding Logan, and especially his cynical behavior when it came to women.

"Now," Logan said as he handed Aaron his drink, "where's the letter you got from this lawyer in Elko?"

Aaron reached for the inside pocket of his tweed jacket, pulled out a letter, and handed it to him. Logan read silently while Aaron nursed the brandy.

"But we don't know a thing about taking care of children," Logan protested when he'd finished and handed the letter back to Aaron, who shoved it back into his pocket.

"Well, one of us had better learn fast," Aaron said. "Because she's on her way."

Logan began pacing the floor, trying to think, his tall solid frame tense and determined. "There's got to be a way," he insisted angrily, and strode to the window that overlooked the side gardens, where he stood staring out into the darkness.

"A governess," he finally said, turning back to face Aaron. "We'll need a governess."

"A governess?"

"We certainly can't take care of the kid ourselves. And who else is better qualified than a woman?"

"But we don't have time to hire a governess."

"Why not? Surely there's someone in town we could hire."

"Who?"

Logan shrugged. "Addie Trundel?" he suggested.

Aaron laughed. "That hawk-faced prohibitionist wouldn't be caught dead within ten feet of the Highland."

"Well . . . how about Millie Teasdale?"

"She doesn't have a brain in her head. You know damn well she'd do more harm than good. She's barely able to take care of herself."

"There's got to be some woman in town who'd be suitable."

Aaron frowned. "Oh yeah, there's lots who'd be suitable, but let's face it: With your reputation there isn't one mother in town who's going to let her daughter stay in this house with you, even if she were along as a chaperon, and any other woman in town who might be available, excluding women like Addie and Millie, would jump at the chance, only they wouldn't pay any attention to the kid, and you know it. You'd be fighting them off all day."

"Then we'll have to hire someone from San Francisco or someplace. Someone experienced."

"And where do we get the time? Even if I sent a wire, by the time she was hired and took the trip, it'd probably be another week. The letter said the kid's due anytime now."

"So we find a fill-in till she gets here."

"Who?" Aaron asked irritably. "Don't you think I haven't tried to think of something?"

Logan's expression changed, and there was a shrewd gleam in his eyes. "There's only one woman in town who'd be willing to stay in the same house with me, yet wouldn't try to sink her hooks in."

Aaron's eyes widened. "You wouldn't!"

"Wouldn't I?"

"But the Duchess? What would people say?"

"That she was taking her payment out in trade, I suppose." He grinned. "And they'd probably be right, but what the hell do I care."

"What about Aunt Delia?"

"By the time she gets back, we'll have a regular governess hired. All we have to do is talk the Duchess into it."

"If you can talk her out of those fancy low-cut dresses and all the lip rouge, you're a better man than I thought."

Logan rubbed his chin thoughtfully. "That's right, she has to at least look the part, so the kid won't know the difference. Well, I'll have to give it a try."

"You think it'll work?"

"It has to. I don't intend to play nursemaid to any sniveling adolescent."

"You'd better start working on the Duchess tonight, then. That kid could be on tomorrow's afternoon stage."

Logan checked his pocket watch. It was eight-thirty. The Duchess and her girls would just be coming to life. He squared his shoulders.

"Wish me luck," he said, and left the library hurriedly, while Aaron headed for the whiskey decanter, shaking his head.

The walk to the Duchess's place revived Logan after the long stagecoach ride, but he was still apprehensive. She wasn't going to go for this masquerade, and he'd have to do some tall talking. If it wasn't for the Duchess's precarious position in town she was ideal for the part because she'd gone to school back east when she was younger.

At the age of eighteen the Duchess had married a man who claimed he was a duke, and a year later had a daughter. Unfortunately, the following year, her husband was drowned in a boating mishap, and since her parents were both dead, and with no other relatives to help, she made her living the only way open to her at the time. She'd been a beautiful woman, and still was, with dark hair and flashing brown eyes, and her figure was still that of a young girl, even though she was all of thirty. Her daughter had died of pneumonia at the age of five, and she'd headed west afterward, settling in Goldspur, Nevada, where she opened up her unusual boardinghouse.

Paying customers soon made it possible for her to build a private house of her own next door, and for the past few years she was able to run the business without taking an active part. Unknown to Logan, she'd been in love with him since she'd first set eyes on him, but knowing men, especially men like Logan Campbell, she'd always been content to take his favors without making demands on him. As long as he was consistent, she never complained.

As Logan lifted the door knocker and let it

fall with a somewhat hesitant gesture, he wondered how he was going to approach the subject of Poetica Yancey.

The door was opened by Peko, the Duchess's Mexican servant girl, whose eyes widened as she stared at him.

"Señor Campbell, you are in San Francisco!" she blurted, very much surprised.

He grinned. This small fragile girl of twelve amazed him with her devotion to the Duchess, and she never minced words, saying the first thing that came into her head, whether it made sense or not.

"Now, do I look like I'm in San Francisco?" he asked as he stepped into the entrance hall.

"*Sí, señor* . . . I mean, *no, señor*. You are here," she answered, quickly grabbing the long black braid that hung down her back, pulling it over her shoulder, and twisting it excitedly.

"Then you know why I'm here," he said. "Is she upstairs?"

The girl nodded. "*Sí.*"

"Then I'll find my way," and he headed toward a staircase at the end of the hall while Peko stared after him, wondering why he wasn't in San Francisco like he was supposed to be.

He turned at the top of the stairs and reached down, quietly opening the first door he came to. As he did, the fragrance of the Duchess's favorite perfume filled his nostrils, sweetly provocative.

She was sitting at the vanity in a flimsy red negligee, her back to him, the dress she intended to wear spread out on her bed, and he saw her straighten as she sensed that someone had come into the room.

"Peko?" she asked hesitantly.

"Logan," he replied softly, and stepped inside, shutting the door behind him, leaning back against it.

She whirled around, and her eyes widened. "Logan!" She stared at him for a minute, then composed herself and stood up. "How could you do this to me without even a warning?" she asked, her voice soft and sultry.

He walked over and pulled her into his arms. "You shouldn't need a warning," he said huskily, and kissed her long and hard. However, his mind wasn't really on what he was doing, and as soon as his lips left hers, he dropped his arms and walked over to her liquor cabinet, pouring himself a drink while she stood aside.

She continued to stare as he walked to the fireplace at the other end of the room, leaned one arm against the mantel, and stared absentmindedly at the dead ashes in the grate while he sipped his drink.

"All right, what's the matter, Logan?" she finally asked, and walked over to stand behind him.

He was trying to think of some way to broach the subject, and he finished his drink quickly, then turned to face her.

---

"I need your help," he said, his voice rather unsure for the first time since she'd known him.

"You need my help?" Her eyebrows raised. "You mean Logan Campbell's finally in a mess he can't get out of?"

His eyes flashed. "What is that supposed to mean?"

"If you think I'm going to play nursemaid to some pregnant Nob Hill debutante you've been sleeping with just to keep your neck out of a noose, you're sadly mistaken, lover," she retorted, guessing at his reason for coming. "Your kisses mean a lot to me, Logan, but not that much!"

"You think . . . ?"

She turned her back on him flippantly. "Why else would you come running back from San Francisco? What other kind of trouble could you possibly be in where I could help? Not business, that's for sure."

He lost some of his anger, and walked over, plunking his big frame down on her plush velvet settee. "Oh, hell!" he exclaimed, twisting the empty brandy glass around and around in his hands.

"Well, if you don't want me to play nursemaid to one of your fillies, what do you want me to do?"

"That's just it," he said, sitting up straight, and he glanced at her out of the corner of his eye. "I do want you to play nursemaid, but not to one of my so-called 'fillies,' as you put it."

The anger rose in her big brown eyes.

"Come here, please," he said quietly. "Let me explain."

She hesitated, then walked over and sat down beside him. He took one of her hands in his and held it tightly, then took a deep breath.

"Aunt Delia has been made guardian to a little girl named Poetica Yancey," he blurted quickly. "And since Aunt Delia's in Scotland and I know absolutely nothing about kids, I was hoping you'd help."

Her fingers went limp in his hand and she stared at him incredulously. "You want me to be nursemaid to a kid?"

He nodded.

"How old is she?"

He shrugged. "'Nine or ten . . . hell, I don't know, but she's on her way here, and I've got to have somebody."

"But I don't know anything about taking care of kids." She took her hand from his and stood up. Now she needed a drink, and she walked over and poured herself a good stiff one.

"Oh, come on," he answered. "You mother those girls next door as if they were your own daughters, and little Peko thinks more of you than she did her own mother. You could pull it off."

She took a large swallow of the brandy.

"You're crazy, Logan. I run a whorehouse, I'm not a governess."

"Duchess!"

"Well, let's face it. That's what I do."

"You're a woman, Duchess. That's what I need."

"There are plenty of women in Goldspur."

He stood up and walked over to her, putting his hands on her shoulders. "You know why I can't hire any of them . . . and it'll only be until we can get an ad in the city papers and hire an experienced woman."

"But I don't even look like a governess."

He eyed her, his head cocked to one side. "We could fix your hair different, take off the lip rouge, and get some different clothes."

"And make me look like a dried-up prune, I suppose."

He smiled. "You could never look like a prune."

She frowned. "I'd feel naked without my frills."

He leaned over and nuzzled her neck, kissing her behind the ear, raising gooseflesh on her arms. "You'll do it for me, won't you?" he whispered softly.

She shoved him away and took another sip of brandy as she walked back to the dressing table.

"You're good at that, aren't you?"

"At what?" he asked innocently.

"You know very well what I mean," she

insisted. "You think all you have to do is make love to me and I'll jump at your bidding." She drained the rest of the glass.

"Have I ever disappointed you?" he asked.

She looked up into the mirror at his reflection as he stood behind her. No, he'd never disappointed her. His lovemaking was always above reproach, but that was just the trouble. He was making love, not feeling it. It was an act with him, not a spontaneous feeling from the heart. He knew how to make a woman feel loved, and he made the most of it, but it was only make-believe, and she knew it. It really didn't matter, though. She'd go to hell and back for him if he wanted her to, and he knew it.

"Damn you, Logan," she said as her eyes caught his in the mirror. "All right, I'll do it, but only until you can find someone else."

He reached out, took her by the shoulders, and turned her around, pulling her into his arms.

"I hate you, Logan Campbell," she whispered. "I hate you," and as his mouth came down on hers and she melted against him, they both knew damn well she was lying.

# 2

# The Arrival

The tall young woman sighed, glancing about apprehensively as she rode down the main street of Goldspur, heading her mount toward a place about midway along the line of buildings. She shifted uncomfortably in the saddle and flicked her long red hair back off her shoulder. It was a couple of hours past noon and the constant drumming of the quartz-crushing machines seemed to be keeping time with her horse as she ambled along, then reined the black gelding to a stop in front of a group of men loitering on the boardwalk in front of one of the saloons.

Her right leg moved swiftly in a graceful arc over the horn of her saddle and she slid easily to the ground, then stood surveying the men who were gawking at her wide-eyed.

She was long and tall, almost six feet in her heeled boots, and the black pants and shirt she

35

wore, although well worn, rumpled, and in need of a good washing, were so tight they looked like they'd been pasted on her, emphasizing a number of eye-catching curves. A flat-crowned, wide-brimmed black hat lay low on her forehead, shading her face from the hot afternoon sun, and she tilted it back a bit with her right hand, revealing a pair of large blue-green eyes that seemed to mock each man as they passed over him. She took a few steps toward them, still holding her horse's reins, the twin six-shooters on her hips swaying up and down in a tantalizing motion with each step, and the men continued to stare, speechless.

"Any you gents know where I can find some-one named Campbell?" she asked as she looked them over disdainfully.

The men still stared, but didn't answer.

"Well, goddammit!" she exploded, the faint outline of freckles near the tip of her nose deepening. "What the hell's the matter with you varmints anyway? Can't any of you talk?"

One wizened old man reared back, squinting at her, then pointed across the street. "At the Highland," he offered through broken teeth, and she nodded to him, giving the others a look of disgust.

"Thanks, old fella, much obliged," she said, and pulled her hat down again to shade her eyes, gave the other men another dirty look, and turned, heading across the street, leading her horse behind her, the men's eyes following the unusual motion of her six-shooters all the way.

A few minutes later Aaron looked up from his desk just in time to see her silhouette in the doorway a second before she closed it. He stared in disbelief, and slowly stood up, realizing he was looking into a pair of huge long-lashed blue-green eyes that were boring a hole clear through him.

"You a Campbell?" she asked, stopping dead in front of his desk.

"No, ma'am," he answered willingly. "But I represent Delia Campbell. I'm Aaron Goldbladt, her attorney. What can I do for you?"

"I'm Poe Yancey," she stated flatly, and watched the expression in his eyes change from one of admiration to one of shock.

"You're . . . ?"

"I said I'm Poe Yancey," she repeated irritably. "What's the matter with the goddamn men in this town anyway? Those gents over at the saloon can't talk, and you can't hear."

"Oh, I heard you," Aaron answered, his voice breaking. "It's just that I don't believe it."

"Well, you're expectin' me, ain'tcha?"

He nodded, barely able to talk. "We were and we weren't." He sat back down in his chair slowly and swallowed hard, then suddenly started to laugh. Now it was her turn to stare.

He laughed so hard there were tears in his

eyes, and she watched in dismay, shaking her head.

"What the hell you laughin' at?" she demanded, but it only brought on more peals of uncontrolled laughter. "Are you sure you're all right?" she asked after a few minutes, and he finally wiped his eyes with a handkerchief, trying to control himself.

He nodded. "I'm fine," he answered when he'd managed to catch his breath. "Only . . . only you're supposed to be so . . ." and he measured about half her height with his hand, then almost broke down again, but managed to control himself, although it was hard. "How old are you?" he asked, realizing she was every bit as tall as he was, maybe a shade taller.

She frowned. "Almost seventeen. Why?"

He tried to look serious, but there was still a hint of laughter in his eyes. "We thought you'd be much younger."

Now she understood. "Well, don't that beat all. You thought I was gonna be a little kid, is that it?"

"That's about it."

She let out a stream of cuss words that would've curled Addie Trundel's hair. "Didn't that old son of a bitch up Elko way tell you how old I was in that letter he wrote?" she asked.

Aaron shook his head. "Only that Delia Campbell had been appointed your guardian until you turned twenty-one or married, and that you were on your way here."

"He's a stupid jackass," she stated, pushing the hat back off her head till it hung down her back, revealing a head of dark mahogany-colored hair with short wipsy ends that played about her face, while the rest curled and bounced generously off her shoulders. "Ain't no sense me even comin' here," she went on. "I don't need any guardian. I got my own," and she patted her guns lovingly. "Ain't no one gonna take care of me, except me."

"But you have to," Aaron said as he stood up again and walked around the desk. "You have no choice."

"I don't have to, and I ain't gonna," she replied firmly. "I only came here to tell the old lady I don't want any charity, and I don't want any damn guardian either!"

"Your mother left a will, and the court ordered it. If you don't stay, you're in contempt of court, and they'll put you in a girls' home."

"A girls' home?"

"Where bad girls go."

"You're joshin' me."

He shook his head. "They'd probably send you to some big city—"

"They'd have to catch me first."

"You think you can hide from the law?"

"Hell, there's plenty of country around here to get lost in."

"Let's face it, honey," Aaron said, and his eyes appraised her from head to toe. "There isn't any place in God's country a female like you could hide, at least not for long."

Her eyes narrowed. "You makin' fun of me?" she asked.

"Hell no." He seemed sincere. "You're about the neatest thing I've seen in a long time."

Her head jerked back, and she frowned. "You get those damn eyes back where they belong," she stated emphatically. "Ain't no man gonna ogle me!"

"I'm sorry," he apologized, and backed away, walking over, picking up his hat. "No offense meant, okay?"

She pointed to his hat. "Where you goin'?"

"Well, I've got to take you up to the house. You can't just walk in here and then leave without going out to the house."

"Why not?" she asked, watching him uncertainly.

"You don't seem to understand." He tried to explain the best he could. "It's not your decision to make. Look," he suggested, "go out to the house with me, then wait in town long enough to have a talk with Delia Campbell. She's a fair woman, and being independent herself, she'll probably understand. If she gives you leave to go, then you can go any blessed place you care to. Is it a bargain?"

Her long hair had found its way onto her shoulder again, and she flicked it off as she eyed him suspiciously. "I told you I ain't stayin'."

"I know, I know," he argued. "But look at it from Aunt Delia's point of view. If you get ornery and just take off, she can put every sheriff in Nevada on your trail, and probably will. But if you talk her into letting you leave, you're free. You can come and go as you please."

"What if she ain't havin' none?"

"Why not give it a chance?" he pleaded. "It can't hurt anything. Just stay in Goldspur till you get a chance to talk to Delia Campbell. What's it going to hurt?"

She breathed a deep sigh. "Well . . ."

"Look . . . make me a promise. You won't leave the Highland until after you've talked to Delia Campbell . . . promise?"

She shrugged.

"It won't be that bad."

"I don't like kowtowin' to any old lady," she protested stubbornly.

"But you'll do it?"

"I'll talk to her, but I still ain't stayin'."

"But you promise you won't leave the Highland or Goldspur until you've talked to her?"

"All right, I promise," she finally gave in.

"You won't back down on your word?"

Her eyes bored into his as she pulled her hat back on top her head, sliding the bead up the rawhide ties, tightening it beneath her chin. "You sayin' my word ain't any good?" she bridled.

He looked aghast. "Hell no, I'm just making sure you won't back down."

She jammed the hat down tighter. "I don't welsh, sir," she said, and hitched her gunbelt up, settling it tighter on her hips. "Now, let's go. I don't have all day to hang around this damn place."

Aaron set his hat on his head and opened the door, stepping back politely, waiting for her to go through first, but when he saw that she wasn't about to, he walked out into the late-afternoon sunshine, letting Poe Yancey follow close at his heels.

Logan was pacing the floor of the library. He'd spent all morning with the Duchess, helping make her over into some semblance of a governess. She succumbed to the plain-looking high-necked dress all right, and having her hair pulled into a bun at the nape of her neck, but she refused to be seen with a naked face.

The afternoon stage was due anytime, and he'd given orders to Clive that the minute Aaron arrived with Poetica, he was to tell the Duchess and have her give them about ten minutes or so, then make her appearance.

He was just getting ready to pour himself a drink when he heard the front-door knocker, and froze for a moment, watching, as Clive passed the door to the library on his way to the foyer. Then Logan set the glass back down and hurried over to the other end of the room, where he sat on the top of the big mahogany desk by the bay window, and picked up a book, browsing through it, trying to look unconcerned, so that he was totally unprepared for what he saw coming through the door.

It was Aaron all right, only he was followed by a tall young Amazon of a woman with dark red hair, blue-green eyes, and a figure that looked like it was poured into a well-worn pair of black pants and black shirt. He stood up, startled.

"What the . . . ?"

Aaron was holding his hat in his hand, and he stepped aside, waving it toward the young woman with a flourish. "May I introduce Miss Poetica Yancey," he said, eyes twinkling mischievously. "Miss Yancey, Mr. Logan Campbell."

Logan stood stock-still, staring at her, his mouth gaping open, eyes wide. "But . . . but it can't be . . ." he blurted.

"But it is," Aaron answered, and his eyes were gleaming.

"Who's he?" Poe asked as she hit Aaron's arm an unladylike belt, while motioning toward Logan.

"He's Delia Campbell's nephew," Aaron quickly explained, rubbing his arm where she'd hit him.

"You didn't say anything about any relatives. What the hell're you tryin' to pull?"

---

Aaron hurriedly stepped behind her and reached his arm out, blocking the doorway. "I'm not pulling anything," he said. "Remember your promise."

"I promised to talk to Delia Campbell, not some damn relative. Now, you bring her out here, or I leave!"

He shook his finger in her face, his eyes almost level with hers. "Ah, ah! You don't welsh, remember? You promised to stay here until you talked to Delia Campbell, and you can't back out."

"I know what I promised," she answered. "You bring her, I'll talk."

"That's the trouble," Aaron confessed sheepishly. "She isn't here."

"She . . . !" Her face went livid. "What do you mean, she ain't here?" She looked at Logan. "Where's your aunt?"

He'd managed to find his composure, and stood looking down at her, one of the few men who could look down on Poe Yancey.

"My aunt happens to be in Scotland at the moment, Miss Yancey," he stated coldly. "And while she's gone, I have power of attorney to handle her affairs."

The anger in Poe's eyes increased as she turned around to Aaron, who stood his ground in the doorway, hoping she wouldn't resort to violence.

"You polecat!" she shouted, her eyes flashing. "You miserable, no-good polecat." Then she resorted to a few other choice names that even made Logan cringe. "You knew she wasn't here," she shouted. "You made me promise!"

"He made you promise what?" Logan asked, now that the initial shock was over.

"I made her promise to stay at the Highland until she talked to Aunt Delia," Aaron offered, still blocking the doorway. "She said she only came to Goldspur to tell the Campbells where they could go, and she was ready to take off for parts unknown."

"Why didn't you let her?"

"Come on now, Logan," Aaron argued. "You know very well I couldn't do that. The court's appointed Aunt Delia her guardian, and since you're in charge till she's back . . . maybe Aunt Delia knows all about it . . . how do we know? She could get mad if we didn't do right by the girl."

Logan gave him a dirty look. "You always think of the right things, don't you, Aaron," he said sarcastically, then looked at Poe. "What do we do with her, pray tell?"

"What the hell do you mean?" Poe asked. "You ain't doin' anything with me. I'm leavin'," and she made a bolt for the door, only she wasn't fast enough, and Logan caught both arms, holding her back.

She kicked and cussed, and finally, after realizing her protests were hopeless against a man who literally towered over her, she relaxed and stood defiantly while he still held her arms.

"Are you going to behave yourself now?" Logan asked.

When she nodded, he released her, but gingerly at first, expecting her to make a break for the door. She glanced at him and began rubbing her arms. Her hat had fallen to the floor in the struggle, and she bent down, picking it up, then walked over and plunked herself down in one of the easy chairs the other side of the desk.

"Okay, big man," she said sarcastically. "You know so damn much. So here I am, so what the hell you gonna do with me?" and she slung one leg up over the arm of the chair and leaned back, lifting her arms up as far as she could, stretching her shirt to its full capacity, almost popping a button in front.

Logan's eyes flashed as he deliberately walked over and hit her leg, knocking it off the arm of the chair. "First we make a lady out of you," he answered furiously. "At least we try."

"You ain't makin' any lady out of me!" she yelled, and started to get up, but he pushed her back down.

"Shut up!" he shouted. "Let me think," and he walked to the liquor cabinet and poured himself a drink, while Aaron, who'd been standing in the doorway watching their little charade, stepped aside just in time to let the Duchess step confidently through the doorway, looking quite dignified and serene. However, the Duchess had eyes only for Logan, and missed seeing Poe sprawled defiantly in the chair.

"Well, Mr. Campbell, where is this darling little charge of yours?" she asked beguilingly. "I can hardly wait," and her voice made a liar out of her words.

Logan drank a good stiff jigger of brandy and pointed toward the chair just as Poe decided she was tired of sitting down, stretched her long frame, and stood up.

She was almost a head taller than the Duchess, and looked down at her as if she were a nasty bug that had to be stepped on; then she turned and strolled leisurely to the window behind the desk and stood looking out, keeping her back to them.

The Duchess drew in a sharp breath, her face turning pale. "That's Poetica Yancey?" she asked incredulously, then nodded. "That's Poetica Yancey," she answered herself, still nodding in disbelief, and Logan watched the fire begin to rise in her dark brown eyes as she turned toward him. "You expect me to—"

"You can't back out now," Logan interrupted. "I need you now more than ever."

"Need me? You need me?" Her face was livid. "If you think for one minute I'm going to play nursemaid to that . . . that Amazon, you're sadly mistaken!"

———

"But, Duchess—"

"You stay where you are, Logan Campbell. Don't you dare come near me," she said, putting her hands up to keep him away. "You can look after your own 'little girl.' Only I'll give you a piece of advice. You'd better get yourself a chaperon instead of a governess, honey, and a damn good one too, because from the looks of your 'little girl,' I'd say you're gonna need one!" and she flew out of the room in a rage.

Logan knew there was no use trying to stop her. She had that look in her eye, and he knew that nothing he could do now would persuade her to change her mind.

He glanced over at Poe, who still had her back to him, and suddenly he realized the young woman was shaking to keep from laughing out loud. Without warning Poe turned to face him, threw her head back, and guffawed, slapping her leg with her hat.

"What's the matter, lover boy?" she said sarcastically, a broad grin on her face as she watched his expression. "You losin' your touch?"

He stared at her hard, while Aaron waited for the explosion, but instead, although Logan's eyes snapped vigorously, he seemed quite calm.

"How old are you?" he suddenly asked.

She stopped chuckling, and stood stock-still, her head held high, her face suddenly serious again. "I'll be seventeen in two weeks," she answered, then asked suspiciously. "Why?"

He ignored her question. "Where did you live in Elko?"

"We didn't live in Elko. Ma and me lived in the mountains up at Ruby Lake."

"You went to school?"

"What school?" She snickered. "I didn't need any school. Ma taught me how to read, write, and do numbers, and I can keep up with the best."

Logan turned around, walked to the bookshelf, took down a book, opened it, flicking the pages, then stopped somewhere in the middle of the book and walked over to her.

"Here, read this," he said, and she took the book from him rather gingerly, holding it out in front of her.

She glanced down at the page, then back to Logan, then at the page again, and with a sly smile she read the balcony scene from Romeo and Juliet with feeling, and without missing a word, then flipped the large volume of Shakespeare shut.

"I cut my teeth on him," she stated. "Got any more ideas?"

Logan took the book from her. "At least you're not completely uncivilized," he said as he put it back in its place on the shelf.

"What do you mean by that?" she asked. "Who's uncivilized?"

He turned to face her. In spite of the dirt on her face, and the men's clothes, he had to admit she was rather pretty, and at first glance, with her tanned complexion and soft curves, she even looked feminine. But the minute she opened her mouth, although her voice was warm and husky, her language and attitude were enough to make any man back off.

"In the first place," he stated flatly, "your language is atrocious. If you intend to stay here, it'll have to change, and in the second place, nice girls don't wear clothes so tight they look poured into them. Most ladies wear dresses or riding skirts."

"I told you before, I ain't a lady," she answered defiantly.

"I'll go along with that." He straightened authoritatively. "But unfortunately I'm afraid you're going to have to start acting like one."

Suddenly he inhaled, his eyes widening as he found himself looking into the barrel of one of her six-shooters leveled right at him.

"I said I ain't gonna be a lady for you or anybody," she shouted. "Now"—she pointed with her left hand to the doorway—"I'm gonna go out that door and you ain't gonna stop me . . . ain't no one gonna stop me, understand?"

"You can't leave," Aaron pleaded unhappily. "You promised."

She gave him a dirty look, then quickly glanced back at Logan, who started to take a step toward her.

"I wouldn't advise it," she stated boldly. "I

can shoot a candle out without touchin' the wick, and drive a nail into a four-by-four, and I sure as hell ain't gonna miss a big hunk like you."

"And hang for murder?" he asked.

She eyed him for a minute as if weighing his words, and he continued.

"As far as I'm concerned, I don't care if you stay or not. You could walk out that door anytime, and I'd be happy," he went on. "But I'm no longer acting for myself, I have Aunt Delia to think of. Now, either I try to stop you and you shoot me and hang for murder, or you act like a sensible young woman, put the gun down, and we talk things over. What's it going to be?"

She stared at him; then her eyes narrowed. "Keep talkin'," she said.

"All right. Suppose you keep the bargain you made with Aaron. Suppose you stay here till Aunt Delia returns. She's due back from Scotland in about a month or so, the end of July or first part of August. In the meantime, we'll try to make a lady out of you—"

"I told you. I don't wanna be a lady."

Logan sighed. "Look," he said. "For one month, only one month, try! By the time Aunt Delia gets back, if you still don't like being a lady, and if you still insist on going off on your own, I'll help you try to persuade her, and you can say good-bye to the whole thing. It's not a bad bargain, and acting like a lady one month out of your life won't kill you. It's either that or hang, because I don't intend to let you go through that door."

She was so enraged her face was red, yet for a second Logan thought he saw a tear in her eye.

"Only for a month?" she asked.

"Until Aunt Delia gets back, that's about a month."

"And you'll help talk her into letting me leave?"

"Nobody talks Aunt Delia into anything, but I'll try," he answered, and was relieved to see her twirl the gun back into its holster as she made up her mind.

"All right," she finally said. "I don't wanna hurt anyone, but I warn you, I ain't much for this lady business, and you can bet your bottom dollar I'll kiss the lot of you good-bye when it's over. I'll stay till your aunt comes home, but no longer, mind you. No longer!" and the two men looked at each other, breathing a sigh of relief.

Later that evening, Logan wasn't sure whether he'd done the right thing or not. He probably should have told Aaron to send Poe packing, but there was every chance there would have been repercussions from Aunt Delia if he had.

Now he glanced across the dinner table at her as she enjoyed her meal, and smiled to himself. He'd never seen a female who could put so much food in her stomach, and he wondered if she ate like that all the time. All the ladies he knew picked at their food as if it were contaminated, and hardly ate a bite, but Poe seemed to be enjoying it with gusto.

He remembered the argument she put up when they made her take her guns off to eat. In fact, it was guns she and Aaron were talking about now.

"I taught myself how," she answered when Aaron asked her about shooting. "There wasn't anybody to teach me except Ma, and she wasn't that good."

"And you said your mother taught you to read?" Logan said, joining their conversation.

Her face flushed. "But I don't like Shakespeare."

"Any special reason?"

She shrugged. "Maybe 'cause I got tired of it. It was practically the only thing I had to read till I was thirteen."

"The only thing?"

"That and the instructions on the boxes of things Ma bought, and an old worn Bible."

"How far back in the mountains were you?" Aaron asked.

"Far enough back so we didn't have to worry about any stinkin' bastards botherin' us."

Aaron looked quickly at Logan, who cleared his throat loudly, then addressed her.

"Miss Yancey, if you don't mind," Logan began slowly, "there are a few words I want you to start eliminating from your vocabulary."

"What's wrong with them?" she asked, her voice vibrating dangerously.

"There are certain words, such as 'bastard,' 'polecat,' 'son of a bitch,' and some others I don't care to repeat that are not only grating to the ear but also quite vulgar. Surely you realize this."

"Men say them, don't they?"

"Have you heard me say them?" he asked calmly, and she blushed.

"You would if you got mad enough."

This time his face reddened too.

"Well, you would, wouldn't you?" she asked.

Aaron grinned sheepishly. "Would you, Logan?" he asked, pretending to be shocked.

Logan could have killed him. "All right," he said. "I'll concede that under certain circumstances, there are times when all men may lose their tempers and say things they wouldn't ordinarily say. But you, young lady, use them when you're simply passing the time of day."

Her eyes were hostile. "Nobody ever complained before."

"But ladies don't swear."

"Lady Macbeth swore."

"Oh?"

" 'Out, damned spot! Out I say,' " she quoted dramatically. "Or have you forgotten your Shakespeare?"

---

He closed his eyes defensively, breathing deeply, trying not to explode. "All right, so ladies forget sometimes too. But for the rest of the month, will you please refrain from using them? If not, I'll be forced to take drastic measures."

"Wash my mouth out with soap?" she asked insolently, and he stared at her hard, wondering how he'd ever gotten into this mess.

"Speaking of mouths," he replied, ignoring her remark about the soap. "Who told you to fill yours as if you were a stoker filling a furnace?"

She straightened abruptly, fingers tightening on her fork. "Food's for eating, ain't it?" she asked.

"You're holding your fork like a shovel." He lifted his own fork, holding it properly in his right hand. "Do it like this."

She looked down at his hand, then at her own. "The food gets there," she said stubbornly.

He set his fork down, rose from the chair, and walked over, standing a little behind and to her right; then he reached out, grabbed her hand, and started to remove the fork, only she wouldn't let him.

"Why must you be so blamed bullheaded," he asked as he fought her, finally prying her fingers loose until the fork was free. "Here." He held it out to her. "Now hold it the way I showed you."

---

She didn't move.

He picked her hand up, put the fork into it, and forced her to hold it the right way.

"That's better," he said, and walked back to his seat, sitting down again, only Poe still didn't move or make any attempt to use the fork.

Instead, she sat stoically holding it for almost a full minute, then gently set it back on the table, picked up the napkin, wiped her mouth, then set the napkin back down again beside her half-empty plate.

"I ain't hungry anymore," she said quietly.

"You mean 'I am not hungry anymore,'" Logan corrected her.

"Am not, ain't, who the hell cares!" she burst out bitterly. "Can't eat right. Can't talk right. That's why Ma and me lived by ourselves, so we could do things our way. What difference does it make anyway whether I hold my pinkie out at the side of my cup when I drink tea or not? No one's gonna treat me like a lady!"

She pushed her chair back, stood up, walked away from the table, and went to one of the dining-room windows, turning her back on the two men so she could stare outside.

"Nobody treats a girl with respect when she doesn't even look like a lady," she went on, then turned to face them. "Look at me!" she said, her hands gesturing down her body. "Just look at me! I tower over all the so-called ladies around, and the men . . . well, let's just forget about the men.''

"But you're beautiful," Aaron gasped.

"Beautiful?" She laughed cynically. "I've got freckles on my face, a stupid nose, and I stand out like a sore thumb. You even said yourself that I'd have a hard time hiding anyplace. What good's it gonna do for me to try to look or even act like a lady? No one would ever mistake me for one."

Aaron wasn't about to give up. "Have you ever tried being a lady?" he asked softly.

"Once," she answered, and bit her lip. "When I was thirteen, Ma took me to Elko—that's when she went to see that Mr. Wimpole to make out the will. She insisted I wear a dress and try to act real nicey nice. Well, I did, and all I got for it was spit on!"

"Spit on?" Aaron was shocked.

"There were some kids comin' from the schoolhouse, and I was waitin' for Ma outside the store, and I was wearin' a dress with my hair fixed real proper and everything. Well, they started makin' fun of me 'cause I was so tall, and I kept my mouth shut as long as I could. But when they spit on me, I tore into the whole lot of 'em with my fists, and you can bet they fared the worse. Well, I ain't grown much since I was thirteen, and I decided right then and there that if they didn't want to treat me like a lady, I sure as hell wasn't gonna try to act like one." Her eyes sparked as they bored into Aaron's. "Why should it be any different now?"

"But you're not a kid anymore, you're a grown woman."

"Am I?" She took a deep breath. "Funny, but I don't feel like a woman."

"Then maybe you need a man to treat you decent and make you feel like one," Aaron suggested, and Logan, who'd been watching her closely, saw her cringe.

"I don't need a man, and I don't want a man, ever," she said fiercely. "All I want is to be left alone."

Logan gestured for her with his hand. "Poetica, come back to the table."

"My name's Poe."

"All right then, Poe," he corrected softly. "Come back to the table, Poe."

"Why?"

"Because you didn't wait for dessert," he said, surprising her, and she just stared at him for a minute, then reluctantly returned to her seat at the table and they finished their meal in silence.

However, Aaron noticed, as did Logan, that when she ate her pie, she didn't seem to have to try too hard in order to hold her fork properly, and as the men exchanged glances, Aaron sensed a satisfaction in Logan's eyes.

After dinner Aaron and Logan stood in the library watching Poe from the window as she headed for the stables to take care of her horse.

"Well?" Aaron asked.

"Well what?"

"Think you can do it?"

"Do what?"

"Make a lady out of her."

Logan looked studious as he watched her enter the stables and disappear from sight. "Methinks the lady doth protest too much, Aaron," he finally said.

"Come again?"

Logan turned and walked over, settling himself in the chair behind the desk. "You heard her read Shakespeare, and saw her use her fork properly with hardly any trouble at all. She knew how before I showed her, I'm sure of it. I honestly think it isn't so much that she doesn't know how to act like a lady. I think it's more like she doesn't want to try because she's afraid she'll succeed."

Aaron couldn't believe it. "But why?"

"If I knew that, I wouldn't be here wondering."

"Wondering what?"

"How we're going to get her into a dress."

Aaron rubbed his chin thoughtfully. "Ask her?"

"Like I asked her to stop cussing?"

Logan frowned, and Aaron smirked.

"Don't you dare laugh," Logan warned Aaron. "She can't keep wearing that pair of pants and shirt around. If we can only get them off her."

"She has to go to bed. Hide them."

"You know, that just might work," Logan said, straightening abruptly.

"Hiding her clothes?"

"Well, why not?" Logan stood up now with more conviction. "I'll sneak into her room after she's asleep tonight and make sure there's not a pair of pants or shirt left for her to put on in the morning."

"What if she sleeps in them?"

"Sleeps in them?"

"Let's face it," Aaron replied. "You aren't fooling around with any normal female, Logan. I'll bet she either sleeps with them on, or in the nude."

"You aren't serious?"

"Ah, but I am. There was only one bundle on the saddle of that horse, and it didn't look big enough to hold more than her bedroll and another pair of pants and a shirt. Now, how will you know either way?" Aaron asked, but Logan found out that evening after Aaron was gone and he and Poe started talking about retiring.

They had been sitting in the library playing a game of chess, and Logan was amazed at her alert mind. She was a formidable opponent, and he'd been surprised she even knew how to play.

"I suppose your mother taught you chess too?" he said, noticing the dirt under her fingernails and how grimy her hands still were, even though they'd been washed.

"Ma hated chess," she answered studiously.

"Then . . . ?"

"The sheriff up at Ruby Lake arrested a fella had one of them sets on him, and he taught me to play before they hung him."

"They let you play chess with a man in jail?" he asked incredulously.

"Hell, I helped the sheriff bring him in. Hadda stick around for the trial anyway."

"When was this?"

"About three months ago."

Logan stared at her in amazement, then shook his head. She'd told him earlier about her ride here from Elko, and about a skirmish she had with some Shoshones up that way. It's a wonder she was still alive. She didn't seem to be a coward, that's for sure.

"By the way," he said, changing the subject. "I noticed you travel light. Are your suitcases coming later?"

She frowned. "What suitcases?"

"Surely you have more clothes than what you have on."

"I got two pair of pants, two shirts, two pairs of drawers, and one pair of boots. That's all I need."

"Your nightclothes?"

"Who needs nightclothes?"

"But you can't sleep in your clothes."

---

"Don't intend to." She moved one of her men. "Checkmate," she said, then went on. "Been sleepin' in the raw all my life. No reason to change now."

Aaron was perceptive, Logan thought, and tried not to grin as he remembered his earlier conversation with the lawyer.

"I'm afraid you're wrong there, Poe," he informed her. "That's another habit you'll have to change. You can't sleep in the nude."

She pushed her chair away from the card table, rolling her eyes upward. "I know, I know," she said disgustedly. "Ladies don't sleep without clothes on."

"And besides," he offered, "what if an emergency came up . . . a fire . . . you'd be pretty embarrassed having to run out of your room stark naked."

"I would, or you would?" she asked, eyeing him head-on, and Logan could feel the heat rising in his face, turning it crimson.

He stood up quickly, remembering the Duchess's words about needing a chaperon. "Since you don't own any nightgowns, I'll go see what Clive can rustle up for you to put on," he said as he headed for the door.

She was grinning smugly as he left the room, but he was back in less than five minutes, handing her a blue-and-white striped man's nightshirt that looked brand new.

"Aunt Delia's nightgowns would never fit,"

he said as she took it from him. "This is a new one I haven't worn yet. You can use it until we buy you something of your own."

She unrolled the nightshirt and held it up under her chin. "I'll swim in it," she remarked, looking down at herself.

"So." He shrugged. "You won't feel all confined. It's just for one night anyway."

"Well, I guess it's all right," she conceded reluctantly. "If you can wear somethin' like this to bed, I guess I ain't too good to."

Logan sighed. At least she wasn't fighting as hard anymore, but the battle was a long way from being over.

A short while later, after a much needed bath and hair-washing, Poe stood in the middle of her bedroom and looked down at the blue-and-white nightshirt she had on. It was the first time she'd ever had anything on that was too big for her. Usually her clothes were so tight she could hardly breathe. The sleeves were way too long so she rolled them up, but there was no way to roll up the bottom of it. So she just held it up while she walked across the soft carpeting to look at herself in the full-length mirror on the closet door.

She looked ridiculous. This whole thing was ridiculous. She shouldn't have let them talk her into it, but really, what else was there? He'd been right, they'd have hung her if she'd shot him. Or at least sent her to jail. It had been stupid of her to come here in the first place, but that jackass up in Elko had warned her that she had to.

Well, she was here, and she'd try it, but she wasn't gonna make it easy for them, no sirree! She wasn't gonna get laughed at and ridiculed again for tryin' to be somethin' she never could be.

Picking her clothes up off the floor where she'd dropped them, she folded them neatly and set them on the chair by the dresser. Her other outfit was in the top drawer. Then she set her boots beside the chair and stood looking around.

The room was a beautiful one, with a canopy bed, plush carpeting, soft boudoir chairs, and frilly curtains, and Poe felt out of place. She was used to bare wood floors, bulky four-poster beds, handmade patchwork covers, and shabby but clean curtains at the windows. This room even had its own fireplace to take the chill off in the evenings.

She blew out the lamps on the dresser, climbed into bed, and pulled the silky plump comforter up under her chin, then shut her eyes tight to hold back the tears. She didn't want to be a lady, and she wasn't gonna be a lady, she couldn't ever be a lady, and she fell asleep repeating it over and over again to herself while tears rolled down her cheeks onto the pillow.

---

\*   \*   \*

It was well past midnight when Logan took off his quilted blue robe and finally slipped back into bed, a grin on his face. He'd stuffed her clothes, boots, everything, under his bed, way up beneath the head of it. She'd never think to look there, and he wondered what she'd do in the morning when she found them gone.

She'd been sleeping so soundly when he'd slipped into her room, and he was glad he'd given her the nightshirt, because the covers were almost all the way off her, and she was sprawled on her back with her arms stretched above her head. For a minute he'd been afraid she'd waken, especially when the dresser drawer creaked, and he almost lost one of her boots on his way out the door, but all had gone well. Now as he fluffed up his pillow and settled down to sleep, smiling to himself, content with his night's work, he suddenly realized that for the first time in years he was looking forward to what tomorrow might bring.

# 3

## The Making of a Lady

The sun was far from being up yet, and only a faint glimmer of light was begging to make its appearance on the horizon toward the eastern hills of Goldspur as Poe stood beside the bed staring down at Logan sleeping peacefully. His hair was ruffled, and his face was turned toward her, with his left hand holding the edge of the covers, and his right hand, resting close to his forehead, was open and relaxed.

She studied him quietly for a few minutes with the large glass of cold water poised in her hand; then quickly, before having a chance to change her mind, she let the water fly with a flourish, covering his torso, which was bare to the waist.

Logan's eyes flew open in shock, and he sputtered, letting out a yelp, then stared dumbfounded at Poe. "What the devil!" he gasped, water dripping from his face.

---

"I want my clothes!" she shouted, slamming the empty glass down on his nightstand.

"Your clothes?"

"Yes, my clothes, you miserable son of a bitch! You stole 'em!"

"That's why you threw water on me?" His eyes were blazing as he sat up in bed, the wet covers plastered against his bare skin.

Her eyes narrowed as they settled on his bare chest. "So that's why you made me wear this thing," she said as she grabbed the side of the striped nightshirt. "It's all right for you to sleep in the raw, but not me, because you knew you were gonna sneak in and steal my clothes. Is that it? So that's why the nightshirt was new. What was it, last year's Christmas present? I oughta rip the damn thing off!" and she grabbed the neckline, starting to rip it down the front.

She was standing close to the bed, and his hand shot out. "Stop it!" He seized her arm, but as he did so, the covers began to slip, and in order to keep them from sliding off all the way, he had to snatch them with his other hand.

She started to fight, but he wouldn't let go his hand tightening on her arm, and he pulled her down onto the bed, forcing her to sit beside him on the wet covers.

"I want my clothes!" she snarled through clenched teeth.

He was holding her arm in a viselike grip and

stared into her eyes. Light was beginning to filter into the room now, and he could see her face clearly. In spite of her anger, she looked softly feminine with her hair cavorting about her head haphazardly and her blue-green eyes misty.

A strange feeling began to pulsate through him. He'd never felt quite like this before, and suddenly he remembered again the Duchess's remark about a chaperon, and he pushed the feeling aside irritably.

"You'll get clothes," he answered gruffly. "You'll have a whole new wardrobe before the week's out."

Poe's eyes began to falter as they stared defiantly into his, and she lowered them self-consciously. Him and his know-it-all ways. She'd fought men, cussed them, and watched them cower under her tirades, but not Logan Campbell. And he was unpredictable. Just when she thought she had him figured out, he'd do an about-face. Like now. He was trying to be nice.

"I won't wear any dresses," she said softly, her eyes still lowered.

"You won't, or you don't want to?" He was still holding her arm, keeping her on the bed.

"I look horrid in dresses. Besides, you'd never find one to fit."

"I've already given Clive orders to have the dressmaker out here first thing this morning."

She glanced up quickly, eyes alert. "Ain't any

dressmaker gonna paw all over me," she began protesting, but he stopped her.

"Poe, will you quit the nonsense! You have to have clothes."

"My pants and shirt are fine."

"For a man, yes. You're a woman, and it's time you started acting like one."

She lowered her eyes again, staring at the floor. "I haven't worn a dress for almost four years," she said, almost as if she were talking to herself. "What will I look like?"

He felt the tension in her arm relax, and realized she was through fighting for the time being, and he released her. Reaching up slowly, she rubbed her arm where he'd been holding it, but still remained sitting on the edge of the bed.

"I'll look horrible," she whispered, and her eyes were frantic as she looked at him.

"Don't underestimate yourself, Poe," he said, his gray eyes studying her intently. "You may be taller than most women, but you have the same equipment . . ." Something he saw in her eyes made him stop. "What's the matter now?" he asked.

She stood up quickly, suddenly aware that he was a man, a good-looking man, and she was sitting on his bed while he lay stark naked with only a few covers between them.

"All right," she said, ignoring his question. "I'll wear the dresses, only it won't make any difference. I'll still be a monstrosity." She held her head up high so she didn't have to look him in the eye, and fidgeted with the front of the nightshirt. "But what do I wear till I do have clothes, this nightshirt?"

Lord, he hadn't thought of that. His eyes narrowed thoughtfully and he frowned, then pointed to the closet in the corner of the bedroom. "There's another robe of mine hanging in the closet. It's a green one, on the back of the closet door. You can eat breakfast in that, and by the time you're finished, the dressmaker should be here."

She went to the closet, took the robe down, came back to stand beside his bed and put it on, tying the sash firmly. The sleeves were far too long, the same as the nightshirt, and she turned them up, then took a deep breath, straightening. The room was light now, and the first rays of the early-morning sun streaked across the floor in front of her.

"I'm not sorry about the water," she said defiantly as she stood near the foot of the bed. "That was a dirty, low-down trick you pulled on me."

His eyes softened. "Would you have relinquished the clothes willingly?"

She shook her head but refused to answer aloud.

"I thought not, so I had no other alternative, did I?"

---

She glanced at him quickly. He was still surrounded by the wet sheets, and even though he tried to look stern and severe, instead he looked quite undignified with his hair all wet and tousled. His chest, covered with curly dark hair, was broader than she'd suspected, and she watched the muscles ripple under his bare skin as he moved, trying to get into a more comfortable position on the wet bed, and suddenly, not realizing why, she felt self-conscious.

"I'd better go," she said, and held up the bottom of her clothes, heading for the door.

"Suddenly becoming modest?" he called out to her.

She stopped, glancing back toward the bed, her eyes hostile again as they warred with his.

"Oh, go to hell!" she retorted furiously, and left, slamming the door hard behind her.

The dressmaker arrived shortly after breakfast, and was ushered into the parlor where Poe waited impatiently, pacing the floor, still dressed in Logan's nightshirt and robe. The dressmaker took one look at Poe, however, and shook her head.

"Where, sir, do I find clothes to fit her?" she asked, gesturing toward Poe's long frame.

"You make them," Logan stated arrogantly.

"But you said she needed something for today."

"She does." He looked at the dressmaker hopefully. "Surely you have something . . ."

---

The dressmaker inhaled irritably as she took another good look at Poe, then shook her head.

"Mr. Campbell, I'm sorry," she apologized. "But the young lady is far too tall. The dresses I have would not only stop well above her ankles, but I'm sure they'd be too short in the bodice."

Logan eyed Poe himself, studying her for a minute while he rubbed his chin. "Would they fit her otherwise?" he asked.

"Fit her?"

"Yes, ma'am, in the shoulders, the waist . . . ?"

The woman looked Poe over again more closely while Poe stared back at her warily. "We could lower the waist, I suppose, but otherwise, yes, I think I have something that might do."

"Can you add material to the bottom?"

She nodded slowly, beginning to understand what Logan was getting at. "Ah yes, I see," she said knowingly. "Yes . . . it should work," and she smiled. "I have a dress," and she opened one of the boxes on the floor, pulling out a dove-gray dress of *peau de soie* trimmed with a wide flounce that was edged with black lace. The square bodice was low in front, edged in the same lace, with the slash sleeves also tucked with lace. "I have some of the gray material left back at the shop, and I can put another lace-edged flounce along the bottom to make it longer, and add some bands of black lace to the bodice to lengthen it, and it should do nicely," the woman said, holding the dress up, but Poe backed away hesitantly.

Logan's eyes flashed. "You made a promise," he reminded her, and she looked disgusted.

"I have to wear that?" she asked, pointing to the dress.

"For a starter." He made the seamstress take all of Poe's measurements, then proceeded to order a whole new wardrobe for her, including some decent riding clothes, with part of it to be ready by the end of the week, and each piece brought to the house as it was finished.

Two hours later, Poe stood in her room in front of the mirror, studying herself. The dress had turned out beautifully, and the gray made her hair all the redder, while deepening the blue-green of her eyes, only she felt uncomfortable in it. They had managed somehow to find a pair of shoes to fit her, but she was used to her heeled boots, and the shoes felt light on her feet.

Reaching up, she touched her hair. Besides Clive, there were two kitchen maids, a cook, and two household maids at the Highland, and the upstairs maid had fixed her hair for her, piling it on top of her head, with curls clustered toward the back and down along to the nape of her neck.

She sighed. So this is what she'd come to. She just knew Logan was going to laugh when she went downstairs for lunch. She was nothing like the delicate women he probably knew. They were no doubt small and dainty, not big and clumsy like her. Well, he wanted it. If he laughed, she'd clobber him, dress or no dress. Taking a deep breath, she straightened, walking reluctantly toward the door.

They were just finishing lunch when Logan set his napkin down and looked across the table at Poe. Her appearance a half-hour before had certainly been a surprise. The dress had done even more for her than he figured, but it was going to take more than a dress to make a lady out of her. It was going to take a change of heart on Poe's part, and that was going to be harder to come by.

He stood up and addressed her. "Shall we go to the library?" he said, and it was a command rather than a suggestion.

Poe followed close behind him until they reached the library door and he opened it, waiting for her to enter first. There was a strange expression on her face as she quickly glanced up at him, and he wondered if it was the first time anyone had ever shown her the simple courtesy. After a moment's hesitation, Poe stepped into the room ahead of him, and he shut the door behind them, then walked to one of the bookshelves and began picking up first one book and hefting it for a few seconds, then another, until he seemed to find one that suited him. He turned, handing it to Poe, who accepted it cautiously.

"You want me to read it?" she asked.

"I want you to wear it," he answered. "Lay it flat on top of your head and see if you can walk across the room without letting it fall off."

"On my head?"

"That's what I said."

She glared at him dubiously for a second, then shrugged, reaching up, trying to set it on top of the curls the maid had piled up, only it kept sliding off.

"Damn!" she blurted, trying unsuccessfully to flatten them.

"Wait." He reached out, stopping her. "Let me," and his hand moved into her hair, deftly undoing the hairpins, letting it fall through his fingers back onto her shoulders.

She frowned, bewildered.

"You can put it back up after you learn how to walk," he explained. "You not only have to look like a lady, you have to walk like one too."

Her jaw tightened. "I walk just fine."

His eyes were steady on hers, his face determined and unyielding. "You walk like a barroom hussy," he snapped.

"I do not!"

"My dear young lady," he said, watching a flush spread over her face as her blood pressure rose, "when you walk, your hips . . ." He cleared his throat. "Shall we say, they do things no lady's hips are supposed to do."

She glowered at him for a few seconds, then lowered her eyes, looking away. "Dirty-minded man!"

He fought a smile. "What do you know about dirty-minded men?"

She threw her head back, her red hair tumbling about her shoulders, and once more her eyes were drawn back to his. "Oh, come now, Mr. Campbell," she answered. "I may not be a lady, but I'm not dumb either. As you so aptly put it, I have the same equipment, and there are men who've noticed from time to time, and they're dirty-minded men who mentally undress every woman they see, whether she's a lady or not, so what difference does it make how I walk?"

"Poe." His voice was low and husky. "Don't spoil it now, please?"

She hesitated momentarily, then heaved a sigh. "What the hell's the difference," she said, throwing her hands up in defeat, and she set the book on top her head. This time it stayed, and she held her head stiff, trying to balance it.

The first time across the floor was fine, and the book stayed put.

"Except you look like you're walking a tightrope," Logan said.

He straightened her shoulders, pushed her chin up to hold her head high, steadied the book so it was level, then walked over and sat at the desk, where he could survey her as she walked.

Two frustrating hours later she was still walking, and he was still watching, unsatisfied. Again she walked to the other side of the room, slowly, rhythmically, her back to him, and again he shook his head.

"No! No! No!" he shouted wearily, leaning across the desk toward her. "You're not wearing guns anymore, so why the hell do you think you have to keep hitching them up every time you take a step?"

She stopped a few feet from the far wall, her back to him, and held her breath, her eyes closed. Her neck was stiff, her back ached, sweat was trickling down between her breasts, making her clothes stick to her, and most of all her feet hurt. The stupid shoes didn't fit right, and she had blisters on both heels.

She bit her lip, then whirled around, catching the book as it fell from her head. "Oh!" she gasped in frustration. "So my hips aren't right, are they?" Her eyes were blazing as her temper flared. "So why the hell don't you watch something else for a change?"

"Because something else isn't swinging like it was unhinged! And what's wrong with your feet? You weren't walking like that before."

"Because I didn't have blisters before," she yelled back, and there were tears glistening in her eyes. "Here!" she screamed. "Take your damn shoes!" and she reached down, pulling them off one at a time, throwing them at him.

He quickly took refuge in the desk chair, whirling it around, ducking behind it as the shoes hit it, bouncing off onto the floor.

"And you can keep your damn book too!"

Logan saw it coming and ducked behind the chair again, letting it hit with a splat; then he peeked back around just in time to see her reach for a vase on a stand against the wall.

"Don't you dare throw that!" he warned, but it was too late, and the vase flew straight at him. He ducked again and kept his big frame behind the chair as two small china figurines followed close behind the vase, all of them shattering into bits, and he winced. Good God, if he didn't stop her, she'd smash everything.

"I won't! I won't! I won't!" she shrieked as loud as she could, and reached out, looking around for something else to throw.

Logan took advantage of her empty hands and the fact that her eyes were no longer on him, and quickly vaulted over the desk.

"Oh no you don't!" she yelled as he bore down on her. "I'll not wear the shoes, not today, or ever!" and she made a break for the door, Logan in hot pursuit, his long legs eating up the space between them.

However, Poe reached the hallway first and was just in time to collide with Aaron, who stood gaping as she hurriedly pushed him aside, half-running, half-falling up the steps, heading toward her bedroom.

Poe's collision with Aaron finally stopped Logan, and he pulled up at the foot of the stairs, staring after her. Then, as she disappeared down the hall and he heard her bedroom door slam shut, without saying a word to Aaron, his face somber and disagreeable, he turned and stalked back to the library, with Aaron cautiously following behind.

"What on earth happened?" Aaron asked as he watched Logan walk over and pick up the shoes. Then he saw the broken figurines and vase littering the carpet. "She did that?"

"She's a hellcat," Logan exclaimed furiously as he jammed the shoes together in his hands. "Got a temper worse than a mule's, and she's as unpredictable as a rattlesnake, with a disposition to match."

Aaron had never seen Logan so upset, at least not over a woman. He frowned. "What set her off?"

Logan's gray eyes were sparking dangerously. "I was teaching her how to walk like a lady."

"I like the way she walks," Aaron said, grinning. "Especially when she's wearing her six-shooters."

Logan glared at him. "That's just the trouble," he said. "She throws her hips around with that seductive walk, then wonders why dirty-minded men make remarks."

"Dirty-minded men?" Aaron scratched his head, puzzled.

"Forget it," Logan said, then walked over to look out the window at the back of the room, deep in thought.

Aaron was amused. "I see you got her into a dress," he finally said as he stared at Logan's back.

"And got water thrown on me for my efforts too." Logan turned, his voice cynical and sarcastic. "The mattress is still in the yard drying out, and if it dries in time, I may get to sleep in my own bed tonight."

"She threw water on you while you were in bed?"

Logan pointed a finger at Aaron. "Don't you dare laugh," he cautioned, as he saw Aaron's eyes crinkling at the corners. "It isn't funny. I've never seen such a temper in all my life."

"Bite off a bigger hunk than you can chew?" Aaron asked, managing to stifle the smile that tugged at his lips.

Logan tilted his head back and closed his eyes disgustedly. "I'll either make her or break her," he replied, and the amusement left Aaron's eyes as he caught the hard determination in his friend's voice.

"Why don't you just try sweet-talking her?" he suggested abruptly, and this time it was Logan's turn to be amused.

———

"Ever had any success sweet-talking a bob-cat?" he asked.

Aaron shrugged. "It works on the Duchess."

"The Duchess is a warm, affectionate woman who appreciates a man's attentions." Logan hesitated, fidgeting with the shoes in his hands. "And speaking of the Duchess," he continued, "have you seen or talked to her since yesterday?"

Aaron grinned sheepishly. "Getting worried?"

"Not in the least. I'm just curious."

"I saw Peko this morning and she said the Duchess is furious. Came home storming about some redheaded Amazon, and she's been biting everybody's head off ever since."

"The Duchess?"

"You have an unusual effect on women, my friend," Aaron said complacently.

"She's jealous of that . . . that . . ." He waved his hand in the air disgustedly as he walked over and set the shoes on the desk. "That's ridiculous."

"Not really. Poe's competition, and young competition too."

"Competition?" Logan's eyes narrowed. "I wouldn't touch that female with a ten-foot pole, and I'm sure the feeling's mutual."

"Then you'd better inform the Duchess."

Logan laughed softly. "Why? Let her stew awhile." He straightened, once more sure of himself. "It'll do her good. Besides," he added irritably, "since when do I have to account to her for what I do?" He walked back to the window and stared out, then turned once more to face Aaron. "Just a bit of advice, my friend," he said with authority. "Never tell a woman you love her, or even give her that impression by making her think you have to make excuses for anything, or she'll think she can sink her hooks in and run your life for you, and there isn't a woman on the face of the earth who's worth that. Not one. Enjoy them, flatter them, and take all you can get, but make sure you keep them in their place."

"Their place? Come on, Logan, you know damn well how I feel about women."

Logan eyed his friend knowingly. Ah yes, he knew women held a special place in Aaron's life. Aaron fell in love with them regularly, and Logan was surprised he'd managed to stay single so long, assuming the only reason was that although Aaron loved the ladies, he was far from being a lothario.

Logan had once heard one of the Duchess's girls describe his lovemaking. "It's like kissing a man with ten hands, three mouths, and an unquenchable thirst," she'd said, and Logan smiled to himself now as he remembered the description. There was nothing suave or polished about Aaron. He blundered into lovemaking like a lovesick adolescent, and enjoyed every minute of it, even though the women didn't.

"You're incorrigible, Aaron," Logan said, finally calmed down some from his altercation with Poe. "You're a disgrace to the male ego. Women are for amusement, and when one no longer amuses, there's always another to take her place."

Aaron shook his head. "Someday, Logan," he said, glaring at his friend hopelessly, "you're going to meet a woman who's going to get under that thick skin of yours and push your cynical heart around, whether you want her to or not. And you know, I sure hope I'm still around to see it, because I'd love to see a woman bring you to your knees."

Logan grinned. "You've got a long wait, friend," he said. "A long, long wait."

But Logan didn't see the amused look that once more covered Aaron's face, nor the grin that followed as Aaron watched Logan snatch the shoes Poe had been wearing off the desk and leave the library, heading upstairs.

Poe sat on the edge of the bed and reached down, gingerly touching the blisters on her heels. They were broken open and raw already, and she cursed Logan with a vengeance.

The egotistical bastard! Women weren't people to him. They were things to order around. He had no heart, no feelings! What did he care if she had blisters on her feet, just so she wriggled her rear end the way he wanted her to.

She stood up in her bare feet and surveyed

herself in the mirror, then slowly walked toward it, holding her head high, her eyes on her hips. She didn't walk that badly. So her hips moved a little. Good God, she wasn't a statue.

"To hell with you, Logan Campbell!" she mumbled to herself, and walked over to the bedroom window and looked out. A self-satisfied grin transformed her face as she looked down into the yard and saw his mattress drying out. Now she wished it had been a whole bucket of water instead of a glass.

There was a hesitant knock on the door and she could hear the slightly muffled voice behind it. "May I come in . . . please?" Logan asked.

She turned toward the door. "No!" Her answer was too late as he walked in. She'd forgotten to lock the door.

"Get out!" she screamed. "I hate your guts!"

He stood looking at her a moment, then calmly shut the door behind him. "I don't intend to leave until we've talked."

She flicked the hair back off her shoulder, standing her ground. "I'd rather talk with a rattlesnake."

He ignored the remark. "Let me see the blisters," he said, and she eyed him suspiciously. "You did say you have blisters?"

"Yes."

"Then sit down." He pointed to the chair beside her while she stared at him dumbfounded.

He was more forceful. "Sit down," he commanded, and walked over, staring down at her, his eyes threatening.

She sat down in the chair slowly; then, much to her surprise, he knelt in front of her, picked up her right foot, and turned it so the blister was visible. She saw him wince.

"My God, girl," he exclaimed, and there was actually concern in his voice. "Why didn't you tell me earlier?"

Her jaw tightened stubbornly. "Because you were too busy yelling at me."

He stared at her for a minute, then stood up. "I'm going to send the downstairs maid up with salve and bandages," he said. "Let her take care of your feet, then don't even bother to put the shoes back on, but come back down to the library when she's through."

"The library? Why? So you can bully me around some more?"

He glared down at her. "Did it ever occur to you that if you were a little more cooperative none of this would have happened?"

"You mean, if I play up to you and roll my eyes, and say yes all the time, like that lady who was here yesterday, you might not yell at me? No thanks!"

He took a deep breath, and she could tell he was trying to hold his temper. "What you need, young lady," he said harshly, "is a good hard spanking."

"You aim to try?" She stood up, challenging him, her feet firmly planted.

"At the moment, no," he replied. "But don't tempt me." Then he turned and walked to the door. "I'll see you in the library as soon as you're finished," he said, looking back for a second; then he started to leave.

"If I feel like it!" she countered, only her words were lost on him as the door closed behind him, and fuming with rage, she sank back down into the chair to sulk.

It was almost an hour later when the library door slowly opened and Poe came in barefoot.

Logan was sitting in one of the chairs by the fireplace, slumped down relaxing, his hands clenched together and held in front of his mouth, contemplating. He glanced over, suddenly aware she'd entered the room.

"Come, sit down," he said, straightening, motioning toward the chair opposite him, and as she walked across the room, his eyes traveled to the bandages on the back of her heels.

She sat down in the chair, folded her hands in her lap, and looked docile.

He stood up and went to the desk, taking something off it, then came back to the chair where she was sitting. "Put these on," he said, and handed her a pair of doeskin moccasins.

They were beaded and fringed, and soft as velvet. She fingered them a moment, then leaned over and carefully slipped them on her feet.

———

"Blisters hurt with them on?" he asked.

She shook her head.

"Good." He looked pleased again. "Wear these until they're healed, and we'll have the bootmaker fix you up with shoes that fit. Meantime we'll start again tomorrow morning on the walking."

She glared up at him, her eyes alert. "You intend to parade me back and forth again tomorrow?" she asked.

Again he looked stern and authoritative. "I intend to parade you, as you call it, until you walk like a lady. Is that understood?"

She winced. "And I thought maybe you were trying to be nice for a change." She looked down at the moccasins, then back up at him. "Come to think of it, though, you probably don't know what the word 'nice' means, do you?"

"I suppose you were being nice when you threw all those things at me?"

"You deserved it!"

"Why? Because I want you to be something more than a saddle tramp? Because I think you've got the makings of a lady, if you'll only try. What's wrong with you, Poe Yancey? What's the real reason you don't want to be a lady? Why won't you even try? What are you afraid of?"

"I'm not afraid of anything."

"You're afraid of being a lady."

---

"I am not!"

"Then be one. I dare you!"

Her face paled and she didn't answer. Instead, she stood up and faced him squarely. "I'll be what I want to be, and nothing more," she answered. "Now, may I go?"

He studied her thoughtfully for a moment, hesitating, as if trying to decide what to do with her, then sighed. "For the moment, I guess," he said. "But tomorrow we start again." She was still glaring hatefully at him as she left without saying another word.

That evening, after a rather uncomfortable dinner, Logan found himself walking toward town. He was frustrated for the first time in years. There was no method to handling Poe Yancey. She was a law unto herself, and she was fighting him every step of the way.

At dinner, when he'd corrected her speech and criticized her manners, he'd run up against hostility again. She'd complied, but reluctantly, and her compliance was without the finesse a lady should possess, and he knew she was doing it on purpose.

The night air as he walked felt warm and balmy, and before realizing it, he found himself in front of the Duchess's house, staring at the door. He wanted to go in, yet didn't, and felt restlessly out of sorts.

"Oh, hell," he finally mumbled aloud to himself as he turned, walking on toward one of the saloons. "Maybe a game of poker will settle my nerves instead," and he spent the rest of the evening losing every cent in his pockets. Something that rarely happened to Logan Campbell.

The next morning Poe walked stoically into the library and stood staring at Logan, who was standing with his back to her as he gazed out the window. She stood just inside the door, not saying a word, and it wasn't until he turned around that he realized she was there.

She had on a different dress today, of pale green silk, soft and feminine. The dressmaker had fixed it over for her, and sent it out to the house late the night before so she'd have something to wear. Her hair was down on her shoulders as it had been the day before so the book wouldn't slip off her head. Much to Logan's surprise, she reminded him of a wood nymph one would expect to see rising from the morning mists on a summer day.

"I didn't hear you," he said hesitantly as he stared at her.

She held her head up straight and erect. "Well, I'm here."

"Then shall we start?" He walked to the desk, sat down, then gestured to her, and she began walking slowly toward the bookcases on the opposite wall.

At first he watched halfheartedly, expecting

the same response he'd gotten the day before, only suddenly he straightened in the chair, staring dumbfounded as he watched her walk gracefully across the room. Her walk was beautiful and smooth, carriage perfect, shoulders at just the right angle, hips swaying gently, with a grace of movement he'd seen in very few women. He couldn't believe his eyes.

She picked up the same book they had used the day before from its place on the shelf, and started to set it on her head, but before she had a chance, he stood up, a menacing look on his face, and walked toward her, grabbing the book from her hands.

"You little vixen!" he snarled, his face wreathed in anger, and her eyes widened.

"You're not pleased?" She was bewildered.

"Pleased?" he yelled. "Pleased? Because you made a fool of me? You knew all along what you were doing yesterday, didn't you?"

She started to protest.

"Don't lie!" he said heatedly, not giving her a chance to even talk; then he pointed toward the other side of the room. "Walk," he commanded, and she hesitated. "Walk!" he ordered her again, and she walked gracefully across the room and back, his eyes never leaving her.

"Why?" he asked when she stood before him again. "Yesterday . . . why did you pretend?"

"I . . . I didn't . . ." she stammered unhappily.

But he paid no heed. "You're a liar, do you

hear me?'' he yelled viciously. "A goddamn liar!'' and he slapped the book on the desk with such force the lamp shook, then turned and stormed from the room, slamming the door behind him.

Poe stood motionless, her face drained of color, and she was still standing in the same spot only seconds later when the door opened and Aaron walked in. He came over and stood beside her, frowning.

"Hey, what is it? Logan just bit my head off, and look at you . . . What happened?''

Her eyes were misty. "He . . . he called me a liar,'' she murmured softly, her voice barely a whisper. "I stay up half the night practicing, hoping I've got it right, hoping it's what he wants, and he accuses me of pretending, and calls me a liar.''

Aaron was puzzled for a second, then slowly understood. "You mean you stayed up all night practicing how to walk?''

She nodded.

"Why?'' he asked, knowing that only yesterday she'd fought him stubbornly.

"Be-because I believed him when he said I could be something,'' she stammered. "Be-because I was a stupid fool and thought it didn't matter how tall I was . . . that maybe he was right and I could be a lady. Then when I do it right, he says . . . he says . . .''

Aaron whistled low. Logan had really put his

foot in this one. "He said you'd been playing him for a sucker, right?"

She moved away from in front of the desk and walked over to the window, looking out toward the stables. "Where's my horse?" she suddenly asked.

"In the stable, as far as I know. Why?"

She turned abruptly and headed for the door.

"You don't intend to ride, do you?" Aaron asked as he followed her from the room, down the hall, and on out the back door, heading down the back walk toward the stables.

"Don't I?" she answered.

"But your dress?"

"To hell with the dress," she stated angrily. "If I don't get out now and cool off, I just might kill that bastard the next time I see him!"

Aaron gasped. "But you can't," he protested.

They reached her horse's stall, and she picked up the blanket and saddle, throwing them on her horse, straightening them and pulling the cinch tight.

"You gonna stop me?" she asked.

He winced as he watched her finish saddling the black gelding. "Not me," he answered, backing away from the fury in her eyes, and a few minutes later he shook his head in dismay, watching her ride out of the yard and on up the back slope, heading toward the Monitor Range, her frothy green silk dress floating out on each side, red hair flying.

---

Poe was so upset she hardly saw where she was headed. All she knew was that she wanted to get away. Last night after she'd gone to bed, she'd thought over what he'd said, and how he didn't want her to be a saddle tramp, and she made up her mind to at least try, and she'd gotten back up, pacing the floor until way past midnight, when she'd finally decided she was doing it right, and she thought he'd be pleased.

Pleased! Ha! You couldn't please a man like Logan Campbell, or any other man for that matter. They were all alike. Ma had warned her about men. They took what they could from a woman and gave nothing in return except heartaches.

She rode for over an hour, keeping her horse at a hard pace as she moved on up to where the hills were steeper, going deep into the pine timber. Branches snagged her dress and snatched her hair, yet she paid no heed. She had to get away. As far away as possible, and as she conquered each new hill with a reckless indifference, it somehow seemed to soothe some of the anger inside her. Maybe that's why, when she rode up to another hill, steeper than all the others, she let her emotions guide her instead of her common sense. It wasn't until she was halfway up the hill that she finally came to her senses and realized her mistake, only it was too late.

Her horse was winded, and began to falter,

breaking stride. She tried to calm him, but instead he reared up, taking her off guard, and she flew through the air, landing unhurt on her back in a bed of weeds at the bottom of the ravine, from where she watched dismayed as the horse bolted the rest of the way up the hill alone.

"You damn ornery critter!" she screamed after him breathlessly, struggling to her feet. "You come back, you stinkin' no-good . . . !" But it was useless.

The horse kept right on going until he was out of sight over the top of the hill, and slowly, as Poe straightened, looking around, taking in her surroundings for the first time since she'd left the house, the ravine grew quiet until the stillness lay all around her, overwhelming her, and suddenly, with tears in her eyes, she sank to the ground, physically and emotionally exhausted.

# 4

## A Change of Heart

Logan took the front steps of the Duchess's house two at a time, then fidgeted nervously as he waited for Peko to open the door.

"Señor Logan," the young girl said as she let him in, a surprised look on her face. "The Duchess, she's not up yet."

"Good." He headed for the stairs.

The scent of her perfume seemed stronger than usual as he opened her bedroom door and slipped inside, and for a moment he was almost repelled by it. Closing the door softly behind him, he walked over, staring down at the woman on the bed.

Dark shades were drawn to keep out most of the sunlight, but he could see her clearly. Her dark hair was spread out against the pillow and he studied her face. There was still beauty in it, but there was a hardness too. She'd fought her way in the world, and it showed in her face now as she slept. There was none of the youthful freshness he'd once thought was there, and for the first time he saw her as she really was: a woman trying to hold onto her youth as long as she could. He remembered what Aaron said about her being jealous of young competition. She was trying to cling to the past and fight against age with determination, and he watched the crow's-feet at the corners of her eyes wrinkle as she slowly stirred, opening them.

"Logan?" she whispered, blinking, surprised to see him; then she stretched sensuously, revealing a black lace nightgown that barely covered her. "Sit down," she said, and patted the side of the bed.

He sat down, heaving a sigh, and she knew something was wrong.

"The girl?" she asked hesitantly.

He swore as he rubbed his knee with his hand, and she could see he was agitated. "That goddamn little hellcat!" he blurted, and stood up again, suddenly beginning to pace the floor.

The Duchess rose on one elbow, watching him for a minute, then smiled seductively. "Come here, Logan," she said, her voice soft and warm.

He stopped, staring at her.

"Logan, please?" she purred.

He walked over slowly, sat back down on the edge of the bed again, and reached out, pulling her into his arms. Her body was soft and yield-ing, but he was still enraged, his kiss stiff and awkward, not the warm caress she was used to.

She drew away, staring at him, at the frustra-tion all too apparent in his eyes, and reached up, running her fingers through his hair, then touched his cheek.

"You're losing your touch, pet," she whis-pered provocatively.

He pushed her away, and she fell back on the bed. Surprising her, he stood up and walked to the liquor cabinet while she quickly composed herself and slid from the bed, slipping on her black lace negligee. Her satin slippers were un-der the edge of the bed, and she put them on, then walked over to stand beside him, watch-ing while he poured himself a good stiff drink.

"She's really gotten to you, hasn't she?" she said.

"What's that supposed to mean?"

"I told you you needed a chaperon."

He laughed cynically. "You think . . . ?"

"What else am I supposed to think when you kiss me like that?"

He drained his glass in one swallow, set it down, then reached out and drew her to him. "Is this better?" he said, and kissed her again, long and hard.

When his lips left hers again, she drew away, eyeing him skeptically. "Something's wrong, lover," she said softly. "Your mind's not on your work."

He shrugged. "You don't know what I've been through." He shook his head. "I've never seen anyone so cussed ornery and foul-tempered. She's enough to try the patience of a saint."

"Which you definitely are not."

He pulled her closer and kissed her neck just below the ear. "Which I am not," he confirmed, continuing to kiss her neck, caressing the hollow at the base of her throat with his lips.

Maybe this was what he needed, he silently told himself, and his hands began to fondle her affectionately, desire rising in him. Sweeping her up in his arms, he carried her to the bed, and for a while all thoughts of Poe were pushed to the back of his mind as he made love to her.

Here was a woman he could master, he kept telling himself. A woman who gave everything to him and asked nothing in return except the joy she found in his arms. For the next hour or so he used the Duchess's body hungrily, trying to forget all his troubles, losing himself in a world of pleasure where he was sure Poe Yancey couldn't exist.

Logan went to the mines after leaving the Duchess, and from there to the lumber mill, and it was close to dinnertime when he decided to stop by the office in town.

Aaron was at his desk as usual, working on

the books, and he looked up as Logan stepped inside. "When you disappear, you really disappear, don't you?"

"You wanted me?" Logan asked.

"I was looking for you earlier, but I imagine she's cooled off and come back by now."

Logan straightened. "Who's come back by now?" he asked sharply.

"Poe."

"Poe?"

"You treated her rather shabbily, you know."

"I . . . ? Look, my friend," he said hastily, "that good-for-nothing excuse for a female made a fool of me yesterday."

"You should have hung around for an explanation," Aaron said, disappointed in Logan. "But it probably wouldn't bother you that the kid changed her mind about being a lady, would it? That she'd been up half the night practicing just to please you."

Logan stared at him, unable to believe what he was hearing.

Aaron continued. "You really did it this time, didn't you? You'll be lucky if you ever see her again, the way she took off on that horse."

"What are you talking about?" Logan demanded. "What horse?"

"Her horse!" Aaron yelled back. "She was so upset after you left, I couldn't stop her, and the last I saw of her, she was headed for the Monitor Range as if the devil himself were on her tail."

"And you let her go?"

"How was I to stop her, pray tell?"

Logan's gray eyes darkened like clouds before a storm, and without saying another word, he whirled around and left, completely surprising Aaron, who cringed as the door slammed so hard behind Logan that the glass almost shattered.

Logan ran all the way to the house, and it took no time at all to discover that Poe hadn't returned. A few minutes later he was cursing as he saddled his horse. Why hadn't she told him? He hadn't given her a chance, that's why. He'd blown up and accused her of lying, and with her temper, she'd done the obvious thing.

He had to bring her back, not only for Aunt Delia's sake but also for his own peace of mind.

Still wearing his suit and fancy shirt with the ruffles down the front, he reined his horse out of the yard, looking warily toward the sky that was beginning to darken ominously as the storm clouds that had been forming for the past few hours began to take shape, emitting low rumbles off in the distance.

It took a good half-hour to pick up what he thought was Poe's trail, and now, as he headed toward the mountainous Monitor Range, lightning suddenly shattered the sky a short distance ahead, and he frowned.

Ordinarily he wouldn't worry about Poe. She'd ridden down from the Ruby Mountains alone without any trouble, but she'd been wearing six-guns then, and pants, boots, and shirt. All she had on now was a thin, filmy silk dress and moccasins, and she knew nothing about the lay of the land. It was so easy to get lost.

Spurring his horse harder, watching the storm clouds continue to gather in the lowering sky, he suddenly wished he'd taken time to at least grab some blankets or a slicker. He'd even left his guns behind, but felt a little more reassured as he glanced at the rifle he'd remembered to grab at the last minute and shove into the sheath on his saddle. Only a rifle wasn't any protection from the elements, and he shivered slightly, listening to another clap of thunder that sounded much closer than the other rumblings had.

He was working his way into the pine country now, taking it slow to make sure he wouldn't lose the trail, and he could tell she was riding hard, without caution or care.

He'd been riding for well over two hours already, and it was getting darker by the minute. Now he really started worrying. Especially when he rounded a bend and came out into a small clearing where a lone horse was restlessly grazing, his saddle empty. The black gelding was skittish, so Logan stayed in the saddle, hoping his own horse would keep it from spooking. But just as he reached it and started to lean over to grab the horse's halter, a bolt of lightning crashed, hitting a nearby tree, and the gelding took off, breaking through the trees at the side of the clearing. Logan stared after it. He could chase it down, but if he did, he'd lose Poe's trail altogether, and it was getting too dark. If he didn't find her by nightfall, there was a good chance he never would, and the empty saddle had comfirmed a gnawing fear at the back of his mind that she was in trouble. She might have stopped for a breather and the horse had run off, but he had his doubts. The way she was riding, she was more than likely thrown, and could even have a broken arm or leg, or worse.

Picking up Poe's horse's trail where it came into the clearing, he started backtracking, and every once in a while he'd stop to call, quickly becoming discouraged as his voice seemed to lose itself in the wind that was blowing up. And when he waited, listening, the only answering calls he could hear were the wild calls of the birds warning each other of his approach, and the rumble of thunder overhead.

As he called her name once more, then waited for an answering call with no luck, he suddenly felt the first few drops of rain on his face, cold and wet, and his heart sank. Nights could be cold in these mountains when it rained, without proper clothing or shelter, and if she was hurt she wouldn't have much of a chance.

He urged his mount forward, and topped a small hill, riding down the other side into a ravine. It was getting darker and harder to see, and the intermittent raindrops were being blown into his face by the wind, which was growing stronger by the minute.

Suddenly he stopped, straining his eyes as he saw movement up ahead. "Poe!" he yelled, only to have his words lost again in the rush of wind.

This time he didn't wait for an answer, but spurred his horse hard, and hearing the noise of the pounding hooves behind her, Poe whirled around, recognizing him instantly. She tried to run, to get away, but he was out of the saddle in seconds, standing beside her, his fingers tightening on her arm.

"What are you doing, you damn fool!" he shouted as he pulled her toward him, the rain starting to fall harder. "I've been searching for hours!"

"Leave me alone," she yelled. "I don't need your help."

"Well, you're going to take it whether you want to or not," he stated angrily, relieved that she wasn't hurt.

The rain was coming down harder now, and he had to find shelter of some kind or they'd be drenched. Remembering a cave nearby, he pulled her toward his horse, ignoring her continuing protests.

"Get on," he ordered firmly, but she just stared at him stubbornly. Disgusted, he picked her up, and despite her yelling and kicking deposited her in the saddle. He then jumped on behind, warning her to stay put, or else, as he dug his horse in the ribs, urging him quickly into a full gallop, heading for where he was sure the cave was. Even at that, it took over ten minutes to find it.

He rode inside just as the sky opened up, unleashing a flurry of wind and rain that seemed to drown everything in its path. Once inside, he jumped from the saddle, turned and lifted her down, then stood surveying their shelter.

It was so dark he could barely see, but he'd been in here before and knew it was big enough for at least one horse, even though it was barely a hole in the side of a hill.

Poe walked over and stood near the entrance, looking out at the deluge. She couldn't run now, it was like a wall of water out there, and she stood for a long time staring out before moving back to sit on the ground and lean her head against the side of the cave, her back to him.

He sat down directly behind her, and for a few minutes they both watched the rain in silence.

"Why didn't you tell me?" he finally asked, and she looked back over her shoulder at him curiously.

"Tell you what?"

"That you'd been practicing."

She shrugged. "It wouldn't have mattered. I'm a liar, remember? Why don't you just leave me alone?"

He didn't answer, then saw her shiver as she reached up, trying to hug her arms to keep warm. His suit jacket was wet on the outside, but the inside was still dry. Slipping it off, he reached over, trying to put it around her shoulders, only she'd have no part of it, and pushed her arms back, letting the jacket fall to the ground behind her.

"I don't want your damn jacket! I'd rather catch pneumonia."

He took a deep breath and picked up the jacket, more determined this time. She moved quickly, but not fast enough, and as the jacket covered her shoulders, his arms went around her, and he pulled her close, turning her toward him, holding her tightly against him.

"Leave me alone," she snarled, continuing to squirm, but instead he held her all the tighter, his jacket still about her shoulders.

"Don't be a pigheaded ass, and hold still," he said furiously; then his voice warmed a little. "Pneumonia is nothing to fool with, and those clothes you have on couldn't keep anything warm."

She was unable to move because of the way

he was holding her. "Please, let me go," she pleaded stubbornly.

He refused. "You might as well give up," he said calmly. "Because I don't intend to let go. It's cold and wet, and we can keep warm like this, so why don't you relax? We've got a long night ahead of us."

"All night?"

"All night," he confirmed, and she was at a loss for words.

She had never been this close to a man before, and tensed, afraid. The ruffles on his shirt touched her face, tickling her nose, and she moved her head. Then, realizing there was only a shirt between her head and his chest, and remembering how broad it had looked yesterday morning when he lay in bed, muscles rippling under his bronzed skin, and the soft hair scattered across it . . .

He was right, though. Her chills were subsiding, and she was warming up. Even her legs began to get warmer, only she had the strangest sensation that it had nothing to do with her outward physical condition, because her skirt was still soaking wet, and by all rights her legs should still have been cold, but they weren't.

Logan was in a sitting position, leaning against the hard rock wall of the cave, his legs stretched out close to hers, and although the mere closeness of his body seemed to be what was warming her clear through, it was a peculiar warmth, one she'd never felt before. Not only was her skin warm on the outside, but inside she felt hot and flushed.

No man had ever put his arms around her before, or held her close like this, and it was unnerving. She put her hand up against his chest and felt his heart beating. Although in some ways it was frightening being so close to him, it also gave her a surprising feeling of security, and she began to relax, admitting reluctantly to herself that it did feel good. She'd never known a man's arms could feel like this, and, contented, she nestled her head closer against his chest.

"Comfortable?" he asked as he felt her body relax.

Her voice was soft, barely a whisper. "Yes."

He sighed, relieved, and leaned his cheek against her hair, watching the rain outside. It was pitch dark now, and although the storm was raging wildly outside, inside the cave it was quiet and secure, as if they were the only two people in the world.

Logan's horse, standing only a foot or two away, changed his position, nickering, and he hoped the animal would stay put, since there'd been no place to tether him.

Poe's hair was wet from the rain, yet felt soft against his cheek, like silk. She stirred, sighing contentedly, and he smiled to himself, breathing deeply. Strange, he thought as she moved her head again, brushing her hair against his nostrils. There was no strong perfume smell on Poe's hair, only a faint sweet fragrance mixed with the fresh smell of the rain, earthy yet sensuous. And she felt so different in his arms compared to all the other women he'd ever held. Most women were small and fragile and often felt as if they'd break in two. But Poe, although soft and warm, felt firm and alive.

He could feel her body pressed against his, and for some strange reason he began to wonder uneasily what it'd be like to make love to a woman like Poe. A woman with fire. One he could caress without worrying about breaking. A passionate woman. And he was so sure Poe would be passionate, for she hated with too much vehemence. It was only logical she'd love with the same fervor.

The thought was intriguing, but he quickly pushed it to the back of his mind. At least he tried to, but she stirred in his arms again and a warm sensation shot through him, and he inhaled, holding his breath. She might be barely past adolescence, but she was more woman than he'd realized. Slowly he let his breath out again as he cuddled her closer, his body beginning to ache with longing.

My God! He'd never ached for a woman like this before. Of all the stupid . . . what had he gotten himself into? He'd held women before, and they'd never had this effect on him unless he wanted them to, and he certainly didn't want to feel like this now, with Poe.

He leaned his head back against the cave wall, closing his eyes. He'd told her it was going to be a long night, and by God, he thought to himself as he fought the natural instincts that were trying to control his body, he'd been right: It was going to be a terribly long night, longer than he'd ever imagined.

It was almost dawn. They had both been dozing, and now Logan became conscious of Poe stirring gently against his chest. She'd been warm and cozy all night and hated to move because it felt so good in his arms, but now Poe also felt something else. There was a stirring inside of her she'd never known existed, and one that frightened her, making her restless, but she didn't know why. All she knew was she wanted something, but what?

Logan began to stir too, and they both sat up, his arms loosening from about her. The first rays of dawn were starting to filter into the cave, and Logan straightened, stretching his arms above his head.

She followed his lead and stretched too, then leaned back against the wall of the cave, pulling his jacket closer about her.

"You stayed warm?" he asked, his eyes catching hers off guard.

She stared at him, unable to look away, and

something went through her, making her whole body tremble, leaving her speechless.

He reached out and took her chin in his hand, holding her face toward him so he could look into her eyes, and he held his breath.

Then quite abruptly he dropped his hand, avoiding looking at her this time, and he stood up. "Looks like the horse has forsaken us," he said briskly, and walked toward the mouth of the cave, then spotted him a few feet away, grazing.

Everything was dripping with water. The trees, grass. Water even dripped intermittently down over the mouth of the cave.

"At least the rain has stopped," he continued, then finally looked down at Poe again, holding his hand out to pull her to her feet.

She took his hand reluctantly, letting him help her up, then stood staring at him for a few seconds. Finally he let go of her hand and went after the horse while she waited in silence.

Maybe he was right. Maybe she could be a lady, she thought hesitantly, and for no logical reason she began to wonder about the way Logan had held her last night, and if it would feel the same no matter what man held her. She'd never known she could feel like that in a man's arms. She'd liked the feeling it gave her, then suddenly remembered her mother's warning. But then, her mother never said it didn't feel good. In fact, her mother said it felt too good, and that was the trouble. Ma had told her repeatedly that no man could be trusted, and the pleasure wasn't worth the heartaches. If only she knew . . . Just maybe . . . She was so mixed up and confused.

"Are you ready to go?" Logan asked, interrupting her thoughts, and she stepped out of the cave into the fresh morning air, leaning her head back to breathe a deep sigh.

"I'm sorry I caused so much trouble," she said softly as she strolled to the horse, nuzzling his nose with her hand.

"No need to be sorry," he replied. "I don't think either one of us can take laurels in the temper department. Now climb on, and I'll ride in back."

His jacket was still about her shoulders, and she slipped her arms in the sleeves, then mounted. He climbed up behind her, both of them settling comfortably on the horse, and as the first few brilliant rays of the sun peeped over the tops of the pine trees on the horizon, they headed away from the cave back in the direction of Goldspur, both lost in their own disturbing thoughts.

It was about an hour before lunch when they rode down the back slope and on into the stables at the Highland, and after depositing their horse in its stall, they were met at the back door by Clive.

"We were quite worried, sir," the butler said

while escorting them to the kitchen where the cook began trying to put together some food for them.

Logan ushered Poe ahead of him, and pulled a chair out for her.

"We're starved," he said as she sat down gingerly on the chair.

It was the first time Poe had been in the kitchen. There were two kitchen maids, besides the cook, scurrying around, as well as a down-stairs maid and an upstairs maid who were flitting in and out of the room, surreptitiously eyeing Poe and Logan where they sat together at the table.

Poe was still wearing Logan's jacket, and self-consciously pulled it tighter around her, feeling their curious eyes on her. Logan glanced over quickly, sensing her discomfort, and ordered them to stay out of the room. All except the cook, that is, who was setting hot soup and fresh-baked bread on the table in front of them. When she was through, she went back to the sink and started washing some vegetables while they began to eat.

After a few minutes Logan glanced over at Poe. She looked restless, and was only toying with her food, having eaten hardly a thing.

"What's the matter, Poe?" he asked.

She shook her head. "Nothing." Her eyes strayed hesitantly toward the cook, then back down at her bowl of soup.

Logan had been watching her closely, and he frowned, momentarily puzzled, then dismissed the cook before turning to Poe again when the cook was out of earshot. He set his spoon down. "All right, Poe, we're alone," he said, reassuring her. "Now, I asked you before, what's the matter?"

Her face paled, then started turning pink as she glanced over at him, trying hard to avoid his eyes, but she still didn't answer.

"Don't go coy on me," he said irritably. "You haven't had food since yesterday morning, and I know you've got to be hungry, so why aren't you eating?"

"I can't."

"Why?"

Her eyes lowered. "I'm all confused."

"About what?"

She sighed, and suddenly looked up at him, straight into his eyes. "Logan, what did you feel when you held me in your arms last night?" she asked, her voice trembling.

The question took him completely by surprise, and he stared at her big blue-green eyes that were gazing into his so innocently.

Her eyes faltered again, and she lowered them shyly. "I'm sorry, I shouldn't have asked," she murmured.

He was still shocked by her question, and just kept staring at her, then suddenly realized why she asked it. "Poe, hasn't any man ever held you in his arms before?" he asked abruptly.

She looked troubled. "No," she answered; then her eyes suddenly took on a faraway look. "I never thought it would be like that. It felt so strange . . ."

"How did it feel?"

She still had a dreamy expression on her face. "I was so warm and alive deep down inside. It was as if . . . as if I wanted to crawl inside of you and become a part of you." She paused for a second, then without warning asked, "Is that how you felt?"

He closed his eyes and sighed, then opened them again, frowning. She was so honestly innocent. "Yes, Poe, that's how I felt," he answered truthfully.

"Will it always feel the same when a man puts his arms about me?"

He frowned. "I don't know, Poe."

"Do you always feel the same way when you hold a woman?"

"No."

"Why?"

He stared at her dumbfounded, unable to answer. Why did he feel differently toward different women? Some left him unmoved, most bored him. But holding Poe had been a sensation he hadn't felt before. Even the Duchess had never aroused the sensuous feelings in him he'd had when he held Poe.

"Does it really matter?" he asked.

"Yes." She picked up her spoon and stared at it absentmindedly. "You see, I've been taught to hate men, all men."

"I see."

"No, you don't see," she went on irritably, and the dreamy, faraway look began to vanish from her eyes. "Oh, never mind. I shouldn't have said anything," she said flippantly, "and I'm not hungry."

Logan's eyes darkened. She was the old Poe again, fighting herself and everyone who crossed her.

"Well, at least you'll admit you need a bath," he said. "Clive will have a tub set up in your room, and he said some of your clothes are here. So if you don't mind, after you've changed I'll see you in the library."

She stood up and started for the door, then turned back, her hand on the knob. "One thing," she said defiantly as she stood glaring at him, her voice threatening, face pale. "Don't ever put your hands on me again, ever! Do you understand?" she warned. "Because if you do, I might just have to kill you!" and she left the room while he stared after her in surprise, wondering what had brought that on.

An hour later, his clothes changed, Logan was sitting at the desk in the library when Aaron walked in.

"Took you long enough to find her," Aaron

said as he came over and sat in a chair near the desk.

"Don't be funny." Logan's eyes were snapping.

"You sound like you enjoyed the evening," Aaron teased sarcastically.

"You want your throat cut."

He laughed. "It was that bad? After all, you did spend the night with her."

"So?"

"So she's a beautiful young woman . . ."

Logan stood up and walked around to the front of the desk, ignoring Aaron's remark. "I've decided what we're going to do with Poe, Aaron," he said, and stopped in front of his friend. "We're going to make a lady out of her, then marry her off to any nice eligible gentleman we can talk into taking her."

Aaron's mouth fell, and he shook his head. "You don't really mean that."

"Oh, don't I?"

"But you can't. Aunt Delia . . ."

"Don't worry," Logan replied. "We won't let her marry anybody until Aunt Delia gets home, but by that time the stage'll be all set."

"You sure you're all right?" Aaron asked suspiciously. Logan was talking about a woman who hated men. "What makes you think she'll be so anxious to get married?"

"She's a woman, isn't she?"

———

"I hadn't noticed. Is she?" Aaron answered, only his sarcasm seemed to be lost on Logan.

"She'll respond to a man just like any other woman," Logan went on.

"You know by experience?"

"Never mind how I know," Logan snapped. "I just know. And once we turn her into a lady, letting nature take its course, by the time Aunt Delia gets back, Poe Yancey will be ready to be a blushing bride."

"What does the young lady have to say about your plans?" Aaron asked as he settled back in the armchair.

Logan straightened, frowning. "She knows nothing about it. And you're not to tell her," he warned. "Do you understand? I don't want her to know what we're trying to do."

Aaron's eyes narrowed shrewdly. "You know, I do believe you've a little larceny in your soul, Logan," he said as he studied his friend, and at that moment there was a knock on the door.

When Poe entered and walked across the room toward them, both Logan and Aaron stared speechless. She was wearing a velvet dress the color of her eyes, with a low-cut heart-shaped bodice that accentuated her firm round breasts and small waist. Her hair was pulled back with velvet bows tucked in the sides, making it cascade down her back in a blaze of red.

"Well," Aaron finally said as she stopped a few feet from them. "Come into my parlor, said the spider to the fly," and Logan gave him a dirty look, then sat on the edge of the desk.

"You said you had a birthday, Poe. When?" Logan asked.

"A week from next Friday," she replied. "Why?"

"Think you can learn enough about being a lady in . . . let's see . . . we have about twelve days . . . to attend your seventeenth birthday party and be the belle of the ball?"

"I . . . I don't know," she answered hesitantly. "I never thought . . ."

He stood up, looking down at her in that strong domineering way of his that made her hair bristle like a cat ready for a fight.

"A week from next Friday," he announced to Poe and Aaron, "if all goes well, and Poe tends to what she's doing, Goldspur is going to see a coming-out party like it's never seen before. And you, my dear," he said to Poe, "are going to be the main attraction."

Her face paled because she could tell by the determined look in his eyes that Logan meant every word, and there'd be no use trying to put up an argument.

The next few days at the Highland were hectic. Poe paced the library until walking like a lady seemed to become a natural way of walking for her, especially since Logan dressed her down with a tongue-lashing whenever she'd start to lapse into her old hip-swinging gait. She practiced not only walking like a lady and talking like a lady but also eating like a lady, until she wanted to scream from frustration because of the pressure Logan was subjecting her to.

It was, "Remember to put the napkin on your lap! Stop waving your fork in the air! Quit swinging your hips! Glide, don't bounce! And for heaven's sake, it's 'isn't,' not 'ain't'!"

"And you don't blurt out 'dammit' when you make a mistake!" he admonished as they practiced dancing in the parlor the night before the party.

She pushed him away, even though the music hadn't stopped, and walked to the fireplace, leaning both hands against the mantel, staring into the dead cold ashes. She was fed up. Just plain fed up, and that was the last straw.

"I don't really care anymore," she cried softly, then straightened, whirling to face him. "I'm so sick and tired of being yelled at." Her eyes sparked furiously. "I don't care about your damn party, or your damn guests, or anything else. I just want to be left alone!" She was almost screaming. "So what if I say 'ain't,' and wave my fork in the air when I'm eating, so who the hell cares!"

"I'll tell you who cares," he shot back angrily. "I care!"

"You care?"

---

"That's right, me. I promised myself that when Aunt Delia came home she was going to meet a lady, and by God, Poe, I'm counting on you to help me keep my promise."

Poe inhaled sharply, and stared at him for a few minutes, then suddenly felt guilty. She guessed the past few days hadn't been much fun for him either. She gazed at him sheepishly, a half-smile curling the corners of her mouth as she once more conceded.

"All right, Simon Legree." She walked over to him, sighing as she held her arms up, waiting. "Let's go."

The music had stopped by now, and he walked over to the Victrola, cranking it up again and replacing the needle at the beginning of the record, then returned, taking her right hand in his left hand, with his other hand at her waist. Only this time, instead of holding her at arm's length as he'd done before when they danced, he pulled her close in his arms, resting his cheek against her temple.

Poe squirmed, trying at first to protest, then reluctantly she began to relax as he started waltzing her about the room to the lilting strains of the music.

She hadn't wanted to surrender like this, but as they danced she suddenly felt that same strangely wonderful feeling begin surging inside her that she'd felt with his body next to hers that night in the cave. It was such a wonderful feeling, and her heart started pounding restlessly, making her feel weak all over as they moved gracefully together, as though they were one, his body caressing hers in the rhythm of the dance. How exhilarated she felt. It was an intoxicating feeling, making her light-headed, as if she'd had too much to drink.

Logan instinctively pulled her closer, breathing deeply, his eyes intense. It seemed so strange to be dancing with a woman and feel her head close to his without him having to practically break his back bending down to reach her. And he wasn't just propelling her carefully about the room as if she were a delicate china doll that might break, either. Instead, Poe's body moved with his as if they were molded together.

The Victrola began running down as the record neared its end, and Logan stopped, but still held her in his arms. For a long time they stayed like that, neither of them moving, until the room grew so quiet they could hear each other breathe. Then very slowly Poe's head moved up, and her hot breath on his neck sent chills down his spine. Only her lips didn't stop there, they kept moving higher until they suddenly pressed sensuously against his ear.

Logan held his breath, waiting, letting his body enjoy the pleasurable sensations that were flowing through him. Then quite abruptly a shock went through him as Poe took a deep breath, then whispered venomously, her clenched teeth touching his ear, "I told you I'd kill you if you ever touched me again. Now let go!"

He froze, continuing to hold her close, but barely for a moment longer, then slackened his hold on her. Only instead of taking his arms from her, when her head went back and she started to move away, he suddenly leaned forward, and his mouth came down hard on hers.

Poe had never been kissed before, and fire shot through her whole body clear to her toes.

His lips were tense and demanding at first, then softened, caressing her mouth slowly, seeming to draw the breath from her body, making her tremble deep down inside. She hated responding like this, but couldn't seem to help herself as her lips moved beneath his, opening to let his tongue have its way, and answering instinctively with her own until she felt as if she'd explode inside.

Finally Logan drew back and looked down at her. Her lips were parted, face flushed, and the small pulse at the base of her throat was throbbing.

"I hate you!" she whispered breathlessly. "Leave me alone!"

He licked his lips, savoring the memory of her kiss for a moment, then straightened, inhaling deeply as he took a step backward away from her.

"You'll do beautifully tomorrow evening," he said calmly, as if nothing had happened. "And, oh yes," he said, as if it were an afterthought. "Thank you for the dance." Then he turned quite abruptly and headed for the door.

"Didn't you hear me, Logan Campbell, I said I hate you!" she screamed after him, and her eyes were misty. "I hate your guts!"

The door closed quickly behind Logan; then he hesitated, leaning back against it, cocking his ear, waiting. He knew he wouldn't have long to wait, and cringed knowingly barely seconds later as something crashed violently against the other side of the door. All he could do now was pray that it wasn't one of Aunt Delia's valuable antiques, as he hoped that by tomorrow evening Poe's temper would be controllable again.

The white satin dress Poe was wearing for the party tonight shone with a slightly pink cast beneath the lights from the overhead chandeliers in the dining room at the Champaign Hotel, as did the seed pearls that adorned it. It was more what one would see at the opera in New York or on Nob Hill in San Francisco than in a small mining town like Goldspur. However, after only two weeks under Logan's tutelage, for the first time in her life Poe felt at home in something other than shirt, pants, and leather boots.

Logan had wreathed the hotel dining room in flowers that Aaron said he'd imported from the coast by way of Tonopah and a fast carriage. A huge birthday cake was on the banquet table, where there was plenty of food, and potent punch flowed freely.

Poe stood her ground well. On the outside she was every inch a lady, calm and serene, but inside, she was still seething. The kiss Logan had bestowed on her last night had made a profound impression on her. One she didn't like, and all day she had been extremely quiet, speaking to him only when it was impossible for her not to, and when she did, her words were sarcastic and biting.

"Look," he'd finally said on the way to the hotel in the carriage while she sat stoically beside him, "I don't care what you say to me when we're alone, but tonight, in front of all those people, you'd better toe the mark or by God I'll give you the spanking you've been asking for since you arrived. Lady or no lady!"

She had eyed him stubbornly. "Don't worry, Mr. Campbell," she'd promised, "you've done your job only too well. No one at the party will have the slightest suspicion that I can't stand the sight of you." Now Poe stood inside the ballroom greeting people she'd never seen before, politeness dripping from her tongue, as if she'd been born to it.

The Champaign Hotel was owned by Delia Campbell, who'd imported most of the furnishings from Europe, and it was every bit as beautiful as the Cosmopolitan Hall in Belmont, even though Goldspur had nowhere near the population Belmont had, although tonight almost all the inhabitants of Goldspur were present. Not because they liked Logan, but because they knew if they didn't show up, Delia Campbell would learn about it when she got home, and there were very few people in Goldspur who didn't like Delia. Besides, they were curious. Even the Duchess was there, although she was receiving the usual cold shoulder from the rest of the town ladies.

Everyone in Goldspur had heard of Poe's arrival, but only the men who'd been in front of the saloon the day she arrived, the Duchess, and the dressmaker had seen her, and because of them, the stories were already all over town about the tall, gawky girl who'd suddenly become Delia Campbell's ward.

Consequently the townsfolk's surprise was genuine when they were introduced to Poe, who was now a graciously beautiful, statuesque young woman, quite feminine and genteel, but so tall she either towered over all the men in town or met them on eye level. All but a few, that is.

One was big Jim Slattery, a brawny lumberjack who insisted he was cousin to Paul Bunyan. Then there was the preacher, the Reverend Willard Ambrose, who was as thin as he was tall, and another man who arrived at the party late.

"Who is he?" Poe asked Aaron as she caught sight of him out of the corner of her eye.

Aaron was at her side, trying to help her sort out the townspeople, and she noticed the newcomer had been staring at her ever since stepping into the ballroom, the look in his eyes making her uneasy.

Aaron grinned. He always made it his business to know everyone in town. "He checked in at the hotel this afternoon," he answered, watching her sip at her punch. "Name's Lord Merriweather. He has a short little gent who usually follows him around like a shadow, name of Tyson. I assume he's something like a valet."

Poe was surprised. "Lord?"

"Claims to be a titled Englishman."

"What's a man like that doing in Goldspur?"

"At the moment, my dear," Aaron replied, "he's staring a hole right through you, and there's a definite gleam in his eyes."

"Well, he'd better lose it," she retorted, so low only Aaron could hear.

But the gentleman didn't lose it. Instead, he approached Aaron, keeping his eyes steadily on Poe.

"Mr. Goldbladt," he greeted, extending his hand. "I believe we met earlier in the day?"

Aaron returned his handshake. "May I present my employer's ward, Miss Poe Yancey,"

Aaron said, gesturing toward Poe. "Lord Merriweather, my dear."

Poe extended her hand, expecting Lord Merriweather to shake it courteously. Instead he held her hand gently in his, his eyes searching her face, then lifted it to his lips and kissed the back of it, while Poe stared in surprise.

She had to admit he was rather nice-looking. His hair was a sandy color, with a trimmed mustache to match, and sideburns that grew thick along his jawline. His deep blue suit was immaculate, fitting him nattily, with a pearl stickpin peeking from the folds of his dark blue cravat.

Pale brown eyes studied Poe inquisitively as he straightened, releasing her hand, and he smiled, showing a set of gleaming white teeth. Poe's eyebrows raised when she found herself looking up at him. He was every bit as tall as Logan Campbell.

"I heard this is your seventeenth birthday, Miss Yancey. Is that right?" he asked, his accent very British.

"Indeed it is, sir," she answered politely.

"May I say then that the Americans are fortunate to have such beautiful women because today, my dear, you are truly a woman, and quite lovely."

Poe frowned slightly, and for a moment Aaron thought she was going to say something derogatory. Instead, she smiled sweetly.

---

"You flatter me, sir," she replied, and lowered her eyes coyly.

Aaron had a hard time keeping a straight face, because it was so unlike Poe.

A small orchestra was playing at one end of the room, and Lord Merriweather glanced toward it momentarily, then back to Poe.

"Ah, Miss Yancey," he said. "Since the music is so inviting, would it be too presumptuous of me to ask if I might dance with the guest of honor?"

Poe froze, her eyes darkening cautiously.

Here it goes, thought Aaron. She's going to tell the sissified dandy where to go. But instead, Aaron stared dumbfounded as Poe extended her hand in a gesture of acceptance, then let the Englishman link her arm in his, ushering her toward the dance floor.

From the look on Poe's face as she walked beside Lord Merriweather, it was hard to tell what she was thinking, except that she seemed quite in command of the situation. However, beneath her veneer of calm, she was writhing in agony.

The only man she'd ever danced with until now was Logan, and she was terrified at the thought of having another man hold her. What if the same thing happened that always happened when she danced with Logan? What if she got so flustered she forgot the steps? She wanted to run and hide, only at that very moment she spotted Logan across the room and all thoughts of fleeing quickly left her. The Duchess was hanging onto Logan's arm as if she owned him, her gold lace dress complimenting her dark hair, which was adorned with yellow flowers. Logan's eyes, as they deliberately captured Poe's, challenged her recklessly.

Poe took a deep breath and held it as Lord Merriweather stepped in front of her, lifting her right hand with his left and circling her waist with his other hand, drawing her gently to him. She felt his body press against her, and her eyes widened. She'd been expecting a reaction to the contact, and much to her surprise, there was nothing. No intoxicating feeling, no strange warmth inside.

Lord Merriweather whirled her onto the floor with a flourish, but instead of being conscious of his arms about her, Poe discovered that all she was conscious of were the movements of her feet and the flattering words that flowed so easily from him. There wasn't even any tingling or throbbing in her head, and she certainly wasn't light-headed. She relaxed a little, breathing a sigh of relief, and began to enjoy the dance.

Logan was watching Poe intently as the tall man with the sandy hair, mustache, and dapper clothes whirled her about the room, and the Duchess followed his gaze.

"They make a striking couple, don't they?" she said.

Logan frowned. "Who is he?"

Her hand tightened on Logan's arm. "His name's Lord Merriweather, and he arrived in town this afternoon with his valet, a man he calls Tyson."

"English?"

"Very English, and very aristocratic. At least he gives that impression."

"You don't believe it?"

"Who knows?" She shrugged. "There are a lot of titled men who've forsaken their depleted estates and looked for new fortunes in new lands. He could be what he says."

"But you don't think so."

"Now you're putting words in my mouth." Her eyes narrowed as she studied the man who was dancing with Poe. "There's just something about him . . ."

At that moment Aaron strolled over, stopping next to Logan. "Do you suppose maybe we've finally found one tall enough?" he asked, gesturing with his head toward Poe and her partner.

Logan understood, and smiled. "Maybe we have at that."

The Duchess glanced first at one man, then the other. "I have a sneaking feeling that you two are plotting something you shouldn't be," she said cautiously. "I only hope the young lady is willing to cooperate."

Logan glanced down at her. "What do you mean?"

She smiled sweetly. "I know what you're talking about, love," she replied knowingly. "And if you don't know what I'm talking about, you're more of a fool than I thought. Both of you."

"You mean because she hates men?" Aaron asked.

The Duchess's throaty laughter took him by surprise. "My dear Aaron," she said, "the girl doesn't hate men. Whatever gave you that idea? She merely hasn't learned to appreciate them yet. I'm sure, given the right man, it won't take her long. However"—and her eyes moved back to the couple on the dance floor—"I don't think the gentleman you have in mind is the right one."

Logan was surprised. "What makes you say that?"

There was a brutal look in her eyes as she continued to watch Poe and the tall good-looking newcomer; then she glanced up at Logan, whose arm she was still holding tightly. "Because, my dear Logan, I'm a woman and you're a man," she announced curtly. "Only I know how a woman's mind works. Call it instinct if you want, or just plain horse sense, but I'll bet you that's one little filly out there who won't say yes to any man, at least not until she's sure."

"Sure of what?"

"Of not getting hurt, of course." Her eyes

darkened passionately. "Let's face it, love," she explained reluctantly, "the only reason a woman hates a man is that she's afraid she'll get hurt. To a man-hater like Poe Yancey, all men are cads, brought into the world only to break women's hearts. And until the day some man proves to her that all men aren't heels, she'll go on hating all men, whether she really wants to or not."

"You think we're wasting our time?" Aaron asked.

The Duchess smiled, pleased with herself. "If you intend to marry Poe off," she answered. "That is, unless you pick a better man than Lord Merriweather. He's too suave, too insincere with his flattery to get past the wall she's built around her feelings. I met him earlier today, and believe me, he's a ladies' man if I ever saw one."

"Who told you we were trying to marry her off?" Logan asked, and the Duchess smirked.

"Because I know how your minds work." She looked at Aaron, then back to Logan, and her eyes mocked him. "You two have a nasty habit of trying to get rid of anything you don't understand or can't master, and I suspect Poe Yancey fits into both categories. Am I right?"

"You're far too perceptive." Logan's eyes left the Duchess's face and settled once more on the couple dancing. "I can only hope you've missed the mark where Poe's concerned, though, because I intend to have her ready to walk down the aisle with someone by the time Aunt Delia comes home."

The music stopped, then started again, and now Poe was dancing with another gentleman, only this one was short and bald. As the evening wore on, Logan continued to watch off and on from the sidelines and saw Poe dance by with quite a succession of men. They were all sizes and shapes, both young and old, and all seemed to be enjoying themselves. However, Logan did notice that her most frequent partner was Lord Merriweather.

Occasionally Logan would dance with the Duchess, then mill about visiting with some of the guests, but most of the time he was keeping a close eye on his young protégée.

It was about ten forty-five when he finally stepped up and took Poe's arm as she finished dancing with Aaron.

"I'm afraid the dancing's going to have to wait for a few minutes," he said. "It's time to cut the cake," and he instructed Aaron to have the orchestra give a fanfare while he escorted Poe to the front of the room.

Poe was apprehensive by the time they reached the banquet table. She'd been holding up well all evening, but for some reason Logan's sudden attention was unnerving her, although no one in the ballroom seemed aware of her discomfiture.

As the fanfare stopped, Logan released her arm, then held up his hands, gesturing, and the hall grew quiet.

"I'm glad to see so many of you here enjoying yourselves," he began, while the people moved forward, gathering around them. Then he explained: "As you probably know, you were invited here tonight to help my aunt's ward, Miss Poetica Yancey, celebrate her seventeenth birthday, only I specifically asked that no one bring gifts because this was more our way of introducing her to you than an actual birthday party. However, before she cuts the cake, there is one gift my aunt has asked me to present to her, and I'd appreciate your indulgence for a moment."

He reached in his pocket, pulled out a small package, and held it out to Poe, who stared at it curiously, knowing he hadn't had time to receive an answer to any letter he might have written to his aunt. Suddenly realizing that giving her a gift was only his way of putting on a show in front of the guests, she wished she could expose his deception. She couldn't bring herself to, though, and instead took the package, unwrapping it hesitantly to reveal a small blue box that contained a gorgeous lavaliere made from a huge pear-shaped diamond clustered about with smaller diamonds, and there were matching earrings.

Poe gasped, staring at them, remembering the day she got her ears pierced. She'd screamed, yelled, and fought with Logan so hard that he finally had to hold her down in a chair while the downstairs maid did the honors. The maid was an older woman who'd pierced many an ear in her day, but had never worked on an unwilling victim. And that's exactly how Poe had felt, like a victim. She'd cursed Logan all the rest of the day, threatening to tear the gold loops out the first chance she had, and only her better judgment kept her from doing it.

Now, as she gazed into the box at the small pair of matching earrings, she did so with mixed feelings. She was glad she could wear them because they were so exquisite, but she was still angry because Logan had had a part in it, and had once more managed to get his own way.

"They're lovely," she finally said, and glanced up, her eyes meeting Logan's. Somehow she knew he was remembering that day too, and she was embarrassed. "Thank you," she murmured almost incoherently, and reached up, fingering the pearl drop earrings that hung from her earlobes now. Her lobes were still sore, but they were healing, something she felt her heart would never do.

She closed the little box and handed it back to him. "You'd better keep them for me until we leave," she said, and Logan agreed, slipping it back into his coat pocket. Then he turned to the table, reaching out, taking a knife, and handing it to her, handle-first. Someone had lit the candles while she'd been opening her present, and the flames drew her eyes hypnotically until Logan's voice cut through her reverie.

"Make a wish, blow out the candles, and make the first cut," he was saying. She glanced at him, frowning for a second, then closed her eyes, made a wish, blew the candles out, then put a cut right down the center of the cake before relinquishing the knife to one of the waiters to do the serving.

Poe stepped aside to stand in front of Logan so the waiter could finish cutting the cake, and Logan gestured with his head toward the orchestra.

"I believe the next dance is mine," he said from behind her as the musicians started to play again and the people started to disperse.

Poe's face went white. She'd been afraid of this all evening. She stood motionless.

"Poe?" Logan questioned.

She took a deep breath, and her head tilted stubbornly. This was ridiculous. What was she afraid of? Hadn't she danced with almost every man in the room tonight? They'd all held her close, yet none of them had had any weird effect on her. Not even Aaron. Could it be she was finally over the silly notion that a man's arms held some special sort of meaning? That night she lay in Logan's arms had been the first time a man had touched her, and it had been new to her. Now, after being in the arms of so many men tonight, she just knew there was nothing to fear.

She forced her misgivings aside and smiled smugly to herself as she turned to face Logan. "If you wish," she said, keeping her voice as steady as possible. But even though she was more confident than ever before, her heart was pounding as he escorted her to the dance floor.

When they reached the other dancers, he caught her hand, turning her, pulling her into his arms, and for a brief moment his eyes caught hers and she felt her heart sink discouragingly. Oh no! She started to panic as that same familiar surge began to swell deep down inside her, making her knees weak.

Not again! Not again! she screamed silently. This wasn't supposed to be happening. It wasn't supposed to be like this. She wouldn't let it happen, she couldn't, and she tried to ignore the weird sensations that were spreading through her as he pulled her even closer, his lips lightly brushing her forehead, and she felt herself tremble.

His arm tightened just a bit more. "Relax," he whispered softly against her hair. "You're doing beautifully."

Poe wanted to die, but wasn't about to let Logan know anything was wrong. "You're holding me too tight," she gasped breathlessly.

"Tightly," he corrected her. "But I hadn't noticed."

---

"Please, Logan," she begged. "Please," and slowly he loosened his arm from around her, drawing his head back so he was looking into her face.

"What did you wish when you blew out the candles?" he asked as they continued dancing slowly to the waltz the orchestra was playing.

Her eyes were hard and cold, an artificial smile on her lips as she stared back at him. "I wished you were dead," she said politely. Only her voice quivered as she spoke, and Logan's eyes mocked her.

"Don't be ridiculous, Poe," he countered, smiling wickedly. "If I were dead you wouldn't have anyone to fight with, now would you?" and before she could come back with an appropriate retort, he pulled her closer in his arms again and she had no recourse but to keep on dancing.

Either that or make a spectacle of herself in front of all these people, and that's one thing she wasn't about to do. These people had all been treating her just like a lady, and by God, for once in her life she really felt like one. But oh, she thought as she simmered deep down inside, how she hated Logan Campbell. Hated him with a passion, and her eyes were smoldering dangerously as they finished their dance.

# 5

## A-Courting We Will Go

Even though the dance with Logan lasted only a few minutes, it seemed to spoil the whole evening for Poe, who continued to seethe inside with rage, although it wasn't apparent to those around her. Her appearance was still that of a lovely, well-composed young woman, and as the evening continued to wear on, it became quite evident by the attention being paid her that Poe had captured the hearts of not only Big Jim Slattery, Reverend Ambrose, and Lord Merriweather but also close to half the bachelor population of Goldspur, even though she was as tall as, or taller than, most of them.

It was almost one in the morning when the party finally broke up, and now Poe stood next to Logan near the entrance to the ballroom, saying good-bye to everyone. Among the first to leave was Lord Merriweather.

"You will let me come visit tomorrow, won't you, my dear?" he pleaded after kissing her hand ardently. "I could hire a carriage . . . we could go driving."

"Driving?" How horrible, she thought, and was about to decline the invitation when Logan cut in.

"Yes, driving, Poe." Logan seemed rather eager as he addressed the Englishman. "I think that's a marvelous idea, Lord Merriweather. Really I do," he went on. "She's been out so little since her arrival. And I happen to know that she doesn't have a thing planned for tomorrow. In fact"—and he glanced at Poe again for a brief second before continuing—"why don't you come about four or so, enjoy a nice afternoon ride, then stay for dinner?"

"My dear fellow." Lord Merriweather's face was beaming as he accepted. "I'd be ever so delighted. Miss Yancey?" His eyes settled on Poe, waiting for her confirmation.

"I . . . I think that would be just lovely," she answered reluctantly.

What else was there for her to do? She glanced over at Logan, her eyes flashing dangerously while Lord Merriweather gushingly bid her good night, kissing her hand one more time just for good measure. And a few minutes later, as she watched the Englishman leave, she cringed inside. She hadn't wanted to see Lord Merriweather so soon again, or any of the other men for that matter. What did Logan expect from her anyway? Wasn't it enough she'd been nice to them tonight? She turned toward Logan again, and suddenly a horrible thought struck her as she saw the gleam in his eyes. It *hadn't* been enough. Not for Logan. She was sure of it, and before the last good-bye was said, he proved her suspicions right by making plans for Reverend Ambrose to escort her to church Sunday morning, then accompany her to lunch at one of the restaurants in Goldspur before bringing her home, where afterward she'd be met by Big Jim Slattery for a picnic supper late Sunday afternoon. And as if that wasn't bad enough, Logan made sure she'd have plenty of escorts for assorted buggy rides, singing bees, dinners in town, and taffy pulls during the rest of the week, and then some, the three taller men alternating for honors, with a few of the bachelors from Goldspur sandwiched in between, so that by the time they were in the carriage headed for home, Poe was furious. She glanced over at Logan, fuming as the carriage pulled away from the hotel and headed toward the house on the hill. It was her first chance to retaliate, and she was determined to make the most of it.

"You had no right to do that, and you know it," she yelled angrily.

Logan's eyes hardened. "If I hadn't, you'd have let every one of them leave without even so much as a thank-you."

"Thank you for what? Having my toes crushed by that monster of a lumberjack who dances like an elephant while he sizes up my child-bearing possibilities?" she stormed. "Or would it be for listening to the pious reverend expounding on your sins, and warning me about the den of iniquity I'm living in while his eyes stray to my cleavage and his hot hands paw my waist like a cat on a pillow? Or maybe," she finished, taking a deep breath, "I should thank your precious Lord Merriweather for slobbering all over my hand and trying to bundle on the dance floor."

"How do you know about bundling?"

"Never mind how I know, I just do." She straightened haughtily. "Only I thought you wanted me to be a lady."

"I do."

"Well, if that's what ladies are subjected to, I'd rather go back to being what I was."

There was a light inside the carriage, and Logan watched Poe closely. "Poe, aren't you even glad the men liked you?" he asked.

"Why?"

He shrugged. "I don't know . . . I guess . . . it's just something most women would enjoy, that's all."

"Well, not me. I hate the whole lot of them!"

" 'Hate' is a strong word." He frowned. "Are you sure it's not that you're more afraid of them?"

"Afraid of them? Don't be ridiculous." She tried to look confident. "I'm not afraid of anyone."

"Aren't you?" His eyes narrowed shrewdly as he continued to bait her. "I bet that after only a week or two of their sweet talk and flattery you'd fall head over heels for one of them, just like any other women would, and you know it," he went on. "That's why you don't want to be around them, isn't it? That's why you say you hate them. Why, Poe, you're afraid of them!"

"I am not!"

"Then prove it."

"How?"

"By keeping every one of those engagements I made for you. If you do that without reneging on any of them, I might be inclined to believe you."

She sneered, and her eyes grew intense. "We'll just see who's afraid of men," she said, and he watched her jawline tighten.

"Remember, Poe, you're a lady," he cautioned.

Her eyes danced mischievously. "I will, if they will," she answered, and turned, looking out the carriage window, and for a brief moment Logan wasn't sure he should have challenged her, because if anyone was unpredictable, it was Poe Yancey. He sighed. Oh well, he couldn't back down now, nor could she. Not if she wanted to save face.

---

Poe continued to stare out the window for a few minutes longer, then slowly drew her eyes from the passing darkness and gazed over at Logan. He wasn't watching her anymore, but was staring out the other window, deep in thought, a self-satisfied look on his face. Arrogant bastard, she thought indignantly. Thinks he's so smart. Well, she'd show him. There wasn't a man on the face of the earth who could sweet-talk her into acting like a lovesick ninny. No sirree! Besides—and she smiled smugly—Delia Campbell was due home soon, and when she showed up, this whole stupid thing'd be over and she could kick the dust of Goldspur good-bye.

With that conviction in her heart, Poe drew her eyes once more from Logan's face to lean back on the seat, content with the knowledge that the ride from the Champaign Hotel to the Highland was a short one, and she wouldn't have to put up with Logan's superior attitude much longer tonight.

The next afternoon was Saturday, and like it or not, Poe found herself riding about the countryside in a handsome carriage with Lord Merriweather at her side and his man Tyson at the reins.

"I like to have my hands free," Giles Merriweather had told her when they were first settling into the carriage, but now, after close to an hour of riding, Poe began to doubt the honesty of the Englishman's earlier statement, because since starting their excursion, the man's hands hadn't really been empty at all. He was either holding her hands, or playing with her hair, or any number of things.

However, she had to admit the two of them probably did make an attractive couple decked out in their fancy clothes. And Giles Merriweather did wear clothes well, there was no denying that. And he was quite handsome. It was just that he was so conceited. According to him, he fenced better, rode better, sailed better than any other gentleman in England, or even the States, for that matter. And on top of that, he made sure she knew that he was quite well known as one of Queen Victoria's closest advisers.

"Why, when she discovered I was coming to the States, she was quite upset," he was saying as they rode along, his arm creeping across the back of the seat until his hand ended up close to Poe's shoulder. "But then, one does have a commitment to one's own life, doesn't one?" he added.

Poe eyed him skeptically, wondering just how much of his prattling was the truth and how much was wishful thinking on his part, because after all, about the only thing she noticed he did do better than any of the other men she'd met was flatter the ladies and brag about himself.

"Yes, I guess one does," she finally said, figuring it was easier to let him think she believed his nonsense than argue the truth of the matter. Only, all during the rest of the ride, she felt so foolish trying to be nice to a man she couldn't stand, and even later that evening, during dinner, while Giles and Logan talked about mining, lumber, cattle, and life in the big cities, she prayed fervently that the Englishman wouldn't overstay his welcome. Unfortunately, this time God didn't see fit to answer her prayers, however, and when Logan made it a point to disappear soon after dinner, Poe found herself having to entertain the Englishman all by herself again. A situation that quickly became quite disagreeable for her, as Lord Merriweather tried to prove to her, and undoubtedly to himself too, that his prowess with the ladies was no less than that of an experienced Don Juan. He flattered her, teased her, and did everything he could think of to break down her reserve. Only he'd never had to deal with anyone as stubborn as Poe, and in spite of everything he did and said, by the time she stood at the door bidding him good night, Lord Merriweather knew that he was still no closer to winning her heart than he had been the moment they'd first met. As he rode away from the Highland, he was more determined than ever that the next time she'd succumb to his charms, or he'd know the reason why.

For Poe, dragging herself upstairs to bed that evening, there was nothing more than relief at having finally gotten rid of him. Only her relief didn't last long, because the next day things didn't go much better, and after a hurried breakfast with Logan in the dining room, she found herself dressed in a delicate pink dress of silk and lace, with her hair half-hidden beneath a matching hat that sported frothy ostrich plumes, sitting reluctantly beside Reverend Ambrose, headed for town and Sunday morning at church. There was one consolation for her this morning, however. The reverend was driving his own carriage, and at least she wouldn't have to put up with roving hands like she had the day before. But she did have to put up with his roving eyes, and all during his sermon, as he looked out over the congregation, he kept coming back to her. Especially when he made it a point to expound on the evils of money, and the licentiousness it brought with it, corrupting men's souls and causing them to lead innocent young women astray.

However, later, while having lunch with the good reverend in the dining room of the Champaign Hotel, Poe was inclined to take a much closer look at the man.

Although at least an inch or so shorter than Logan, Willard Ambrose almost seemed taller. Possibly because he was so thin. And it was this lean quality that often made his face look as if it were chiseled from granite, with eyes like pale blue agates that could make the worst of sinners squirm beneath their gaze. But at the moment they were busily studying Poe, and the look in them was somewhere between that of a hungry man and a simpering adolescent.

"Why, I'd even be willing to take you into my own home to save you from that sinful environment you've been forced to live in," he was offering while using his fork to toy with the mashed potatoes on his plate.

Poe watched him carefully. "Don't you think it's rather unchristian of you to talk about the town's benefactors in such a manner?" she asked, trying not to sound too rude, yet irritated by his pious attitude.

Willard Ambrose was unruffled. Now thirty-two, he'd realized years before that doing the Lord's work wasn't going to be an easy task, and he'd conditioned himself for barbs far worse than the one Poe had just thrown at him. However, he hadn't conditioned himself for anyone like Poe. She was not only the loveliest young woman he'd seen in years but also the first and only woman who'd ever brought out such strange, vibrant feelings inside him. Feelings he unfortunately was having a hard time ignoring. The kind of feelings he felt sure a man of the cloth shouldn't be having.

He set his fork down and picked up his napkin, playing with it instead. "Miss Yancey . . . may I call you Poe?"

She nodded.

"Poe, it's common knowledge in Goldspur, and you should know by now yourself, that although Delia Campbell is a woman of virtue, her nephew not only frequents the saloons and gaming tables but also is very often seen in the company of . . ." He cleared his throat. "Shall we say, questionable young women."

"What are questionable young women?" she asked, feigning innocence.

He reached over, taking her hand. "That, my dear, you wouldn't be expected to know." He was all concern, and overly solicitous. "But believe me, they're women living in the lowest form of sin known to mankind."

"You mean like the Duchess?"

"Exactly." He stroked her hand affectionately— only the gesture was unnerving, since his hand was hot and clammy.

Poe drew her hand away, lowered her eyes demurely, then looked up at him again. "But you don't understand, Reverend," she reminded him. "I have no other choice but to stay at the Highland. Delia Campbell's my guardian, and the court's ordered me to stay there, at least until I'm twenty-one or marry."

"Then marry me, my dear," he whispered anxiously. "I'd be more than willing to sacrifice my freedom, if it meant saving you from that dreadful place."

Poe fought the urge to laugh. The reverend was so serious, and yet she could tell by the gleam in his eyes that his sole interest wasn't just in seeing that she wasn't corrupted by living under the same roof with Logan Campbell, and she wondered what his congregation would think if they could see the feverish way he was eyeing her from across the table.

Hypocrite, she thought, while refusing his proposal, and she tried to keep a straight face while she told him that there was no way she could ask him to sacrifice himself just for her, yet let him know that even if she wanted to say yes, it was completely out of the question, since she'd have to have Delia Campbell's permission, and her guardian was still in Scotland.

She smiled smugly to herself later after he deposited her at the door and she watched him driving away in the buggy, still mumbling to himself over losing a bout with the devil.

Man of God, ha! she thought, and turned, entering the house, closing the door behind her. He was no different from any other red-blooded man, just fought the urges harder, that's all, and she made sure she let Logan know all about the good reverend later that afternoon while they sat in the parlor waiting for Big Jim Slattery to arrive.

Logan didn't seem too disturbed about her

appraisal of the town preacher, however, and since her suggestion that she be released from her engagement with the lumberjack fell on deaf ears, when Big Jim Slattery did arrive, Poe had no alternative but to join him on horseback, heading away from the Highland into the hills, his booming voice grating on her ears as they rode along.

After returning from her lunch with the reverend, Poe had changed into a dark green riding skirt with a matching fringed jacket, and a white silk blouse beneath it, her red hair tied back in a queue and covered by a wide-brimmed black hat. And with boots of black tooled leather on her feet, making her feel quite feminine, she probably would have been enjoying herself if she hadn't been with Big Jim Slattery. She was beginning to like wearing nice clothes. Something she'd never admit to Logan. But she glanced over at Big Jim riding beside her, wishing with all her heart she could be out here riding alone.

Big Jim was exactly what his name implied: big. About an inch taller than Logan, his frame was massive, and his face looked like it had collided with somebody's fist, which it probably had, and his usual attire was a scratchy woolen shirt, leather pants, thick-soled boots, and a floppy old fur hat even in the middle of summer.

"Makes a man a man" was his motto. None of those sissified dandy suits for him, and he smiled at Poe as they rode along, complimenting her enthusiastically on the ease with which she sat a horse.

Poe had been studying him closely while they were riding, and now as they reined in near the edge of a small stream to spread their picnic supper, she came to the conclusion that he was probably nice enough in his own way; at least so far he hadn't tried to ply her with dishonest flattery. And in spite of his size he seemed shy and rather awkward, but she just didn't care all that much for him.

"I bet havin' little ones would be real easy for someone like you, huh?" he said seriously, a short time later while they sat beside the picnic basket munching on fried chicken the cook had fixed for them.

Poe glanced at him furtively, realizing he was blushing. A trait strange in a man so big. "If you don't mind," she answered, "I'd rather not try to find out," and she continued to pick delicately at the piece of white meat she'd been toying with for the past five minutes.

Big Jim frowned. "Don't you like babies?" he asked.

"Certainly." Her eyes danced. "As long as they belong to somebody else."

"You mean you don't want a family of your own?"

"It's the furthest thing from my mind."

Big Jim stared at her hard for a minute, then

shook his head. "Just ain't natural," he said softly, then tossed the chicken leg he'd cleaned off onto his plate and reached over, grabbing her hand. "Miss Poe, I gotta change your mind," he began earnestly. "Why, it ain't right for a gal like you who's just built for havin' kids to be so determined not to. Why"—his hand tightened on hers—"there ain't hardly no women built like you no more."

She smiled hesitantly, knowing it'd be foolish to even try to pull her hand away from his viselike grip. "I'll go along with that," she said congenially.

He sighed. "You know, you ain't one of those frail little females what's always ailin'," he went on fervently. "No, sirree. Why, they ain't fit to be a man's wife. Not a real man anyway. But you . . . my God, gal," he sighed passionately, "why, you fairly set my heart a-goin'," and without warning, he suddenly tried to pull her into his arms, only instead she fell sideways, right onto the picnic basket, almost crushing it, and knocked over the bottle of lemonade they'd been enjoying, spilling it all over the tablecloth they'd spread out.

Big Jim gasped, then tried to untangle her from the mess, only he was so frustrated, he grabbed her the wrong way, and her knee landed smack dab in the middle of a berry pie they were going to have for dessert. Tears were close to the surface of Poe's eyes and she let out a soft cry, then finally managed to stand up, staring down in dismay at her riding skirt.

"I'm sorry, honey. Here, let me help," Jim said anxiously, once more reaching out to touch her, but Poe pushed him away.

"No . . . please . . . I'm all right. I'm all right. I'll do it myself," she insisted, and looked down again at her knee, dripping berries and pie crust; then she reached over, grabbing a napkin, and started to wipe it clean. "I don't think I'm hungry anymore, Jim," she said as she finished cleaning the last of the mess from her knee as best she could and tossed the dirty napkin down with the rest of the unsightly clutter. Then she straightened as Big Jim, too, stood up. "Do you suppose maybe we could go home now?" she asked uncomfortably. "I do look rather a mess."

"Hey, now, that don't matter to me," he answered. "Shucks, I'm the only one who'd see it, and I don't care."

"But I feel horrible."

"Nonsense," he insisted. "Besides, I ain't had a chance yet to show you my favorite sittin' place." He sounded so enthusiastic. "You did promise on the way out, you know, and I've really been lookin' forward to it."

Poe stared at him, aware of the anxiety in his eyes and realizing how disappointed he'd be if she said no. She shrugged. Oh well, what did it matter. She was already a mess.

"All right, Jim," she finally agreed, straightening her jacket while trying to ignore the purple patch on her knee.

Big Jim grinned from ear to ear. "Come on, we'll pick up this mess when we get back," he said agreeably, and grabbed her hand again, this time pulling her after him, and for the next half-hour they climbed over fallen trees, trampled along a path that led through a lot of thick underbrush, and went up and down at least three steep hills before finally coming to a wall of solid rock that looked as formidable as some of the cliffs up by Ruby Lake where she used to live.

"This is it?" she asked breathlessly when he stopped.

"No, ma'am," he answered. "That's it," and he pointed to the top of the cliff some fifty feet up. "I sit up there all the time when I ain't workin', and look out over Goldspur, and you know, sometimes I get to thinkin' that that must be how Miss Delia feels when she sits in that tower room of hers up at the Highland, lookin' out over the town."

"How nice." She was still gazing up. "Now may we go back?"

"Without seein' the top?" He was mortified. "Not on your life. Come on," and once more he grabbed her hand, pulling her after him, while ignoring her feeble attempt at a protest, and he guided her toward a place in the cliff wall where he'd hewed out a makeshift path, with rude steps going up.

"You expect me to go up that?" she asked incredulously.

He laughed. "Don't worry, honey. You can make it. I'll help, and I can climb it like it wasn't even there."

"Oh, great." She knew he was trying to reassure her, but it didn't do much good. She remembered the last time he had tried to help her.

"I promise you'll be all right." He smiled warmly and there was no way she could refuse. "Now, come on."

So with Big Jim's help and a lot of exertion on her part in which she added dirt and grass stains to the berry stains on the knee of her riding skirt, Poe did finally manage to reach the top and see what it was like. She stood beside Big Jim panting and surveyed the town. He was right, it looked so different from up here, and as she cocked her head, listening closely, she could still faintly hear the pounding of the unceasing quartz-crushing machines that had greeted her the day she rode into town, while out on the horizon to the northeast, her eyes caught sight of the mountains rising again, varying in shades from green to purple in their density.

"It's lovely," she told Big Jim thoughtfully,

and for a few moments she envied him his quiet place.

Only the quiet and peace didn't last long, and later, when they finally arrived back at the fancily trimmed pale yellow house known as the Highland, even though it wasn't quite dark out yet, Poe was completely exhausted. Her clothes were dirty, every muscle in her body ached, and although she admitted to herself that of all three men, Big Jim had been the nicest, if the most naive, she silently cursed Logan Campbell for giving her one of the worst days of her life. She promised herself as she fell into bed that night never to let it happen again.

Much to her dismay, however, the rest of the week was almost a repeat of what she'd put up with over the weekend, as she diplomatically fought off Lord Merriweather's roaming hands again, time after time, refused the parson's repeated offers of marriage and whatever else he had in mind, and wore herself ragged following Big Jim over hill and dale while he clumsily tried to court her. And the worst part was that all of this was accomplished between visits from every one of the bachelors in Goldspur who had made previous engagements with her, at Logan's insistence, the night of the party.

For almost the next two weeks life went on like this for Poe until finally, late one evening, during a boring game of cribbage with Lord Merriweather, made tolerable only by music from the Victrola, Poe stood up, walked over, lifted the needle, turned over the record on the Victrola, set the needle back in place, then began to wind up the machine. Suddenly she stiffened.

"Get your damn hands off me, Giles," she hissed angrily as she felt Lord Merriweather's hands on her waist, and her hand tightened on the Victrola handle, although she'd quit cranking it. He had crept up behind her, and now his breath was hot against her ear, but his hands didn't move. "I said off!" she repeated.

Instead he whirled her around, pulling her into his arms. "Now, Poe, love," he whispered fervently. "You know you don't really mean that."

"Oh, don't I?" She tried to push him away. "All you ever want to do is paw me!"

"Paw you?" He looked shocked, then frowned. "I'm in love with you, Poe," he pleaded passionately, and his eyes were troubled. "I've been trying to tell you that for days now, if you'd only listen."

"I have been listening," she said furiously. "I've been listening to you and all the others until I'm sick of it." Her eyes were blazing. "Well, I'll tell you," she went on, staring straight at him. "There was nothing in my bargain that said I had to keep on being nice to the lot of you for the rest of my life, and by God, I don't intend to. It's going to stop right here and now, or else."

Now he was really confused, and his mustache twitched a bit above his upper lip as he stared back at her. "What are you talking about?" he asked, bewildered.

"Oh, never mind," she answered, and began to squirm again, trying to get free. "Now, let go!"

"Let go? Never!" he said forcefully, and instead, his hand caught the back of her head, forcing her to hold it still, while his arm held her close, and without warning his mouth covered hers clumsily.

His teeth were bruising her lips and she tried to keep her mouth closed to escape him, but there was no escape. The harder she pushed and shoved, the tighter he held her. It was horrible. Like being kissed by a slimy leach. Then, suddenly realizing she wasn't about to get free, she froze, stiffening like a board.

Giles was ecstatic. She wasn't fighting him anymore, and he mistook her stillness for surrender, his mouth slowly softening on hers while he eased his hold on her, then drew his head back so he could look into her eyes. Suddenly a chill ran through him.

"Get out of here!" she gasped breathlessly, and there was fire in her eyes.

He frowned, but didn't move, while her eyes continued dancing dangerously.

"I said out!"

"But . . . I'm sorry, love. What . . . what did I do wrong?" He was at a loss.

"Everything," she answered, managing finally to pull free.

"But I don't see—"

"That's just the trouble. None of you see, do you?" She walked toward the card table where they'd been playing cribbage, then turned to face him. "I don't intend to carry on this charade any longer," she replied, deliberately hoping to disillusion him. "Giles, the only reason I went out with you or any of the rest of the men from Goldspur in the first place was that I promised Logan I would."

"Poe, please," he begged, walking toward her. "You don't know what you're saying. I'm in love with you, you know that. I was hoping someday to ask you to marry me."

"Don't be ridiculous, Giles." She frowned momentarily, then sighed. "You might as well know. I don't intend to marry anyone, ever."

"But . . . Logan . . ." His voice died away.

"Logan what?" she asked suspiciously.

His eyes searched hers. "Logan led me to believe . . ."

"He told you I was in love with you?"

He flushed. "Not in so many words, no. But by Jove, he let me think I had a chance."

"Oh he did, did he?" Her eyes narrowed, and she gazed past him as if contemplating, then her jaw tightened stubbornly. "I'm afraid Logan's misled you, Giles," she said abruptly. "I made up my mind years ago that I'd never marry anyone, and he knew it."

Giles shook his head. "That can't be . . . don't say that, love," he begged frantically. "You can't mean it. I know you can't. I know you love me. I've seen it in your eyes."

"You've seen nothing but contempt in my eyes," she insisted.

He reached out to take her hand, but she pulled it away.

"Good God, Giles, what do I have to do to make you understand?" she cried. "I don't love you now, I never did, and I never will."

"Oh, but you do," he went on, then smiled confidently. "You're just a little mixed up, that's all, and I've been a bounder to spring it on you so sudden like this. I realize that now. However"—and he straightened, waving a finger at her as if she were a naughty child—"I know that in spite of what you've been telling yourself, you do love me, my dear, and believe me, I can be patient. Only I shan't give up trying to convince you, you can be sure of that."

She stared at him incredulously. The stupid fool! He hadn't listened to a word she'd said. Was he that dense?

"Please, Giles!" Her hands went to her head and she closed her eyes briefly, massaging her temples, then opened her eyes again to look at him. "Not any more tonight, please," she pleaded. "If you don't mind, I have a terrible headache." She shook her head disgustedly. "It's just been too much."

He reached out, and this time he took her hand, ignoring the fact that she was trying to pull it away. "Forgive me, my love," he cooed tenderly. "I didn't mean to upset you." His eyes twinkled as they caught hers. "But you do look so delightfully scrumptious when you're angry, you know."

"No, I don't know," she said, managing to free her hand again before he had a chance to kiss it. "Now, if you'll just excuse me, I'll have Clive show you out," and she brushed past him, heading for the door before he could say anything else to stop her.

She had felt Lord Merriweather's bewildered eyes on her as she stalked from the room, and knew he must have felt foolish standing there alone, and now, as she walked toward the kitchen, hoping to find Clive, she knew she'd been rude, but at this point she didn't much care. All she wanted was to be left alone. Just one day to call her own, and by the time she ran into Clive at the end of the main hall, she still wasn't in a very good mood.

"Will you please show Lord Merriweather out, Clive?" she said briskly, then added hesitantly, "By the way, is Mr. Campbell home?"

"No, miss."

She frowned. "Do you know where he is?"

The servant's gray head nodded congenially. "Said he was going to play a bit of poker tonight, miss," he answered matter-of-factly, and she hesitated for a moment as if she were going to ask him something else, then seemed to change her mind.

"Thank you Clive," she said softly, then turned, heading for the stairs and her room while the gray-haired servant went to the parlor so he could escort Lord Merriweather to the door.

The rest of the evening went by so slowly for Poe, and now she lay in bed listening intently for Logan's footsteps on the stairs. She had stayed up, sitting in the chair by the window, waiting for him as long as she could, then finally gave up and got into bed. Only she wasn't about to fall asleep. She had to talk to him. And it had to be tonight, it just had to.

She kept her ears strained, hoping she wouldn't miss hearing him. After all, the stairs were carpeted, and on top of that, he always tried to be as quiet as he could when he came in late.

Finally, well past midnight, she heard a faint noise. Slipping from the bed, she opened her bedroom door a wee crack just in time to see Logan enter his room and close the door behind him. Good.

Grabbing the pink lace wrapper that matched

her nightgown from off the chair, she opened the door, crept into the hall, and closed the door quietly behind her, slipping the wrapper on as she headed for his room, her bare feet sinking into the hall carpet.

She knocked on the door, waited until she heard his muffled "Come in," then opened the door and stepped inside, closing it behind her.

Logan hadn't bothered to light the lamp when he came in because he was still angry over losing again at poker, and he couldn't for the life of him understand why he couldn't seem to keep his mind on the cards anymore. He'd been sitting on the edge of the bed taking off his boots when she knocked, and thinking it was Clive, he'd called for him to come in. He turned when he heard the door close, expecting it to be the butler, and suddenly froze, but only for a brief second as Poe straightened, walking toward him.

He stood up. "What are you doing here?" he asked, staring at her apprehensively.

Poe tried to keep her eyes on Logan's face, but it wasn't that easy. His shirt was unbuttoned and pulled out at the waist, and he was still clutching one of his boots, the other already tossed aside.

"I have to talk to you." She took another step toward him so she could maybe see his face a little better, since the only light in the room was the dim moonlight from the window.

"About what?"

"Why did you tell Lord Merriweather I was in love with him?"

"Aren't you?"

"You know damn well I'm not," she answered heatedly. "I've done nothing but fight him and those other men off for weeks now. And tonight that . . . that . . . He kissed me!"

A smile began to play about the corner of Logan's mouth. "He kissed you?"

She stared at him hard for a moment; then suddenly all the fight seemed to drain from her and she felt miserable. Her eyes lowered. "I can't do it anymore, Logan," she murmured, close to tears. "If being a lady means I have to subject myself to somebody's slobbery lips all over my mouth . . ."

"I presume you didn't like it."

"I hated it." She felt herself flush, and trembled slightly.

"Are you cold?" he asked.

She shook her head. "No . . ." But her voice faltered. "It's just that it was so horrible, and I was remembering."

"It was really that bad?" His voice had softened.

"Please, Logan," she begged, her eyes rising once more to meet his, and it was only the second time he'd ever heard her plead with him, the first being when they were dancing at the party. "Please." She went on, "I can't stand them touching me. I can't take it anymore. Tell me I don't have to do it again," and much to his surprise, as he stared back at her, tears sprang to her eyes and began running down her cheeks. "I hate them, I hate them all!" she cried helplessly, and without warning she threw herself at him, her arms encircling him, as if for protection while she raved on. "I can't stand their pawing hands on me. Please, Logan." She was sobbing against him. "The parson doesn't care about my soul, he only wants my body, and Big Jim and the rest—they all want the same thing. I hate them!"

Her head was on his chest and she was clinging to him desperately. For a moment Logan wasn't quite sure he was really seeing what he was seeing, or feeling what he was feeling, but then slowly, as the realization that she wasn't putting on an act just for his benefit sank in, he tossed the boot he was still holding aside, and his arms encircled her, holding her close. It was the first time he remembered seeing her cry, and his left hand caressed her head, pressing it even closer to him until he felt hot tears on his bare chest.

She felt soft and feminine, and he trembled inside, his heart beginning to pound as that same warm sensation he'd felt that night in the cave began to spread through him, and suddenly he wanted to run. Instead, his hand moved down her hair and curved into the nape of her neck. How easy it would be to pull the hair back and touch his lips to her flesh just below the ear. He could soothe her fears. He knew he could. The thought made him start to ache inside. He hadn't been to the Duchess since the morning Poe ran away. He hadn't seemed to need her, but now . . . It would be so easy. The bed was so close, but Poe . . . ?

He glanced down at the top of her head. The shadows had all but swallowed her against him, yet the soft, sensuous, earthy smell of her floated up to him and he felt intoxicated. If only he dared pick her up, carry her to the bed, and make love to her. But it was impossible, and he knew it, and it took all the strength he had to fight his conscience over it.

Reaching down with his other hand, he took hold of her chin, turning her head up so she had to look at him. For a second he was certain he'd made a mistake, because her mouth looked so inviting, and he had such a hard time concentrating on what he wanted to say, but after another stubborn battle with himself, he finally managed.

"Poe," he whispered softly, gazing into her misty eyes. "I had no idea. I thought maybe, if you knew a little more about men, you wouldn't hate them so."

"Not hate them? I despise them," she answered helplessly. She hadn't wanted to break down like this. She'd planned to just tell him off, then leave in the morning. But when she'd stood staring back at him a few moments ago, she remembered what her life had been like before, and thought how different life here at the Highland was and how she was beginning to like being a lady. "Please, Logan," she pleaded, her lips trembling slightly. "Don't try to make me go out with them anymore . . . don't force me to go back on my word and leave the Highland before meeting your aunt, please!"

"You won't have to," he conceded reluctantly. "I got word this evening that Aunt Delia got into San Francisco early this morning and should be in Goldspur by tomorrow night."

Poe froze, staring at him curiously, the tears no longer blurring her eyes; then slowly, hesitantly, as if she were suddenly realizing where she was and what she was doing, her face reddened and she squirmed in his arms, trying to get loose.

"What's the matter?" he asked, knowing full well what was wrong, but stubbornly keeping his arms where they were.

"I . . . I shouldn't have come here," she said self-consciously.

"Why?" He was looking straight at her, his voice hushed. "Because you hate me?"

"Yes," she replied breathlessly, fighting the weakness in her knees and the tingling sensation that was working its way to her toes. "I'm sorry, I wasn't thinking." She wrenched free of his arms, only to have his light laughter tease her.

"Poe, you amaze me." His eyes were crinkling at the corners. "You insist you can't stand me, yet come to me for help."

"Well . . ." Her chin tilted stubbornly, her mouth forming a pout. "Where else could I go?"

"Besides," he added, teasing her affectionately, "I don't slobber when I kiss, so you picked the lesser of the two evils, right?"

"Oh! How could you!" she gasped, mortified, and her eyes grew hostile. "You're impossible, Logan Campbell," and without any warning she gave him a hard shove, catching him unprepared, and he fell back on the bed, sprawling awkwardly, while she turned and left the room, slamming the door behind her.

Logan lay on the bed, holding himself up on his elbows, watching the door shut, then let his head fall back, to lie where he'd landed, staring at the dark ceiling overhead.

What the hell was the matter with him anyway? What was it about her that always seemed to goad him into doing things he knew would irritate her? There just didn't seem to be any answer. He closed his eyes and brought back the sight of her standing there only a few minutes ago in her lace nightgown with her hair catching lightly at the moonlight, deepening it to mahogany. The sight had been breathtaking. Then, when she'd hurled herself into his arms . . . Damn!

He'd come so close to trying to make love to her that it was frightening. Would she have surrendered, or fought like a wildcat? he wondered thoughtfully, then had a strange premonition she'd have chosen the latter, and was glad he hadn't forced the issue.

Opening his eyes again, he took a deep breath and got up from the bed, once more starting to undress. Funny how a person's feelings could change so drastically, he thought. He'd wanted women before, plenty of them, but being denied the satisfaction had never brought him the anguish that denying himself Poe had caused him, because there'd always been another woman to take the other's place. But there just didn't seem to be anyone who could take Poe's place, and deep down inside he knew it. That was the trouble; he knew the truth yet fought against it, even though he was aching miserably, and he cursed her for being a nuisance and tried to put her out of his thoughts. It wasn't that easy, however, and as he finished undressing and climbed back onto the bed between the cool sheets and laid his head back on the pillow, he knew as he closed his eyes that his dreams would be filled with her as they always were, and he swore silently, telling himself that his desire for the inexperienced young girl was just that, a physical desire, and that's when he made up his mind. Tomorrow evening, just to prove he was right, he promised himself he was going to stop by and see the Duchess, and with that thought in mind he punched the pillow into a ball beneath his head, turned onto his side, and sighed, determined that tonight he wasn't even going to dream.

# 6

## Aunt Delia Returns

$P$oe spent the next day in her bed in her room feigning an upset stomach and a headache, and all the threats and coaxing from Logan did nothing to make her change her mind. She wouldn't even come downstairs to turn all the suitors away, so he was obliged to do the honors, a task he soon came to resent. However, as the day wore on, he slowly realized how unfair he'd been to her. Why, with all the suitors he'd been turning away, she had had barely a minute to herself these past few weeks. No wonder she had called him a Simon Legree. He'd been enjoying himself, doing the things he wanted, while she'd been doing everything she hated, and he soon found himself counting the hours until the stage was due.

Finally, early that evening, about half an hour before stage time, he walked into Poe's room after a brief knock on the door and found her resting against propped-up pillows, reading a book.

"You don't give a person much chance to get decent, do you?" she said, dropping the book and trying to pull the covers up over herself.

She was wearing the same lace nightgown she'd had on last night, and Logan tried to ignore the stirring it brought deep down inside him as he caught sight of it just before the sheet and blanket covered it.

"I think this has gone far enough," he said roughly as he stared at her. Her tousled red hair was plastered back against the propped-up pillows, making her appear soft and angelic, but he knew far different. "You have no more stomachache than I do," he continued in the same tone. "I went along with you because I knew how you felt, but I'm leaving to meet the stage in a few minutes and I want you dressed and downstairs ready for dinner by the time I get back with Aunt Delia. Is that understood?"

The covers were up to her chin. "I don't have much choice, do I?"

"Not really."

"Are you sure Giles and the others won't be showing up again?" she asked apprehensively.

He shrugged. "I can't make any promises, naturally, but I think I discouraged them thoroughly enough that they won't be back today." He studied her for a minute, then straightened.

"If they should show up, though, Clive has instructions to get rid of them, so you shouldn't have any worries." He checked his pocket watch. "Now, I'd better get along," and he started for the door, then turned back to her. "Remember, I want you ready to meet Aunt Delia," he said, and left the room.

Poe stared after him. He'd been wearing a black suit with that same ruffled shirt he'd been wearing that night in the cave, and the sight of it always had the weirdest effect on her. Last night when she went to his room she'd been all set to tell him she was leaving, but when she'd seen him standing there staring at her like that she knew she didn't want to leave, not really. He'd shown her a new way of life. He'd taken away her pants and shirt and replaced them with frills and manners, and she wanted no part of the old Poe anymore. She had suddenly felt as if Logan was the only one who could help her, and now her face reddened at the thought.

She slid from the bed, remembering his words of last night, then smiled. She had to admit he'd been right. He didn't slobber when he kissed. In fact, what he did do was quite different, and as she walked over, staring at herself in the full-length mirror on the wall, she flushed even more, feeling strange inside.

Sometimes he made her so angry. Still, she had to admit he didn't paw her or embarrass her with a lot of nonsensical flattery. That was why she always had such a hard time trying to figure out just what he did do to her, and why. However, he was a stubborn, egotistical male, and that was all she needed to know to stamp her disapproval on him. Yet he was the only friend she had. If you could call him that. It was really frightening at times.

She went to the wardrobe and took out the velvet dress that matched her eyes. Well, at least with Delia Campbell home, maybe she wouldn't have to depend on Logan for everything anymore, and she threw the dress on the bed, pulling the bell cord that hung near the window so she could have the servants bring up the tub. A warm, soothing bath would do wonders for her right now.

Logan nervously paced the boardwalk at the Champaign Hotel, waiting for the stage. It was just past dusk already and he was irritated as he watched the lights going on in the different establishments here and there down Main Street. As usual the damn stage was late again. Glancing over toward the darkened offices of the Highland Spur, he wished Aaron hadn't had to go to Carson City because he could sure use some moral support when he told Aunt Delia about Poe. Ah, well. He stopped pacing, sat down in one of the chairs in front of the hotel, then suddenly sprang up seconds later, hearing the faint rattle and clank of the stagecoach nearing town, and by the time the driver pulled the team up in front of the hotel, Logan was standing at the side of the road anxiously waiting. He watched the driver get down and waited for him to open the door, then sighed as Aunt Delia stepped from the stage.

Delia Campbell was the only passenger this evening, and when she stepped from the stage she did it with a flourish, as was her usual custom. Not a tall woman compared to Poe, she was still a little taller than most, with a slightly plump figure, and her ebony hair, streaked with gray, curled delicately, framing an attractive face for a woman of fifty.

"My dear, boy," she exclaimed, kissing Logan on the cheek when he came to greet her; then the big blue eyes that matched her silk traveling suit studied him curiously as she drew back. "I thought you'd be pleased to see me," she said wistfully.

"I am . . . I am," he answered quickly, then began ushering her toward the carriage he'd driven to town. "Only you have to admit you weren't due back for another few weeks."

She glanced about. "Where's Aaron?"

"Had to go to Carson City about some new equipment some fella wants to sell you." He helped her into the carriage. "Figured he'd find out all the particulars before you got back and save you some time."

She smiled, nodding. "Good, because I don't intend to go anywhere now for ages." She settled the skirt of her traveling suit smoothly over her legs as she talked. "I was never so glad to see anything in my life as I was to see San Francisco harbor when we sailed in."

"Sounds like you didn't enjoy the trip."

"On the contrary." Her smile was warm and comfortably reassuring. "I loved seeing all the old places. Scotland's still as beautiful as ever, but I'm afraid I'm a landlubber at heart and I made up my mind that I'm never going to cross that horrid ocean again. I was sick the whole while. I guess I forgot what it was like when I crossed it years ago as a little girl."

Logan grinned. "I never thought I'd see the day when you'd admit anything ever got the best of you."

She patted his hand. "Don't get cheeky, Logan," she admonished lightly. "I don't generally, and you know it. But since you're a relative and I can swear you to secrecy . . . after all, I have to complain to someone. Now"—she motioned with her head to where a large trunk and some lighter baggage lay in the dusty road in front of the hotel—"how about gathering up the luggage?"

Instead Logan came around to the other side of the buggy. "Don't have to," he said as he climbed in beside her. "If you'll glance back, you'll see the hotel's taking care of it. I had the clerk at the hotel hire someone to haul your trunks out to the Highland."

"I might have known," she said as she glanced sideways at him. She'd been watching Logan closely ever since her arrival, and for some reason he seemed exceptionally nervous. Or was he? No, it wasn't really that. It was more like unsettled, and usually he did everything with such a confident air of authority that this change had taken her by surprise. His face was shadowed in the dim light from the hotel window seconds before the buggy pulled away from it, but she'd swear his eyes were strangely alive and expectant.

"All right, what's the matter?" she asked as the carriage rolled down the dark street toward home.

He straightened, then looked over at her, frowning. "You didn't get my letter?" he asked.

"What letter?"

"Oh, Christ!" He ground his teeth, then continued talking as he drove the carriage toward the edge of town. "I sent a letter almost three weeks ago, hoping you'd get it before you left. I guess you didn't."

"Obviously." Her eyes narrowed. "What's happened, Logan?" she asked, a little more worried now. "What was the letter about?"

He cringed momentarily, then shrugged. Might just as well get it over with. Besides, except for the fact that Aunt Delia never liked to have unexpected disruptions in her life, she usually took them pretty well. He cleared his throat.

"You know a Joe Yancey!" he asked abruptly, then glanced at her quickly as he felt her tense. Her mouth was firm, eyes hesitant, waiting.

"Go on," she said, her voice unusually strained.

"Well." He drew his eyes from her face, tending to his driving again. "It seems a lady named Hester Yancey, who used to be married to Joseph Yancey, died, naming you guardian of her daughter, Poetica, and she's up at the house now waiting for you to get back," he blurted quickly. "She's been here at Goldspur for about a month now."

"Oh my God!" she exclaimed breathlessly, and Logan reined the horse to a halt, then looked over at his aunt.

Her face was pale, the knuckles on her hands white as she clutched the sides of the carriage, and her eyes were staring off into the distance, transfixed. For a second he was afraid she'd faint.

"Aunt Delia?" he asked, concerned, and she slowly drew her eyes from whatever memory had captured them and looked straight at him. "You know about Poe Yancey?" he asked.

She nodded hesitantly, her breathing shallow, voice unsteady as she spoke. "I know all about Poetica Yancey," she answered unhappily. "Only please, don't stop. Go on."

He started the buggy up again.

---

"We have to talk," she said slowly.

He hesitated. "Now?"

"Yes, before we get to the house."

"Go ahead."

She was apprehensive. "Did . . . did she say anything about money or anything?" she asked.

"Poe?"

"Yes, Poe."

"Should she?"

Delia sighed. "Oh God, Logan, are we in trouble," she said, and he'd never heard her sound so strangely hopeless before in his life.

"What kind of trouble?" Now he was worried.

"Don't worry, I'll tell you about it later," she said, then seemed to get her emotions a little better under control. "Only tell me, what's she like?"

"Now, or when she came here?" he asked.

Her eyebrows raised curiously. "There's a difference?"

"A big one." He chuckled, amused. "She came to town cussing like a banshee and fighting like a wildcat. Wasn't even going to stay. Just stopped long enough to tell you off, only Aaron tricked her into promising to stay until you got back. She's a real lady now, though. Only trouble is, she still won't have anything to do with any of the men from town. Aaron and I were hoping we could get her interested in one of them and make her change her mind, so that by the time you got back she'd be ready to settle down and get married, to get her off your hands. But it hasn't worked.''

Delia's hand flew to her breast. "Thank God!" she sighed in relief. Logan glanced over at her, bewildered, as he maneuvered the buggy off the main road, starting up the long drive toward the house.

"Is she pretty?" Delia asked quickly as they neared the front entrance.

"I guess you could call her pretty."

"I was afraid of that." She shook her head as he pulled the buggy up to the door and stopped.

"I wish you'd tell me what this is all about," he complained, puzzled by her reaction.

"Not now, dear, later," she assured him, and he climbed down, hitching the reins to the post for one of the stableboys to retrieve, then came around to her side of the buggy. "After I've met the girl, we'll have a long talk in the library," she said while he helped her down. "Only I'm afraid Aaron's going to have to know too if we want to avoid a scandal." She sighed, her mind seemingly quite preoccupied. "Oh dear, I'm afraid I'd really forgotten about Poetica Yancey. How stupid of me," she mumbled as if to herself, and Logan was frowning, more bewildered than ever as he helped his aunt up the walk and into the house.

Delia was extremely tired from all the riding, and just before the stage arrived in Goldspur, she had sworn that nothing was going to keep her from coming home, taking a long luxurious bath, then climbing into bed. Nothing short of Poe Yancey, that is, because now she stood in the library staring at this magnificently tall young woman with the red hair and blue-green eyes, all thoughts of rest and relaxation having vanished.

Poe had been reading when they walked in, and she closed the book, setting it on the arm of the chair, then stood up facing the woman she assumed was Logan's Aunt Delia, who was staring back at her with the same intensity Poe knew was in her own eyes.

"My dear," Aunt Delia said after recovering from her initial shock of discovering that Poetica Yancey had turned into such a lovely young goddess. "I never dreamed you'd be so grown up."

"And so tall?" Poe offered caustically.

"Well, yes. I must admit you are taller than I imagined." She smiled, embarrassed. "But I'm not exactly short myself, dear," she went on. "As you can see. Only on you it's much more becoming," and she walked over, taking Poe's arm, surprised that she actually had to look up to the young woman, and ushering her toward a leather couch beneath the bookcases on the far wall. "Sit down, let's talk," she said, hoping that by sitting down she'd feel more in command of the situation. She settled them both in the middle of the couch while Logan stood nearby, wondering what the hell kind of trouble Aunt Delia could be in that would have anything to do with Poe.

"Now," Delia said as she studied Poe thoughtfully. "Has Logan been treating you right while I was gone?"

Poe gave him a dirty look, then looked back at his aunt. There was a definite family resemblance between the two—both had dark hair and similar facial features, only Delia Campbell had brilliant blue eyes, nothing like Logan's hard gray ones.

"If you call trying to marry me off to anybody who'd have me, taking good care of me, I guess you could say he did fine," she answered.

Logan had turned his back on Poe when she'd glanced over at him, and he was staring out the window. Delia looked over at him. "Don't worry, my dear," she said solicitously. "We'll forget all about that for the moment."

"But will they?" Poe interrupted. "They've been coming to the house all day, and Lord Merriweather insists he's going to haunt me until I say yes. And Big Jim Slattery won't take no for an answer."

"Would you eventually say yes to either of them?" Delia asked as she glanced back at Poe, noticing the loathing that filled the girl's eyes when she talked of the men.

"Never!" Poe sounded more than just determined. "I'll never marry any man, ever," she went on. "I hate the whole lot of them!"

"Never's a long time, my dear," Delia replied softly. "Don't ever be too quick to make such emphatic statements where the heart's concerned. Remember, the heart's such a fickle thing, and can be so traitorous. Believe me, you'll change your mind a hundred times before you die."

"Not me!" Poe insisted, and glanced over again toward Logan, who still had his back to them.

Delia watched Poe curiously, then sighed. How could she blame the girl really? Hester Yancey had been hurt so badly when Joe left her and her baby that she'd turned against all men. Evidently she'd brought her daughter up to hate them too, and it was no wonder now that, even with Hester dead, the girl would hold to those beliefs. Still . . .

"We'll see," Delia replied. "But for now, I just want you to feel that this is your home, Poe, for as long as you care to stay," and as she reached over, taking Poe's hand, squeezing it, and Poe acknowledged the gesture, Delia hoped with all her heart that the girl's coming wouldn't end up being their downfall.

Aaron arrived back from Carson City about half an hour after the stage that brought Delia home rolled into Goldspur, and after stabling his horse, he went directly to his rooms over the Highland Spur offices, changed clothes, then headed toward the Highland, wishing he could have gotten back sooner. Logan's telegram had informed him that Delia was due home this evening and he cursed himself for not making better time so he could have been with Logan when the stage pulled in. As he trudged up the drive toward the house, he wondered how Delia had taken the news about Poe.

Fortunately Aaron arrived at the Highland just as Logan, Delia, and Poe were sitting down to eat, and Delia, happy to see him, yet anxious over how she was going to explain things to him later, welcomed him warmly, instructing the servants to set a place so he could join them at the table, and although it looked on the surface as though Delia had welcomed Poe without any qualms, all during dinner as she talked about her trip to Scotland, he felt the trepidation running just beneath the surface of her calm veneer.

Unfortunately, they were only halfway through Aaron's favorite dessert when he saw the veil of composure finally begin to slip from Delia Campbell's mannerisms, and realized things weren't all they seemed to be. Then he knew he was right as she turned toward Poe, addressing the girl a little more sharply than was her usual manner.

"If you don't mind, my dear," she said, trying her best to sound affectionate and caring, "after dinner I have some important business affairs to talk over with Logan and Aaron in the library, so if you could perhaps find something to occupy yourself with until our discussion is over . . ."

"I'll go to the parlor and finish the book I've been reading," she answered, and Delia was pleased, even though her eyes still appeared troubled.

So after dinner Poe settled on the sofa in the parlor with her book, while Logan, Aaron, and Delia faced each other behind a locked library door.

"So now what the hell's going on, Aunt Delia?" Logan asked as he walked over and flopped on the leather sofa, stretching his legs out. "You've kept me hanging ever since you got back. Why the big mystery, and what does Poe have to do with it?"

Instead of answering, Delia turned to Aaron, then motioned toward one of the overstuffed chairs. "You might as well sit down too, Aaron," she said sternly. "Your pacing is only making me more nervous than I already am!"

Aaron obliged.

"Well?" Logan asked again.

"All right!" Logan had never seen Aunt Delia so upset before, but her hands were actually trembling. She had changed from her blue traveling suit, and the red dress she had on only made her look all the paler. "We'll start at the beginning," she began slowly. "Poe's mother's maiden name was Hester Campbell and she was about my third or fourth cousin somewhere along the line. I really lost count but she and her parents came over from Scotland years ago with mine and we settled in the same town, which happened to be St. Louis, living side by side until I left home in my late teens. Although Hester was younger than I by about four or five years, we grew up together and were very close. Unfortunately, Hester was a shy girl, with none of her daughter's assets. Her hair was more of a carrot red, and even though her eyes were the same color as Poe's, they were set in a face full of freckles that wasn't exactly homely, but she wasn't very attractive either, so there were few men who courted Hester." Delia wrung her hands as she began to pace back and forth, then went on. "That's why, when Joe Yancey came along, she fell for him so hard. Hester was a romantic from way back—you can proba-bly tell that by the peculiar name she gave her daughter. When Poe was born, Hester took one look at her and said she was as beautiful as all the poems she'd ever heard, all rolled into one. She said she was a poet's dream, so she named her Poetica. Anyway, that's neither here nor there . . ." She took a deep breath. "What I'm getting at is that she was the sort of woman who thought love came as a knight in shining armor. Well, he came all right, but not until she was in her late twenties, and his name was Joe Yancey. Only he wasn't a knight. He was handsome, virile, and quite a ladies' man. That was the whole trouble. He liked the ladies too much, and the worst part was that I introduced them during one of my frequent trips back to St. Louis. When I realized what was happening, I warned Hester about him before leaving St. Louis again, but it did little good. She just knew she'd found her Prince Charming."

Delia walked to the window, staring out for a minute as if remembering, then turned back toward Logan and Aaron.

"She came back down to the ground soon enough, however, when her father was forced to hold a gun on Joe while the minister performed the ceremony so her child wouldn't be born out of wedlock."

Again she paused, studying their faces for a moment before going on.

"You might know the marriage was a farce from the very start," she went on, beginning to pace the floor again. "Hester had been so sure that once she had a ring on Joe's finger he'd act like a loving husband, but he only champed all the harder at the bit. And he wasn't even discreet about his infidelities, flaunting them right in front of her. Finally, after Poe's birth, she wrote and told me that he did settle down for a while. From the way she said he acted, it sounded like he really took a liking to the baby, and even tried to toe the mark, trying to be a good husband. Only it didn't last. Seems he just couldn't keep his hands off women or liquor, and one day, after an awful row with Hester, he finally took off, leaving her and the baby to shift for themselves."

She stopped in front of them again, her face grim. "Hester just couldn't seem to face anyone anymore after that," she went on. "And when her mother died unexpectedly a few weeks later, she talked her father into leaving town. They ended up in Elko, Nevada. She and I still kept in touch for the next couple of years. You see, my parents, your grandparents, Logan, died in a fire in St. Louis about twelve years before Hester got married, you might remember it, I don't know, and except for my brother, your father, who was married and still living back in St. Louis, I'd really been on my own all that time. So Hester had been almost like family to me. Anyway, when Poe was about three, her grandfather passed away, and I guess something just seemed to snap inside Hester, because she moved out of Elko and up to Ruby Lake, away from everyone and everything. By that time I'd already been in Nevada for a number of years and was running the Goldspur mines."

"So what does that have to do with Poe?" Logan asked.

"I'm getting to that." She gave Aaron a quick glance, then continued.

"Well, somehow Joe Yancey happened to show up in Goldspur. It was right about the time you came to Goldspur, Logan. Anyway, he'd been gambling, speculating, and drifting, and he'd managed to accumulate quite a bit of cash over the years. I think Poe was about four or five at the time, and unfortunately, or fortunately, however you want to look at it, I badly needed cash right about then, so I let Joe buy shares in the mine. Only I guess his conscience got the better of him, because instead of buying them in his name, he bought the stock in Poe's name, with the stipulation that all monies accrued by the stocks were to be put into a trust fund for the girl until she either turned twenty-one or married."

She saw the look on both their faces and realized they'd caught the implication.

"That's right," she said wearily. "And over the next few years until he died, he continued to help, until he had practically as much money in the mine as I had."

"But I never remember seeing anyone named Yancey around," Logan said, frowning.

"You didn't have to." Delia's hands felt clammy as she clapped them together. "Joe was never one for staying too long in the same place, so he'd just come and go, but he always left instructions and money for buying shares in

Highland Enterprises, with all dividends going into the trust fund. So you see, gentlemen, since I used the money that was supposed to be put in Poetica Yancey's trust fund, even though it was put back into the mines and was used for the good of Highland Enterprises, we're in trouble, real trouble."

The room was dead silent for a moment; then Aaron moved forward in his chair. "She has proof of this?" he asked.

"No, Poe doesn't, but don't worry, Aaron, it was all done legally," she answered. "However, the stock certificates are in my possession. The only trouble is, they were recorded, and Joe said he had a lawyer who was notified every time and knew all about the whole thing."

Logan's eyes snapped. "Who?"

"I wish I knew. He never told me. All he ever said was, 'Delia, don't ever try to cheat my kid because I've got a lawyer friend who's kept track of every cent I've given you over the years, and if, when Poe reaches twenty-one or marries, you don't give her her due, he'll see you rot in the nearest jail.'" She straightened, her mouth twitching nervously. "And I'm afraid Joe Yancey meant every word of it."

"You have no idea who the man is?" Logan was astounded.

"Joe traveled all over. It could have been anyone. But you can bet whoever it is has kept track of Poe over the years."

"What if he didn't?" Aaron cut in. "What if he's dead?"

"I don't dare take that chance."

"Why not?" Logan asked. "Surely he'd have shown up by now. Poe's been here a good month."

"That doesn't really mean a thing," she said unhappily. "After all, she isn't supposed to inherit until she's twenty-one or married." She stared hard at Logan. "And you were trying to marry her off!"

He shrugged, sputtering as he tried to defend himself, but she waved his explanation away.

"It isn't your fault, it's mine," she said disgustedly. "I thought I still had at least three or four years to figure some way out of the mess."

Logan couldn't believe it. "You mean you've been putting all her money into the Highland?"

"And everything else we own."

Aaron shook his head, then frowned. "That means, by all rights, she owns almost everything."

"We're penniless?" Logan asked.

"Not penniless." Her lips pursed deliberately. "It's just that she always had more money from her shares to put back in than I did, since I had to live on mine. Oh, we have some money, true, but if you consider everything, we don't really have enough to afford living like we do."

"Oh, great." Logan stood up and walked to the window, staring out.

"So what do you do now?" Aaron asked, and Delia tried to stay calm.

"I've had an idea forming all evening," she said quickly. "Only I don't know if I can convince Logan to go along with it."

He whirled around. "With what?" he asked suspiciously.

"Well . . ." Her eyes sparked expectantly. "If you were to marry the girl . . ."

"Marry her?"

"That's right." She was desperate. "Logan, as her husband you could handle all the legal matters, and we could stay in control of the money. Maybe that way we could keep the whole thing quiet."

"I don't think that sets too well with Logan," Aaron said as he caught the expression on Logan's face.

"I don't really care how it sets with him," she said stubbornly. "It's either sink or swim now, and I don't intend to spend my last days in jail."

Logan shook his head angrily. "I won't be a scapegoat, Aunt Delia. I won't sacrifice my freedom."

"You have to. It's the only way out." Her eyes darkened. "What if she changes her mind and decides to marry one of those men you sicced on her? What then?"

"You heard her," he tried to explain. "She

hates men. Won't have anything to do with them. Why would she marry one of them?"

"She might if she got suspicious, or learned about the money she could inherit." She was pleading with him. "Please, Logan, it's the only way out."

"It's ridiculous." He sneered. "She won't marry anyone else—what makes you think she'd marry me?"

Delia smiled, amused for the first time since they'd entered the library. "Come now, dear boy, you seem to have an extraordinary way about you where women are concerned. They flock around you like moths to a flame. A little lovemaking on your part should put her right where we want her. Surely you aren't averse to making love to a beautiful young woman like Poe?"

Logan's face wore an expression neither Delia nor Aaron could fathom. "I'm afraid the young lady has an all-consuming hatred for me, Aunt Delia," he answered coldly. "That in itself would eliminate all thoughts of making love to her. Now, any other suggestions?"

Delia sighed. "You're giving up too easily, Logan," she said, and her eyes flashed dangerously, but Logan still frowned.

"I don't intend to even try," he answered. "There'd be no use. Evidently her mother did a magnificent job in turning her into a man-hater.

It'll take more than an attempt at lovemaking to make her change her mind."

"Then we try another way," Delia replied, and her eyes bored into his. "If I can talk her into marrying you, will you do it?"

His jaw set stubbornly. "I said I don't want to get married."

"I didn't ask whether you wanted to or not," she said stubbornly. "I asked if you'd do it?"

Aaron leaned back thoughtfully in his chair, trying to come up with a better solution while Logan stared hard at his aunt.

"Remember, Logan," Delia added, "if I go to jail there's every chance you and Aaron could go too."

"Us?" Logan glanced at Aaron, then back to his aunt. "Why us?"

"My dear boy," she answered, and her face was solemn, "I brought you here from St. Louis fifteen years ago after my brother and his wife passed away—that means you were around here before Joe Yancey died, when he was still buying shares of stock for his daughter, and as soon as you were old enough to work in the business, you were included. As for Aaron here, he's my lawyer. He's been with me ten years. Do you think any court would believe he could take care of the books, handle all my legal affairs, and not know what was going on?"

"But I didn't!"

"Nor did I," Logan added.

"I know that and you know that, but can you prove it?"

Aaron took a deep breath and looked at Logan, his eyes troubled. "She's right, Logan," he said.

Logan ran a hand through his dark hair. Damn it! She was right. Who'd believe they hadn't been a part of it all along? He turned again, staring out the window. If he did marry her, what then? Oh, but that was impossible, she'd never consent to it—he was sure of it. He turned back to face Delia.

"Well?" she asked again. "Will you do it?"

"Do I have any choice?" he asked.

"I'm afraid not." She stepped toward him, looking into his face sympathetically. "Thank you, Logan," she said softly.

He stared down at her, his gray eyes intense. "Don't thank me yet," he offered. "You'd better convince Poe first."

Delia's mouth twisted into a wicked little smile. "I think I know the way to do just that," she said smugly. "Now"—she glanced over at Aaron, then back up to Logan—"if you two will wait here, I'll go talk to Poe," and she left the two of them waiting for her in the library, still in a mild state of shock over the night's happenings.

Poe was curled up on the sofa with her book, when Delia came in, and she quickly sat up straight, her feet back on the floor, the book closed.

"Business talks over?" she asked.

Delia watched the way her blue-green eyes shone. She was such a likable girl.

"Not quite," she answered, and walked over, sitting beside her, turning sideways so she could face her. "There are a few things I have to talk over with you too, Poe."

Poe was surprised. "Me?"

Delia nodded, then smiled warmly. "Poe," she asked, "did your mother or Attorney Wimpole ever say anything at all to you about money?"

Poe frowned thoughtfully. "They did say something about Pa making arrangements with you so I wouldn't ever have to worry about money anymore," she answered. "That's why Mr. Wimpole said I had to come here first before doing anything else. And then one time Ma told me she got a letter from Pa once, and he wrote telling her that if anything ever happened so I was alone, she was to send me to you."

"I thought as much," Delia said, and smiled, trying to hide her discomfiture. Well, she'd have to make at least a show of good faith now. She reached over and squeezed the girl's hands. Only she wasn't really a girl anymore. She was a woman, and that was the whole problem. "First of all, let me explain, my dear," Delia said with a show of affection. "You see, years ago, I guess your father had a stroke of guilty conscience, and . . . well, it was right about the time he had some money in his possession. To make a long story short, my dear, he found me here in Goldspur and bought some shares in the Highland Mines for you, hoping someday if you were ever in need you could fall back on it. It wasn't really a great deal of money to start with, to be sure, Poe," she went on. "But over the years, since you weren't around to collect any of the dividends from it, I reinvested them in the mines for you, and I'm happy to say, my dear, that the increase on the initial investment has been so great that right now you happen to be quite a wealthy young woman."

Poe stared at her. It didn't seem possible.

"I know it's probably hard for you to believe," Delia continued. "But it is true, my dear."

"But Logan . . . Aaron—neither of them said a thing."

"They wanted me to be the one to surprise you. That's why Aaron tricked you into staying. Naturally, compared to the rest of the Highland Enterprises, your share is a small one," she lied. "But unfortunately it's one that is causing me quite a bit of a problem."

"What kind of a problem?"

Delia stood up and began to pace the floor, then stopped, watching for Poe's reaction. "You see, my dear, although your money isn't an enormous amount, you are an heiress, at least you will be when you reach twenty-one or marry, whichever comes first, and that's what's bothering me. There are so many fortune hunters in the world. Men who'd take advantage of the fact that you have money. And you are a beautiful woman, my dear."

Poe smiled. "You don't have to worry about that, Aunt Delia," she assured her. "I hate men, and I'll have no part of them."

"That's just the trouble," Delia ventured. "They'll want a part of you." She came back over and sat down again beside her. "Don't you understand, Poe?" she went on, hoping she could pull it off. "Already half the men in town are fighting over you, if what Aaron and Logan have told me is true. When they learn that you're due to inherit a small fortune when you marry, they'll never leave you alone, and you won't be twenty-one for four more years. You'll be trying to keep them at bay all that time."

"We could keep it a secret," she suggested hopefully.

"A secret? You just don't understand business, my dear," she said, and hoped the guilt didn't show in her eyes as she went on. "You see, as I said before, your money was invested back into the company for safekeeping. If I intend to give you your full share when you reach twenty-one, I'm going to have to start selling some of my holdings now to make sure I have enough capital, because it takes time. And I'm afraid when that happens, the news is bound to leak out one way or another. It'd be too suspicious for people not to talk and speculate about."

"You have to give it to me all at once?" Poe asked.

"Those were your father's orders, and they're legal, my dear. You're to get a lump sum when you reach twenty-one or marry, whichever is first."

Poe's eyes were troubled. "But I really need money now, and besides, I don't want to spend the next four years fighting off men," she pleaded with Delia. "What can I do?"

"Well," Delia said, pleased that the conversation was going her way, "there is one solution," she went on hesitantly. "And it would solve everything."

"What's that?"

Delia took a deep breath. "Marry Logan," she said quickly, and saw Poe's mouth fall open, her face turn livid.

"Marry Logan?" she gasped, astonished.

"Yes, dear," Delia began, only to be cut off by Poe's anger.

"You're out of your mind!"

"But it's—"

"I don't care what it is!" Her blue-green eyes were sparking dangerously as she continued to yell at Logan's aunt. "I wouldn't marry that egotistical bastard for all the money in the world. You can keep the damn fortune. I want no part of it. I'd rather be what I was before than let any man touch me, let alone Logan. Do you understand? No man will ever do to me what my pa did to my ma, and that goes for Logan Campbell or any other man!"

Delia shook her head as she stood up facing Poe. "Please, Poe, let me explain. There's no need—"

"Isn't there?" Poe yelled, her face flushed, and she too stood up, attempting to brush past Delia; only Delia caught her hands, stopping her.

"Please, dear, listen to me," Delia pleaded hurriedly, her hands tightening on the girl's arms. "It won't be like you think. You'd be his wife in name only. He'd never lay a hand on you . . . I can promise you that."

Poe hesitated, staring at her, and Delia went on.

"Don't you understand, dear," she said, all warm and solicitous, "it would be a marriage of convenience, that's all."

"Convenience?" Poe asked, calming a little, but still bristling with anger.

"That's right, convenience. As far as the town's concerned, they'll think you married for love and the men will leave you alone, but in truth you'll have only taken Logan's name." Delia's hands dropped as she realized Poe was no longer trying to run off. "You can have separate bedrooms and go your separate ways, I promise you that, and Logan will never touch you."

Poe stared hard at Delia Campbell. She'd liked her right from the start, even though she had felt a little intimidated by the woman's commanding presence. Her eyes seemed warm and caring, though, and Poe needed someone to care the way her mother had cared. Only she still wasn't quite sure she understood.

"You mean I wouldn't have to really be his wife . . . I wouldn't have to . . . to give myself to him?" she asked, her face turning crimson.

"That's right, my dear."

"But how would that solve anything?"

"Come, sit down again and I'll explain," Delia offered, and once more Poe sat beside her, listening as Delia explained. "As Logan's wife, my dear, the men in town will have no reason to pursue you, yet you'll be free to come and go as you please, without the restraints of a regular marriage."

"Oh, I understand that part," she answered. "I just don't understand how that's going to help you as far as the money goes, because no matter whom I marry, if I do it right now you'll still have to break up Highland Enterprises and sell off part of your holdings, won't you? I don't want you to have to do that."

"That's just the good part of the whole thing, my dear," Delia confided hopefully. "You see, as Logan's wife, any property either of you has will automatically belong to both of you jointly— what's yours will be Logan's and what's Logan's will be yours. And since Logan is already my partner and sole heir, you'd automatically take over your shares and I wouldn't have to sell anything. The Highland holdings could stay intact. That way, you'd have your inheritance legally without having to change anything physically, only on paper. But most of all, Poe," she said, straightening reassuringly, "you could still go on being a lady with pride and dignity."

Poe looked heartsick. "But Logan—of all people."

"Oh, I admit he isn't the best choice a girl could make for a husband," Delia agreed. "But I know I can trust Logan. He'll not only take good care of your money for you, but he'll do what I say."

"Will he?" Poe wasn't so sure. "Will he stop visiting the Duchess?"

Delia flushed. "The Duchess?"

"I'm no fool, Aunt Delia," Poe said stubbornly. "If you told everyone in town that Logan and I were happily married, do you think they'd believe it when his visits to the Duchess didn't stop?"

Delia held Poe's hands, her fingers tightening. "I see what you mean. You're far more perceptive than what you've been given credit for, my dear," she said. "But yes, I think his visits to the Duchess will stop."

"Ha! I bet," Poe said. "He's no different from any other man."

---

Delia patted her hands solicitously. "You just leave that part of it to me. All I want to know now is, will you do it?"

Poe pulled her hands from Delia Campbell's and stood up, then walked to one of the windows, staring out. Delia Campbell was right about one thing. Being married was probably the only way she could ever get the men in Goldspur to leave her alone. Especially Big Jim and Lord Merriweather. Besides, if she couldn't get any of the money until she was twenty-one, what was she going to live on in the meantime? She sure didn't feel like going back to living out of a bedroll and a saddle. And if it was a marriage in name only . . . What to do? Suddenly she thought of something and turned back to the woman on the couch.

"What about Logan?" she asked curiously, and Delia frowned.

"What do you mean?"

"Just what I said. What about Logan?" She looked at Delia suspiciously. "Why would he ever consent to marrying me?"

Delia smiled smugly. "My dear girl," she answered, pleased with the way things were going, "you evidently don't know Logan like I know Logan. I already have his consent. You see, Logan likes money better than he likes his freedom. Now, he knows that if you don't marry him I'll have to start selling things and we could possibly lose a fortune, so since he's my partner and is just as interested in keeping Highland Enterprises intact as I am, he's chosen the wisest course.''

"Then he's doing it for the money?"

"That's one way of putting it. I like to think he's willing to do it for Highland Enterprises rather than just money."

"I see." Poe contemplated for a moment. "And you can promise he won't touch me?"

"He won't touch you, my dear."

Poe bit her lip, pondering; then, "All right," she blurted reluctantly. "I'll do it. But remember, there'll be no more Duchess, and he keeps his hands off me. Agreed?"

"Agreed." Delia was ecstatic as she stood up, walked over to her young ward, and gave her a big hug. "You won't be sorry, my dear, believe me," she said affectionately. "I promise, you'll never be sorry."

"You just make sure Logan Campbell keeps his part of the bargain," she said as Delia pulled back, and Delia saw fire in Poe's eyes as she said it.

"He will, don't worry, he will," Delia answered hurriedly, and she couldn't have been happier.

# 7

# The Engagement

$\mathcal{D}$elia Campbell shut the library door carefully behind her, breathed a sigh of relief, then glanced toward the desk and the overstuffed chair where Logan and Aaron were still impatiently waiting.

"Well?" Aaron asked, and she strolled across the room, smiling. "You must have been successful," he went on. "You don't usually smile so smugly."

Her smile broadened. "I was successful," she offered complacently. "Only before the definite plans are set, I'm afraid I have to extricate a few promises from my dear nephew here," and she glanced over at Logan, who was sitting at the desk, fidgeting with one of the paperweights on it.

"Now what do I have to do?" he asked belligerently.

"It's really what you *don't* have to do," she

answered matter-of-factly. "Rather, I'd say, what you'd better not do. First of all, she'll marry you, but only on the condition that you keep hands off. And I'm sure you know to what I'm referring."

Logan wasn't surprised. "I figured as much," he said. "What's the other promise?"

"Second," she said, and her eyes hardened, "you stay away from the Duchess and her kind."

This time she saw Logan flinch. "Dammit all!" he yelled as he shot from the chair. "What the hell does she think I am, made of stone?" He saw Aaron smirk. "And you!" he went on, staring down at him, his gray eyes blazing. "You're supposed to be a lawyer, yet you can't even find a way for us to legally finagle our way out of all this. What the hell good are you?" He turned on his aunt again. "You know damn well I can't promise a thing like that," he said. "Especially not under the circumstances."

"It's either that or go to jail, Logan."

He was fuming. "I'd rather go to jail. Same difference."

"All right then," she conceded. "I know it was asking a lot, but for God's sake, Logan, you have to marry her. We have no other choice. Look, keep the first promise—you can do that can't you?"

He mumbled something incoherent that she took to be an answer.

"As for the second, I'll tell her you agreed,

but you'd better promise me to be discreet or I'll have your hide, do you understand?"

He stared at her furiously, but didn't answer.

"If anyone should get wind of what we're doing, there could really be repercussions," she tried to explain. "Believe me, dear boy, I don't want it any more than you. But like Poe so delicately put it, a happily married man shouldn't have any reason for visiting the Duchess, now should he?"

"Who says I'll be happily married?"

"Me," she said anxiously. "Because that's the impression we want the town to have. If you spoil it, and anyone in town discovers what we're really doing, we could still end up rotting in jail."

"Don't worry, I'll try the best I can not to spoil my reputation," Logan said sarcastically. "Only if you think I'm going to give up all my pleasures for someone who hates my guts, as she so aptly puts it, you're sadly mistaken."

Delia sighed. "All right, Logan. I get the point. Only please," she begged, "be careful. I told her you'd do what I say."

"Oh, I'll keep my hands off her," he answered. "But that's the only bargain I'll make. Whatever else I do is my business."

"Does Poe know about the money?" Aaron asked, interrupting them.

Delia looked apprehensive. "I told her she's an heiress, yes, but fortunately she doesn't seem to know much about the business world and I'm positive she's not the least bit aware that what I've done is illegal. She thinks it's just a matter of seeing to it that she gets the dividends from her shares of stock. She's definitely not aware that the trust fund she was supposed to get doesn't exist, and as long as we keep her from learning about it, we're all right, at least until she ties the knot with Logan."

"How'd you convince her to do that?" Aaron asked. He was really surprised she'd managed, and so was Logan for that matter.

"It wasn't really all that hard," she answered. "I merely pointed out that if she were married to Logan, a marriage that would be in name only, the male inhabitants of Goldspur would be forced to quit making nuisances of themselves by trying to court her. Naturally, I also pointed out that if she didn't marry Logan and the men in town learned about her inheritance, they'd become even more obnoxious and demanding. So she's willing to marry you so she'll be safe and won't ever have to be bothered by men she can't stand." She smiled. "You might say that I convinced her life as a rich wife would be far more advantageous for her than life as a rich heiress." She paused for a moment and studied her lawyer. "We can get away with it legally, can't we, Aaron?" she asked.

Aaron leaned back in his chair and rubbed his chin thoughtfully for a minute before answering. "We can on one condition," he said. "But it's going to take some maneuvering, and I only hope Poe will be so busy with all the wedding arrangements she won't take time to look into what's going on."

Logan frowned. "Now what?"

"Now the sticky part comes in," Aaron answered. "I'll make sure the papers are all drawn up ahead of time, and as soon as the ceremony's over we'll have Poe sign papers giving Logan, as her husband, power of attorney to handle all her business affairs. Then, while she's changing from her wedding dress into traveling clothes, Logan will sign a paper accepting all monies from Poe's trust fund for her, and no one will be the wiser."

Logan frowned. "But there is no trust fund."

"You know that, and I know that, and Delia knows it," Aaron answered. "But we just better make sure nobody else finds out."

Logan glanced sideways at Aaron. He felt like a cad. "That's the only way it'll work?" he asked.

"The only way." Aaron was emphatic.

"And if we're caught?"

"Once you have power of attorney, unless Poe herself presses charges, there's not much anyone can do," he answered. "Why, what's wrong, Logan?"

"I just don't like cheating her like this," he answered. "Somehow it just doesn't seem right."

Delia reached out lovingly and touched Logan's face. "That's what I like about you, dear boy," she said affectionately. "You still have a little bit of conscience left."

He took her hand from his cheek, his eyes hard on hers. "Just make sure of one thing," he replied. "I don't want any more Poe Yanceys popping up out of your past, because I don't intend to take any more mistakes off your hands, understand!"

She smiled, patting his arm. "Don't worry, dear boy," she said. "Now, if Aaron will go fetch Poe, we have some arrangements to make."

Aaron had scarcely left the room when Delia turned on Logan.

"Before he comes back, I want the truth from you, Logan," she said hurriedly. "Have you tried anything you shouldn't with that girl?"

His eyes were hard and cold, yet he didn't answer.

"Don't look at me like that, Logan," she went on. "She didn't say anything, it's not that. It's just that I have this strange feeling that something's happened between the two of you. Am I right?"

He reached down absentmindedly and picked up the paperweight he'd been fussing with before, and turned it over in his hand as if examining it, but instead his thoughts were on other things.

"Well?" Delia asked again.

———

"I kissed her once, if you call that something," he finally answered, and she frowned.

"No wonder she was so insistent that you keep your hands off," she said sternly. "I assure you, Logan, your behavior is of the utmost importance in all this." She had to make him understand. "If you fail to keep your part of the bargain, and she were to get mad enough, she could revoke the power of attorney you're planning to sign, and husband or no husband, we'd be in one hell of a big mess again. Do I make myself clear?"

"Perfectly," he answered, and set the paperweight back down as he looked back over to where she stood, proud, yet apprehensive. "You've set a hard row for me to hoe, haven't you," he went on casually. "Logan Campbell, a man who's left a trail of fallen women behind him from here to San Francisco and back, and he ends up married to a woman he can't even touch. Ironic, isn't it?" His fist clenched, and Delia saw the tension in his face. "You know, it'd really be funny and laughable if it weren't so tragic."

Delia studied his face, the strong lines she knew only too well, yet there seemed to be a change in him. "You haven't fallen in love with the girl, have you, Logan?" she asked.

"God forbid!" His answer was almost too quick. "Only it just seems a damn shame that so much woman has to go to waste," and Delia looked disgusted.

Ah yes, that was Logan, her Logan. He'd finally found a woman he couldn't master and his ego was hurt. Who knows, she thought as she watched him turn to look out the window while they waited for Poe and Aaron, maybe Poe Yancey was just what Logan Campbell needed, although she'd always planned a better match for him. Oh well, you couldn't always have everything. She smiled, amused at the thought.

Poe walked into the library slowly, as if she weren't sure just what to expect. Delia was smiling and looking quite pleased with herself, but Logan, when he turned to greet her and Aaron, looked mad enough to skin a bear.

"Come in, come in, dear," Delia said as she walked over and took Poe's arm, then glanced back to Aaron, gifting him with the same warm smile. "We have so many plans to make and so much to do. Now, let's see, the wedding should be as soon as possible within the realm of good taste. We'll put an announcement in tomorrow's newspaper . . ."

"Tomorrow?" Poe couldn't believe it. "Isn't that rushing things a bit?" she asked.

"Nonsense," Delia insisted. "The sooner the better." She glanced over at Logan. "Will you quit looking like you're going to a funeral?" she said. "The both of you look like you've swallowed a bottle of vinegar. It isn't going to be all that bad, you know. Now, where were we? Oh yes, the announcement." She released Poe's arm, went to the desk, grabbed a piece of paper and pencil off it, sat down, and began to write. "I also want announcements sent to all the nearby cities and towns, and, oh yes, San Francisco," she rattled on, and Logan stared at her unsmiling.

"Rubbing salt in the wound?" he asked bitterly.

"I forgot." She looked up at him, then pushed a stray gray hair back in among the dark ones that still covered her head. "You do have friends there, don't you, dear?" she said, then shrugged, smiling again, a little more self-satisfied than necessary. "Well, everyone has to know, you know," and as she bent her head again, working on the list in front of her, Logan wondered what Cassie, Rachel, and all the others were going to think when they learned about his intended marriage.

"I'd say six weeks from tomorrow should give us just about enough time, what do you think?" she asked, then didn't even wait for an answer. "But of course, now, there'll have to be a trousseau . . ."

"A trousseau?" Poe looked bewildered.

"Why, certainly, my dear." Delia wasn't about to be swayed otherwise. "And we'll make arrangements for a short honeymoon. Maybe San Francisco . . ."

"Now, why the hell do we need a honeymoon?" Logan asked, interrupting her.

"For appearances' sake, dear boy," she answered. "And while you're in San Francisco the two of you are to pretend you're honeymooners," she went on, unperturbed by his interruption. "Now, you can at least hold hands once in a while and smile at each other, can't you?"

She saw the glance exchanged between Poe and Logan.

"Well, good heavens," she retorted. "It won't hurt either one of you, you know. Now, as I was saying. We'll plan the wedding for six weeks from tomorrow," and she went right on making her plans while the two of them stood glaring at each other, and Aaron sat in the overstuffed chair, taking everything in.

Later that evening Delia stood in her tower room surveying the town spread out before her. It was well past midnight and few lights were on at this hour; however, the moon was full tonight and it crested on the tops of the houses and buildings, making it look like something out of a fairy tale, only Delia knew better. Goldspur was a full-blooded town, with real people who could be nasty if they wanted to be. Only right now they were her people, and she was determined they were going to stay her people.

She'd dug for gold with her bare hands in those days, right alongside the men, to get where she was today, and by God, she wouldn't give it up for anything. Not even Poe Yancey.

Suddenly a frown creased her forehead as she caught sight of a figure heading for town, and instinctively she knew who it was and where he was going.

"Damn," she whispered softly to herself, determined to chew him out for taking such a risk, and she prayed silently, hoping Logan's unexpected nighttime excursion wouldn't ruin everything for them.

The night air was humid and dry as Logan moved down the road heading toward town. He was restless and all out of sorts. Had been ever since Aunt Delia's arrival back in Goldspur. Or maybe it was even before that. He wasn't quite sure anymore when the restlessness had started. After all, Poe had left him in a miserable state last night that had given him nightmares, and he'd woken this morning in a cold sweat. Then to top it off Aunt Delia had to spring her nasty little surprise on him and Aaron.

Marriage! Even the word sounded confining. He kicked the dust in the road ahead of him, then stopped, watching momentarily as it whirled up, catching bits of moonlight before settling down to the earth again. Damn women, he thought angrily. He wanted to lash out at something, anything. Instead, he started walking again, and by the time he walked up the step and pounded on the Duchess's door, his mood was anything but congenial.

The door opened hesitantly and Peko poked her head out.

"Where's the Duchess?" he snapped.

Peko straightened, opening the door farther. "She's next door, Señor Logan," she answered timidly. "We hadn't expected you."

"I know that," he said irritably, and pushed his way past her into the house. "Go tell her I want her," he ordered. "I'll be in the sitting room," and Peko stared after him for a moment before shrugging her shoulders and heading next door, while Logan went straight to the liquor cabinet in the parlor.

He was leaning with one hand on the mantel and the other wrapped around a half-empty brandy glass, staring into the fireplace absentmindedly, when the Duchess walked in.

"As I live and breathe," she sighed sarcastically. "If it isn't Logan Campbell. I thought Peko was having hallucinations."

"You're not funny," he said as he turned to face her.

"Well, it has been quite a while, love," she reminded him bitterly.

He stared at her hard. She was a beautifully seductive woman, and the red dress she had on tonight with its satin sheen and low neck hugged every curve, while her dark hair was pulled off her shoulders and piled high, leaving her neck and earlobes free to show off the rubies and diamonds that graced them. A touch of lip rouge at the mouth, a slight blush of rouge on the cheeks, and the flawless way her eyes were made up gave her a haunting beauty he knew she didn't naturally possess.

"You think I wanted to stay away?" he asked.

"Oh, come now, Logan." She walked over and poured herself a brandy. "The Highland isn't that far away."

"With Poe there it might as well be a thousand miles," he answered, and drained the rest of the glass.

"Are you getting scruples?" she asked winsomely, and sipped at her drink, gazing at him over the rim of the glass.

He strode over, took the glass from her hand, set both their glasses down, then reached out and picked her up, cradling her in his arms.

"Logan—?" she started to question, but his mouth came down on hers, hard and demanding, then he drew his head back.

"Shut up," he commanded, and headed for the stairs with her in his arms.

When he reached her bedroom, he kicked the door open, stepped inside, still carrying her, and kicked the door shut behind him, then set her on her feet with her back to him and began unfastening the back of her dress.

"Logan, I didn't say—"

"I said, shut up," he told her again, and this time the timbre of his voice was enough to make her blood run cold.

———

It was just the way he said it. Logan had always been tender and gentle, and although the Duchess sensed that his actions before had always been well-thought-out and deliberate, she hadn't cared. Tonight, however, his actions seemed more rash and reckless, and there was a savagery about him that frightened her.

Her dress fell to the floor and he proceeded to unfasten her underclothes, divesting her of them completely, until she stood quietly in front of him, her clothes crumpled at her feet.

The scent of her perfume was strong about him now as Logan reached out, feeling the softness of her skin, deliberately running his hand down her back, waiting for something to happen, but what? For some reason, there was nothing exciting about the Duchess's back tonight. It was just like any other back. Disappointed, he picked her up again and crossed to the bed, where he laid her on her back, then bent over her, looking deeply into her eyes.

"What is it, honey?" she asked softly, trying to understand, but instead of an answer, a strangled sob seemed to wrench its way from him, and his mouth covered hers again, this time even more hungrily.

The Duchess clung to him wantonly, and moved sensuously on the covers in ways guaranteed to entice any man, and Logan began to break out in a cold sweat. He drew his lips from hers and buried his face in her breasts. It just wasn't working tonight. There was something wrong, but what, dammit?

"You've been away too long, love," the Duchess murmured huskily, and ran her fingers through his hair, feeling his hand on her left hip pressing into the flesh.

Logan hesitated momentarily, his lips on her breast, her perfume filling his head, and a shiver ran through him.

"Now, love, take me now," she whispered softly, and before he had a chance to change his mind, he released her, stood up, yanked off his suit coat, and began unbuttoning his shirt.

A short while later Logan swore silently to himself as he shut the door behind him and walked down the steps, leaving the Duchess's house. It hadn't been what he'd expected, and it hadn't gone well at all. The Duchess had been no different than any other time; it was him. He was still aching inside. There just seemed to be a void there that he couldn't quite fill. An emptiness inside, as if something were missing. There was no satisfaction, no warmth, no fulfillment. He still felt the same longing and yearning inside he'd felt last night when he'd held Poe in his arms. He felt restless inside, as if he'd never even been to the Duchess.

Shoving his hands in his pockets, he started the long trek back toward the Highland, his tall frame bent slightly with disgust. Damn girl! he mumbled to himself. He'd set out to prove something tonight, but . . . He cringed. Well, he'd proved it all right. He'd proved that that damn girl had spoiled everything for him, everything, and as he melted into the night shadows, watching the moon descending on the horizon, he swore softly to himself again, cursing the day he'd met her.

The next afternoon Logan rode through town on his way back from the lumber mill northeast of town. He was riding his favorite horse, a palomino Aunt Delia had given him on his twenty-fifth birthday three years before, and he reined the horse over toward the side of the main street, drawing him up short as he saw the Duchess coming his way, waving a piece of newspaper in her hand and yelling.

"You no-good son of a bitch," she cried, reaching him, and she grabbed his horse's bridle, staring up at him. "What did you do, go straight from my bed to hers?" she asked venomously, and Logan slid hurriedly from the saddle, ground-reining his horse.

"Shut up!" he ordered sternly, and grabbed her arm, pulling her off the street. They were in front of the Highland Enterprises office and he opened the door, shoving her inside, oblivious of the fact that Aaron was sitting at one of the desks at the back of the room.

"Now, what the hell are you talking about?" he asked as he released her.

"This," she answered, waving a sheet from the local newspaper in front of his nose. "You're engaged to that . . . that Amazon," she spat at him. "When did you propose to her, before or after you left me last night?"

"There are some things even I have no control over, Duchess," he said forcefully. Only she didn't look any too pleased.

"You mean it's Delia's idea? Ha! I'll never believe that," she added caustically. "Not after last night's performance, anyway."

"What do you mean by that?"

"Last night, honey, you made love like a man whose mind's on another woman," she replied bitterly. "From another man I could understand it, but not from you. You always enjoyed making love to me before, but last night you . . . you acted like it was an experiment. As if you were waiting for something to happen. As if you had to make love to me to prove something to yourself."

"You're crazy." Logan's eyes were like steel. "I made love to you because I wanted to."

"Then why are you marrying Poe?"

He took a deep breath. "Maybe I figure it's time I settled down. After all, when I'm gone, what's left? Aunt Delia isn't going to live forever, and neither am I, so whom do I have to leave Highland Enterprises to when I'm gone? Besides, why not Poe? She's young, beautiful."

"And you're in love with her?"

Logan's eyes were flashing. "All right, I'm in love with her," he yelled angrily. "Is that what you wanted to hear?"

"And that's why you came last night? To make sure?"

"If that's what you want to believe. Have it any way you like."

Her face was as colorless as the pale gray dress she had on as she crumpled the paper in her hands, and there were tears in her eyes. "If you marry her, you'll never be able to come back to me, you know that, don't you?" she said.

He reached out, his hand beneath her chin, tilting her head up so he could look into her eyes. "Won't I?" he asked cynically, and she stared back at him, her lips quivering.

She had guessed it would come someday. That someday he'd fall in love, only she'd so wished it could be with her. Suddenly she pulled his hand from her chin, and her head went up haughtily.

"Don't count on it, lover," she snarled, glowering at him, then turned abruptly and walked out, closing the door firmly behind her.

Logan watched as she walked briskly down the street, while behind Logan, Aaron still sat at the desk watching him.

Finally Aaron leaned forward. "Did you mean what you just said a few minutes ago, friend?" he asked.

---

Logan whirled about sharply.

"How long have you been here?" he asked irritably.

"Since you walked in." Aaron smirked. "But you didn't answer my question."

"What question?"

"Did you mean what you told the Duchess?"

"What's that?"

"Are you really in love with Poe?"

Aaron saw Logan's eyes narrow testily and his face grow dark and sullen.

"Oh, go to hell, Aaron!" he growled furiously, and stormed out, slamming the door behind him so hard Aaron was afraid the glass would break; then he mounted his horse and headed down the street toward the Highland.

In a plush suite at the Champaign Hotel, the marriage announcement was having even more repercussions.

"You and your damn ideas," Giles Merriweather said as he stood looking out the window onto the main street of town.

"Well, you're the one who claimed to be the ladies' man," Roger Tyson answered. "Not me."

"But you were the one who said it'd be so easy." Giles turned. His face was almost the same color as the tan suit he was wearing, and all the rides with Poe in the warm Nevada sun had bleached his hair and mustache a shade lighter. "Sweep her off her feet and marry her, you said," he went on. "That way we can return to England and the manor house with enough money to last us a lifetime, as well as pay the back taxes on the estate, you said. You bloody well made it sound so easy. Well, you botched this one up royally, cousin, didn't you?"

"Me?" Tyson countered. "I botched it up? Look here, dear cousin," he exclaimed. "You were the one who was supposed to do the sweet-talking, not me. I'm beginning to think all those things you told me about you and those English ladies were figments of your imagination."

Tyson stood up. He wasn't as tall as Giles, and his hairline had started to recede, but there was a strong family resemblance in the square jawline and classic nose. However, since his face was minus the mustache, and his eyes green rather than brown, few noticed the family resemblance.

"That girl's worth millions," he said as he walked over next to his cousin, pulled the curtain on the window back slightly, and glanced into the street below. "She's got to be. Joe Yancey gave Delia Campbell enough money to buy shares in ten mines before he died, and the dividends have been accumulating interest in that trust fund of hers ever since, and I don't intend to let it slip through my fingers that easily. Why do you think I went to Elko and hung around all those years after Joe's death trying to compete for clients with Wimpole while I waited for the girl to grow up?" he asked. "Just to let it get away from me? If you hadn't happened to send that telegram telling me you were on your way and shown up when you did, I'd have found someone else to do your job." He glanced over at his tall cousin. "Maybe I should have anyway," he said disgustedly. "Do you happen to realize what all we could do with the kind of money Poe Yancey could bring to us?"

"Would have, you mean," Giles said heatedly. "There's nothing we can do now."

"Oh yes there is," Tyson was quick to disagree. "You can go back out there and make another try for the lady, that's what you can do," he said. "Remember, she's not married yet, and meanwhile I'll see what else I might be able to come up with, just in case."

At that moment he looked back out the window, and suddenly his eyes narrowed shrewdly as he saw the Duchess step from the Highland offices and walk briskly toward the bordello, followed a few moments later by Logan Campbell, who mounted his horse and rode off in the opposite direction, as if he were riding for his life.

"Hmmm," he mumbled thoughtfully to himself as Logan disappeared down the street.

Giles frowned, staring at him. "What's that?" he asked.

---

"Strange, isn't it, dear cousin?" Tyson answered. "That Logan should be consorting with his—shall we say—close ladyfriend the very morning his engagement is announced in the papers," and he proceeded to tell Giles what he'd just witnessed while Giles's back was to the window. "And Mr. Campbell looked anything but happy," Tyson concluded.

Giles eyed his cousin curiously. "You think something's going on?" he asked.

"I think maybe they're trying to pull a fast one on me."

"Like what?"

"Like I'm beginning to wonder if maybe Delia Campbell might have forgotten to set up that trust fund," he mused. "After all, not a word's been said about money since we arrived in town. Now, let's face it, since Poe Yancey's scheduled to inherit what would be considered by most people as a sizable fortune, don't you think word would have gotten out about it by now?"

Giles frowned. "How could they get away with that?"

"Not very easily, but it could be done."

"I'm listening."

"First of all, if there is a trust fund and they're just not advertising the fact to keep fortune hunters away, then when Poe marries Logan Campbell, as her husband he'll just enjoy all the benefits, but if there is no trust fund, and Delia Campbell used the girl's money illegally over the years, then the only way to cover it would be for Campbell to sweet-talk the girl into marrying him, then have her sign power of attorney over to him. With him holding the purse strings, who's to holler fraud?''

"You think they'd do that?" Giles asked.

"I think Delia Campbell would stoop to anything for money. Look at this town," he said, and gestured toward the window. "She practially owns the whole thing." His hands dug into his pockets and he began to pace the floor. "God-damn parasites," he growled. "Either way, they're going to get that girl's money and she probably won't even know she's been had."

Instead of looking angry, Lord Merriweather began to chuckle, and Tyson stopped pacing.

"What are you laughing about?" he asked.

"That's rich," Giles answered, still grinning. "That's jolly well rich. They're beating you at your own game."

Tyson's jaw tightened stubbornly. "I'm not beaten yet, cousin," he said. "There may be only one way to milk a cow, but there's more than one way to pick a pocket."

"Then we don't leave?"

"We don't leave." He walked back over and looked out the window again, watching the activity below. "I'll get money from the Campbells one way or another, you'll see," he said. "Besides, it's still several weeks till the wedding, and until Logan Campbell actually gets that ring onto her finger, you don't give up, understand?"

"You mean you still want me to try courting her, even though she's engaged?"

"Why not? Until she's Mrs. Logan Campbell she's still fair game."

"For an attorney, Roger, you have a thick skull," Giles retorted. "I'll be bloody well lucky if I can even get near the Highland, let alone try courting her again."

"Well, she won't be at the Highland all the time," Tyson reminded him, "and I expect you to take every chance you can to get to her. Remember, we can't fix up Weatherby Hall or pay the back taxes without any money, and there isn't even enough in our coffers now to get either of us to England, let alone fix up your estates. So keep remembering, Poe Yancey's worth money to us."

"And Joe Yancey, poor chap, thought you were his friend," Giles said, and his eyes caught his cousin's, settling on them knowingly.

For the next few weeks Poe and Logan were kept so busy they didn't even have time to wonder whether they might be making a mistake. Delia saw to that. There were teas and luncheons and all sort of soirees, as well as rehearsals for the main event. And Poe had to stand for hours on end while the dressmaker fitted her with new clothes for her trousseau, and she blushed profusely when she caught sight of the diaphanous nightgowns that were being included, knowing what the dressmaker was thinking. Yet there was no way she could protest their inclusion without admitting that her marriage was going to be nothing more than a farce.

There was no regular engagement party as such, but there was a diamond ring which was presented to Poe in the sitting room five days after the engagement was announced, because it took that long to have a man come from San Francisco with some rings from which she was to choose.

"I feel ridiculous," Poe said as she started to slip the ring on her own finger after the jeweler had gone, only Logan reached out and grabbed her hand, stopping her.

"Wait," he snapped sharply, and took the ring from her, then grabbed her hand, heading for the door with her while Delia and Aaron stood watching. "Not like this," he said.

"Where are you taking me?" she started to protest, but he didn't answer, only continued dragging her after him, on outside to the flower gardens, to a bench near the walk, where he stopped.

"Sit down," he commanded roughly, and plunked her on the bench a little less gracefully than he'd planned.

"I'm sorry, Poe," he apologized. "I didn't mean to be so rough with you."

"What is it?" she asked breathlessly, and for a minute he didn't answer, only stared at her, marveling to himself at how lovely she looked in the pale green dress she was wearing, even though it clashed with her eyes.

"Logan?" she asked again, puzzled.

"All right, Poe," he finally said, remembering why he'd brought her out here. "I promised Aunt Delia I'd respect your wishes and wouldn't touch you, but dammit all to hell, you're not going to put your own engagement ring on your finger. That's going too far. I may be a heel, but I'm not that bad. Now, give me your hand."

Poe was speechless as she stared at him.

"I said, give me your hand," he insisted, more softly this time, and she held her hand toward him, the words she knew she should have uttered still caught in her throat.

He slipped the ring on the third finger of her left hand, then drew her to her feet, looking down into her face. "Will you marry me, Poe?" he asked huskily, and her blue-green eyes widened in astonishment as she drew in her breath quickly.

"Why . . . why did you do that?" she asked hesitantly.

"I know this whole thing is a farce, Poe," he explained gently. "And I know you hate me, but please, let's have some semblance of civility in this whole mess. Now, will you marry me?"

---

Her lips quivered as she continued to gaze into his eyes. It was a hot day, the sun was lowering on the horizon, and the breeze rustling the leaves on the trees nearby was warm, yet Poe shivered, her voice almost inaudible.

"Yes," she half-whispered. "I'll marry you, Logan," and he reached out, cupping her chin in his hand.

"Thank you, Poe," he acknowledged softly, and after staring at her for a long moment, wanting to give her more than just words for an answer, yet knowing it could spoil the moment for them, he let his hand drop from her chin, grabbed her hand, and turned, heading back toward the house, dragging her with him again to where Delia and Aaron were waiting, wondering what was going on.

All during the time preceding the wedding, Lord Merriweather continued to make a nuisance of himself, trying to see Poe every chance he could. When she was in town he followed her around like a lovesick puppy, and if she went riding he usually showed up somewhere, trying to join her, but his strategy didn't seem to be working. Not only did she pay as little attention to him as she could, but his constant pursuit made her even more determined than ever that the decision she'd made to marry Logan had been the right one, because she knew, as Logan's wife, she'd be beyond the Englishman's reach.

---

Delia had planned for the ceremony to take place in the town church. That is, until Poe got wind of it.

"Oh, no," Poe exclaimed that evening at dinner, after hearing of the plans she'd made. "I won't be married by the Reverend Ambrose, and that's that. You'll have to find someone else."

"Someone else?" Delia asked. "Why?"

"Because I said so." Poe was determined. It was her wedding, and by God, if she was going to get married, it'd be her way. "I won't be married by him and I won't be married in his church, and that's final."

"That's unreasonable," Delia said, throwing up her hands. "Please, Poe," she begged anxiously.

"What's so unreasonable about it?" Logan cut in, and Delia glanced at him in surprise. "Why can't we have the preacher from Tonopah," he went on, as if it were the natural thing for him to side with Poe. "And the ceremony could take place in the ballroom at the hotel, where we had the birthday party."

"I see." Delia studied him for a minute, then shrugged. "I guess it doesn't really matter, we could do that," she said. "But it seems so unnecessary when there's a church with a preacher right here in town."

"Maybe the folks in Goldspur consider him a preacher," Poe said belligerently. "But I don't.

As far as I'm concerned, he's no more than a dirty-minded hypocrite."

Delia's eyes widened in astonishment. "Good heavens, girl, what did he do?" she asked.

"It isn't what he did that counts," Poe stated firmly. "It's what he wanted to do."

"Poe!" Delia gasped.

"Well, it's the truth," she said stubbornly. "Pretending he wanted to marry me to save my soul from being corrupted by living out here at the Highland . . ."

"He said that?"

"He certainly did."

"Well," Delia said, her eyes sparking, "I guess I'm just going to have to have a long talk with the right Reverend Willard Ambrose, aren't I?" She took a deep breath. "In the meantime, my dear, you'll have your preacher from Tonopah," she assured Poe, and as the days went by, the plans for the wedding proceeded according to the suggestions Logan had made that evening at dinner.

# 8

# Wedding Bells

The morning of the wedding was more like a circus in Goldspur than like the solemn nuptials most weddings were. Flowers overflowed in the ballroom at the Champaign Hotel, drinks flowed freely in all the saloons, and the atmosphere was anything but staid.

Only four people in the whole town seemed not to be enjoying themselves. Reverend Willard Ambrose was still smarting over the confrontation he'd had with Delia Campbell and the fact that another minister was called in to perform the ceremony, while the Duchess, Lord Merriweather, and Roger Tyson sulked as they stood with the rest of the guests and watched Poe slowly make her way through the crowd toward the ballroom where Logan and the minister waited, with Aaron as best man.

Poe's dress of slipper satin had a gently

flounced overskirt that was held in place by white satin roses, and delicate seed pearls graced the heart-shaped bodice, scattering down onto the underskirt below the flounces. The pearls on the dress matched beautifully with the pearls that lay across her throat and hung gracefully in clusters from her earlobes. The veil covering her luxurious red hair was so sheer it floated as she walked, and was held in place by a tiara of pearls intertwined with real white rosebuds that complemented the roses and baby's breath in the nosegays that hung from the Bible she carried. She was a vision of loveliness, tall and statuesque as she walked down the length of the ballroom, then gracefully stepped up beside Logan, who was resplendent in a midnight-blue suit worn over a lace-ruffled white shirt.

Their eyes met, the orchestra at the far end of the room that had been playing the wedding march stopped, Logan took Poe's hand in his, they turned toward the minister, and the Duchess held her breath.

She was standing at the top of the stairs that came down into the lobby, where she could look directly down into the dining room, and her heart sank as she watched the elderly minister begin reading the ceremony.

It wasn't happening! It shouldn't be happening. She couldn't believe it. Logan Campbell, the man who swore no woman would ever drag him down the aisle, was parroting the preacher's words as the ceremony went on for all to hear in the suddenly quiet room. It seemed sacrilegious somehow. He couldn't be in love with her, that's for sure, the Duchess thought. Logan didn't have the capacity for love. Then quite abruptly as she watched the proceedings with tears in her eyes, she froze, her eyes glued to the couple in the ballroom, as she caught the scattered words of a conversation going on just behind a curtain to her left, at the top of the stairs.

"Well, there goes a million dollars," Giles was whispering to Tyson. "Now what do we do?"

"We bide our time," Tyson answered thoughtfully. "Like I said before, there's more than one way to make them pay." He straightened arrogantly as he watched the ceremony below them. "You know, I don't think Logan and Delia Campbell would like it if the folks in Goldspur discovered he married the girl just so they wouldn't all go to jail, do you?" he asked. "And they just might even be willing to pay us for not telling. What do you think?"

"Then it's definite?" Giles was frowning. "She didn't set up a trust fund?"

"Not according to the banker here in Goldspur. And I've had people check for me in every bank from here to San Francisco, back East, and in the South in the past few weeks, and the final answer came this morning. There isn't a bank officer around who'd even heard of Poe Yancey until she showed up in Goldspur. Not even at the local bank."

"Then shall we hang around until the honeymoon's over, dear fellow?" Giles asked.

"Exactly." Tyson sneered. "And you know, I have a feeling this whole affair may prove interesting, what say, cousin?" and they both concentrated once more on the ceremony going on below them.

The Duchess's eyes had narrowed expectantly while she eavesdropped on the men's conversation. Now she breathed a sigh, smiling smugly. So that was why he was marrying Poe. Her smile changed to a frown. Only, why would marrying Poe keep him and his aunt out of jail? And what was all their talk about a trust fund?

She drew her eyes from the room below, and turned toward the curtain where the two men stood watching the ceremony. Maybe it's time I got to know this Englishman a little better, she told herself thoughtfully. It just might be worthwhile, and she slid her hands along the rail that edged the balcony over the lobby, edging toward the spot where the two men stood.

Downstairs in the ballroom, Poe's hand trembled as Logan slipped the wedding ring on her finger.

"With this ring I thee wed," he was saying, but Poe barely heard him.

The ceremony was going so quickly and she

was hardly aware of the words, her heart was pounding so loudly. She felt the ring slip onto her finger; then Logan took her hand in his.

"By the powers vested in me by the state of Nevada," the preacher was saying, "I now pronounce you man and wife," and Poe was conscious of a stillness about her as all present held their breath.

"You may kiss the bride now," the kindly old preacher was saying as he stared at them over the top of his prayer book. "It's customary, you know," and Poe's heart fell to her stomach as she glanced up at Logan's face for the first time since the ceremony had started.

She stared at him, her mouth quivering, and he reached out, putting his arm about her waist, drawing her to him. She'd forgotten about the kiss at the end of the ceremony, and there was nothing she could do to stop him.

His lips came down on hers deliberately and a cheer went up from the crowd. Her face flushed, her knees weakening, and a tingling warmth spread through her from head to toe.

Suddenly their kiss was interrupted by the sting of rice against their cheeks, and before Poe had a chance even to realize what was happening, the dance music had started up and she was in Logan's arms being whirled about the floor.

Her head was spinning and she felt disoriented. "I think I'm going to faint," she gasped breathlessly, but Logan wouldn't let her.

He pulled her closer in his arms as they danced, his voice murmuring soothingly against her hair, close to her ear.

"Don't spoil it now, Poe," he whispered softly. "You're doing beautifully, and I'm right beside you. Some music, a bit of food, then we'll be out of here." Poe tried to believe him.

Almost an hour later, after shaking hands and accepting congratulations from everyone while trying to choke down some wedding cake, Poe had gone upstairs with Delia, quickly changed into a dark blue traveling suit with a fancy flowered hat, and now she found herself being ushered through the hotel lobby, out the door, and into a waiting carriage. While she was upstairs she had signed some papers Delia had had for her, and now she leaned back on the seat of the carriage, took a deep breath, and closed her eyes. It was over.

The carriage was closed because the ride to Tonopah was a long one, and Logan sat across from her in a plain gray suit and gray silk tie, his eyes studying her face. She'd been on the verge of collapsing more than once from the heat and excitement, something he felt was probably alien to her, because he was sure she was basically a strong person.

"Feel better?" he asked as the carriage headed out of town with a hired driver at the reins.

She opened her eyes, sat up, and looked at him. "It really happened, didn't it?" she said.

"It did."

"It was like a dream." Her eyes widened, as if in a daze. "I can't even remember saying the words."

"You did," he assured her.

"Did I sound nervous?"

He laughed. "Poe, you were not only nervous, you were scared to death."

"I was not," she retorted indignantly. "It was just all those people. I'm not used to so many people, but I wasn't scared." She glanced out the window. "How far is it to Tonopah?" she asked, changing the subject.

"About forty miles."

"We'll make it in one day?"

"We should, and by tonight we should be on the train headed for San Francisco," he answered. "You don't mind spending your wedding night on the train, do you?" he asked. "If you want, you can sleep on my shoulder."

"I don't really care one way or the other," she said irritably.

"Look," he said after watching her for a few minutes while she tried to ignore him, "I don't like this any better than you do, but since we have no one else to talk to but each other, I do think maybe we could be a little more civil about it, don't you?"

Her eyes were smoldering as she looked directly at him. "Why did you kiss me?" she asked bluntly.

Logan sighed. "Didn't you hear the preacher, Poe. It's customary."

"But you didn't have to do it the way you did."

"How did I do it?" he asked, surprised.

She flushed. "As . . . as if you really enjoyed it," she stammered.

"Maybe I did." He fought a smile. "Why shouldn't I enjoy kissing you?" he asked softly, and saw a frightened look creep into her eyes. "Don't worry, though," he assured her, "the incident will not be repeated. Now, can we at least try to be friends? Remember, I am supposed to be your husband."

She hesitated a moment; then, "All right," she said. "If you'll just make sure you keep your part of the bargain."

"I assure you, dear lady," he stated emphatically, "I'll never touch you again—unless you want me to, that is," and his mouth curved into a smile as she gave him a dirty look, while the carriage continued on toward Tonopah.

By the time they reached San Francisco the next day, and entered the lobby of the hotel to register, they'd managed to bury some of their hostilities, and were even acting cordial toward each other. They were greeted enthusiastically by Soong Lee, who didn't even try to hide the fact that he was amazed to discover there was now a Mrs. Campbell.

"She, missy, so high," he said in his musical accent while he helped the bellboy carry their baggage upstairs behind them, and Poe smiled at his open friendliness.

"He likes you," Logan said after Soong Lee had left.

She took off her flowered hat while gazing about the extravagantly furnished suite of rooms, and set the hat on a stand near the sofa, then walked to the window. "How do you know?" she asked.

Logan watched the reaction in her eyes as she took in all the activity in the street below. "Because he smiled," Logan answered. "Soong Lee rarely smiles unless he likes something. And I think that something is you."

The window was open partway, since it was a hot day, and Poe leaned forward a little to watch as she heard the clang of one of the cable cars Logan had pointed out to her earlier. After it was out of sight down the hill, she turned, once more looking about the room.

The management had given them the bridal suite. It was beautiful and plush, with white brocade draperies at the windows and dark green velvet furniture. Logan walked across the luxurious carpet, joining her at the window, and he pulled the drapery back, looking down on the scene she'd looked down on only moments before.

"It's so big compared to Elko and Goldspur, isn't it?" she said, and turned back around, looking out the window again. "It's almost frightening."

"I thought you weren't afraid of anything."

She glanced over at him. He was no longer looking out the window.

"I'm not," she said, gazing into his steely gray eyes. "Not even San Francisco."

Only, later that evening, as Logan settled down on the green velvet sofa for the night, leaving the soft, comfortable bed for her, he knew there was one very real thing she was afraid of, and he cursed her mother for the part she had played in molding her daughter's emotions.

During the week of their honeymoon in San Francisco, Logan escorted Poe to the theater and opera, where she was introduced to a number of his friends, including a young woman named Rachel, who gave her such a hateful look the night they were introduced that Poe instinctively knew she was one of Logan's former lady friends. Even the young woman's parents, who were with her at the time, treated Logan coolly, only proving to Poe that they had undoubtedly planned for their daughter to become Mrs. Logan Campbell.

In spite of Poe's apprehension over Rachel's reluctant reception of her, however, they ate in exclusive restaurants, went sailing on San Francisco Bay, a pastime Poe took to surprisingly well and seemed to really enjoy. Even the fireworks they watched in Chinatown one evening brought a glow of delight to her eyes, and much to Logan's surprise, Poe didn't even make a fuss or protest when he put his arm about her while they were sailing or held her hand during the fireworks. Sometimes the way she smiled and looked at him, there seemed to be a quiet intimacy between them that no one else shared, and he began to feel slightly hopeful.

The honeymoon was almost over. They were to leave the next afternoon for home, and had come back to the hotel in the wee hours of the morning from an after-theater party at the home of a friend of Logan's. Some big businessman who claimed to own a number of ships and warehouses. Poe hadn't liked him too well, but his wife seemed nice, although rather talkative, and shortly after the carriage pulled away from their front walk, Poe, weary from all the talk, and not used to the late hours, leaned her head on Logan's shoulder and was soon fast asleep.

She was still sleeping when the carriage pulled up and stopped in front of their hotel, and Logan glanced down at her head with a smile.

"Come on, sleepyhead," he said, waking her

gently, and she opened her eyes hesitantly, then lazily sat up.

Logan moved off the seat, then stepped from the carriage and reached in to help Poe down. Suddenly his eyes lit with amusement. She was still so sleepy that her head had fallen back on the seat, and her eyes were closing again. Reaching out, he pulled her toward him, catching her into his arms, and carried her into the hotel, through the lobby, and on up the stairs toward their rooms.

Poe nestled against his shoulder half in and half out of sleep as he moved up the stairs and stopped in front of the door to their suite of rooms.

"Poe," he whispered softly. "Wake up, Poe," and he stood her on her feet while he fished into his pocket for their room key.

Her legs were wobbly, so he let her lean against him, practically holding her up, one arm around her waist as he unlocked the door, then swung it open. As soon as the door was open, Poe came a little more alive, and with Logan's help she straightened, then stretched slightly, staggering lazily into the room, unfastening her black velvet cape as she went. Slipping it from her shoulders, she held it in one of her hands, dragging it after her across the room, then tossed it on the sofa as she headed toward the window.

The room was dark, and she stood looking out over the city, quiet now in the dead of night. "I never thought I'd like San Francisco," she said as she stared out the window.

Logan walked over, standing behind her. "You had a good time?" he asked.

She nodded sleepily. "Oh yes," she sighed. "Everything was so grand here. I never knew there were places like the theater, and the opera, and all those other places we went." She turned around to face him, and the faint light coming through the window fell on her face. "Thank you for showing them to me, Logan," she said softly, and her eyes drooped, still languid from sleep.

"There are other ways to thank me," he murmured, and reached out, pulling her slowly into his arms.

He expected her to protest, but instead she melted against him comfortably, setting his whole body on fire. He reached up and cupped her chin in his hand, turning her head, kissing her just below the ear, and he felt her tremble.

Drawing his head back, he looked directly into her sultry eyes, then leaned down, his lips barely touching hers. However, as if suddenly waking from a deep sleep, instead of answering his lips, Poe pushed him violently away and gasped indignantly.

"How could you!" she raved furiously, then stepped away from him, trying to compose herself, but her voice was still unsteady. "We have a bargain, or have you forgotten?"

"To hell with the bargain," he stormed back at her. "My God, Poe, I can't take much more."

"Then it's good we're leaving tomorrow," she answered heatedly, her voice menacing as she brushed quickly past him. "Good night, Logan." She strode quickly into the bedroom, shut the door hurriedly, and he heard the lock being set.

He stood rooted to the spot, staring across the room at the door, the urge to break the damn thing down so strong he could almost feel splintered wood against his shoulder. Then he closed his eyes, swallowed hard a few times, fighting the idea with all his strength, finally succeeding; then he moved over to the sofa, sat down, kicked off his shoes, and stretched out, still in his evening clothes, only he couldn't sleep.

He could go see Cassie, he supposed. But it would do no good, just as it had done no good when he went to see the Duchess that night. He didn't want Cassie, or Rachel, or the Duchess, or anyone else. He wanted Poe and she made it quite clear that she'd have no part of him. When he finally did fall into a fitful sleep, he did so with an ache still gnawing deep inside him, a yearning he knew only Poe had the power to still, and he swore softly to himself, yet prayed someday he'd be able to fulfill that yearning and get past the barrier she'd purposely built up between them.

\*      \*      \*

They arrived back at the Highland with little fanfare, and life at the lovely Victorian mansion on the hill took on the same unpredictable nature that had existed before they were married—only a little more so. Poe had deliberately crawled back into her coat of armor, and froze if Logan so much as looked at her. All the warmth and friendly intimacy they'd shared during their stay in San Francisco had completely vanished now, only to be replaced by a reserved aloofness, as if they were squaring off for a good fight.

Their first night home, they sat at the dinner table jawing at each other like two grizzly bears, disagreeing on everything they saw and did on their honeymoon, while Delia watched anxiously, wincing.

"I certainly hope you two didn't act like this in San Francisco," she said indignantly after watching Poe march from the room in the wake of some biting remarks from Logan.

"Don't worry," he answered, his voice sullen. "We were sickeningly sweet to each other. It's a wonder everyone wasn't nauseated."

"Oh Lord," Delia sighed, catching the look in his eyes. "Now what did you do?"

"What do you mean, what did I do?"

"You know very well what I mean, Logan," she said. "If you've touched that girl . . . !"

His face was dark and belligerent. "So what if I did!"

"Logan, you didn't!" Her face drained of color.

"If you call kissing her neck touching her, then yes I did, but she asked for it."

"What do you mean, she asked for it?"

"I'm a man, not a cigar-store Indian, Aunt Delia. I've got feelings too, you know," and he stood up arrogantly. "Someday that hellcat's going to roll her eyes at me just once too often," he stated furiously. "And no door is going to stand between us, bargain or no bargain!" and he left the room.

Delia sat stupefied. She'd never seen Logan like this before. He was livid, and she frowned, suddenly having misgivings. Maybe having him marry the girl hadn't been such a good idea after all. But then she brushed the notion aside. It was either that or jail, and she shuddered at the thought.

Besides, she reasoned, Logan was only frustrated because he'd found a woman who didn't succumb to his charms, and it irritated him. Yet, what would she do if he ever did force himself on Poe? It would be a disaster. Good heavens, she mused thoughtfully to herself, why didn't the idiot go see the Duchess or something? He'd have to be discreet about it, naturally, so Poe didn't find out, but he was going to have to do something. Maybe she could talk some sense into him, and in the meantime she'd also have a little talk with Poe. It might help.

Delia found Poe in the library with her nose in a poetry book. She was still sulking.

"All right," she said as she stood staring down at the younger woman. "What's it all about?"

"You promised he wouldn't touch me," Poe said stubbornly.

Delia sat in the chair next to Poe. "What did he do?" she asked, knowing full well what he'd done.

Poe stood up and walked to the window and Delia couldn't help admiring her. Logan was right. She was a beautiful woman, and the emerald-green silk dress she was wearing today made her even more striking.

"Everything was fine," Poe said. "I was having a wonderful time. For a while he seemed so different, and he didn't even yell or criticize either." She stared out the window. "We went sailing, and to the opera and the theater. I'd never been to any of those places." She kept her back to Delia as she spoke. "Then that last night in San Francisco we came home late, and somehow everything seemed to get out of hand."

"Oh?"

"I was tired and he took advantage of it."

"Just what did he do that was so terrible?"

"He kissed me, and tried to make love to me," she said nervously; then her face flushed as she turned around and faced Delia Campbell. "We had a bargain. You promised me he wouldn't touch me."

Delia smiled. "Oh, Poe. One kiss isn't so bad. He kissed you after the marriage ceremony, and you weren't angry."

"Wasn't I?" Her jaw set stubbornly. "It's wrong. Ma said it's wrong."

"Poe," Delia said quietly. "Will you come here and sit down a minute, please?"

"What for?" she asked suspiciously.

"Because I think there are some things your mother didn't tell you."

Poe was still sullen. "Ma wanted to make sure I didn't make any mistakes, so I know where babies come from and how they get there, if that's what you mean," she answered. "I'm not dumb."

"No, you're not dumb, Poe," Delia agreed. "That's why I'm hoping you'll understand what I'm going to say." She took a deep breath, then waded in. "My dear," she began, "do you believe in God?"

"I'd be a fool if I didn't," Poe answered indignantly.

Delia stood up, walked to one of the bookshelves, and took down the Bible. "Here," she said after opening it to the book of Genesis and finding the passage she wanted. "Read this," and she handed it to Poe, who read the passage silently to herself, then glanced up.

"I've read it."

"Good." Delia clasped her hands firmly while Poe still held the Bible. "Now," Delia said quickly. "Do you think God would ask people to do anything sinful?" Delia asked, and Poe looked surprised.

"No, ma'am," she answered.

"Then for heaven's sake," Delia said. "You just read in the Bible where God told Adam and Eve to be fruitful and multiply, and, Poe, the only way man can multiply is by making love. If God sanctioned it, then how can it be wrong?"

"But Ma said—"

"Your mother was a disillusioned woman, Poe. She was in love with a dream, only she forgot her dream was human. Your father was a man with frailties, and she deliberately closed her eyes to them. Joe Yancey was too free with his protestations of love, much like Lord Merriweather is, and your mother believed his words rather than his actions. But love can be a beautiful thing, it doesn't have to be what your mother had. Love can be special, Poe."

Poe laughed. "For whom?" she asked bitterly. "There is no such thing as love. You say Ma was in love with a dream. Well, my pa wasn't any dream, he was a man, and you're right there. He walked out on Ma and me because men are fickle, with only one thing on their minds, and believe me, no man's going to make a fool of me. Especially not Logan Campbell. If he touches me again I'll kill him."

Delia sighed, shaking her head as her bright blue eyes searched Poe's face. "You've got a lot to learn, Poe," she said after a few seconds. "Only I'm afraid you're going to have to learn it the hard way," and she left Poe alone to think over the conversation they'd just had.

The next afternoon Logan went back to work, dividing his time among the mines, lumber mill, and the Highland offices, and life looked like it would go on as before. But that very afternoon as he and Aaron worked in the Highland offices, they had a rather unusual visitor, Lord Merriweather.

The man had been in the offices for only some fifteen minutes, and already Logan had to fight to keep from strangling him.

Lord Merriweather was staring out the big front window, a grin on his face. "You act like you don't like my proposition, gentlemen," he said as both Aaron and Logan stared at him. He was dressed in the natty blue suit he'd had on the night Logan had first laid eyes on him, only as Logan watched him now he realized it looked a little worn around the edges. Although Giles was trying to be impressive, his hands were moving nervously along the brim of the hat he was holding. "It's quite simple really," he went on as he turned to face them. "I don't think the inhabitants of Goldspur would take it too kindly if they discovered you swindled an innocent young girl out of a fortune, now would they? So you see, my cousin and I—"

"Your cousin?" Aaron interrupted.

"That's right, my cousin," he continued. "You see, the chap I've been telling everyone is my valet, Tyson, is really my cousin Roger Tyson, and he just happens to be the barrister Mr. Joe Yancey had keeping records of all the transactions he had with Miss Delia Campbell, and it just so happens he has everything down in writing, intact, in a ledger, along with receipts, I believe they're called, with Delia Campbell's signature on them verifying the dates and amounts. Now, Tyson and I thought it quite foolish to let it all go to waste."

Aaron started to speak again, but Logan put his hand out, stopping him. "Go on," he told Lord Merriweather.

Giles straightened haughtily. "All we're asking, gentlemen," he said, looking directly at Logan, his pale brown eyes mocking him, "is that, since you so neatly outmaneuvered me in the romance department, the least you can do is be willing to let me receive some sort of compensation for the loss."

"In other words," Logan said, his jaw tightening, "you're trying to blackmail us."

"Blackmail? My, my, Mr. Campbell, you are being crude." Giles stroked his mustache, then grinned maddeningly. " 'Blackmail' is such a harsh word. It just seems to us that you've really taken undue advantage of the young lady. After all, a man with your experience with the fair sex, what chance did the poor girl have? The rest of us chaps probably weren't even in the running really. And that, my dear sir, brings us to the question of whether or not the young lady might even throw you out if she knew you had only married her for her money and to keep from going to jail." His eyes darkened. "I could bloody well tell her, you know."

"But you won't!" Logan stated emphatically.

"My dear fellow," Giles replied, his voice touched with a slight inflection of nervousness, "if I don't tell her, Tyson undoubtedly will. Unless of course you do as we ask. About a hundred thousand should do for a start. Of course, we may need a little more later on, but we don't want to appear greedy."

Logan was managing to control his temper beautifully because down deep inside he wanted to kill the bastard. "What makes you think I married Poe for her money?" he asked, feigning a calmness he neither felt nor showed.

"Oh, come now." Giles laughed, amused. "The great lover, Logan Campbell. The man the Duchess said vowed there wasn't a woman on the face of the earth worth sacrificing his freedom for . . . a man like that falling in love? I'd say you were having more of a love affair with her money than the lady herself."

"What goes on between my wife and myself

is my business," Logan answered, giving him no satisfaction.

"And the trust fund that never existed, that's strictly your business too?"

Logan's eyes narrowed.

"How did you manage it, Logan?" Giles asked shrewdly. "Just ignore the fact that it was supposed to exist, or take control of an imaginary one? Either way you look at it, my dear chap, it's fraud."

"I'll discuss your offer with my aunt," Logan answered, knowing he was over a barrel. "But don't be surprised at her answer. She isn't a very patient person."

"Nor am I," Giles replied, and smiled smugly. "So if you'd tell her my cousin and I'll wait until Sunday. She can give us her answer at the annual Goldspur Day picnic. I assume the royal family will be attending?"

"I'll tell my aunt," Logan said, his eyes flashing as he ignored the remark. "Now, if you're through, I'd suggest you leave before I forget you're supposed to be a gentleman."

Lord Merriweather's eyes crinkled, amused, but he didn't back down, since he felt he was a fair match for Logan. "My, my, we do have a temper now, don't we," he said flippantly. "But since I detest fisticuffs I'll take my leave, gentlemen, but I remind you, the deadline's Sunday," and he walked out, leaving both Logan and Aaron staring after him apprehensively.

"What now?" Aaron asked as he and Logan moved to the window, watching Lord Merriweather disappear down the street into the hotel.

Logan shook his head. "I wish I knew," he answered softly, then walked to the coat rack, grabbed his hat, and headed for the door. "I might have to strap on my guns."

"I hope not," Aaron yelled after him. "You aren't that good a shot." Only Logan acted like he hadn't heard the statement as he left, slamming the door behind him.

When Logan arrived home, as he came in the front door he instructed Clive to have his aunt meet him in the library. Then he sat at the desk tapping a pencil impatiently while he waited. Irritated that she hadn't arrived yet, he threw the pencil down and picked up the paperweight, absentmindedly toying with it, remembering that he'd been holding it the night Aunt Delia had told him her deep dark secret and demanded he marry Poe, and his mind was miles away when Delia finally did come in and walk over to the desk.

"Clive said it was urgent," she said, and stopped, gazing down at him.

"Oh yes," he answered, looking up, then set the paperweight down. "We're in trouble again," he said reluctantly, and leaned back in the chair, watching her reaction closely. "I know who Joe

Yancey's lawyer friend is," and he saw her eyes widen.

"Who?"

"Lord Merriweather's omnipresent valet, who happens not be a real valet, but his cousin, one Roger Tyson. He has all the records Joe Yancey kept, including receipts signed by you."

She drew in a sharp breath. "He told you this?"

"Merriweather told me," he answered. "He came to the Highland office this afternoon and demanded one hundred thousand dollars, to be given to them the day of the picnic, and that's only for a starter, or they blow our whole scheme sky-high."

"That's blackmail!"

"That's right. But it's no worse than what we did," he said cynically. "I believe they have a name for what we did too, don't they? Something like fraud?"

"Shut up!" she snapped, and flipped her head angrily. "That girl wouldn't know anything about running the Campbell business anyway, and you know it. Besides, I wasn't about to sell out and end up with hardly anything, just to ante up her share."

"So what do we do?" Logan asked.

She waved her hand impatiently. "Let me think," and she began pacing the floor. After a few minutes she stopped, staring at him. "Does Aaron know?" she asked.

"He was with me when Merriweather showed up."

"Good, at least that saves us having to tell him." She started pacing again, then once more stopped. "The records and receipts," she said thoughtfully. "He must have kept some sort of ledger, and the receipts would be with it, and if it weren't for them, it'd be merely my word against his, right?"

"What are you getting at?"

"Look, dear boy, he's got to have them someplace," she said, leaning across the desk toward him. "If we could get our hands on them . . . Do you have any idea where the two men were before coming to Goldspur?"

"He never said, although from his scarce knowledge of things I'd say Merriweather hadn't been in this country too long. But he never said where Tyson came from. Besides, how would knowing that help?"

"Because they have to keep that ledger and the receipts in a safe place." She straightened, her eyes narrowing shrewdly. "I'd say their best bet would be to bring the things with them for safekeeping," she said wisely. "That means they might even have them in their rooms at the hotel, or maybe even the safe there."

"They're not fools," he agreed. "They'd bring the evidence with them, so how do we find out where it is?"

---

"That, dear boy, I'll leave up to you," she said.

"And now the intrigue begins."

"Well, what else would you have me do?" she asked. "Kill them?"

"Now, that's not a bad idea," he said, pointing at her purposefully. "And I'd be glad to start with one bullet right between Lord Merriweather's eyes."

"Don't be ridiculous, Logan," she retorted. "I've done a lot of things in my life, but I won't condone murder."

Logan stood up, walked to the window behind him, and stared out. Poe was in the yard sitting on the bench near where he had proposed to her, a glass of lemonade in her hand, and she was looking up at Aunt Delia's tower room, a strange faraway look on her face.

"Too bad," Logan said as he watched Poe, and he sighed. "That's one man I'd enjoy killing," and he winced, remembering how he had practically shoved Poe into the man's arms.

Later that evening, shortly after a dinner that neither Logan nor Delia enjoyed, Logan told Poe he had an errand to run, excused himself, and headed for town. He'd learned earlier from Aaron that Lord Merriweather spent nearly every evening gambling in one of the saloons until well past midnight, so he had only Tyson to worry about.

When he arrived at the Champaign Hotel, a

furtive conversation with the desk clerk confirmed to Logan that the Englishman's valet, Tyson, was still upstairs in the room he shared with Lord Merriweather, and probably would be there all night. Unless I do something about it, thought Logan, and so, undaunted, Logan gave the clerk a message to take up, telling Tyson to meet him at the lumber mill the other side of town, and that it was urgent, regarding the matter that had been discussed earlier in the day. It was a wild-goose chase, but he had to do something.

The desk clerk obeyed without question, although he did frown slightly when he saw Logan step behind the hotel desk and hide behind the curtains at the back. However, he shrugged as he went up the stairs, realizing it really wasn't any of his business. After all, the Campbells owned the hotel, and he wasn't about to lose his job by being too curious.

When he came back down a few minutes later, he was followed closely by the Englishman's valet, and Logan watched through a slit in the curtains while Tyson went through the lobby and on out the front door; then he slipped from behind the curtains, hurried to the front window, and made sure the masquerading lawyer disappeared in the direction of the mines.

Once Tyson was out of sight, Logan went back over to the desk clerk. "Give me the passkey to his room," Logan said quickly, but this time the clerk did hesitate. "Evidently you must not like your job, Bill," Logan continued, and watched the man squirm.

"It . . . it ain't that, Mr. Campbell," he answered unsteadily. "It's just . . . it's . . . well . . ." Think of something quick, he told himself then. "It's just that you took me by surprise, sir," he went on, and sighed, relieved as he lowered his eyes from Logan Campbell's and took the duplicate key from a drawer in the desk. "You want I should go with you?" he asked.

"Not likely," Logan said. "Just keep your mouth shut," and he went on upstairs alone while the desk clerk scowled after him.

Unfortunately the room was at the front of the hotel and Logan had to pull down the shade before lighting the lamp and starting his search. A good half-hour later saw him finish searching the last possible place without any luck, and he finally went over, blew out the lamp, and left, after making certain everything was back in place.

As he handed the key back to the desk clerk a few minutes later, he happened to think of something. "Did either Lord Merriweather or his man Tyson give you anything to keep in the hotel safe when they arrived?" he asked.

The clerk shook his head. "No, sir, but Lord Merriweather did inquire as to the name of the man who runs the bank."

---

Logan took a deep breath. If they went to pompous old Frank Zentner, who was also the mayor, he and Aaron would have to rob the bank to get the ledgers. Damn! Frank was too honest. He'd never just hand the ledgers over to them, and especially without an explanation, even though Aunt Delia's money did practically keep the bank in business. He was as stubborn as he was honest, yet there had to be a way.

Logan left the hotel, strolled slowly down the street, and stopped in front of the darkened Highland office, staring at it thoughtfully. Suddenly a thought hit him. He walked over to the office door, unlocked it, walked in, lit a lamp, and began rummaging through the drawers of his desk. Finding an envelope with the Highland Enterprises imprint on it, he looked further until he found three sheets of blank paper, folded them neatly, slipped them inside the envelope, then sealed it before writing his name across the front of it. This done, he blew out the lamp and left, locking up again, then headed south of town.

Frank Zentner's house was on one of the side streets, and he opened the door himself to Logan's knock, surprised to see him this time of night.

"Well, well, what brings you here, Logan?" he asked, gesturing for him to come inside.

"I've got some papers here, Frank," he said as he stepped into the hallway, and he showed

Frank Zentner the envelope. "I was hoping you could keep them in your private safe at the office for me for a few days. You see, it's rather important."

"Now?" Frank asked in surprise.

"Business is business, Frank, no matter what time of day it is," Logan said, and stuffed the envelope back into the inside pocket of his suit coat. "I'll pay you extra for your trouble if you want, but they've got to be somewhere where no one can lay hands on them."

Frank sighed, pulling his pocket watch out, checking the time; then he shoved it back in his pocket. "All right, if it's that important. But there'll be no extra charge. Your business is all I ask," and he excused himself, went into the parlor where he'd been sitting, made apologies to his wife, put on his suit jacket, grabbed his hat, then followed Logan out the door.

They entered the bank through the back door, went straight to Frank Zentner's private office, where he lit a lamp, then opened the safe.

"I'll take the envelope," Frank said, reaching out, but Logan held back, delving into his pocket slowly as he pulled out the envelope.

"Not this one, Frank," Logan said quickly. "This one doesn't get out of my hands. I'll put it in myself."

"Suit yourself," Frank answered, and stepped away, watching Logan curiously.

Actually Logan did nothing that could be construed as looking suspicious, because all he did was move the kerosene lamp a little closer to find a good place to put the envelope. However, Frank Zentner was not aware that all the while Logan's eyes were on the inside of the safe they were searching, until they spotted a brown-paper bundle tied with string, with Lord Merriweather's name on it. It was just the right size to hold some ledgers, and he set the envelope right next to it, quickly made a mental note of what the package looked like and how it was wrapped, then stood up.

"I really appreciate this, Frank," he said a few minutes later as he watched the banker turn the key in the door, locking the bank again. "I'll let you know when I need it."

"Must be mighty important," Frank said as they headed back toward Main Street. "Bothering with it this time of night."

"It is," Logan answered, relieved. "They're about the most important papers I think I've ever handled in my life," and he shook hands and watched the banker leave before heading for home himself. The first part of his plan was completed; now he had to go see Aaron, then go back to the Highland and arrange the rest of it. It took longer to convince Aaron that it would work than he'd planned, so by the time he returned to the Highland, found some books in the library, wrapped them in brown paper and string, and finished writing Lord Merriweather's name on it, it was close to midnight.

Smiling, pleased with himself, he tucked the package under his arm and crept toward his room, trying to be quiet as usual, only he didn't hear when Poe's door opened ever so slowly behind him until her voice startled him.

"How's the Duchess?" she asked sarcastically.

He whirled and looked straight at her. The hall was dark and she was barely visible, and he watched her lean back against her door-jamb, her arms folded, partially covering the pale yellow satin nightgown she had on. Her long red hair was resting loosely on her shoulders, and just looking at her was a pleasure.

He stared at her curiously. This was a new wrinkle. "You really want to know?" he asked.

"Not really." She straightened. "But that is where you were, isn't it?"

"If you say so."

"Don't be cute!" Her eyes hardened. "You weren't to see her anymore."

"Oh?"

"It was part of the bargain."

"Your part, maybe." His arm tightened around the package under his arm. "I never said I wouldn't. I merely said I'd be discreet."

"But Aunt Delia said . . . I told her it had to be part of the bargain!"

He took a step toward her, reached out with

his free hand, and took hold of her chin so she had to look directly into his eyes.

"Why, Poe," he asked, "why does it have to be part of the bargain?"

"Be-because I don't want the whole town making fun of me like they did Ma," she stammered. "I don't want them whispering behind my back, feeling sorry for me, saying my husband goes to other women."

"He doesn't have to," he answered huskily, and she closed her eyes, unable to look at him.

"I can't," she whispered softly. "Please, I . . . I can't . . ."

"Then unless you're ready to give me what I want at home, Poe, don't ask me to stay in nights," he replied sharply. "Because I don't intend to." The pressure of his fingers on her chin made her wince; then he let her go and walked away, leaving her staring after him.

He opened his bedroom door, then looked back. "Good night, Poe," he said softly, then went into his room, closing the door behind him.

Poe stared at the closed door to his room, tears filling her eyes; then she stepped back into her own room, closed the door behind her, and ran to the bed, flinging herself on top, trying to choke back the sobs. She was such a fool. Such a stupid fool. She was no better off than Ma had been. There was one consolation, though, she thought as she opened a drawer on her bedstand and took out a handkerchief, blowing her nose: At least I'm not in love with Logan. She wiped her nose deliberately, then sighed. At least I don't think I am. No! She shook her head as she climbed under the covers again. I know I'm not, I just know it, and she kept repeating the same thing over and over to herself as she tucked the damp handkerchief under her pillow and stubbornly closed her eyes.

In the room down the hall, Logan dropped his package on the chair, then stood in his darkened room contemplating. Why? Why hadn't he denied her accusation? Why had he let her believe he'd been to the Duchess? He felt like a heel, yet . . . for a minute he'd thought she was jealous. Had she been? Or had he read something in her eyes that wasn't really there? He shrugged, sighed restlessly, and started to undress.

# 9

# A Switch in Plans

Late the next afternoon, with Aaron at his side, Logan entered Frank Zentner's private office. It was a hot day, and he had his suit coat flung over one arm, but unbeknownst to the banker, wrapped between the folds of the brown suit coat was a package almost identical to the one Logan had seen in the banker's safe the night before.

"Well, Logan, back so soon?" Frank asked, greeting them, then nodded. "Aaron, good to see you."

"I hate to do this to you, Frank," Logan said after Aaron was through saying hello to him. "But I'm going to need that envelope back today."

Frank's eyebrows raised. "So soon?"

"Something's come up." Logan moved over to stand beside the safe. "Business can't always be predicted, you know."

"That's for sure," Frank said, and followed Logan to the safe, bending down to open it.

"I'll take it out myself if you don't mind,

Frank," Logan said as Frank swung the door open. Frank stood up, then stepped aside.

Just at that moment, as Logan stooped down to pick up the envelope, Aaron suddenly doubled up, holding his stomach, his face contorted with pain.

"My God, I must have indigestion," he gasped frantically, and right away Frank Zentner was all concern.

"Breathe deeply," he urged, moving to his side, and he made Aaron sit in the chair behind the desk.

So while Frank helped Aaron, Logan moved quickly. Taking the package from between the folds of his coat, he switched it with the package in the safe, then tucked the one he had taken out into the folds of his suit coat. This done, he picked up the envelope with the blank papers inside, then hurried to the desk just as the banker shoved a glass of water he'd poured from a pitcher on his desk into Aaron's hand and told him to drink.

"I keep telling him to quit eating the cabbage rolls, but he insists," Logan said as he folded the envelope up and stuffed it in his pocket, then joined the two men at the desk. "I'll take him over to see Doc Barrett and have him mix up something for his stomach," he said. "And maybe he'll listen to me the next time he wants to gorge on cabbage rolls for lunch."

Frank wiped his forehead in relief as Aaron

finished sipping from the glass of water he'd given him, then started to breathe easier.

"Never again," Aaron gasped breathlessly. "I love the damn things, but this happens every time. No more!" He waved a hand in front of his face and shook his head, exhaling disgustedly. "I don't care how much I'm tempted."

"With me it's onions," Frank said, sympathizing with him. "Fried onions. Every time the wife fixes them, I suffer." He rolled his eyes. "And how I love fried onions."

Logan kept his suit coat folded on his arm, and it took about five more minutes before Aaron had recovered sufficiently to get out of the chair to leave.

Meanwhile Frank examined the contents of the safe, closed it, after being reassured by Logan that he'd retrieved his envelope, and the two men left the bank, sheepish looks on their faces, while Aaron still complained some about his stomach, and Logan held tightly to his suit coat so the package didn't fall out.

Half an hour later, locked in the library at the Highland, Aaron, Logan, and Delia rifled through the ledger and sorted through the receipts.

"Thank heavens, it's all here," Delia said triumphantly, then clenched her fists and looked at her nephew. "If I'd only had these sooner, you wouldn't have had to go through with this farce of a marriage to that little idiot," she said.

"Whom are you calling an idiot?" Logan asked sharply.

Delia tilted her head up haughtily. "Oh, come now, Logan," she said. "I must admit the girl's pretty and she'd be quite desirable, yes, but she's been reared by a man-hating hermit, and although her education in the basics has been adequate, it certainly isn't very well-rounded. I think she's a dear girl, but not the wife I'd have chosen for you if it hadn't been for necessity."

"Just what kind of a wife would you have chosen for me?" he asked.

"Oh!" She thought for a minute. "Someone like Rachel Flood in San Francisco, I suppose. You know, someone with breeding."

"Then I'm glad you didn't," he said, and his eyes bored into hers. "And in the future," he went on, "if you don't mind, I dislike my wife being referred to as an idiot."

Delia's smile faded and she stared at him, a frown creasing her forehead. "Are you serious?" she asked incredulously.

"Quite serious," he replied. "We took an innocent girl and tried to pawn her off on anybody who'd take her," he said bitterly. "And as if that wasn't enough, if it hadn't been that Roger Tyson was somewhere with these ledgers, we'd probably have cheated her out of everything. Well, thank God Joe Yancey thought of getting someone like Tyson to keep ledgers," he went on. "Because at least I can still look at myself in the mirror without being completely ashamed."

"Oh, Logan, you're being so melodramatic,"

Delia offered. "One would think you really wanted her to marry you."

"Maybe I did," he said belligerently, and started for the door, then turned back, pointing to the ledgers, and he verily towered over his aunt and Aaron. "This time make sure you put them in a safer place. No, better yet, burn them," he said caustically. "Then there'll be no proof left against you for sure," and he walked out, slamming the door behind him.

Delia watched the door vibrating slightly from the force with which it had been shut; then she glanced over at Aaron. "My God, what did I do?" she asked in surprise.

Aaron grinned impishly. "You still haven't caught on, have you?" he said, and suddenly her eyes widened as she stared at him.

"It can't be!"

"But it is. He's in love with her. Of course, he doesn't know it yet."

Delia laughed. "Logan in love with Poe? Impossible!"

"It won't work, Delia," Aaron said, his soft brown eyes mocking her. "He's in love with her, and nothing either you or I can do would change it."

"But . . . but she won't even let him touch her."

"I told Logan a long time ago that someday some female was going to make mincemeat out of him, and by God, you know, the Duchess was complaining to me that he hasn't been to her for so long she's about given up hope."

Delia turned to stare out the window and was just in time to see Logan leading his palomino from the stables; then he mounted hurriedly and took off toward the hills, his face dark and sullen. She turned back toward Aaron.

"You know, you just might be right at that, Aaron," she said thoughtfully. "And you know, it also might prove interesting to watch the results." There was a gleam in her eyes this time as she turned back toward the window, watching Logan disappear into the hills behind the Highland.

The day of the Goldspur picnic proved to be one of the most beautiful days of the year. The azure sky had a few mounds of white clouds that looked like cream puffs, and the temperature, although hot, was kept even by a breeze blowing downhill from the Monitor Range.

The picnic was at the northeast side of town on Campbell property donated every year for the event, and on that day even the mines shut down. Everybody came, young and old. There were horse races, buggy rides, log-rolling in the pond, tree-climbing contests, wood-chopping, tugs-of-war, arm-wrestling, and the women competed with quilting, dressmaking, preserves, baking, and flower growing. It was almost like a fair, only without the games of chance so readily found on midways. However, over the years people from all the neighboring towns had heard about it and tried to win prizes, but Delia Campbell had other ideas, and only residents of Goldspur who'd lived in the community at least two months could enter any of the contests, because money for the blue ribbons and trophies was donated by the town women's committee, and raised by them during the year from bake sales, dinners, and dances. Money was never even considered as a prize as far as the people in the town were concerned, and that way it discouraged outsiders from coming.

Frank Zentner, his wife, and several town merchants were on the committee that handled the picnic, and as Logan and Poe rode onto the picnic grounds on their horses, Logan spied Frank talking to Lord Merriweather near a corner of the bandstand that had been erected a short distance away from the picnic tables. Logan frowned, hoping the theft of the ledgers hadn't been discovered just yet.

"Anything wrong?" Poe asked as they dismounted and fastened their horses to a rope strung between some trees. She was wearing black pants and a black shirt similar to the ones she'd been wearing the day she'd ridden into Goldspur, and for a moment, as Logan glanced over at her, he was reminded of that day, almost expecting her to cut loose with a string of cuss words.

"What made you buy that outfit?" he suddenly asked, staring at it.

"You don't like it?"

"I didn't say that."

"But you don't."

He had to admit she didn't look poured into them, and the shirt wasn't gaping in front, but my God, she was built. She'd been on horseback already, waiting for him, when he'd come downstairs to leave for the picnic, and he'd been so absorbed in wondering what Tyson was going to do when he discovered the ledgers missing, and not wanting to look at her, ashamed of his own part in the mess, that he hadn't paid any attention to what she was wearing until now.

"You aren't really going to wear that here, are you?" he asked.

"Why not?"

"Do you realize how you look in that, Poe?"

She shrugged. "So what? I'm your wife, so who's going to bother me?"

His eyes were flashing. "You don't really realize what you can do to a man, do you?" he said half under his breath.

She smiled, glancing down at herself. "Don't worry, I won't swing when I walk, if that's what you're worried about. No one will notice me."

"Not notice you?" His eyes were intense. "They can't help but notice." He began to plead with her, in a demanding way. "Poe, please, you are my wife, even though you hate having to admit it. I don't want other men ogling you."

"And I didn't want you to go see the Duchess the other night, either, but you did anyway, didn't you?"

"That's my business!"

"And what I wear is mine." She flipped her hair back arrogantly. "Now, if you'll excuse me, they said I was eligible to enter the women's horse-racing contest, and I would like to sign up," and she sauntered off with just a bit of an extra swing to her hips at first, like the old Poe, before straightening her walk and heading for the tables where everyone was signing up for the events.

Logan stared after her, his gray eyes blazing. She *was* jealous, dammit. The little fool. Why didn't she just admit it? Instead she was going to parade around the place making an ass of him, and he stalked off, angry enough to tangle with anything or anyone.

"Well, well," the Duchess said sometime later as she caught Logan leaning against a tree watching Poe as she and Aaron laughed hysterically with everyone else, trying to win a sack race. "You didn't join?" the Duchess went on. "You're missing all the fun, lover. Or are you?"

He drew his eyes from the race for a second, just long enough to look at her with disdain, then straightened indifferently, his eyes returning to the race. "So my wife enjoys sack races and I don't," he answered. "So what?"

"So she enjoys a lot of things you don't," the Duchess answered, and reached up, straightening a curl that was trying to pop out from beneath her straw hat, the bright blue flowers on it matching the color of her silk dress. "I've been watching her all morning."

"That is unusual, isn't it?" he said sarcastically. "Especially since you had to get up so early to do it. Losing your beauty sleep, aren't you?"

Her eyes gazed up into his, and she was puzzled. "What's wrong with you, Logan?" she asked, her voice soft, caressing. "What's she done to you? You don't even come over anymore." Her voice dropped to a whisper. "Is she that much better in bed than I am?"

His eyes narrowed and he looked down at her, and suddenly the thought that he'd ever made love to this painted woman was nauseating. Poe was so utterly different. She was alive and refreshing. Full of vitality, her lithe young body just waiting for a man to claim it. The Duchess was too predictable. She knew every gesture, every deliberate move to entice a man. He was tired of the game she played. Tired of the perfume that seeped into his nostrils, tired of the painted eyes, and tired of the hard-set rouged mouth.

The whole thing suddenly seemed ridiculous to him as he saw the Duchess in a new light, and he smiled cynically. He wasn't about to let her know the truth about his marriage.

"My dear, there's no comparison," he said, answering her question, and he looked out over the crowd again, watching Poe, who was wildly exhilarated, and with her hair flying loose, hopped toward the finish line, then fell just short of it, laughing hysterically as someone else finished. "She's everything any man could want, and then some," he continued. "I have no need to go elsewhere."

The Duchess's mouth twisted. "You're lying!" she spat vengefully. "You married that Amazon for her money, and you know it."

"What money?" Logan asked, feigning innocence as he glanced back at her again.

"The money Lord Merriweather talks quite willingly about when he's been drinking."

"And even more so in bed, I suppose."

"So what!" She was hoping he was jealous. "You haven't been around."

"Nor do I intend to be." He looked back over the heads of the crowd again, his tall frame solid and formidable in black pants and shirt that he suddenly realized matched the clothes Poe was wearing. "Now tell me, Duchess," he said, motioning with his head toward where Poe was standing by Aaron, congratulating the winner, her head thrown back, blue-green eyes alight with warmth and laughter. "Can you honestly think I'd marry a woman like that for her money, then trade her off for you?"

The Duchess's face went from white to red, then paled again as she glanced over to Poe, then back to Logan, and without saying another word, she turned and stalked off, hoping no one would notice the hurt on her face and the bitterness in her eyes.

After lunch, Delia remained at their picnic table sipping a glass of lemonade. At first she'd been mortified when Mrs. Zentner told her about Poe signing up for the horse-racing and joining in on most of the games. But when the banker's wife praised Poe, lauding her for taking a part in everything and leading the fun, Delia was quite surprised, and actually a bit pleased, although she felt it wasn't exactly the thing a lady of quality would do. But the ladies of Goldspur were taking a different attitude toward Logan now that he was married, and after watching today's proceedings, Delia had a definite feeling Poe had a lot to do with it.

She took another long sip of lemonade, then froze, startled as she heard footsteps behind her, and turned, to face Lord Merriweather and Tyson, and she watched them walk over to the other side of the table, where they sat down facing her.

"Good afternoon, Miss Campbell," Giles greeted her. "Jolly good fair we're having, what?"

Her sharp blue eyes bored into his, yet her words were sickeningly polite. "We always have a good outing in Goldspur, Lord Merriweather," she said calmly. "I hope you and your cousin are enjoying it," and her eyes shifted to Roger Tyson.

"I'm sure we'll enjoy it much better after our conversation, dear lady," Tyson replied, and a greedy smile twisted the corners of his mouth.

Her eyes hardened. "I doubt that."

Tyson was surprised. "Logan told you about our offer?"

"Logan told me you tried to blackmail him, yes indeed," she answered. "But I must say the thought's repugnant to me. Especially since you've shown me no proof whatsoever to support your claim, if indeed any proof exists."

"I assure you, Miss Campbell," Tyson said, "the ledgers are intact."

"I think you're lying." She flicked a speck of dust from the sleeve of her pink frock, then reached up, tilting her straw hat a bit to shade her eyes, since the sun seemed to have found a weak spot in the tree branches overhead. "In the first place," she said quite confidently, "Joe Yancey and I had an agreement, and that agreement has been fulfilled. So I'm afraid you gentlemen are just plain out of luck. And in the second place, I don't like being blackmailed." She finished her lemonade, set the glass down, and stood up. "So now, unless you can prove otherwise, I'll ask you to excuse me, gentlemen, I have some things to attend to." She started to leave, then turned back to them. "Oh yes," she finished, "if at any time you ever make any accusations about me or my nephew to anyone, without having written proof to back you up, I'll have you tarred and feathered and run out of town. Do I make myself clear? And I believe even you, gentlemen, will realize I mean every word I say. Now, good day," and she left them staring after her, their mouths gaping open.

"Did you hear the woman's gall?" Tyson asked his cousin when they'd both recovered from the shock. "She's acting like she hasn't done a thing wrong."

"She's trying to call your bluff."

Tyson glanced over at Giles. "Well, we'll just see who calls whose bluff," he said angrily, and stood up. "I've already talked to Mayor Zentner, and he said he'd be willing to go back to town with me today if it was really that important for you to have that package from his safe. And I have a strange feeling it is. So while I'm gone, you find Poe and try to find out if she's in on this, if you can. And for God's sake, Giles, be subtle about it."

"Don't tell me how to do things," Giles answered indignantly. "You're the chap what's been messing things up."

"Don't start that again," Tyson warned him. "Just find out what you can without tipping our hand. In case she doesn't know what her husband and his aunt did to her, and she's madly in love with the guy, don't spoil it." His eyes narrowed shrewdly as he cautioned Giles. "We may need her on our side."

"Don't worry, old boy," Giles assured him,

and stroked his mustache egotistically. "I'll be so subtle she'll never suspect a thing, but I'll find out exactly where she stands in all this, you can count on that. You just make sure you don't mess up your end of it," and he strolled off, catching sight of a figure in black pants and shirt disappearing into the trees at the other end of the small lake where the log-rolling contests were being held.

Poe was hot and tired. The games had been fun but exhausting too, and now she picked a leaf off one of the bushes as she went by and pulled it apart absentmindedly, making her way out of the crowd, and off by herself.

She'd seen Logan standing by the Duchess earlier, before lunch, when she fell on the ground laughing during the sack race, and for some strange reason it had hurt. She remembered looking up at them as they stared at her, and now again that same hurt feeling filled her. It was an actual physical pain, hurting deep in her breastbone. He was flaunting the Duchess in front of her, that's what he was doing, she thought as she strolled along amid the trees. Just like her Pa had done with her Ma, and she flinched, her jaw setting stubbornly.

Well, she wasn't going to take it like Ma did. She could fight back, that's what she could do. She'd show Logan Campbell, but how?

She pondered hard as she walked, tossing

the idea back and forth in her head until suddenly she came up with an idea. She could do the same thing he was doing, that's what she could do, and she smiled smugly. What would her dear husband think if the whole town started whispering behind his back, like they did hers? That'd fix him. Of course she couldn't really take a lover—that'd be going too far. But if she gave them the impression . . . But who? The thought was repulsive, but she had to do something.

She wandered up a small hill, then down the other side, and found a soft patch of grass at the foot of a huge tree and sank to the ground, leaning back against it, and she sighed. She had to have time to think.

Her eyes were shut for a long time as she tried to think of some way she could make Logan think she was having an affair, and she was so deep in thought that she didn't even hear Lord Merriweather approach until he was standing directly over her, and spoke.

"A lovely sight on a lovely day," he remarked, and her eyes flew open.

She sat up quickly. "What . . . what are you doing here?"

"I followed you."

"Oh," Poe answered hesitantly; then she began to wonder. Maybe if she played up to Giles Merriweather. After all, he had been courting her. But could she? She stared at him as he sat down beside her, sitting in the opposite direction so he faced her.

His eyes were fixed on her greedily, and she fought an impulse to get up and run. She had to stay here, she had to make a fool out of Logan like he'd done to her, and if this was the only way, then she'd have to do it.

Forcing a smile to her lips, she gazed at him coyly. "Why did you follow me?" she asked, rolling her eyes.

He reached out, taking her hand, and Poe sighed. Here we go again with the roaming hands, she thought, only this time she forced herself to accept the gesture.

"Is he making you happy, Poe?" Giles asked softly, and she drew her hand away slowly, trying to appear provocative.

"Why shouldn't he?" she asked.

"Let's face it, my lovely," he said, reaching for her hand again, only she avoided him, "your husband wasn't noted for being the marrying kind, and since he managed to maneuver me right out of the picture, I want to make certain he's made you happy."

"I am," she assured him, only he caught a faint tremor in her voice.

"You don't look happy, Poe," he said, and this time when he took her hand he held it tightly so she couldn't pull it away. "If he's made you miserable, my dear, Poe, I'll . . . I still love you, you know," and before she realized what he had in mind, she was in his arms, his mouth covering hers.

This time, instead of fighting, which was her first instinct, Poe forced herself to stay passive. Only the feel of his body against hers was making her sick, and his lips crushing against her mouth were not only suffocating but also nauseating. Still she strained to keep from pushing him away.

His lips finally left her mouth and she took a deep breath, then felt them wet and hot on her neck, his mustache lightly scratching her skin.

"Please, let me go," she pleaded frantically, but his lips moved down to the cleavage where the top button on her shirt had somehow come unfastened, and she realized things were getting out of hand. "Stop . . . don't touch me . . . please . . . !"

But it was too late. His hand traveled to her breast and she felt the pressure right through her shirt as if the material wasn't even there. Kicking and shoving with all her might, she finally managed to wrench free of him, and rolled away on the grass, then sprang quickly to her feet, staring at Giles Merriweather, who looked like he was ready to spring after her.

"Don't you dare!" she yelled hysterically, holding her hands to her breast. "Don't you dare touch me. No one touches me, do you hear! No one, not even my husband!" Then suddenly she realized what she'd just said as she saw the expression on Giles's face change.

He was on his feet now, staring at her. "Not even your husband?" he asked incredulously, and a strange look came into his eyes.

She closed the top button on her shirt, trying to compose herself as she continued to stare at him. "I . . . I didn't mean that," she said hesitantly. "I just don't want you to touch me, that's all."

She couldn't do it. Much as she wanted to give Logan a taste of his own medicine, she couldn't. The thought of Giles's lips on hers again was nauseating, and she shivered.

"So your husband doesn't even touch you," Giles remarked again as he stood staring down at her. "Must be quite a marriage."

"I told you . . . what I said was a mistake."

He shook his head. "Oh no, Poe, you can't make me believe that," he offered. "And I have a feeling you know exactly why Logan Campbell married you, don't you? That's why you won't let him touch you, right? Just what do you know about Logan Campbell, Poe?" he asked, his eyes suddenly intense.

She shifted her feet and stared at him, unable to answer because she was certain he'd known about her marriage before she had even said anything. Otherwise why would he have acted the way he did? Now she began to wonder just how much he did know, and why he was even concerned, because although he kept telling her he loved her, for some reason she knew he didn't really mean it. If he found out that she married Logan just so Aunt Delia wouldn't have to sell off some of her properties, and so she wouldn't have to worry about dodging fortune hunters, he might make it unpleasant for the Campbells. She held her head up, staring at him defiantly.

"I haven't the slightest idea what you're talking about," she answered haughtily, and without saying another word, she turned and took off up the hill, heading back toward the picnic grounds.

In town at the hotel, Tyson swore as he threw the poetry book on the bed, the brown paper and string that had held it crumpled in his hand. He crushed the paper with his fingers, threw it into the wastebasket, then walked to the window, staring out. How? How could they have switched packages? Mayor Zentner had been nice enough to come back to town with him so he could get the damn thing, and he didn't dare try to find out from him what had happened to the original. He knew the minute the banker handed it to him that it wasn't the same package.

He'd told Zentner that Lord Merriweather needed it right away. Ha! Lot of good a poetry book would do them, and by now Delia Campbell had probably burned the real ledgers and receipts. He stood for a long time and stared

out the window, his eyes snapping dangerously.
All those years of waiting wasted! He couldn't
even accuse Logan of switching the packages or
he'd have to admit that he and Giles were trying
to blackmail the Campbells.

Still fuming inside, he left the hotel, heading
back toward the picnic grounds at a brisk canter,
his horse skittish, sensing the rage that drove
his owner on.

Giles Merriweather was just settling down in
a good spot to watch the women's horse race
when Tyson caught up to him. Most of the
women racing were quite young, and Poe was
the only one that was married.

"Well, we're done now," Tyson said between
clenched teeth as he walked up behind his
cousin, startling him.

Giles turned sharply. "You back already?"

"What does it look like?"

"You don't look any too happy, old boy, and
what did you mean, we're done?" Giles asked.

Tyson shoved his hands in his pockets as he
gazed off toward the area where the riders were
lining up for the race. "They switched packages
on us somehow," he answered.

"But they couldn't!"

"They did!"

"How?"

"Don't ask me." He looked up at his cousin,
wishing as he did so often that he could have
been as tall and commanding, with a title to go

with the good looks. If so he'd never have squandered his inheritance on women and good times like Giles had. He'd have built it into a small empire. He sighed. "No wonder Delia Campbell was so smug earlier," he said. "A fortune, right through our fingers."

"Not necessarily," Giles said, and he watched Poe holding her horse in line while she waited for the starting signal. "We may not be beaten after all."

"How's that?"

"I discovered something very interesting this afternoon," he answered, and his mustache twitched slightly as the corners of his mouth tilted in amusement.

Tyson grabbed his cousin's arm just as the race began, and started pulling him away from the crowd.

"Let's go where we can talk," he suggested, and Giles followed beside him until they were some distance away from the crowd and noise.

"Now, tell me what you learned," Tyson said.

So while the women raced their horses along the half-mile stretch beside the lake, Giles told his cousin all about his brief encounter with Poe.

"Well, well, well," Tyson clucked when Giles had finished. "Imagine that."

"My sentiments exactly." Giles took a deep breath. "And I just wonder what the mayor and all his cronies would think if they knew the bride wasn't really a bride after all," he mused.

"It might be worth a try," Tyson said.

Lord Merriweather sneered. "Here all along we thought Logan had sweet-talked Poe with his lovemaking in order to beat me out," he said furtively. "When all along it seems the young lady must have been forced into the marriage somehow. Let's face it, when a woman won't let her husband touch her, there has to be a bloody good reason."

"Seems the lady is either unduly modest or, if not, well . . ." Tyson rubbed his chin thoughtfully. "You know, I just wonder how much the Campbells would be willing to pay to keep the townsfolk from starting to ask questions."

"If they did coerce her somehow into becoming a Campbell, they may be willing to pay a jolly good price. At least enough to make up for some of what we missed out on."

"It's nothing like what we would have had if you'd married the girl, I agree," Tyson replied. "But as with the blackmail, it's better than nothing." Suddenly a gleam crept into his eyes. "Say, you know, we just might have something here, cousin," he went on as he glanced back over to where the races were still being run, with people milling all around. He tried to keep his voice down. "Now, look, if they forced Poe into marrying Logan, and there was anything criminal about it, we could call in the law, they'd have to have the marriage annulled, and she'd be so happy with us for turning the tables on them and saving her, she might even marry you. Who knows?"

Giles eyed his cousin skeptically. "You aren't serious, old boy?"

"Why not?" His eyes narrowed. "But first we try the obvious. If we can get the money from them without any fuss, it's all the better."

"Then tomorrow I pay another visit to Logan Campbell, right?" Giles said.

"Right," Tyson agreed, and they both glanced over to where Poe was in the process of crossing the finish line first, her hair flying as she leaned forward on her black gelding.

Later that evening, after returning to the Highland, Poe was feeling a trifle ornery as she and Logan left their horses at the stables and headed for the house. They had ridden home in comparative silence, which Poe found annoying, since Logan kept glancing at her dubiously the whole while.

"Did you see me win the horse race?" she asked as they started up the walk toward the side door.

"I wasn't watching," he mumbled sullenly.

She glanced over at him. "You were too," she said. "I saw you . . . and you watched the sack race too. Did the Duchess enjoy it?"

He returned her questioning look, only it was dark out by now and he couldn't see her face too clearly. He didn't bother to answer because they'd reached the door and Aunt Delia was waiting to greet them.

Delia had left the picnic grounds earlier and was a little worried about them after her conversation with Lord Merriweather and Tyson during the afternoon.

"Well, Poe," she said as they all walked toward the parlor, then sat down, "you know you made quite an impression on the townspeople today."

"She sure did," Logan added. "She took all my weeks of training her to be a lady and threw it away in one afternoon."

"I did not!" she retorted, and for a change Delia agreed with her.

"Oh, Logan, don't be so stodgy." She smiled, pleased. "Even the women in town loved the way she joined in on everything, although I must say, Poe, your taste in clothes today could have been a little more conservative."

"I'm tired of being a lady all the time," Poe said, and put her hands behind her neck, stretching, letting her hair fall through her fingers. "It's fun just to be me for a change, and I discovered something today. I discovered that I can still be me without all the cussing I used to do, and folks still think I'm a lady. It isn't as much what you do that makes you a lady as how you do it."

"Don't tell me it's finally sunk in," Logan said.

She glanced over at him. He was lounging in one of the overstuffed chairs nursing a glass of brandy he'd poured for himself when they'd first come in.

"Oh, shut up!" she said. "What do you care anyway? You wouldn't have cared if I'd busted my neck out there today."

"I didn't know you wanted me to care," he said, and as his eyes bored into hers, Delia saw a strange look pass between them that she'd never seen before.

"I think I'll go up to bed," Poe said, changing the subject. "It's been a long day," and after saying good night, she left the room with Logan's eyes on her all the way.

She was barely out the door and out of sight when Delia turned to Logan.

"How long have you been in love with her, Logan?" she asked, and quickly caught the startled look in his eyes as he almost choked on his drink.

"What the hell are you talking about?" he asked irritably.

"Oh, come now, dear boy, don't be naive," she answered. "It's written all over your face every time you look at her."

"You're seeing things." He stood up, changing the subject. "Speaking of seeing things, I saw you with Merriweather and Tyson earlier. How did it go?"

She eyed him hesitantly, not wanting to give

up on the subject of his feelings for Poe, yet aware that it wouldn't do to aggravate him any more than she already had, so she went along with him.

"Better than I expected," she said smugly. "And I wish you could have seen the look on Tyson's face when he came back from town empty-handed. As it was, he had nerve enough to ask Frank to go back into town and open the safe, today of all days. The little weasel," she said irritably. "There's only one thing I don't like, though."

"What's that?"

"Well, when he got back from town, I was watching, and he went right to Giles Merriweather and the two had their heads together for quite a long time. Then, as I was getting ready to leave, Lord Merriweather came over to the buggy and said, and I quote, 'Tell your nephew I'll stop by the Highland offices tomorrow to have a word with him. The first round was his, the second will be ours,' and he walked off, joining Tyson a short distance away, and both were smiling like Cheshire cats when they left. They're up to something else, and I don't like it."

Logan finished his drink. "Don't worry," he said, walking over and setting his glass next to the decanter on the liquor table. "You burned the ledgers and receipts. What can they possibly do?"

"I don't know." She shook her head. "I just don't like it. They looked far too satisfied with themselves."

"You're worrying unnecessarily," he assured her. "Now, believe me, there's nothing they can do," and he stretched. He was tired, yet restless. "Think I'll go upstairs, get comfortable, then go to the library and read for a while," he said, and Delia agreed she was quite tired too and went along upstairs with him, retiring to her room up in the tower, hoping she'd get a good night's sleep for a change, since she hadn't really had one from the day this whole mess first started.

A short while later, Logan, wearing slippers, and with a pair of pants on beneath his blue quilted robe, headed for the library, when Clive stopped him in the hall.

"Mr. Logan," Clive said rather nervously, holding a piece of paper out toward him. "There's a young man came to the door and gave me this to give to the young Mrs. Campbell, but I don't feel it's my place to wake her. Would you see she gets it?"

Logan stared at the note in Clive's hand, then reached out and took it. "Who's it from?" he asked.

The old butler shook his head. "Don't know, sir. The young man didn't say."

Logan thanked him, then Clive excused himself and Logan went on into the library, shutting the door behind him.

He stood for a long time, leaning against the door, staring at the small piece of paper in his hand, contemplating who'd be sending Poe a note. Well, only one way to find out. He straightened, unfolded it slowly as he walked over toward the lamp on the desk, then held it down toward the flickering light, and his face turned livid as he read it.

Taking a deep breath, he crumpled the note angrily into his fist and stormed from the library, heading up the stairs, taking them two at a time. He didn't even stop when he reached the door to Poe's room, but threw it open, stepped in, and slammed it shut behind him.

Poe was sitting at the vanity in a diaphanous nightgown that was part of her trousseau, and her long red hair was down over her shoulders, a hairbrush in her hands. She stood up, backing against the vanity, clutching the hairbrush to her as she stared at him.

"Wh-what do you want?" she asked breathlessly, frightened by the fury in his eyes.

He studied her, watching the light from the lamp on the stand by the bed fall on her, accentuating her figure beneath the sheer material, and he suddenly felt a strange yearning deep down inside. Ignoring the feeling, he stepped forward, holding the crumpled note out to her. "Here, read this," he ordered heatedly. "It was sent to you!"

She set the hairbrush on the vanity, reached

out gingerly, took the piece of paper from him and straightened it, then walked to the stand, holding it toward the light so she could read it.

"My dearest, Poe," the note began. "When I held you in my arms this afternoon and felt your lips on mine, I knew I could not live without you. Somehow I must see you again, my darling, we have to talk." It was signed "Yours forever, Giles."

Poe stared at it in disbelief. "But I . . . I didn't . . ." she began.

"You didn't what?" he asked viciously, and his eyes were blazing. "Did he kiss you today?"

"Yes, but . . ."

"You let him make love to you?" he asked incredulously.

"No!" She shook her head. "No . . . you don't understand. I thought I could get even with you for the Duchess . . ."

"You let him kiss you, but I can't touch you?" he yelled, ignoring her explanation, and he reached out, grabbing her arm, pulling her toward him.

"Please," she begged, "Logan!"

"I suppose my kisses aren't good enough for you," he said, and his eyes held hers, hard, unyielding.

"I wanted to make you jealous," she whispered.

"Why?"

"I don't know!" She stared back at him, her heart in her throat.

"Why?" he demanded again.

"Logan, please . . ."

He pulled her closer in his arms, holding her tightly against him, and bent his head until his mouth was barely inches from hers.

"Is this why, Poe?" he cried huskily, and his mouth came down on hers, claiming it passionately. "Is this what you want?" he whispered roughly as he drew his lips from hers and leaned down farther, kissing her neck.

Chills shot down Poe's spine, setting her whole body on fire, and she trembled in his arms as he picked her up, carrying her toward the bed. Her head was reeling and she felt light-headed as his lips continued their assault at the base of her throat, and she began to beg him.

"Please, Logan," she pleaded, her voice barely a groan as she squirmed powerlessly in his arms, trying to get free. "Please, let me go," and she fought him vainly, trying to still the raging in her heart, so that she could escape the feelings that were overpowering her. "You can't . . . Don't!" she cried as he laid her on the bed, but it was too late, and he was bending over her now, his gray eyes alive and warmly passionate as they stared into hers.

She lashed out, but he caught her wrist, pinning it to the bed, and she tried to reach him with her other hand.

"Give up!" he whispered.

Her heart was pounding, eyes frightened. "Never!"

---

He searched her face. "Poe, for God's sake!" He couldn't stop now, he had to . . . It was too late. "Poe, I need you, I love you," he pleaded gently, the timbre in his voice low, vibrant. "Don't fight me, please!"

Her eyes filled with tears. "I hate you, Logan Campbell," she gasped, her voice trembling. "I hate you," but he stilled her protest with his lips again.

For a brief second Poe tried to ignore what she was feeling, but slowly, as his hands slid down her body and his lips caressed her mouth, the hunger and yearning she'd been trying to deny were there broke loose in her like a storm and sent raging torrents of fire through every nerve in her body.

Logan cupped her breast in his hand and felt the nipple harden sensuously. She was giving in. Oh God, how long he'd waited.

Slowly and deliberately his lips left her mouth, and he kissed the tears from her eyes, his breath warm against her flesh. "I adore you," he murmured fervently, and his lips trailed to just below her earlobe, then back to her mouth, brushing her skin lightly, like the flutter of a butterfly's wings.

Poe never dreamed anything could feel like this, so strong, so alive, yet so utterly overwhelming that she could hardly breathe, with every nerve in her body tingling ecstatically. She let out a soft cry, and groaned helplessly as his hand molded her thighs, then found its way between them, probing and stroking her lovingly until there was no fight left in her and she melted against him, wanting him as much as he wanted her.

Then he slipped from his clothes and slid into bed with her, and for what seemed like an eternity in heaven to Poe, she forgot all about hating him.

He was so gentle with her. Gentle and loving, and even the pain as he entered was forgotten as he thrust inside her, bringing them both to a peak of pleasure that made her cry out with a joyous contentment, that at the same time made her feel like she wanted to crawl inside him and explode.

He pulled her closer against him, his body still tingling from the violence of his own release, and groaned, kissing her softly again, and Poe sighed.

So this was love. This was what Ma tried to keep her from knowing about. This wonderful feeling that made her warm and giddy inside, her body throbbing clear to her toes. She never dreamed it would be like this. It was as if she were a part of Logan, and now his soft caresses continued to soothe her as she lay beneath him.

Logan had turned out the lamp before sliding into bed with her, and now the moonlight streamed in the window, falling across her face, lighting her languid eyes as she turned her head, letting him kiss the nape of her neck. He'd never felt like this before with any woman, and had never wanted a woman before the way he'd wanted Poe. And now that he'd finally made love to her, he knew there'd never be another woman in his arms ever again.

She'd been all he imagined, and more. She'd responded to him like a desert wanderer quenching a thirst. Like a wild, untamed animal, and the wonder of it had been a glory to him. He felt fulfilled for the first time in his life, the restless anger that had been gnawing inside him gone, as he knew it would be.

He pressed his lips against her ear. "I love you, Poe," he whispered passionately. "I love you more than life itself."

She turned to him, her lips finding his, and she whispered against his mouth, "I hate you, Logan Campbell. I hate you for making me love you," and there were tears in her eyes as she pressed her mouth hard against his, all the love that had been imprisoned inside her finally turning her into a real woman.

# 10

# The Kidnapping

Dawn was just beginning to creep into the room as Logan slipped quietly from the bed so he wouldn't wake Poe, and put on his pants, robe, and slippers. After pulling the sash on his robe tight, he stopped next to the bed for a minute and looked down at Poe, sleeping peacefully on her back, her breasts bare, and a thrill went through him as he remembered last night.

My God, how he loved her. He had thought he'd never ever love a woman, and then he'd met Poe. Oh, how he'd fought loving her, but now that he'd finally admitted the truth to himself, the restless yearning that had driven him from one woman to another all those years was completely gone. With Poe he'd found perfection. She was a part of him now, and he'd never give her up.

Suddenly he felt guilty for what they'd done

to her, and he couldn't let the money come between them. This afternoon when he got back from the mines, he'd tell her the truth, and just hope she'd understand.

Sighing contentedly, he left the room, closing the door carefully behind him. He'd promised to meet Aaron at the mines at six this morning for a meeting about working conditions, so he went straight to his bedroom, washed with cold water from the pitcher on the dry sink, put on his workclothes, which consisted of pants, boots, shirt, and buckskin jacket, then took a pencil and paper out of one of his dresser drawers and wrote a note.

Tiptoeing softly, he left his room and slipped back into Poe's, where he found a pin on the dresser, then moved cautiously to the bed. She had moved her position while he was gone, and was curled up, cuddling the covers like a small child. He leaned over, pinned the note to the empty pillow beside her, kissed her lightly on the cheek, then left the room.

But before leaving the house, he found Clive and told him to tell the maids to let Poe sleep as late as she wanted; then he headed for the mine.

It was late in the morning. Logan and Aaron had settled things at the mine earlier, and now Logan sat in the Highland offices alone, working on the list of complaints and trying to find a solution, while Aaron headed for the lumber mill.

He looked up as the door opened, and the tendons in his neck stood out, his eyes narrowing as Lord Merriweather walked in.

"What the hell do you want?" Logan asked testily.

Giles Merriweather sauntered over to Logan's desk. The Englishman was dressed in a fancy suit that looked out of place in Goldspur. In fact everything he wore looked more appropriate for Piccadilly Circus.

"Just a little chat, my good fellow," he answered nonchalantly.

Logan stood up, glaring at him. "I have nothing to chat about."

"Ah, but I beg to differ with you, dear fellow," Giles said, and sneered. "I don't think the people in this town would like to discover that an innocent young woman like Poe Yancey was forced into marrying the likes of you, do you?"

"What the devil are you talking about?" Logan asked, bewildered.

"Come now," Giles admonished. "We both know what kind of a marriage you have, now don't we?"

Logan relaxed. So that was it. Now he understood what the two men were up to. They'd guessed at the reason for his and Poe's marriage. Only the Englishman was in for a big surprise. Logan could play cat and mouse too.

"We do?" Logan asked, pretending surprise. "Just what kind of a marriage do I have?"

"Not the kind you should have."

"You know something I don't know?"

"I know you don't dare touch your wife."

Logan laughed, then leaned back in his chair. "Whoever gave you a notion like that?" he asked.

"Your wife!"

"My wife? Now why would my wife be discussing our love life with you?"

"She didn't discuss it with me," he announced nervously. "Actually, it was a slip of the tongue. Nevertheless," he continued quickly, "I know it was the truth."

"Indeed." Logan leaned across the desk defensively, his eyes flashing angrily. "Is that why you tried to make love to her yesterday? Because you felt she was starved for affection?"

Giles's mouth gaped open. He hadn't thought Poe would tell him about their little fracas in the woods.

"You should have asked first," Logan continued. "I assure you, Lord Merriweather, my wife and I have a relationship that is far from platonic."

"So you say." Giles was trying to smile, but now he wasn't so sure.

"So she'll say too if you take the time to ask her," Logan said.

---

Giles was fuming. "Yesterday your wife said, and I quote, 'No one touches me—not even my husband.'" He tilted his head back, looking down his nose at Logan. "So you see, she's already admitted that you've never laid a hand on her."

Logan stood up. "That was yesterday," he said emphatically. "Ask her again today, Giles," he goaded. "The answer may startle you."

Giles stared at him curiously.

"Why don't you just give up, Giles?" Logan continued. "You tried to marry Poe and she'd have no part of you, you tried to blackmail Aunt Delia and it didn't work. Now you're hoping to blackmail me, but I assure you, sir, I asked Poe to marry me because I love her, and she accepted because she loves me. We had a little misunderstanding at first, I'll admit, but that's all been straightened out. So now why don't you and your cousin catch the next stage out of Goldspur and forget about the whole damn thing before you get hurt, because I assure you," and his voice deepened ominously, "if you ever so much as talk to my wife again, I'm liable to kill you. Is that understood?"

Giles's face flushed as he stared at Logan, unable to answer.

"Now, get out!" Logan yelled, pointing to the door, and Lord Merriweather backed away nervously, then turned and hurriedly left without saying another word.

***

Logan was fuming as he stared after the man, watching him walk down the street toward the hotel. The gall of the Englishman, and his cousin too. They were determined to get their hands on the Campbell money any way they could. He watched Lord Merriweather disappear into the hotel, then thought of Poe's confession about her attempt to make him jealous, and blurting out the fact that her husband didn't touch her, and he smiled. She certainly couldn't ever say that again, and he prayed she'd never want to.

He glanced down at the work on his desk, contemplating. He could stay here, get it done, and leave for the Highland in time to spend the afternoon with Poe, or he could let it go, head for the Highland, and try to finish the work later. He started for the door, then stopped, staring at it apprehensively. There was no denying he wanted to be with her so badly he ached with longing. Yet if he left now, he'd only have to interrupt his time with her later, and that would be even worse. Taking a deep breath, he sighed, shrugged, walked back to his desk, then sat down and began digging into the stack of papers in front of him. First things first, he told himself; then he'd have the rest of the day to spend with Poe.

Out at the Highland, Poe stirred and opened her eyes, pulling the covers up to her chin as she curled over onto her side. At first she just stared straight ahead, the memory of last night flooding her thoughts, making her feel all warm and good inside; then slowly her eyes drifted to the pillow beside her with the note pinned to it. Rising hesitantly, she reached out, unpinned it, and held it up to the sunlight that was streaming in at the window so she could read it. There were three words, "I love you," and it was signed "Logan."

She held her breath, pressing the note to her breast as she closed her eyes, then realized she was sleeping in the raw and remembered why. Her face flushed, remembering Logan's hands stripping the sheer nightgown from her shortly after he'd begun kissing her, and she trembled.

This was what love was all about. The fulfillment of unspoken words that had passed between them. Was this what Ma had felt the first time Pa made love to her? Ma said men never meant what they said when they were making love. That they said the same thing to every woman who took their fancy. But that couldn't be. She sat up in bed, fluffed the pillows behind her, and leaned back on them, staring down at her hands, at the note he'd left her.

Logan would never do what her father did. He'd said he loved her, and oh how she loved him! True, she hadn't wanted to. Even now, part of her hated him for bringing her to this. He'd forced his way into her life where he didn't belong. She'd vowed never to love anyone.

Never to let a man touch her, yet at that time she hadn't the faintest idea what ecstasy a man's arms could hold, or how strongly just his mere presence could fill her heart.

Suddenly, as she stared at the note, then glanced toward the open window, she remembered about his reputation with the ladies and his nights spent in Goldspur with the Duchess, and a feeling of dread began to close around her. Was her night with him no different from his nights with the Duchess? And all those other women people talked about—what of them? She cringed, a knot forming in the pit of her stomach. How many women had there been in his life—and could she really expect to be the last?

She was so confused. Tears filled her eyes. Had Logan really meant all the things he said last night, or were they only words spoken in the heat of passion, without any real meaning to them? How did a person prove love, how could she know for sure? If there was only a way.

She wanted to believe him so badly. Her eyes searched the note again, looking for some way, some sign to prove that the words on the paper were really what they purported to be. There was no way, except to believe.

She remembered what it had been like to lie beneath him and feel his body taking hers, and she let out a soft cry as she sprang from the bed. She'd been such a fool, listening to his words, letting him persuade her to forget everything her mother had warned her about. She was so ashamed. She loved him, yes, but now, in the clear light of day she realized that he had acted no differently from any other man, and she'd let herself be taken in. Now there was nothing ahead for her but the same path her ma had taken. There was no guarantee that she wouldn't have to sit back and watch him break her heart over and over again through the years as he flaunted new conquests before her, as her pa had done with her ma. She was so mixed up.

It was so easy to say "I love you." Men said it every day without meaning it. Had Logan really meant it? She looked down at the note in her hands again, then threw it on the dresser and began opening the drawers, yanking out clothes so she could get dressed.

Tears streamed down her cheeks. Had Logan really meant it last night, or was it only a way for him to overcome her defenses? If only she knew for sure. Her heart was aching with indecision as she finished dressing, putting on a pale blue riding habit, pulling the jacket on over a white blouse, then sat in the chair to slip on her riding boots.

Maybe a ride would help clear her head, because as much as she wanted to believe him, her ma's warnings kept haunting her, and she didn't know what to do. After grabbing her hat from the armoire, she snatched the note off the dresser, tucked it deep in her pocket, and headed for the door. She didn't even feel like breakfast, with her stomach tied into so many knots, and as she went downstairs, slipping quietly from the house and on out to the stables, she was glad no one else seemed to be about.

Anxious to find some way to still the uncertainty that was turning her life upside down, Poe didn't even hunt for the stableboy, but saddled the horse herself, rubbing his nose affectionately as she headed for the stable doors. She had forgiven the sleek black gelding for throwing her that night she'd ridden off after Logan had hurt her so, and she'd been so relieved when he'd finally wandered back home. They'd been together for so long, and the thought of not having him to ride her fears away on was as frightening as the fears themselves. A few minutes later she was headed for the hills, paying no heed whatsoever to two lone figures on horseback in the shade of some trees a short distance away, who started following her as she rode off, lagging back just far enough to keep out of sight.

Poe had been riding for about an hour, with her mind everywhere except on her surroundings, when she reined the gelding to a stop, then waited, listening intently. Somewhere in her subconscious she'd realized she'd heard hoofbeats behind her, and now, after pulling the gelding to a halt behind a cover of pine trees, she sat in the saddle, surprised to see Lord Merriweather and his man Tyson ride into view from behind a boulder.

She nudged the gelding in the ribs, riding forward as she addressed them.

"Why are you following me?" she asked warily.

Giles smiled broadly, trying not to look nervous, but his mustache was twitching. "Worried about something?" he replied.

"No." She studied him for a minute. He seemed restless and on edge.

"You should be," he went on, and before she realized what was happening, he had a gun leveled on her. "Come here," he ordered unsteadily, but she sat in the saddle staring at him, a dumbfounded look on her face.

"I said, come here!"

When he quit smiling, she decided it'd be best not to argue, so she nudged her horse forward cautiously, with his eyes never leaving her until she was directly in front of him.

"What's this supposed to mean?" she asked.

"It means that since your husband thinks so much of you, my dear," he answered, "there's every good chance he'll be willing to part with some of his ill-gotten money just to get you back."

"Do you understand now?" Tyson added,

moving his mount up next to his cousin's horse, and Poe stared at him incredulously.

"You're kidnapping me?" she asked.

"I wouldn't actually call it kidnapping, my dear, would you, Tyson?" Giles said, then sighed. " 'Detaining' you seems so much more refined. Don't you think, cousin?" and he glanced sideways at Tyson, who was studying her critically.

"You're crazy," she exclaimed. "You're both crazy!"

"Your husband's crazy if he thinks I'm going to leave Goldspur empty-handed," Tyson snarled at her. "I waited years to cash in on all that money, and he's squelched me at every turn. First he marries you, then he steals my ledgers, and now he laughs in my face. Well, I'll get the last laugh. I figure he'll pay a pretty penny to get you back alive."

Poe winced. She had no idea what the stupid man was even talking about. "You wouldn't dare!" she challenged, and Tyson's eyes narrowed viciously.

"Don't misjudge me, my dear." His beady eyes were hard and cold. "I may look harmless to you, but I assure you, at the moment I'm quite dangerous. In fact, if it weren't for the fact that I love money more than I hate your husband, I'd kill him right now without any remorse. But we both need money, and lots of it. That's where you come in."

Poe wasn't about to sit idly by and let them drag her away, gun or no gun. Besides, she was certain Giles wouldn't have the guts to shoot her, and he was the one holding the gun. Making a quick decision, she pulled on her horse's reins, jerking the animal around, trying to get away, only Tyson had been watching her too closely and anticipated her move before she made it. Digging his horse in the ribs, he lunged forward, trying to stop her, but in doing so bumped against his cousin's horse, throwing Giles off-balance. Startled by the collision, and still trying to stay in the saddle, the Englishman instinctively tightened his finger on the pistol in his hand, and suddenly all three gasped as a shot rang out.

At first Poe didn't feel a thing. Then, as the next few seconds went by, a burning sensation shot through her shoulder, and she let out a cry, grabbing it, a stunned look on her face. As her hand clenched on her shoulder, low, close to her left breast, her eyes grew dazed, bewildered. Unable to shake the blackness that was overwhelming her, she slumped forward in the saddle, blood already soaking the front of her clothes.

"You stupid fool!" Tyson yelled as he got his horse under control, then reached out, catching Poe before she fell from the saddle.

Giles's horse was skittish, and he was frozen in the saddle, staring openmouthed at Poe, the gun in his hand still smoking. "I couldn't help it!" he finally yelled, his face pale, hand trembling.

"Well, for God's sake, don't just sit there like a dunce," Tyson cried. "Help me with her!"

Giles stuffed the gun into his pocket, nudged his horse forward, and leapt down, then reached out, grabbing Poe, lifting her from the saddle so Tyson could let go. She was out cold, her arms dangling at her sides, head falling back as if she were dead.

Walking hurriedly to a nearby tree, he set her on the ground, leaning her against it, and pulled her jacket and shirtwaist aside to get a look at the wound, checking to see if it had gone through.

"Bullet's still in her," he said as blood continued seeping all over her clothes.

"Now we really did it!" Tyson exclaimed. "And you . . . !"

"Me?" Giles scowled, looking up at his cousin. "That's right, that's it, try to blame me for the whole bloody mess," he said, trying to find some way to soak up the blood as he talked, even using his own handkerchief. "How'd I know the damn pistol would have a hair trigger? You and your six-shooters!" He stood up, staring down at her. "I told you we should have left well enough alone, but no, you just had to have the money. We can make millions, you said. Ha! We'll be lucky to get out of this without a rope around our necks.''

''Hey, cousin, you weren't all that averse to heading back to England with a little money in your pockets,'' Tyson snapped as he tried to wipe a spot of blood from his sleeve with his handkerchief.

Giles's mustache twitched nervously. ''You didn't say I'd have to kill her to do it. You said make love to her, cousin, or did you forget?'' he asked, and leaned down again, checking once more to see how badly she was bleeding. ''You didn't say anything about hanging for murder.''

Tyson took a deep breath. ''Don't worry, she's not dead yet,'' he countered, and looked about quickly, taking in the terrain. ''If I'm not mistaken, this path leads to the old abandoned Goldspur mines,'' he said. ''I came for a ride up here one day awhile back. The old section's been shut down for a number of years and nobody ever goes there much anymore since the Highland Spur section opened. It's only a short way, and we can take her there, then decide what to do.'' He motioned toward Poe. ''Pick her up and carry her. I'll lead the horses. It should be just around the corner,'' and Giles did as his cousin asked, picking her up gently in his arms, then followed Tyson some hundred feet or so along the overgrown path until they came to an old tunnel, the timbers shoring it up weather-beaten and shabby.

Giles hesitated at first; then, with his cousin's urging, and assurance that the thing was safe, he stepped inside, but only a few feet, and set Poe down. He slipped his coat off and rolled it up, propping it beneath her like a pillow, only he was worried because she was still unconscious.

There was a little light streaming in from the entrance, but not enough to really see by, and he stood up, looking about quickly; then he and Tyson both scrounged around the place until Tyson came up with an old lamp that still had a bit of kerosene in it, and a bit of a wick. Once the lantern was lit, Giles knelt down again, examining her a bit closer.

"She's going to need a doctor, old chap," he said, but Tyson's eyes hardened.

"Not now, dammit," he answered. "Bring a doctor out here and it'll ruin our plans for sure."

"Our plans?" Giles exclaimed as he stood up, facing his American cousin. "What bloody plans?" he went on. "You still planning to try to get money out of Campbell? By Jove, you're off your rocker, Ty." His pale brown eyes darkened, square jaw tightening angrily. "You turn her over to them dead and we don't have a prayer of a chance."

"She isn't dead."

"Might as well be!"

"We've still got time." Tyson rubbed his chin,

avoiding the fear in his cousin's eyes. "You stay with her and keep her alive."

"How do I do that, pray tell?"

"Any damn way you can."

Giles shook his head, exasperated, but Tyson went on.

"I'll go into town and state our terms," he said thoughtfully. "I'd ask for a hundred thousand, only I think the Campbells are too smart to keep that much cash in Frank Zentner's two-by-four bank. But I don't see why they shouldn't be able to come up with at least fifty thousand. That's enough to get us two tickets to England, with money to spare."

"And how the hell do you plan to exchange her, old boy?" Giles asked. "If Logan gets one look at her, we're done, for sure."

Tyson glanced down at Poe, still unconscious, her face pale, the front of her shirtwaist dark from the blood. "We tell him we'll bring her in after dark," he answered. "And that's just what we'll do. We'll tie her to her horse and let him loose in the hills just behind the Highland, and by the time the horse carries her in, we'll be long gone."

Giles didn't like it, but there wasn't much he could do. He was up to his neck in it now and didn't dare back out. He glanced down at Poe. He'd done some rotten things over the years, things he probably wouldn't have gotten away with if he hadn't had a title, but here in the

States, as these Americans were fond of calling it, the fact that he was an English lord wouldn't matter one twiddle. He'd hang no differently from any other murderer or horse thief. Damn bloody mess they were in . . .

Poe stirred a bit, and Giles grew hopeful, then cursed as she went limp again. She was such a lovely creature, too, even without the money.

"I wish we hadn't started this whole blasted thing," he said bitterly. "Cheating at cards or stealing a bauble or two is one thing, but this—"

"Well, we did," Tyson cut in belligerently. "I agree I didn't think it'd go this far, but I don't intend to leave here without a good chunk of Campbell money in my pockets. I spent years in that stinking town after Yancey died so I could be around when the girl's money was doled out, and I don't intend to lose out now. I may not get all of it, but I'll at least get my share." He hitched up the gunbelt at his hips, then reached out his hand. "Give my other gun back," he said quickly. "I don't intend to go back to town without them, not this time."

"Won't the folks think it's rather strange for my valet to be wearing six-shooters?" he asked, pulling the unfamiliar gun from his suit-coat pocket, handing it to his cousin.

Tyson smirked as he slipped it back into his left holster, then rested his hands on the butts of both guns for a brief moment. "At this point,

dear cousin, I don't give a damn what the townsfolk think," he answered. "Because the minute
I come back with that money, you and I are
going to get the hell out of here, and I sure
don't intend to look back. Now"—he motioned
with his head toward Poe—"try to keep her
breathing until I get back, and we'll still get out
of this," and Giles shook his head, watching
apprehensively as his cousin left the old tunnel,
heading for his horse.

It was shortly after noon. Logan was almost
finished with his paperwork, and he glanced
up at the clock on the far wall. Lunch would be
over at the Highland, but he'd still get to spend
most of the day with Poe.

Suddenly he looked over at the door as Aaron
burst into the office, shoving a reluctant Tyson
ahead of him.

Tyson brushed his clothes, while Aaron pushed
past him, stopping at Logan's desk and glaring
back at the valet, whose eyes revealed the fact
that he didn't like being pushed around.

"Go on, tell him," Aaron urged angrily, his
curly hair damp with perspiration. "Tell Logan
what you told me," and his eyes shot daggers
at the man.

"What the hell . . . ?" Logan stood up. "Tell
me what?" he asked.

"This weasel and his cousin have Poe," Aaron

blurted out, and he saw Logan's gray eyes narrowing.

"What do you mean, they have Poe?"

Aaron's look was deadly. "He said if you want her back alive it'll cost you fifty thousand dollars."

Logan stared dumfounded at Tyson for a second; then his eyes widened. "You kidnapped my wife?" he asked incredulously.

Tyson's smile was crooked. "That's what the man said," he answered confidently. "And it'll cost you fifty thousand to get her back."

Logan stood motionless, staring at him, unable at the moment to believe it; then slowly the anger began seeping into his body as the full impact of what they'd done made his flesh crawl.

The stupid, bungling amateurs had stolen his wife! First blackmail, now this! And they were dangerous, too, because the idiots were as unpredictable as two-year-olds. It was obvious the way they'd planned everything so far that they weren't hardened criminals, and it only made matters worse, because they were more prone to do things on impulse. Dammit! If there was a set pattern to their ways, he could maybe handle them, but there was no telling what they might try to pull next.

He tried to stay calm, and straightened, walking out from behind the desk so that he was gazing down at Tyson, hoping to intimidate him.

"Where is she?" he asked solemnly, never really expecting Tyson to tell him, but giving himself a chance to size things up.

"So far, she's all right. As long as you cooperate," Tyson answered, pleased with himself. He was going to pull it off, he could just feel it, as he watched the look in Logan Campbell's eyes. "Fifty thousand in small bills," he went on. "And I want it now."

"And my wife?"

"We'll bring her back to the Highland and release her within sight of the place after dark this evening."

"No," Logan stated flatly. "In the first place, I can't get money like that together so fast here in Goldspur. My working capital is in San Francisco. Besides, how would I know you'd keep your part of the bargain once you had the money?"

"You'll have to trust me, I guess, that's all," Tyson said, and grinned wickedly, watching Logan's eyes darken as he moved over to the front window of the office, staring out.

Logan was sure Lord Merriweather wouldn't be capable of murder, especially that of a helpless woman. But he wasn't so sure about the man's cousin. Tyson was a greedy bastard, and he wondered if Joe Yancey had known the man's true colors when he'd hired him to keep track of Poe's interests, or if he just happened to be someone he ran into during all his travels. Whatever, Logan was certain he shouldn't trust the man, but right now Tyson had the upper hand. Logan had to get Poe back, but fifty thousand . . .

If he had three days he could come up with twice that much, but it'd be hard scraping up even ten thousand in Goldspur. The bank was small. He had about three thousand in his personal account, Aunt Delia had about six thousand, and there was about a thousand in the safe here at the office. Then, if he could maybe borrow about ten thousand from the bank in Tonopah, between that and the payrolls from the mine and lumber mill, he could maybe scrape the rest up, then replace it with funds from the bank in San Francisco. But he'd still be short.

He turned, facing Tyson, his gray eyes intense. "Twenty thousand is all I can raise on such short notice," he stated.

Tyson shook his head. "Fifty!"

"Good God," Logan argued. "If I had three days I'd get you a hundred thousand if that's what you wanted. But I don't have that much here. It's just impossible."

"Then forty will do, I guess," Tyson relented, and Logan was pleased, yet surprised the man was willing to bargain.

"Thirty's about all I can scrape together," he answered angrily. "And even that'll take time."

Tyson frowned. He didn't like hashing over the money like this, and he'd love to get his hands on that hundred thousand Logan men-

---

tioned, but he sure as hell didn't have three days to wait. Even now there was no certainty that she might not be dead by the time he got back to the mine, and there'd be a murder charge against them. At least this way, if she were still alive there was every chance the Campbells could get her to a doctor tonight, once they had her.

"All right, thirty thousand," he agreed irritably. "By seven tonight, and you and I meet here. My cousin will keep your wife with him until the exchange. But mind one thing, the sheriff stays out of it or you'll never see your wife alive again."

Logan took a step toward Tyson, who backed away quickly.

"If I don't come back, she doesn't have a chance," he reminded Logan, and Logan hesitated.

"Lord Merriweather doesn't have the guts for murder," Logan said.

Tyson laughed sardonically. "He doesn't have to murder her," he answered, and Logan's eyes flashed angrily, knowing only too well what Tyson meant.

"If he so much as touches her!" he yelled furiously, pointing a finger in Tyson's face, fighting to control himself, "he'll never live to tell it!"

Tyson flippantly shoved Logan's hand away from his face. "You're in no position to threaten anything," he said haughtily.

---

Logan took a deep breath. "Get out!" he shouted. "Get out of my sight," and he whirled toward the door, holding it open for Roger Tyson. "You'll get your thirty thousand," Logan added viciously. "And by tonight. Now, get out!"

Grinning confidently, Tyson took his time walking out, hesitating momentarily just outside as Logan slammed the door after him; then he swaggered on down the street, whistling nonchalantly while both Aaron and Logan stared after him.

"Should I get the sheriff?" Aaron asked.

Logan shook his head. "I won't do anything that could endanger Poe."

"But you can't scrape up thirty thousand by seven tonight. That's only six hours!"

"I can try," Logan said, and the agony he was suffering was all too visible in his eyes.

"You've finally admitted it to yourself, haven't you, Logan?" Aaron said, and Logan stared at him, his eyes somber.

"I never dreamed a woman could do what she's done to me, Aaron," he confessed, and his jaw set hard. "I can't lose her now. Life would be meaningless without her."

Aaron frowned. "Then let's figure where we can get that much money, because I have a feeling Tyson means what he says."

Logan strode to the desk, picked up paper and pencil, and started figuring, then glanced up at Aaron. "Wire San Francisco for someone to bring thirty thousand in cash as soon as possible to cover the payroll and other money I'll be using, then wire Tonopah and guarantee a private loan for me for ten thousand and tell them I need the money before seven tonight. We'll have a man meet their man from Tonopah halfway, at Toiyoba Pass. I think I can scrape up the rest between my bank account and Aunt Delia's and maybe what's in the safe out at the house."

"What if Tonopah won't give you the ten thousand?"

"They've got to," Logan answered.

"You going to tell Frank why you're taking the money?" Aaron asked.

Logan's eyes hardened. "What do I tell him?"

"The truth?"

"He'd tell the sheriff. No." Logan shook his head. "I'll think of something," he said. "I have to, because I intend to get my wife back no matter what," and they left the Highland offices, determined to have thirty thousand dollars in cash by the time Logan came back at seven.

Poe tried to move, but the pain was unbearable. Opening her eyes, she slowly tried adjusting them to the dim light and looked around her. There were shoring beams overhead, telling her she was in some kind of a mine, and a lantern hanging from a nail on one of the beams nearby was flickering low, casting shadows against the dirt walls, mingling with a bit of light from outside. That meant it was still daylight.

A noise startled her, and she glanced toward the opening that loomed some distance beyond the light, and she held her breath fearfully as a tall figure moved forward. Then she recognized Lord Merriweather.

He walked over and knelt beside her. "Finally came to, I see," he said, his familiar British accent bringing everything back to her, and he reached for a canteen beside her, holding it to her mouth.

Part of the water missed her lips and ran down her chin. She wiped it away feebly with her right hand. "Where are we?" she asked as she let her head relax back again against whatever she was using for a pillow that was bunched up against the dirt wall behind her. She had no thought that it was his green frock coat.

"At the old original Goldspur mine," he answered, then apologized. "I'm sorry, love, I didn't mean to shoot you, you know. I say there, you shouldn't have tried to run. I had no idea the trigger was so blasted touchy."

Her blue-green eyes deepened, then narrowed angrily as she stared at him. "Ma always told me never to aim a gun at anyone unless I planned to pull the trigger," she said. "And by

God, I wish I'd had my guns on—you'd never have got within talking distance of me."

He smiled. "You're quite a lady, aren't you?"

"I'm not a lady," she answered, trying to keep up her courage. "I'm a stupid dumb female for getting myself in this mess."

"How's your shoulder?"

She winced. "Hurts."

"You've lost a lot of blood."

Her teeth clenched hard as searing pain shot through her shoulder, and her stomach began to churn; then a weak feeling began to sweep over her, leaving her light-headed. She closed her eyes.

"My God, I feel sick," she groaned, and tried to take a deep breath, but it only hurt all the more.

Giles reached out and pulled her jacket and shirtwaist away to check the wound. His handkerchief was still over it, but the handkerchief was thoroughly soaked now with her blood, and the wound was still bleeding, although not as profusely. He knew, however, that the longer the bullet stayed in, the worse it'd be for her, only there was nothing he could do about that.

"How . . . how long have we been here?" she gasped softly, as he stood up, pulled his shirttail out, ripped a piece off, then knelt back down, exchanging it for the blood-soaked handkerchief.

He seemed rather uncertain. "Not long," he said.

"Tyson?"

"He went to make a bargain with Logan. Fifty thousand, even trade."

She laughed bitterly, her voice weak as she opened her eyes and watched him trying to sop up the blood that was still oozing from the wound. "Don't count on it," she said sadly. "He might not think I'm worth it."

He stopped working on the bullet hole, shoved the piece of cloth against it, then stared at her, puzzled, as he set her shirtwaist and jacket back in place. "But he said the two of you . . . Are you in love with him, Poe?"

She stared back at him, unable to lie for some strange reason. Maybe because she felt death so close. "Yes," she replied softly. "I'm in love with him."

Giles sighed. "Too bad," he said callously. "If you'd married me you wouldn't be in this jolly mess now."

"I'd probably be in a worse one," she said, choking slightly as a new wave of pain bit into her shoulder. "And you know it."

He frowned, watching her grit her teeth against the pain. "That bullet really should come out, you know," he mused thoughtfully. "If I could just get you to a doctor . . ."

"Why can't you?" Her eyes were reddening feverishly. "You don't belong here. You're not a criminal. Why don't you give this stupid thing up?"

"Can't!" he snapped.

"Can't, or won't?"

"It's too late now." He stood up, tucking his shirttail back in. "Tyson's still calling the shots, and he'll never back down."

"Tyson? But he's your valet!"

"He's my cousin," Lord Merriweather corrected. "And this whole thing was his idea."

"But why?" she asked breathlessly. "You've got a title . . ."

"That's all I've got, mind you," he said as he gazed down at her in the dimly lit tunnel. "I left England up to my neck in debt, with an estate falling apart, if it isn't taken from me for back taxes first, and three highly irate husbands breathing down my neck. Marriage to you would have solved everything, but you'd have none of it. Then we tried to blackmail the Campbells with your father's ledgers and receipts, only they got their hands on them. Then we threatened to tell the town about how you were forced into marrying Campbell, only that fell through, thanks to your husband. Now we're doing the next best thing."

She had no idea what he was talking about, but the pain was so bad she didn't much care. "And you think it'll work?" she asked.

"Why not?" He smirked. "Your husband should be glad to pay the ransom, and there's miles of open country between here and Canada, and I can return to England in style."

Poe's eyes lowered slightly as she stared up at him. She'd been trying to follow his reasoning, only he'd lost her somewhere between the words "blackmail" and "ledgers and receipts," and now, with the pain that gripped her chest and shoulder, and the weariness that was making her weak all over, she sighed.

"Good luck," she whispered, her voice barely audible. "You'll need it," and she closed her eyes again, drifting into a restless sleep.

When she opened them again it was to see Tyson and Lord Merriweather standing near the entrance to the tunnel, having a heated conversation.

"That only gives us fifteen thousand apiece," Lord Merriweather was arguing. "How far do you expect me to get on that?"

"Well, it was your finger almost killed her," Tyson shot back. "If she didn't have that bullet in her we could hold off long enough for him to get a hundred thousand from the bank in San Francisco, but as it is, we don't dare."

Giles's eyebrows rose in surprise. "He's willing to pay that much?"

"But he doesn't have that kind of money in Goldspur. Besides, it's too late for that now. We'll take the thirty thousand and clear out and be glad we got away, no thanks to you."

Giles gave his cousin a dirty look. "Don't act

like it was all my fault," he said, straightening to his full height so that he was looking down on his cousin, and his mouth twisted angrily. "I wanted to leave this morning when Campbell called our bluff. But no, you had it all figured out. It'd be so easy, you said. We hold her for a few hours, get the money, then let her go. What's to go wrong? you said. Well, we found out bloody well what could go wrong. Oh no, dear cousin, it was your blasted idea to stay!"

Tyson glared at his cousin for a second, then looked farther into the mine, squinting as his eyes adjusted, and he realized Poe had been watching them. He sauntered in and stared down at her. She looked pale and weak, and her eyes, glazed with pain, drooped wearily. She looked more dead than alive, and he swore to himself softly, then turned abruptly and walked back to where Lord Merriweather stood waiting, and Tyson prayed as hard as he could that she wouldn't die before seven.

# 11

# *The Best Laid Plans . . .*

$\mathcal{L}$ogan was moving like a stalking cat as he paced the floor of the Highland offices, the fringe on his buckskin jacket swinging jerkily, his jaw clenched, eyes on the door. It was five minutes to seven and he'd made sure he and Aaron were at the office early enough, just in case Tyson's watch wasn't synchronized with the one here in the office. The thirty thousand was in a sack on his desk, and he glanced at it apprehensively. He'd had to tell Aunt Delia why he needed the money from her personal account, and much to his surprise, she agreed it was the only thing they could do. But then, she had to agree. If anything happened to Poe, it might complicate matters for all of them. Even though Logan was Poe's husband, the less publicity regarding their finances, the better.

"But do you have to use the payroll money?"

she'd asked on the way to the bank. "What will Frank think?"

Logan had told her all Frank had to know was that they needed the money. After all, it was company money, not the bank's, and he remembered the strange look Frank had given them when they walked out of the bank with twenty thousand in cash.

Aunt Delia had taken the buggy back to the house to wait, and now Logan stared nervously at the bag of money, then switched his gaze to the clock on the wall, then back to the door again as he paced.

"Will you slow down?" Aaron said from where he stood watching out the front window; then he tensed. "Here he comes now."

Logan stepped up to the window beside Aaron, and saw Tyson trying to look inconspicuous as he rode his horse down the street, smiling smugly to himself.

"He won't go for it," Aaron said, but Logan swore.

"The son of a bitch had better." Logan's teeth clenched. "I want Poe back now, not when he decides to turn her over."

Tyson spotted them watching, and stopped for a minute, then reined his horse up to the hitch rail, dismounted, and straightened confidently before stepping into the office. He was still wearing a gunbelt, but so was Logan now. A fact Tyson didn't notice at first.

"You've got it?" he asked.

"I've got it," Logan answered. "Only there's going to be a change in plans."

Tyson eyed him skeptically.

"Don't worry, you'll get your thirty thousand. Only Aaron and I go with the money and bring Poe back with us. I don't trust you."

"Don't be ridiculous," Tyson said hurriedly. "I'd be a stupid fool to do anything that'd put a noose around my neck now."

"As you said, however," Logan reminded him, "there are other things that can be done to a woman, and I don't trust either you or that so-called aristocratic cousin of yours."

Tyson's eyes hardened. "I don't like it," he said, frowning. "What guarantee do I have that you won't have the sheriff right behind us all the way?"

"And jeopardize my wife's safety?" Logan took a deep breath, his slate-gray eyes challenging Tyson. "I want her safe and sound, only I want her now. I'm not going to pay thirty thousand and end up with a half-dead wife because one of you suddenly decides to get funny ideas."

Tyson weighed the possibilities. If Logan learned Poe was already hurt, it could ruin everything, yet if he didn't take him along . . . "What happens if you go along?" he asked.

"I take my wife home myself," Logan answered. "And you don't get your filthy hands on the thirty thousand until I know she's safe."

---

343

Tyson glanced down and realized for the first time that both Logan and Aaron were wearing guns too. The situation was getting rather sticky. "All right," he agreed arrogantly. "But I give the orders. We do it my way," and he scowled, putting his hands on the butt of one of his guns.

Logan walked over, grabbed the money sack off the desk, and the three of them left the office, heading for their horses at the hitch rail out front.

All the way out to the old mine, Tyson's eyes kept shifting from Logan to Aaron, to the money sack, then back to Logan again, and instead of leading the way, he kept telling Logan which direction to take so he wouldn't have either man at his back. It wasn't exactly that he didn't trust Logan and Aaron, because he was certain Logan wouldn't try anything as long as he knew his wife could be hurt if he did, but there was always that slim chance that something could go wrong.

It was late, and the sun was low on the horizon, its red rays barely topping the trees as they made their way into the hills behind the Highland, moving northeast, and Logan realized after only a short distance where they had to be heading. Still he kept a slow pace in front of Tyson, especially when it appeared that Tyson was taking a roundabout trail. Logan didn't like it. Maybe because Tyson was too jittery. He was like a man lighting a dynamite fuse, and it worried Logan.

It was almost dark by the time they reached the old abandoned Goldspur mine and reined in some hundred feet or so from the entrance. Some of the shoring had fallen in places, and vegetation was reclaiming it, but Logan quickly caught a glimpse of a light inside the dark opening.

"I go on in alone," Tyson ordered. "After I talk to Giles, we'll come out and leave her tied up inside, you give us the money, and we ride out."

Logan stared at him suspiciously. "How do I know Poe's even in there?" he asked. "I'll see her first, or no money."

Tyson was sweating now, his hands clammy on the reins. "All right, all right!" he answered. "I'll bring her to the entrance and show you, then we take her back inside."

Logan wasn't any too pleased. "Why can't you just bring her out?" he said stubbornly. "Fair exchange out here."

"And have you two turn those guns on us the second we have the money." Tyson frowned. "I'm not that dumb. We do it my way, remember?"

Logan's jaw set hard, and his eyes were like steel. "You win," he said reluctantly. "But make sure I see her first, or no money."

Tyson cautioned them to stay put, then rode

on in and dismounted, tethering his horse to a tree near the entrance, where another saddled horse and a packhorse were also tied, and when he ducked inside, Lord Merriweather was kneeling next to Poe, helping her try to get a sip of water.

She was so weak she could barely hold her head up, and moaned agonizingly as she tried to wipe the water from her chin, but was able to move her hand only a few inches. The water dripped off her chin, falling into the valley between her partly exposed breasts, and it mingled with the perspiration from the fever that was starting to rise in her body.

Giles stood up, fastening the top of the canteen he'd been using.

"She's bad, isn't she?" Tyson said as he stood staring down at her.

"Real bad." Giles's eyes narrowed as he realized Tyson was empty-handed. "Where's the money?"

"Shhh . . ." his cousin cautioned him. "It's right out there with Campbell," and he motioned with his head toward the mouth of the tunnel.

"Campbell?" Giles looked horrified. "What the devil is he doing here?"

"There was no other way." Tyson shook his head disgustedly. "You can buck a man just so far. He won't hand over the money until he's sure she's safe."

"Bully for us!" Lord Merriweather was really peeved this time. "One look at her and we're through for sure," he exclaimed.

Tyson rubbed his chin thoughtfully, then knelt down close to Poe. "Is she conscious enough to know what's going on?" he asked.

"Barely."

"Good." He motioned toward Poe. "Get your coat out from underneath her head and wrap it around her shoulders," he ordered.

Giles frowned. "Why?"

"Never mind why, just do what I tell you. Only make sure when you pull it around her that it covers the blood in front." Lord Merriweather studied his cousin for a brief second, then began to get a glimmer of what Tyson was up to, and complied.

"How's that?" he asked when the dark green frock coat was neatly wrapped around their victim.

Tyson knelt down, inspecting his cousin's handiwork, pulling the coat a bit closer together in front so her breasts were covered a little more, then helped Giles ease her back against the wall of the mine tunnel.

"Now, do you hear me?" Tyson asked Poe as he studied her face, tilting her chin up with his hand.

Her fevered eyes stared at him blankly, but she nodded, slowly forming the word "Yes" with her mouth. However, no sound came out.

---

"Listen," he said, "your husband and his lawyer friend are outside, understand?" and he saw the recognition in her eyes. "Good, because Giles is going to pick you up and keep his arm about your waist, and you're going to stand between us, while I hold a gun on them, and we're going to show them you're all right."

Her voice was shaking and barely a whisper. "I . . . can't . . . I can't . . ." she protested weakly.

"You can, and you will," he insisted angrily, and his fingers dug into her chin. "If you don't, your husband and the lawyer are sitting ducks out there, and you'll all be dead, understand?"

Tears rimmed her eyes. Logan outside? He had come for her after all, and Aaron too, but what good was it now? She was so weak, dizzy, and sick, and with a bullet in her shoulder—her head felt so hot and feverish. She knew an infection had already started to set in.

Tyson's fingers tightened again, maliciously this time. "Do you understand?" he asked.

"Yes," she whispered helplessly.

He released her chin, then glanced over at Lord Merriweather. "Is all our gear still outside on the packhorse I brought from town earlier?" he asked.

The Englishman, although disliking the position he was in, nodded. "All but the canteen she's been drinking from," he answered.

"Good, but bring it along, we might need it

too, and if they ask about why she's wearing your coat, it's to keep her warm because it's cool in here. Now, come on, let's get on with it."

Giles frowned, staring at her legs. "But she can't even stand up!"

Tyson glanced at her feet thoughtfully for a second, then reached in his pocket and pulled out a handkerchief. Kneeling he grabbed hold of her feet, slipped the handkerchief around her ankles, then tied it.

"They can't expect her to stand up too well if her feet are tied, now can they?" He sneered as he stood back up. "Now, pick her up," he commanded, and Giles stuffed the canteen in his hip pocket, then reached down, picking Poe up awkwardly, trying to hold her, only her head kept slumping forward.

"Hold your head up!" Tyson demanded through clenched teeth. "You're not that bad off!"

Tears filled Poe's eyes and rolled down her cheeks; however, with extreme effort she managed to hold her head up, and they put her between them, then slowly headed toward the opening of the old mine tunnel. When they reached it, Tyson lifted one of the guns from his holster into his right hand, aiming it into the growing darkness outside.

Although Poe's eyes were open, everything in front of her was so vague, as if she were seeing it through a heavy mist or fog, and all she saw were dark shadows and trees as she stared straight ahead.

"Here she is, safe and sound," Tyson yelled from beside her, and she heard Logan answer from some distance away.

"Why isn't she standing?"

"Her feet are tied," Tyson explained.

"Poe, are you all right?" Logan called from out of the deepening shadows, and Poe felt Lord Merriweather's arm tighten about her waist.

"Call to him," Tyson demanded, his mouth close to her ear. Poe winced, well aware that she had very little strength left. "Unless you want him dead, you'd better answer."

"He means it, love," Giles whispered in her other ear, and Poe was at a loss.

She knew very well that he meant it. She hadn't been afraid of Giles Merriweather, he was only a bungling fool, but Tyson was different. He wasn't averse to using any means to get what he wanted. So gathering all the strength together she possibly could, she took a deep breath and tried.

"I'm . . . I'm all right, just scared," she managed to gasp, and the effort almost made her pass out.

"Get her back inside, quick," Tyson growled half under his breath. He still had hold of her arm, and had felt her body go limp.

They turned quickly, moving her back inside

to where the lantern hung, and when they laid her down to lean her against the side of the tunnel again, Lord Merriweather retrieved his dark green frock coat from around her, slipping into it while Tyson propped her up against the wall. She was barely conscious.

"Come on," Tyson snapped when he was through, and he handed one of his guns to his cousin. "There's thirty thousand dollars out there. Let's go after it," and after taking one last glance at their half-dead victim, they both walked back toward the mine entrance, stepping out into the darkening dusk with their guns drawn.

Tyson waved his gun in the air, calling for Logan and Aaron to ride in, while Giles hurried to the tree where their horses were tethered and brought both their mounts as well as the packhorse back over with him.

Logan caught Tyson's signal and nudged his horse, moving in slowly, with Aaron close behind, and they reined up a few feet away from the other two men.

"The money!" Tyson demanded.

Logan untied the sack from his saddle horn and threw it at him.

Tyson's eyes gleamed. "Thanks," he said, and opened the bag hurriedly, checking to make sure it was really money; then he looked back up at Logan. "Good. Now, toss your guns in the bushes over there," and he motioned with his head toward a clump of shrubs a few feet away, while both he and Lord Merriweather mounted their horses. "When that's done," he added, his hand tightening on the reins while he tried to hang onto the money, balance in the saddle, and still keep his gun trained on them, "we'll ride out of here and she's all yours."

Logan started to reach for his gun to comply with Tyson's order, then suddenly hesitated. It had been getting darker by the minute but there was just enough light so that he spotted the stains on the front of Giles's frock coat as the Englishman reined in closer to Tyson.

"That's the coat you had around Poe, isn't it?" he asked hurriedly, his hand only inches from his gun.

Giles tensed. "So?"

"So how come there's blood all over the front of it?"

Instinctively both Giles and Tyson looked down. Giles hadn't bothered to button the coat, and dark stains were spattered near the inside edges. They glanced at each other.

"You fool!" Tyson yelled. Then, terrified, afraid of what might happen next, he hollered, "Come on!" and both of them panicked, whirling their horses around unexpectedly, making a break for the woods, with the packhorse in tow.

Logan's hand, already so close to his gun, finished his draw in one fluid motion, and he fanned a barrage of shots after them, emptying it; then he waited.

At first he wasn't sure he'd hit anything. Then, as he held his breath, he saw Giles sway a little in the saddle, followed a few seconds later by Tyson, who even with a bullet in him was still trying to manage the money, his horse, and his gun. Then both men left their saddles, hitting the ground hard while their horses faltered, bucking skittishly.

Thank God he hadn't hit the horses, Logan thought, because he knew he wasn't that good a shot, and he holstered his gun as quickly as he'd grabbed it, then leapt from his horse and threw the palomino's reins at Aaron.

"Tie him. I'm going after Poe!" He headed toward the mine entrance on the run.

Aaron was still sitting on his horse, dumbfounded, staring after Logan as if in a daze; then slowly, after collecting himself somewhat, he slid from the saddle, his own gun drawn now, and glanced in the direction where the two bodies lay. It had all happened so fast. He turned again slowly, watching Logan disappear from view.

Once inside the mine, Logan knew his worst fears were grounded, and adjusting his eyes to the dim light, he moved forward cautiously, then dropped to his knees beside Poe, who was still propped against the wall, the lantern hanging above her. His heart constricted at the sight of her, and he let out a deep sob.

"Poe!" He was frantic, and his hand touched her face, caressing her cheek. "Poe?"

She opened her eyes, looking directly at him, and he saw tears. "Logan . . ." She was so weak, he barely heard her.

"Don't talk," he cautioned, and his hand moved to her forehead. The fever was already too high.

"The bullet . . ." she gasped. "Tried . . . tried to get away."

"Shhh!"

"An accident," she whispered, her lips barely moving, and Logan's eyes filled with anguish. "An accident . . ." she repeated, again ignoring his warning to be quiet, only this time her voice faltered as she tried to take a deep breath, then passed out.

Logan stood up, turning toward the mine entrance as Aaron stepped inside, the sack of money in one hand, his gun still in the other.

"They're dead, both of them," Aaron said with finality, and holstered his gun as he strolled over to stand beside Logan. "Is . . . is she dead?" he asked, his voice choking on a sob.

Logan shook his head. "Only passed out."

Aaron breathed a sigh of relief because he knew if she'd been dead Logan wouldn't be fit to live with. He watched Logan kneel down again beside Poe and reach inside her shirtwaist, removing a piece of blood-soaked cloth; then Logan took a better look at the wound.

"She needs a doctor," he said, grimacing. "And she needs one fast." He glanced up at Aaron. "Leave the money here, then go get Doc Barrett and a wagon so we can take her home." He looked back down at Poe. "I'll wait here with her," he said, and took a clean handkerchief from his pocket, setting it against the wound, then tried to pull her shirtwaist over it as best he could.

Aaron's eyes darkened sympathetically as he watched Logan. "Don't worry, she'll be all right," he said, and touched Logan on the shoulder. "I'll be as quick as I can," and he tossed the sack of money on the ground beside Logan, then turned, hurrying toward the entrance.

"Aaron?" Logan stopped him, and Aaron turned back. "While you're at it, you might as well get the sheriff for those two," he added, and Aaron nodded, waving acknowledgment, then disappeared outside.

It was well over an hour before Aaron got back, and during that time Logan died a thousand deaths as he watched over Poe, wiping the perspiration from her forehead and covering her with his buckskin jacket, trying to do all he could for her. And during all that time she regained consciousness only once, and that was just long enough to recognize Logan, then pass out again.

"In here!" Logan called when he finally heard familiar voices near the entrance, and the doctor was beside Poe in seconds, while Logan, after letting the doctor take over, left the tunnel, taking the sack of money with him.

"Here, take this to the house," he told Aaron, shoving the money at him while the sheriff and his deputy, who were already dismounted, began examining the two bodies.

Aaron started tying the bag of money to his saddle horn. It was pitch dark now, but the sheriff and his deputy had both brought lanterns, and Aaron glanced at Logan, frowning over the worried look on his face.

"What should I tell Delia?" he asked.

Logan shivered slightly without his jacket. The night air was cool this time of year, especially here in the hills. "Tell her the truth," he said. "Then tell her to get things ready at the house because the bullet's still in Poe and I know Doc Barrett can't take it out in there," and he motioned behind him toward the old mine.

Aaron nodded, then mounted up and glanced behind him to the buckboard and driver waiting only a few feet away. "Luther was pulling away from the store," he said. "I just commandeered the first wagon I came to and promised him twenty bucks for helping. Was that all right?"

Logan was also looking back at the buckboard. He'd have preferred someone other than Luther Crenshaw, who was usually more drunk than sober, but at the moment he wasn't going to be choosy.

"There's a couple of blankets from my place in the back too," Aaron went on as his hands tightened on the reins. "And I've explained everything to Sheriff Macklin on the way out."

Logan nodded gratefully and glanced over again to where the two lawmen were rounding up the dead men's horses so they could tie the bodies on. "Good," he said, turning back to Aaron. "Now, get going, and I'll see how Doc Barrett's doing," and he pivoted abruptly, heading back into the mine as Aaron hit his horse across the rump and galloped past the waiting buckboard, heading back down the trail toward the Highland.

The next few hours were frantic for Logan because he'd been right about Poe's condition. So while Sheriff Macklin and his deputy finished tying the bodies of the two dead men to their horses, he and Doc Barrett, with some help from Luther, who was sober, possibly because it was still early in the evening, carried Poe to the buckboard, made her as comfortable as possible, then left the old mine with Logan riding in the buckboard beside Poe all the way to the house. When they finally arrived at the Highland after a torturous ride for Poe, they were greeted hurriedly by Delia and Aaron, who'd been impatiently waiting for them, and Poe was taken directly to Delia's tower room at Delia's insistence, where she lay for three days after the bullet was removed, fighting an infection.

There were times during those first few days when Poe was almost lucid, but most of the time her mind was in a crazy limbo somewhere, filled with strange dreams and weird nightmares. The few times she was half-conscious she was aware of faces, one after another, floating around her like pictures in a kaleidoscope. Some she recognized, others she didn't. There was Logan, and Aaron and Aunt Delia, only more often than not she was unable to distinguish fantasy from reality, and it was frightening. However, Logan's face did seem to be the one she saw the most during those brief moments of reality, and she'd try so hard to cling to him, letting his voice soothe her, his words comfort her. Only it never seemed to last long enough, and just when she was so sure she'd be able to pull the whole world and Logan back into focus again, to be a part of her life again, he'd suddenly be gone and that horrible blackness would consume her once more, pulling her down, down, down, as if into a cold pit where the terrible nightmares dwelt and she had no control over anything anymore, not even her thoughts.

It was in the wee hours of the morning of the fourth day after she'd been shot; however, Poe had no recollection of the time that had passed as she opened her eyes slowly, finally managing to keep them open long enough to look around. The room whirled crazily for a few minutes at first, and she was almost tempted to shut her eyes again; then, as they adjusted, everything started to come into focus and she got her bearings. She was in a room, and it was dark outside, with a lamp lit across the room, but she could tell it wasn't her room. Then she realized she was in Aunt Delia's tower room with its walls of windows, and she tried to turn her head ever so slowly toward the lamp.

Suddenly, as her head started to move, a shadow fell across the bed, and before she even had a chance to speak, she found herself staring up into Logan's warm gray eyes that were deepening with concern.

She stared at him hard, unable to say anything because it was the first time in so long she'd seen him so clearly, and he came even closer now, lowering himself to sit on the edge of the bed, their eyes absorbing each other as if they just couldn't seem to get enough. Then slowly, hesitantly, her blue-green eyes filled with tears.

Logan bent down, burying his face against her hair, and nuzzled the side of her neck. "I thought I'd lost you," he whispered against her ear, and a warm sensation flooded through her.

Leaning her head over, she let her cheek rest

against his head, and his nearness made her feel so secure, yet just a little bit giddy inside.

He drew his head back, took her hand in his, and looked down at her, relieved. "Thank God," he said.

Her voice was so soft at first when she spoke that he had to lean even closer to hear her. "How long have I been here?" she asked.

"It's been three days." There were dark circles beneath his eyes, and he looked like he hadn't slept for ages.

"Lord Merriweather and Tyson?"

"Unfortunately they're dead." His eyes hardened; then he drew her hand to his lips, his eyes softening again, and he kissed her fingertips. "But you're to forget about them," he said bitterly, his voice filled with emotion. "They're not worth it." He saw her try to lick her lips and realized how dry they must be. "Here, have a sip of water," he said, reaching for a glass on the stand beside the bed. She took a sip, then frowned, studying him curiously while he set the glass of water back. "You've been here all the time?" she asked.

"Most of it." He smiled, and reached out, smoothing the dark red strands of hair from her forehead. "Poe, when I said I loved you, I meant it, every word," he assured her.

"But the Duchess? Those other women in San Francisco—?"

He put a finger to her lips, stopping her. "I

admit I've had other women, Poe, only I'm not proud of it," he confessed. "I'm not a saint, darling, and I never claimed to be one, but from the moment you came into my life, things just seemed to change somehow."

"Then . . . then I'm not just one of your conquests?"

He squeezed her hand. "I see your mother did a beautiful job on you, didn't she," he replied, and shook his head. "No, Poe, you're not one of my conquests. You're my whole life now, you're a part of me, and I intend to keep you busy for the rest of your life proving it."

Poe twined her fingers in his, but she was still so terribly weak, and her voice was hushed. "What does Aunt Delia think?" she asked.

"About what?"

"About us."

"Why should she think anything about us, other than that we're in love?"

She swallowed uneasily because it still hurt to breathe, yet tried to smile. "Because," she half-whispered, "she thinks I'm a silly girl from the hills who married you just to keep other men from my door."

"And did you?" he asked.

"You know I did. At least that's what I told myself."

"And now?"

"Now?" Her eyes grew misty again. "I'm so mixed up," she said, her voice hushed. "I know

I love you . . . I think I did then, but it's so hard to understand . . ."

His eyes searched her face. "Let it go, Poe," he said huskily. "Let your feelings take you. Forget what your mother said—she didn't know my heart." He reached out to a vase of flowers on a stand next to the bed and took one, holding it out to her. "See this rose," he said gently. "This rose is as fragile as my heart is where you're concerned, Poe. Believe it, please, because I do love you."

It was still an effort for her to move, but she took the rose from him, then gazed about the room with its plush velvets and brocades in soothing shades of blue. It was a room fit for royalty, with embroidered sheets and pillowcases on the bed, as well as a painting of the Highland hanging over the marble-manteled fireplace where expensive figurines were displayed. Everything about the room exuded luxury and wealth.

"How come I'm in the tower room?" she suddenly asked, surprising him.

He smiled. "Aunt Delia's orders, but as soon as you're well enough you'll be moving downstairs to our room."

"Our room?"

"Yes, our room. We'll be taking over the master bedroom, since it's the biggest."

Poe blushed, her pale face even more red than usual, and he bent down, kissing her lightly on the lips. "But we'll talk about that later," he said huskily. "You look terribly tired, and I don't want you to overdo it."

It had been getting lighter outside while they talked, and Logan glanced toward the windows, watching the first few rays of the morning sun as it started to peek above the hills to stream in at the window, making everything in the room glow with an elegance hard to define; then he looked down again at Poe. Her eyes were drooping lazily, and her breathing was still shallow. She was a far cry from being well yet.

"For now, my love, I think you'd better get more rest," he said.

She sighed. "What about you? When did you sleep last?"

"Oh, I've been curling up over there." He pointed to a blue velvet chaise longue by the windows. "But now that you've finally come to and I know you're going to be all right, I think I'll go downstairs to my own room and collapse until the rest of the household wakes up."

"Why not here?" she asked hesitantly.

He took a deep breath. "Not yet, my love, not yet," he said firmly but gently. "I'm too wild a sleeper, for one thing, and if I accidentally bumped into you, hurting you, I'd never forgive myself. Besides, if I stayed in the same bed with you, I wouldn't want to sleep, and it's too soon for that. No, I want you well enough first, so that the next time we do share a bed I can let you fall asleep in my arms." He reached down, picking up her hand with the rose still in it. "Would you like me to have the maid bring you some soup?" he asked.

She tried to shake her head. "I'm not hungry, but I am tired."

He smiled. "I thought as much." He glanced down at the rose again. "In the meantime, remember. You still have my heart, and I'll be back as soon as I've rested."

For a second Poe wanted to rebel against his leaving; then common sense told her he was right. He looked so weary after what must have been a long vigil for him, and they both needed rest. If he stayed they'd only keep right on talking, even if they didn't do anything else, and both of them would suffer for it.

So after a few minutes more of reluctant good-byes, Logan kissed her gently again, gave her another sip of water, then went down to his bedroom, where he fell across the bed, soon dropping into an exhausted sleep.

Upstairs, in the tower room, Poe let the rose rest against her cheek, filling her head with its sweet fragrance; then she too fell asleep, to dream of Logan and how wonderful it was to be loved. The nightmares were over.

Late the same morning, just a short time before lunch, Poe lay in the tower room dreaming. The warmth of the sun on her face caressed her long before she was fully awake, and the voices in the room with her were incorporating themselves into her dream. Only the man's voice she was hearing wasn't Logan's, even though she was dreaming of him. With all the strength she could muster, she forced herself back to reality again until she was finally fully awake, although her eyes were still shut, and now, as her brain cleared, she recognized the voice as Aaron's.

He was talking to someone other than her, and she was about to open her eyes to see who it was when she caught the gist of the conversation, and instead she held her breath as she heard Aunt Delia answer.

"For heaven's sake, Aaron, what if she hears you?"

"Don't worry, she's still unconscious," he said. "I checked when we came in."

"Then where's Logan? He was so determined to stay with her until she pulled out of it."

"Who knows? Didn't you see him when we were up here last night?" he answered. "That chaise isn't exactly conducive to sleep, you know. I imagine he just couldn't stay awake any longer and decided to really get a good night's sleep. I suppose he's down in his room now, still dead to the world. We can tell him when he wakes up."

"Well, all right, if you think that's it," she said thoughtfully. "Only I really think he should have sent someone up to be with her instead of leaving her alone."

"He no doubt decided to leave in the middle of the night and didn't want to wake anyone. Now, do you want to hear what the sheriff had to say this morning or don't you?"

"All right, go ahead," Delia answered, and Poe sensed that Aunt Delia was standing somewhere near the fireplace, while Aaron sounded like he was nearer the windows across from the foot of the bed.

Aaron's voice was crisp and businesslike. "Seems that when they were making all the funeral arrangements for Merriweather and Tyson, someone found some things in Tyson's suitcase and turned them over to Macklin, and now Macklin wants a few answers."

"Like what?"

"Like why Roger Tyson had three or four letters in his possession with no return address on them, but that were signed by Joe Yancey, and were addressed to Roger Tyson. He'd written to him about his daughter, Poetica, cautioning and warning Tyson to make sure the girl was taken care of properly if anything should happen, and reminding him of his promise to see things through."

"No mention of money?"

"I read the letters and there wasn't a word mentioned about money."

"You're certain there wasn't even a reference to her trust fund?"

"Not even that. Macklin was surprised enough to discover Tyson and Merriweather were cousins. When he found the letters, he really got suspicious, and now he's anxious to find out why Roger Tyson kept the fact that he knew Poe's father a secret, and why Poe's father wrote to him, warning him not to let the Campbells put anything over on his daughter."

"He wrote that?"

"He did."

"Oh Lord!" Delia's voice trembled breathlessly. "What are we going to do, Aaron? If anyone ever discovers that Logan married Poe just to keep us all out of prison because of that stupid trust fund . . ."

"Don't worry," Aaron assured her. "They haven't any proof. Not since you burned those ledgers. All we have to do now is come up with some plausible reason for Yancey writing what he did to Tyson. Like I said, there's no mention of money. Nor is there anything anywhere in any of the letters that could be incriminating. All they do is simply remind him of his promise to see that Poe's taken care of, and warn him not to let you get away with anything."

"Trusting soul, wasn't he?" she said; then added, "But why didn't Logan discover the letters the night he searched their rooms?"

"He probably didn't pay any attention to them.

After all, he was looking for ledgers and receipts. He probably thought the same thing the sheriff thought at first, that it was just a bunch of unimportant personal mail without a return address. The sheriff wouldn't have paid them any attention either, except they were trying to find out who their next of kin were so they could notify them they were dead. If there also hadn't been a letter in the bunch from Merriweather telling Tyson he was coming to the States for a visit, Macklin wouldn't have discovered they were really cousins, either. It's just one of those things. I imagine Logan didn't even realize what they were."

"Damn!"

Poe wasn't used to hearing Aunt Delia swear, and now she opened one eye a wee slit so she could see across the room in the direction of their voices, and she watched the older woman wringing her hands nervously, yet Poe stayed quiet, letting them think she was still unconscious even though she had begun to hurt deep down inside, and was forcing back tears, the shock at what she'd just heard almost overwhelming her.

"Well, we're going to have to make sure Logan knows," Delia was saying heatedly, while trying to keep her voice low. "If Sheriff Macklin should corner him on it, he's going to have to have the answers, and I don't want him saying the wrong thing."

"Look, even if the sheriff discovered what we did," Aaron replied, "there isn't really anything he can do about it, not now, unless Poe presses charges, of course. And from what Logan's told me, and the way she's been acting lately, I'd say it sounds like she's really fallen in love with him, and if I know Poe, and I think I've gotten to know her pretty well these past few months, I don't think she'd ever let anyone she loved rot in jail."

Poe closed her eye again quickly, trying to keep the tears that were forcing themselves against her eyelids from oozing out onto her cheeks. The bastard! she cried silently, her heart tearing to pieces. The dirty bastard! Now she understood some of what Tyson had been rambling about during the kidnapping that hadn't made any sense. And all along Logan had been pretending to be so much in love with her, and here the only reason he married her was to keep them all from going to jail. Something about a trust fund . . . ?

Again she used all the strength left to her to keep the anger and tears from surging to the surface as she continued to listen to their conversation, hoping to learn more about the so-called trust fund and money, but all they talked about the rest of the stay was what kind of explanation they could think of that would keep the sheriff from getting any nosier, and Poe swallowed hard, stifling a sob as she heard

Aaron say, "I'd better check to see if she's still all right." Seconds later she could sense his presence next to the bed.

When his hand touched her forehead she almost jumped, but was so determined not to let them know she was conscious that not one muscle even flinched. She was especially careful now because she knew if she opened her eyes even a little, there'd be nothing but a flood of tears.

"Well, at least her fever's finally down," Aaron said, and his hand left her forehead. "That's probably why Logan figured he could get a little sleep. Now, if she'd only come to."

Poe heard the distinct click of the bedroom door being opened. "Since she hasn't, shall we go find Logan?" Delia suggested. Poe sensed Aaron's step away from the bed, and again she let her eyes become slits in the sun-filled room so that she could see the door, and she watched Delia Campbell, fancily clad in red silk, take one last look about her tower room, then leave, with Aaron, in his usual tweed suit, following close at her heels.

The second the door shut behind them, Poe let the tears come full force, and her eyes, open now, were blurred as she tried to focus on her plush surroundings, a horrible, dread feeling gripping her insides. Why hadn't she died? Death would have been better than this. Damn! Damn! Damn!

Why had they done this to her? Why? And what had they done that was so terrible they could end up in jail? Her fingers were still twined around the rose, and they tightened on it, squeezing furiously, crushing it the way she'd like to crush Logan's heart as her thoughts went back over her wedding day and she remembered the papers they'd had her sign. How stupid could she have been, not to read them? They'd told her they were simply certificates she had to sign for the marriage to be legal, and she'd believed them, not knowing anything about law or contracts. And she'd thought she was so smart. How they must all have been laughing at her! What a fool she'd been. She should have read all those lawbooks down in the library instead of the novels, then she wouldn't have been taken in like this.

A trust fund! She'd heard of trust funds, but never dreamed one of them might have been waiting for her here in Goldspur. A sharp physical pain began working its way deep into her breastbone, but not from the wound in her shoulder; it was from the wound in her heart.

And she'd let him make love to her! She'd given herself to him, and for what? For his pleasure, that was all. The liar! The goddamned liar!

He said he'd married her because he loved her, and it was all a pack of lies! The whole thing was a pack of lies, and she felt the moisture from the crushed rose against her fingers, the scent of it still strong in her nostrils. She was so furious she wanted to scream, but knew it wouldn't help. What an idiot she'd been. How could she have let him make her forget all of her mother's warnings? Oh, she knew very well how. He'd sweet-talked and charmed her, just like Joe Yancey had done to her ma, and all of it just so he wouldn't go to jail for swindling her. Ma was right. There wasn't one good man on the face of the earth. They were all a bunch of devils, the whole lot of them, only why did it hurt so much to find it out? Why did she have to fall in love with one of them? Why couldn't she have done what Ma said, and avoided the heartbreak?

She was still so weak, and the anger inside was only sapping more of her energy. Her nose was full, her eyes still overflowing, and she let the mangled rose petals fall from her fingers so she could grope on the nightstand for a hand-kerchief she'd seen there earlier. The effort almost made her pass out, but she managed to get it somehow and cleared her nose, wiped her eyes, then tucked the handkerchief into her fist just in case more tears came, while she decided what she was going to do.

One thing for sure. She couldn't stay here anymore. Not long anyway. True, she still wasn't well enough to manage on her own yet, but that day would come, and not any too soon. In the meantime, she had to stay here. She mulled the predicament over in her mind and finally came to a decision.

She'd stay, all right. She'd stay now because she had no choice, only she wasn't about to let them know that she knew what they'd been up to. It was bad enough knowing they'd deceived her; she wasn't about to let them see the effect it had on her. No siree!

Logan had made a fool of her. Well, she'd make one of him. Oh, she'd pretend, all right. She could put on a good act too. Reluctantly she remembered the night before the kidnapping when he'd made love to her, and the wonderful feelings he'd wakened within her. Now that was all gone, leaving only sad memories for her because as she lay in the bed sick at heart, the pain from the wound making her only more miserable, and anger beginning to conquer the shame and hurt she'd felt on learning the truth, she knew there was only one thing she could do.

She should turn them over to the sheriff, but something inside, some hostile feeling she tried to dismiss as stupid sentiment, but couldn't, argued the point with her. No, she wouldn't turn them over to the law. That wasn't the thing to do. In the first place, she didn't have any proof except what she'd heard.

For now, until she was well enough, she wouldn't say a word, and Logan would never know she'd learned the truth. But just as soon as she was able to ride, she'd hightail it out of Goldspur and never look back, and the devil take the lot of them!

So with this new resolve strengthening the bitter anger she felt over Logan's betrayal, Poe hardened her heart, then dried her eyes, promising herself she'd shed no more tears over Logan Campbell because he wasn't really worth it. She buried the back of her head deep into the pillow, staring toward the windows and the morning sun, fighting the hurt inside her the best and only way she knew how.

# 12

# The Runaway

Logan had been furious when he'd learned about the sheriff finding the letters Tyson had, because he was so afraid Poe would find out, and he didn't want anything to spoil the love that seemed to flow between them now. However, it took only one afternoon with a few lies here and there to satisfy the sheriff, telling Macklin that, yes, Lord Merriweather and Roger Tyson evidently were cousins, a fact he and Aaron had discovered only the day Poe was kidnapped. Other than that, Logan pretended ignorance about the letters Joe Yancey had written Roger Tyson, explaining that perhaps Joe knew Hester had been planning to make Delia Campbell Poe's guardian in case anything happened to her, and since Delia and Joe Yancey didn't get along too well because of the way Joe treated his wife, he might have been afraid Delia wouldn't do right by the girl, since she was Joe's daughter.

"After all," Logan had said, "who knows what goes through a man's head? Especially when he knows he hadn't done right by his daughter himself."

Sheriff Macklin didn't exactly see Logan's reasoning on the matter, but since it was the only explanation he had, and since the cousins had been killed while perpetrating a crime, he whitewashed the whole thing. The two men were given a quiet burial, and in the ensuing days, after Lord Merriweather's effects were sent back to his ancestral estates in England, and Tyson's belongings, including the strange letters, were shoved into the back of one of the drawers in the sheriff's office for want of something better to do with them, everyone forgot about the whole affair.

Everyone except Poe, that is. As each day went by while Poe lay in the huge luxurious bed, then rested on the plush chaise longue recuperating from her brush with death, the conversation between Aaron Goldbladt and Aunt Delia that day in her room stayed uppermost in her mind, as well as the fate of the two men who'd kidnapped her and the real reason for Tyson's presence in Goldspur.

And although she responded to Logan with the same warmth as before, pretending to love him as much as he professed to love her, he was never aware that hidden beneath her soft blue-green eyes and hesitant smile was a broken heart that, after being broken, had hardened into a brittle shell of what it once had been. And not once in all that while did she ever let her guard down. She played her game only too well, biding her time.

Finally, one morning, a little over two weeks after Poe's heartbreaking discovery, she stirred in the big satiny bed and opened her eyes slowly, to find Logan sitting beside her, studying her face.

"Good morning," he said.

She'd been lying on her stomach with the pillow bunched beneath her head; now she turned over, the sight of him both bitter and sweet, and she took a deep breath, stubbornly remembering her resolve.

"Is it?" she asked.

The corners of his mouth tilted, amused. "It certainly is. The sun's out, the weather fair, and I have a distinct feeling today's the day."

She gazed at him apprehensively. "For what?"

"For us to take over the master bedroom." His eyes twinkled mischievously as he watched her face turn pink. "I do believe you're embarrassed," he said; then added, "Why?"

She was not only embarrassed but also taken completely by surprise. She'd known the day would be coming soon, but she'd been faking a great deal, pretending she was worse off than she really was, and had imagined he believed her. It must have been Dr. Barrett's visit the evening before that had prompted Logan's sudden decision.

She'd been managing to make it downstairs for dinner the past few evenings, although she was pretending a weakness that didn't really exist, and she was so sure she could talk him into one more day, because she knew she really should have at least until the end of the week before taking off on her own. However, the look in his eyes this morning was not the look of a man who could be easily swayed, and her heart sank. Well, she had one advantage. At least he'd told her in the morning. That gave her plenty of time. She could take off this afternoon while he was in Goldspur at the Highland office if she had to.

She took a deep breath, then smiled at him sheepishly. "You have to admit, Mr. Campbell," she said playfully, "I'm not really all that used to this Mr.-and-Mrs. routine."

He laughed. "Why, Poe, you're an old married lady."

"You know what I mean," she countered, the flush on her face turning crimson, and Logan reached out, cupping her chin in his hand, his eyes growing serious.

"That's what I love about you the most, Poe," he said gently, letting his eyes cover her tousled red hair, then settle on her face. "You're so unpredictable, and so lovely."

And so gullible, she thought to herself, and wished she could say it to his face. Instead she stared back at him, then smiled hesitantly.

"You're sure about tonight?" she asked.

"Positive," he answered, and released her chin, then stood up and surveyed the room. "And I intend to stay home today and give Clive and the girls a hand moving the clothes from both our rooms." He walked over and took a hairbrush off the dresser, turning it over in his hand, then took a mental inventory of everything in the tower room that was Poe's, including the brush. "And I think there's enough stuff up here to keep us toting for a couple of hours too," he went on, then turned to face her. "Last night Doc Barrett said you're home free. And you are home, Poe." He set the hairbrush down again and walked back over to the bed, where he sat on the edge again, helping her sit up, bunching the pillows up beneath her head. "So after breakfast, which I intend to share with you, we're going to have the whole day to spend together. Now, how does that sound?"

Poe's insides were fluttering wildly, and she could even feel her heart skipping a few beats as it pounded against her breastbone, while she fought the urge to scream and cry and curse him for what he was doing to her.

"It sounds marvelous," she managed to say with a semblance of warmth in her voice, hoping the anger and resentment didn't show in her eyes.

Evidently it didn't, because Logan seemed to be quite satisfied with her answer, and bent down, kissing her longingly, then promised to go downstairs and bring her breakfast right back up.

She watched him leave the room, then stared at the closed door for a minute, her heart in a turmoil. So soon! It was coming so soon. One part of her could hardly wait to get away from his lying words, knowing full well it was all a show. A sham to make her think nothing was wrong. And yet another part of her wanted so hard to believe him, and could hardly wait for his smile and the touch of his hand.

The touch of his hand! Damn him, she thought angrily, and tossed the covers aside as she slid from the bed and strolled over to the window, gazing out. She had planned to leave before it came to this, but if he was going to be around all day, how the dickens was she ever going to get away? She couldn't spend the night with him. She just couldn't! Yet what else could she do? He certainly wasn't in the mood to be talked out of it, that was for sure.

She stood in her dimity nightgown and stared out the window at the town of Goldspur. If there was any way, any way at all, that she could find enough time alone today to do what she had to do, she'd do it, she told herself bitterly. Because she was sure there was no way she could spend the night with Logan without giving herself away and telling him what she really thought of him. Only that was another thing. What *did* she think of him?

A tear rushed to the corner of her eye and she brushed it away angrily. She knew all too well what she thought of him. But regardless, there was no way she was going to let it change the course she'd set for herself. Not now, or ever. She'd be damned if she'd stay with a man who didn't love her. Once more, her resolve to leave Goldspur was stronger than ever as she turned from the windows and the early-morning sun and walked back to the bed to sit and wait for her husband to bring her breakfast.

Unfortunately, however, Poe never had the chance that day to carry out her plan to run away. It wasn't that her intentions weren't good. It was just that for some strange reason she couldn't comprehend, Logan rarely let her out of his sight. He had her sitting around supervising everything all day—and that meant literally everything. He even made sure her clothes were hung in exactly the right place in the closet for her, the toiletries arranged where she wanted them on the vanity.

Even Logan's oversize bed, when it was brought into the room and the old regular-size bed moved out, was placed where she wanted it. Not a thing was done without her knowl-

edge, although there were a few things done to
accommodate Logan. Some she approved of,
others she thought ridiculous, like the head of
the elk over the fireplace. Fireplaces were for
mirrors and pictures, not heads of dead ani-
mals, she told him disgustedly. But Logan
disagreed.

"I got that on my first hunting trip when I
was fifteen," he argued indignantly. "And it
stays. Please . . . ?"

She almost had to laugh at this big overgrown boy, because that's really the way he
seemed at times, pleading to keep a part of his
youth with him. She was sitting in the chair
near the bed at the time, and when she looked
up at him, he almost seemed taller than usual,
the elk head bulky where it rested on his broad
shoulder.

How could she possibly refuse? Besides, she
kept secretly telling herself, she wouldn't be
here to see it anyway, so what difference did it
make? So she laughed congenially, finally telling him she didn't care what hung over the
fireplace.

It was like that all day, and if Poe hadn't
known ahead of time that it was all a farce, all
playacting on Logan's part, she'd have sworn
she was watching a man actually enjoying himself. But then, why shouldn't he? After all, she
was a woman. She'd found that out all too well
since coming to Goldspur, and any man, even

Logan Campbell, would look forward to the prospect of sharing a bed with her. It had nothing to do with love. She'd learned that too since coming to Goldspur.

The day moved on all too quickly, and before Poe realized it they were leaving the dinner table, and still she hadn't found any time to carry out her plan to leave. Aaron had come for dinner this evening too, so he could talk over some business deal with Aunt Delia, and now they all retired to the parlor, where he and Delia huddled on the sofa engrossed in their discussion of an attempted takeover of a company somewhere downstate, while Logan and Poe waltzed around the room to the music from the Victrola.

It was the fall season already and Poe was wearing a dark green velvet dress with a high neck edged in lace, the long sleeves all the way to her wrists, while small emeralds Logan had bought for her on their honeymoon clung to her earlobes, their color deepening the green in her bluish eyes. Poe knew by the way Aaron kept glancing over at Logan and her that they probably made a striking couple as they danced around the room, but Aaron had no idea that his mere presence here tonight was so great a reminder to her of what a fool she had been.

If it hadn't been for Aaron and Delia's presence Poe might have even forgotten the horrible truth for a little while, while she danced, but life didn't seem to work that way. Every turn around the room past the couple on the sofa was a reminder to her of what lay ahead, in spite of the familiar surge of passion that Logan's nearness was bringing to her.

Logan was dressed casually tonight, his gray frock coat matching the slate color of his eyes, the silken cravat tied at the collar of his white shirt dark, like the ebony highlights in his hair, and Poe wished to God he didn't look so damn handsome.

She felt his lips nibble close to her ear and trembled as the music on the Victrola slowed, the strains drawn out crazily like a tired musician winding down.

"Sleepy yet?" he asked huskily, and she tensed when he stopped, but he didn't release her.

"Not really," she answered.

Once more his lips caressed her ear. "Good, because I want you wide-awake tonight," he whispered. "I've waited so long."

Poe felt her legs weaken, her insides turning to jelly. If he'd just release her, let her go. At least she could try to fight him, but he didn't. Instead he raised his head, his arms still around her, and looked deeply into her eyes.

"I think it's time we went upstairs, Mrs. Campbell," he said, the timbre of his voice filled with emotion, and Poe was at a loss.

How did you fight something you couldn't even understand?" "I . . . I . . ." she began, but never finished, as Logan turned to his aunt and Aaron, excusing the two of them, and the next thing she knew she was being ushered up the stairs, this time to the master bedroom at the end of the hall. And before she had a chance to even muster up enough courage to try to fight the feelings that were growing inside her, she found herself standing in front of the fireplace, staring at the stupid elk's head on the wall, while Logan stood behind her unfastening the hooks on her dress, his lips warm against the back of her neck while he murmured softly to her, telling her over and over again how beautiful she was, and how scared he was at the thought of losing her, and how much he loved her.

Poe tried to resist his onslaught. Oh, how hard she tried to squelch the passionate emotions he was forcing to the surface, but it was so much easier said than done. Every soft word, every warm caress, seemed to sear its way straight to her heart, and it was so hard not to let her heart have its due this one more time. Moments later, as Logan gently laid her on the bed, then stretched out beside her, it didn't matter that deep down inside she knew the whole thing was a lie. All that mattered now was the moment, and the love she gave to him. A love that she was unable to suppress anymore, but a love she knew would have to die come tomorrow.

---

But tonight was tonight, and as Logan's mouth came down on hers, his hands caressing her, his long lean body molding to her softness, she eagerly accepted what he gave her, finally responding with a wanton abandon that not only surprised Logan but also spurred him on. And Logan, unaware of the turmoil in Poe's heart, reveled in the glory of her sensuality. Marveling that someone so young and inexperienced could fulfill the strong yearning so deep down inside him. And as he stroked her softly, his heart beating heavily to the rhythm of each caress, he knew a love he'd known only once before, the love he'd remembered from that other night when he'd finally made her really, truly his wife.

"Oh God, Poe, how much I love you," he whispered softly as he moved above her. And although Poe wanted to say "I love you too," she just couldn't bring herself to utter the words. Just being here with him like this was surrender enough, and she moaned ecstatically, clinging to him with a desperation driven by the secret knowledge that this would be the last time, and as he entered her slowly, almost reverently, thrusting deeply over and over again, enjoying every moment just like he had that first night they'd spent together, he brought them both to a shattering climax that left Poe crying breathlessly, and his own body shaking.

After a few moments he kissed her again, his

tongue slowly savoring the moist warmth of her response; then his lips left hers and he buried his face against her ear.

"Are you all right?" he asked huskily.

She murmured, the words caught in her throat, "Mmhmm."

His fingers moved to the scab covering her wound. "I didn't hurt you, did I?"

She finally found her voice. "No."

He just barely heard her. His hand slid from her wound to the top of her shoulder, and he rose up again, looking down into her eyes. The only light for him to see her by was the light from the glowing embers of the fire that had been built in the fireplace earlier to ward off the chill in the room, and now it cast shadows across her face.

"I wish I could see you," he said gently, but Poe was glad he couldn't, because there were tears on her cheeks.

"Don't talk, Logan, please," she gasped breathlessly. "Don't talk, just hold me," and as he rolled off her, pulling her close in his arms, she knew that tonight would have to last her a lifetime, and eventually fell asleep in his arms.

It was morning, and the first thing Poe saw as she opened her eyes was the elk's head staring down at her from above the fireplace. God, it was an ugly thing. Her eyes widened, and for a moment she didn't move, then slowly turned her head. The place in the bed beside her was empty, but just as there had been before, that first morning after he'd made love to her, there was a note pinned to his pillow.

Rubbing her eyes sleepily, she reached out, confiscated the note, then sat up in bed reading it, pushing her dark auburn hair back away from her face while she read silently.

"My lovely Poe, how I would love to spend the whole day with you today as I did yesterday," it read. "However, business demands that I ride to Tonopah with Aaron, so I will see you later, at dinnertime. You were sleeping so peacefully when I kissed you good-bye, and it was hard not to waken you. But I shall see you later tonight. Meanwhile, remember the rose and my heart. Your loving husband, Logan."

She stared at the note thoughtfully for a long time, remembering not only the rose but also last night and all it had brought to her. However, she also remembered the look on Aaron's face when she and Logan had left the parlor last night, and the glance that had passed between Aaron and Aunt Delia. They'd been laughing inwardly at her—she was sure of it—and suddenly tears rimmed her eyes.

Why had she let Logan make love to her last night? Why hadn't she just used some excuse? Anything to keep him away. The words on the note blurred as she continued to stare at them. She knew very well why, and with a flood of anger the whole horrible mess forced itself to the surface again, and she told herself once more what she'd only been repeating silently the past two weeks. Logan was a fraud! What had happened last night was just an interlude in a string of conquests for him. He'd married her to keep from going to jail, and that was the only reason, and there was no way she could change that truth, no matter how many times she let him make love to her.

Crumpling the note in her hand, she glanced up, her eyes once more resting on the elk's head, only her thoughts had nothing to do with the trophy. Logan was going to Tonopah. That meant he'd be gone all day. She reached up, running her fingers across the little bit that was left of the scab that covered the wound, then clenched her jaw stubbornly. It was now or never. She had the whole day for a good start, and it was just a matter of doing it right.

With all her heart she wished last night hadn't happened, because it only made the going harder; but perhaps it was just as well it had happened, because now, in the light of day, it only made her realize what an unmitigated bastard Logan really was. Business in Tonopah! She wouldn't believe that any more than she'd believe he wasn't still going to the Duchess whenever he felt like it. Not now, not knowing what she knew.

Taking a deep breath, and filled with determination, Poe sighed. Sitting here mooning over a might-have-been certainly wasn't the answer. All it did was waste time, and she climbed out of the big bed, then glanced out the window, her mind set once more on the promise she'd made to herself, and she began to search the room for the things she'd need.

It was still quite early, and she was certain most of the household was still sleeping because the sun hadn't come up over the hills as yet, with morning mists swirling in and out among the pine trees. She found all her clothes, dressed, and pulled on her boots, then stood up, making sure they were still comfortable enough. Her hands ran down the sides of the black pants she had on. They were the same pants she'd worn the day she'd first ridden into Goldspur, only they were clean now. Heaven knows why she'd even kept them, or even the shirt, but she reached up, checking the front button on the black shirt, glad now she had kept them because she was determined to take with her only what belonged to her. At the last minute, however, she did ignore her angry pride, and took one thing she hadn't ridden in with. It was a sheepskin jacket. She was heading for hill country and the nights could be bitterly cold there. Even her gunbelt and six-shooters had been tucked away in one of the drawers, and as she tiptoed about the room, quietly getting ready, trying to make sure no one would catch her, she gave herself a mental reminder to stop in the harness room by the stables where the ammunition was kept and make sure the things were loaded. Even her beat-up old hat was stuffed into a corner of the walk-in closet along with her musty bedroll.

She put the hat on, checked to make sure she had everything, and hitched the gunbelt up more comfortably on her hips, then stood in front of the mirror staring at herself. For a minute it was like looking at a stranger, because except for the old clothes, she looked nothing like the young woman who'd ridden into Goldspur at the beginning of summer, wildly independent and ready to conquer the world.

There was a maturity about her now that had been missing before. She was still tall and statuesque, the hair and figure the same, although the clothes weren't quite as tight on her, as she'd lost weight since she was wounded. But the eyes held a depth of feeling that was new to her, and she felt so much older than her seventeen years.

"Only you're not very smart," she whispered to herself, then walked over and looked out the window again. She was going to miss the Highland.

Suddenly a movement caught her eye and she took a step backward, keeping behind the curtain, then watched as Logan rode out of the stables on horseback. Good heavens! She thought he'd been gone for hours. He must have been finishing breakfast while she was flitting about the room getting ready. It was a good thing he hadn't come back up for a last check on her before leaving. She watched him ride down the drive, then rein his horse out onto the main road, and a sadness filled her. It could have been so good.

Her jaw clenched and she turned from the window to stare at the note where she'd left it on the bed. She stared at it for a long time, frowning, then slowly walked over, picked it up, and read it again. Words, just words, she told herself bitterly, then made another quick decision. She had planned to ride out without even leaving an explanation of any kind and just let them wonder what had happened, but now, for some reason, she felt compelled to let Logan know she wasn't a complete fool. After rummaging around in the nightstand, she found a pencil and wrote on the back of the note he'd left.

Now, where to put it. She gazed about the room, and her eyes fell on the desk on the far wall. Why not? Walking over, she picked up an envelope, wrote Logan's name on the front of it, stuffed the note inside and sealed it, then went back to the bed and pinned the envelope to the pillow where the note had been pinned, so it would be easy for anyone to see.

This done, she made sure she had everything, took one quick glance out the window again to make sure no one was outside, then slipped out into the hall, heading for the stables. The house was quiet, shadows still lingering in the corners, but she knew someone was undoubtedly up somewhere, since Logan had been up and about. She didn't run into anyone, however, and after getting the ammunition she needed from the harness room, she made her way to the stables, sneaking in furtively.

The stableboy was in the far end of the building taking care of one of the horses, so she had to work quietly, taking the black gelding from his stall as carefully as possible, and rubbing his nose to quiet his nicker. Her saddle was hung near the stall, and she had him saddled in no time at all, then tied the bedroll on.

It was cool this morning so she was wearing the sheepskin jacket, and she took a deep breath, peeking around the edge of the stall to make sure the groom was still busy. Satisfied that he was engrossed in what he was doing, she led the gelding carefully away, and left by the pasture door, keeping next to the building until she reached the gate. Then, once through, she climbed into the saddle and took off at a slow walk so as not to attract attention. When she was far enough from the house, she stopped for a minute, reining the black gelding around, and stared at the house with the sun just beginning to hit the windows in the tower room, turning them to golden mirrors.

It had been fun while it lasted. Tears filled her eyes, and her heart felt heavy, the physical pain she was enduring so overwhelming for a brief moment that she wasn't sure she was strong enough to go on. Then suddenly the remembrance of what Logan had done to her began to invade her thoughts, fighting against the reality of her heart, and with stubborn conviction she said one last silent good-bye to the Highland and rode out, heading northeast into the hills. She had no idea whatsoever as to where she was going, just so it was far away from Logan Campbell and her memories.

It was early evening when Logan rode up the drive at the Highland and dismounted, handing the horse's reins to the stableboy after first lifting off the saddlebags. All had gone well in Tonopah. Aunt Delia was going to be pleased. He and Aaron had ridden down together, and the meeting with the railroad men had been successful, although it was still going to be a long time before the plans for a railroad to Goldspur would be finalized.

He sighed, slinging the saddlebag over his shoulder as he headed for the house. He'd left Aaron back in town nursing a headache. Aaron always ended up with his head hurting every time he was in the sun too long. Even with a hat on. A throwback to being brought up in a city, Logan always teased him.

Logan stretched, and tossed the saddlebags with all the paperwork in them onto a stand just inside the back hall, then headed for the parlor, looking for Poe. She and Aunt Delia were no doubt through eating by now, and he was so damn anxious to see her.

He stuck his head in the parlor, then frowned. It was empty. Looking around, he suddenly realized the house was exceptionally quiet. Clive didn't even seem to be around. He was just ready to call out, when Aunt Delia spoke from behind him.

"Thank God you're home," she said anxiously, and he could tell by the look on her face that something was wrong.

"What is it?"

"Poe's gone."

"Gone?"

She reached into the pocket of her dress and took out an envelope, holding it out for him to take. "Here, this was pinned to the pillow on your bed. Her horse is gone, as well as her saddle, and the maid said the clothes she wore when she first arrived here are missing out of the drawer too. We haven't seen her all day."

Logan took the envelope from her, stared apprehensively at it for a second, then opened it and began to read silently to himself.

"Logan," it read. Not even a "dear" or "sweetheart." He read on. "By the time you read this I will be long gone and you won't have to worry yourself about me anymore. I knew when we first married that our marriage was not based on love, but I had no idea it was based on deceit. If I had known then what I know now, I would have said no and let you all rot in jail, although I do thank you for at least pretending to love me so the people in Goldspur did not learn what a stupid fool I have been. However, I shall never forgive you for what you have done to me." It was signed simply "Poe." No endearment, no warmth.

He stared at it dumbfounded, his gray eyes darkening, then straightened to his full height and gazed down at his aunt.

"How did she find out?" he asked angrily.

Delia looked at him blankly. "Find out what?"

"That I married her to keep us out of jail."

Delia shrugged. "I don't know. I didn't tell her."

"Somebody had to."

"Aaron?"

"Hardly. Besides, he was with me all day."

"Maybe last night?"

"I'll kill him," Logan yelled furiously, and whirled abruptly, heading back out the door. He didn't even bother to get his horse, but marched down the drive, the fatigue that had slowed him during the ride home suddenly gone.

All the way to town he cursed Aaron for what he'd done. After all, it had to have been Aaron. Only the three of them knew what had happened, except for Merriweather and Tyson, and both of them were dead. He himself hadn't told her, and Aunt Delia said she hadn't.

Aaron lived in a suite of rooms above the Highland office and Logan took the back stairs two at a time, then pounded on the door until his fist hurt.

"Good God!" Aaron exclaimed as he opened the door, his nightshirt on already, and Logan stepped in, pushing him aside, then strolled over and lit a lamp near the sofa.

"Here," Logan said, handing him the note to read as he put the chimney back down when the wick was high enough, and Aaron just stared at the paper. "Well, read it!" Logan demanded.

Aaron gazed at him skeptically, then opened the paper and began to read. His eyes narrowed as he leaned closer to the light; then he finished it and looked up at Logan.

"You think I told her?" he asked.

"Who else?"

"Aunt Delia?"

"She said she didn't. And I sure as hell didn't, so that leaves you."

"I swear, Logan." Aaron's face was flushed, his eyes bewildered. "I never said a word." He frowned. "How about Merriweather or Tyson?"

"They're both dead."

"But they were with her when she was wounded." Aaron handed the letter back to Logan. "Maybe one of them said something to her."

___

Logan shook his head. It didn't seem possible. "But if she knew all the while she was recuperating . . ."

"She's in love with you."

"Then why did she leave?"

Aaron stared at Logan for a minute, then shook his head. "You may be great at making love, Logan," he said, "but you sure as hell don't know much about the subject itself."

Logan glanced down at the note Aaron had handed back to him, then looked at Aaron curiously. "What do you mean?"

"Just because Poe took off doesn't mean she isn't in love with you," he explained quickly. "But she's got a lot of pride. Evidently she thinks you don't really love her, that you've been playing make-believe all this time, and if I know Poe, she's not about to stay around under the circumstances."

Logan's eyes darkened, and his tanned face looked worried. "But I do love her, Aaron," he said, his voice husky with emotion. "The damn girl just wormed her way right in even though I didn't want her to, you know that. I'd have married her even without the threat of jail."

"But she doesn't know that." Aaron watched Logan's jaw clench stubbornly. "What are you going to do?" he asked.

Logan took a deep breath. "I'm going to go after her," he answered. "And by God, I'll bring her back."

———

"But you have no idea where she went."

Logan tucked the note into the inside pocket of his buckskin jacket, then started for the door. "Well, then, I'll just have to find out," he said irritably, and left, leaving Aaron shaking his head wearily.

Logan knew it was too late to try to start after her tonight. He wasn't that good at tracking, and now he wished he'd spent more time in the woods like the rest of the men in Goldspur rather than at the gaming tables. His walk was brisk as he strolled toward the Highland; then suddenly he stopped, staring as he realized he was in front of the Duchess's house. He frowned, wondering if maybe she might have learned the truth, then quickly brushed the thought aside. No, if she knew, she'd have taken advantage of the fact long ago. No. It had to have been Merriweather or Tyson.

He saw a light go on in the upstairs bedroom of the Duchess's house and sighed. The thought wasn't even appealing anymore, and he thrust his hands in his pockets, starting to walk again down the dark road, his thoughts once more on Poe and whether she was all right. And by the time he got back to the Highland he knew exactly what he was going to do.

Poe had been riding easily the past few miles because of the terrain. She had spent last night huddled in her bedroll, with the sheepskin jacket pulled around her, and a supper of wild rabbit in her stomach. It had been cold and uncomfortable, but today things looked better. The sun was out, the tears she'd shed last night had dried up, and she'd gone through a small town shortly after sunup where she'd managed to buy a few staples so the next meal wouldn't be so sparse.

The only money Poe had taken with her when she left the Highland was a ten-dollar gold piece because that's what she had in her pocket the day she'd ridden into Goldspur. The less she owed Delia and Logan Campbell, the better.

The day moved on wearily. In some ways it felt good to be on her own again, accountable to no one except herself. Yet she had to admit she already missed the Highland. Waking up on the ground this morning with bugs crawling on her face was a far cry from waking up on embroidered linen sheets in the tower room. But then, so was waking up and looking into the eyes of that stupid elk's head. She smiled momentarily, remembering the argument they'd had over the trophy when Logan had insisted on putting it up. For a few minutes she let her thoughts wander where he was concerned.

Logan was a contradiction, really. He always seemed to try to make people think he was so uncaring and unfeeling, yet little things he often did belied the fact. Sometimes she thought he was trying too hard to live up to the reputation he had, and it didn't ring true. But then, since he'd spent most of his life pretending to be something he wasn't, it had probably been easy for him to pretend with her. Resentment filled her eyes, and she swore not to think of him anymore today as she leaned back in the saddle, letting the little black gelding find his footing down the side of a rocky, pine-covered slope.

After crossing a small stream, she dug her horse a bit harder in the ribs and quickened her pace, heading for a stony ridge farther to the north. The air was cool and dry, not a cloud in sight, the late-afternoon sun hazy as she rode along. She reached the ridge and rode along the edge for some distance, then reined her horse to a halt, looking back over the countryside below, where she'd been traveling most of the day. It stretched out before her for miles, the colors of the hills deepening from greenish brown to grayish purple in the distance. It was so beautiful and so vast.

She moved on again, looking forward this time, gauging where the sun was on the horizon so she could keep her direction, and when night finally came again, she realized she was nearing the Diamond Mountains close to Shoshone territory. She'd had a skirmish with them on her way through here the last time, and as she started looking for a good place to bed down, she also kept her eyes more alert than

ever for any sign of them. Ordinarily she'd have
built a fire tonight, but after finding a small
outcropping of rocks with no snakes in sight,
she settled it at her back and made do as
darkness crept in around her and the temperature began to drop. She was higher up tonight
than last night and the air was thin, but with
some cheese, dry bread, and raisins in her stomach, washed down with warm water from a
canteen she'd bought when she bought the food,
she let the night close around her, and fell
asleep.

The next day was a repeat of the day before,
except that she was moving more slowly now,
confident of her ability to survive alone, yet
more aware that she was in Indian territory.
Suddenly she pulled back on her horse's reins
and brought the gelding to a stop, then stretched
her hand above her eyes so she could see better. She was halfway up the side of a small
rock-strewn mountain, and had glanced back to
the valley below just in time to see movement
behind her on the trail.

"Damn," she whispered softly to herself as
she saw a figure ride into the open for a brief
second, then disappear again in among the trees.
It was too far away to see who it was, but
whoever it was had evidently found her trail,
because a few minutes later she once more saw
the lone figure moving along, and watched it
steadily for a few minutes before losing it again
among the trees.

She glanced ahead, looking over the lay of the land. At least she'd have the advantage, and she urged the gelding forward, moving toward a natural fortress of rocks and earth about thirty feet ahead and slightly above her, the gelding kicking up stones in the gravelly path she was following on the way. Once behind the pile of rocks, she slid from the saddle and hurriedly tied her horse behind some bushes, hoping he'd be concealed, then scrunched her hat as far down on her head as she could, lay down with her shoulders plastered against the rocks, and waited, her eyes on the trail she'd just come up, her gun resting on top of the wall of rocks.

It was late afternoon and the sun was in front of her, making it harder for her to see, but as she watched intently, her eyes glued to the trail, she cursed under her breath as the rider came into view and she recognized him. She squeezed off a shot, then watched Logan whirl his horse back into cover among the trees, where he must have dismounted, because the next thing she knew he was on his feet, running a zigzag line toward a tree that was close enough for him to shout from.

"What are you trying to do, kill me?" he yelled.

She gritted her teeth. "What do you think!"

"I think you're going to succeed if you keep that up!"

She raised her head a fraction, eyeing the edge of his hat where it stuck out beyond the trunk of the tree. "Why'd you follow me?" she asked bitterly.

"Because I love you!"

"Hogwash!"

"Dammit, Poe, will you listen?" he pleaded. "I do love you, I've always loved you, and if Merriweather and Tyson told you different, they were lying."

Her eyes narrowed, she squinted, then took a bead on the edge of his hat.

The shot made Logan jump, because he hadn't expected it, and he watched what was left of his hat brim flutter to the ground in pieces. Damn, she was a good shot. He yanked the hat off, then stuck his head around the tree trunk. He could barely make out the top of her head above the rocks, and he took a deep breath.

"Why'd you do that?" he yelled angrily. "You ruined a perfectly good hat."

"Next time it'll be what's in it!"

"For God's sake, Poe, what the devil's got into you?" He was still clinging to the tree, his head almost hitting one of the overhead branches. "I came after you. Doesn't that prove anything?"

"It proves you don't want to go to jail."

"Who told you that?"

"Don't worry, I heard it from a good source."

"Who?"

"Aunt Delia and Aaron."

———

He was taken aback. "But they said . . ." he mumbled to himself, then yelled back at her again, "When?"

"That morning when I first came to. After you were gone, they came up to the tower room and thought I was still unconscious. I heard about the whole thing."

He stared across the uneven ground to where she was holed up. So that's what had happened. Yet, if she knew then, why didn't she accuse him right away? He stuck his head around from behind the tree again, his gray eyes questioning, then pulled it back in quickly as a shot splattered into the tree trunk just inches away. He was breathing heavily, trying to think of how to get her to stop before she killed him. Then suddenly he realized: she wasn't trying to kill him. If she had been, he would have been dead long ago. She was a crack shot. Hadn't the hat brim proved that? She was trying to keep him away, that's what she was doing.

Well, hell, if that was it . . . He jammed what was left of his hat down tight on his head, straightened stubbornly and took a deep breath, then stepped out from behind the tree. A bullet hit the ground at his feet, but he kept walking, only a slight flinch interrupting his gait.

"You and I have some talking to do, young lady," he yelled as he bore down on her, and Poe's lips pursed as she cut loose with two more shots that tore up the ground on each side of him.

"Dammit, Logan, stay back," she screamed furiously. "I don't want to talk to you! I don't want to have anything to do with you!"

Logan's jaw tightened, but he still kept coming, and the bullets still kept pace with him, barely missing each time, but missing, and he knew he had the advantage.

Suddenly Poe stopped. She was on her knees, her head above the jumble of rock and rubble, both guns pointed right at him, only she knew they were empty.

"Why didn't you just leave me alone?" she cried helplessly, and now Logan saw the tears in her eyes.

"I told you why," he said, his voice lowering, and he stared at her hard.

Her face was dirty, her hair tangled from catching in the wind that swept through the mountains, and her clothes were filthy already. Except for the bitterness in her eyes, she looked like the old Poe again. Wild and untamed. Only the eyes made a lie of the first impression, and he watched the tears clear a path down her dusty cheeks.

He opened his mouth, and was just about to add to what he'd just said, when the crack of a rifle split the silence, and he dived forward, hitting into Poe, knocking both of them over inside the fortress of rock.

"Now look what you've done!" he complained disgustedly as he regained his footing and reached out, helping her, while they both stayed crouched behind the barricade. "All your gunplay has probably flushed out some Shoshones."

Her face was rigid, the tears on her cheeks forgotten, as she leaned back against the wall, reloading her guns, while he took off his hat and peeked over the top of the rocks.

"Where are they?" she asked.

His eyes scanned the terrain. He had come up the trail to the left of where they were now, but the movement he saw was off toward the right. That meant they hadn't gotten his horse. He watched quietly for a few minutes, the only sound the faint clicking and scraping as she loaded.

"They're over there," he said quickly as she finished reloading and holstered one gun, then hefted the other with her finger on the trigger, and her head joined his. He nodded partway down the side of the rocky mountain to where some bushes and trees clung to a patch of ground that leveled off slightly before descending into the valley below.

"How many?" she asked.

He had counted at least three, then watched as four more rode into view, slid from their horses, and joined the others behind various rocks and bushes. "There're seven, I'd say at first glance," and she took a bead on the nearest one, then pulled the trigger.

"There're six now," she answered confidently.

---

Logan watched one of the Indians, who'd moved away from his cover to get in closer, clutch his chest and fall forward, then lie still.

"Need any help?" he asked sarcastically as he pulled his gun from its holster, and she gave him a dirty look.

"I'm not showing off," she said.

He grinned. "You're sure about that?"

"Logan, it isn't funny." She looked disgusted. "They're not all going to be that easy."

"Forgive me," he said, watching the old spark come back to her eyes. "I thought maybe you wanted to do it all by yourself."

"Just shut up and find a target," she snapped caustically, and suddenly they both ducked again as a volley of shots split the air, the bullets whizzing over their heads.

Logan glanced over at her, his heart turning flip-flops as he watched the casual way she accepted the fact that she was being shot at, and he wanted to hug her.

"You know, you could have told me you knew," he said.

Her eyes flicked to his face, then back again to where the Indians were reconnoitering, trying to figure a way to get closer. The sun danced off their ebony hair, and their bronzed skin was partially covered by outlandish clothes that were no doubt confiscated from one of their raids.

Poe's only concern was that at least one of them had a rifle, and she wondered if he knew he could stay out of the range of their six-guns and still use it. She hoped not.

"If I'd told you, you'd have only denied it," she said, finally answering his question as she continued to watch the Indians, but he disagreed.

"I'm not denying it now."

She laughed cynically. "Because you can't."

"I couldn't then either."

Her eyes darkened. "Then why didn't you tell me?"

He lifted his head a little and aimed at one of the Indians, then squeezed the trigger, but missed by a good foot.

"So I can't shoot straight," he said before she had a chance to make any comment, then added, "I didn't tell you because I was afraid you'd do some stupid fool thing like this."

"Oh, now I'm a stupid fool."

He inhaled, frustrated. "I didn't say you were a stupid fool."

Another volley of shots whizzed over their heads, making them duck; then Poe raised her head, pressing her cheek against the top of the pile of rocks again, pulling off another shot before the Indians had time to regroup.

"Five left," she said matter-of-factly, and Logan just stared at her.

"You know, I can't understand you," he said curiously. "You're not afraid of facing those damn Indians out there, but you're so scared of me, you won't even admit you're in love with me."

"I am not!"

"You are too."

"Prove it."

His eyes narrowed wickedly. "Oh, I intend to, just as soon as you pick off the last Indian," he answered. "How many did you say were left?"

Her jaw tightened, eyes blazing. "You're a bastard, Logan Campbell," she said furiously. "I should have killed you with the first shot."

"Why didn't you?"

"Oh, go to hell!"

He laughed, then grew serious. "Poe, I didn't want to cheat you," he said huskily. "I didn't even know what Aunt Delia had been doing all those years. I had no idea your father had made arrangements for her to set up that trust fund. Not until she sprang it on me when she came back from Scotland. Besides, she didn't mean to cheat you either. It just slipped her mind."

Logan's head had raised a little higher than he'd intended it to while he talked, and they both ducked again as a shot rang out, just missing the top of his hat.

Poe glanced up again quickly, then plastered her head down against the barricade, but all she could see was the edge of a feather near one of the bushes some fifty feet away. Logan's head was next to hers now, and he saw it too. They both fired, then watched as the Shoshone behind the bush straightened, leaving his hiding place, and stumbled about. His face was covered with blood, and as he stepped backward, he crumpled, falling into a heap on the ground.

"Four left," she said, and they relaxed again. Then she sighed. "You were saying?"

Even though she was relaxed, Poe's eyes were still on the spot where the Shoshones were, and he went on, his own eyes following her gaze.

"I said I had no idea she was even supposed to be putting money in a trust fund for you," he said. "And when I found out, I was furious. Then, when she insisted I marry you—"

"You had a good laugh?"

"I'd never laugh at you, Poe," he said, and her eyes faltered as she glanced over at him briefly, then looked away again. "I didn't really know what to do," he said, desperately trying to make her understand. "I was so used to my freedom and the idea that there'd never be any special woman for me, and yet there you were, constantly on my mind. I fell in love with you a long time ago, Poe, and it has nothing to do with your trust fund, or jail, or any of the rest of it."

She studied him intently. "I'm supposed to believe that?"

"Why not? Why is it so hard for you to believe that I love you?"

"Because you lied to me. You cheated me out of my inheritance and lied to me."

---

"I didn't cheat you out of anything," he said. "You've had everything you've ever wanted as my wife. Have I ever denied you anything?"

She stared at him hard. He hadn't, not really. Even on their honeymoon in San Francisco, all she had to do was say, "Oh, isn't that beautiful, I just love it," and the next thing she knew, it was delivered to their hotel room.

"No, not materially," she answered truthfully. "But that's beside the point. What Aunt Delia did was against the law, and yet you went along with it, covering it up, and denying me what was rightfully mine."

"Now you're nit-picking," he said irritably. "For heaven's sake, Poe, would you rather I'd gone to jail? Then what would you have done? You'd have had all that money after the Highland Spur folded, and you'd have been prey to every swindler and con artist in Nevada. You don't know anything about handling money."

"I could have learned." She'd had her eye on the Indians again, and squeezed off another shot as one of them tried to move from one rock formation to another as fast as he could. "That makes three left," she stated grimly, and Logan sighed.

"Who would have taught you?" he asked. "Lord Merriweather and Tyson? Or maybe Reverend Ambrose or Big Jim would have helped, I suppose."

"I'd have learned somehow. There are books."

"But you can't learn about love in books, Poe," he said gently. "And I've discovered that money without love just doesn't mean a thing."

She flushed, avoiding his eyes, and Logan, taking her cue, glanced to where the Indians were again, just in time to see one of them leave his hiding place and try to scoot closer on his belly. He aimed quickly and pulled the trigger, then watched the Indian let out a yelp and jump up, holding his foot out, blood dripping from it.

Poe too was watching the Indian, and she glanced at Logan out of the corner of her eye. "You missed," she said facetiously.

Logan laughed. "At least it served its purpose," he said. "Look," and as Poe drew her eyes from Logan's amused face, glancing back again to where the Indians were, it was just in time to see the last three Shoshones scurry to their horses and ride away, leading their dead comrades' horses behind them.

"They'll be back for the bodies later," Logan said as he holstered his gun, and she drew her eyes from the retreating Shoshones.

"You're sure?"

"Don't worry, we won't be here."

She frowned. "We?"

"You are going back with me, aren't you?"

"Logan . . . please!"

He reached out and grabbed her wrist, taking the gun from her hand, then dropped it in its holster before pulling her into his arms.

---

"Now look, honey. I didn't come all the way out here to go home empty-handed," he said, and he looked down into her blue-green eyes.

He was half-leaning, half-lying against the rock barricade, and he tried to get into a better position without letting her go.

"Please, Poe, come home with me," he pleaded anxiously. "I love you so damn much."

Her body was trembling as she stared at him. She was still angry over what he'd done, but for some reason now, with his arms around her and his body pleading for her to give in . . . And she did love him. She could never deny that. She could hate what he'd done, from here to kingdom come, but she did love him.

Logan felt her body relax against him, and a pang of yearning filled his heart.

"You'll come?" he asked tenderly.

She sighed. "On one condition," she answered.

"And that is?"

Her eyes bored into his. "You're to promise never to lie to me like that again, and if you ever pull any shady deals on me, or anyone else, Logan Campbell, I'll pin your ears back with a forty-five, understand?"

He grinned. "Then you do love me, don't you?"

"I never said I didn't," she answered softly. "But you haven't promised."

"I promise," he said passionately, and pulled her even closer, kissing her hard on the mouth, bringing back all the wonderful memories to them both of what sharing life together would be like. "Now, let's get out of here," he said as he drew his head back, looking straight into her eyes, "before those damn Shoshones come back to claim their dead." He stood up cautiously, pulling her up with him, then untied her horse, and they made a break for the woods, where his horse was still waiting.

A few minutes later, as they rode back down the trail heading southwest toward Goldspur, Poe glanced over at Logan, who smiled back at her, his eyes filled with longing. Tonight was going to be a wonderful night for a change, she thought happily, and she wasn't going to have to worry anymore. Not ever. Not even come tomorrow.

## About the Author

The granddaughter of an old-time vaudevillian, Mrs. Shiplett was born and raised in Ohio. She is married and lives in the city of Mentor-on-the-Lake. She has four daughters and several grandchildren and enjoys living an active outdoor life.